Supernatural Encounters

The belief in the reality of demons and the restless dead formed a central facet of the medieval worldview. Whether a pestilent-spreading corpse mobilised by the devil, a purgatorial spirit returning to earth to ask for suffrage, or a shape-shifting demon intent on crushing its victims as they slept, encounters with supernatural entities were often met with consternation and fear. Chroniclers, hagiographers, sermon writers, satirists, poets, and even medical practitioners utilised the cultural 'text' of the supernatural encounter in many different ways, showcasing the multiplicity of contemporary attitudes to death, disease, and the afterlife. In this volume, Stephen Gordon explores the ways in which conflicting ideas about the intention and agency of supernatural entities were understood and articulated in different social and literary contexts. Focusing primarily on material from medieval England, c.1050–1450, Gordon discusses how writers such as William of Malmesbury, William of Newburgh, Walter Map, John Mirk, and Geoffrey Chaucer utilised the belief in demons, nightmares, and walking corpses for pointed critical effect. Ultimately, this monograph provides new insights into the ways in which the broad ontological category of the 'revenant' was conceptualised in the medieval world.

Stephen Gordon graduated with a PhD in medieval literature and archaeology from the University of Manchester, UK, and currently works at Royal Holloway, University of London. He is an interdisciplinary scholar of medieval and early modern supernatural belief and has published widely in his chosen research area.

Studies in Medieval History and Culture
Recent titles include

The Charisma of Distant Places
Travel and Religion in the Early Middle Ages
Courtney Luckhardt

The Death Penalty in Late Medieval Catalonia
Evidence and Signification
Flocel Sabaté

Church, Society and University
The Paris Condemnation of 1241/4
Deborah Grice

The Sense of Smell in the Middle Ages
A Source of Certainty
Katelynn Robinson

Travel, Pilgrimage and Social Interaction from Antiquity to the Middle Ages
Edited by Jenni Kuuliala and Jussi Rantala

Supernatural Encounters

Demons and the Restless Dead in Medieval England, c.1050–1450

Stephen Gordon

LONDON AND NEW YORK

First published 2020
by Routledge
2 Park Square, Milton Park, Abingdon, Oxon OX14 4RN

and by Routledge
52 Vanderbilt Avenue, New York, NY 10017

Routledge is an imprint of the Taylor & Francis Group, an informa business

First issued in paperback 2021

British Library Cataloguing-in-Publication Data
A catalogue record for this book is available from the British Library

Library of Congress Cataloging-in-Publication Data
Names: Gordon, Stephen, 1985-author.
Title: Supernatural encounters: demons and the restless dead in medieval England, c.1050-1450/Stephen Gordon.
Description: Abingdon, Oxon; New York, NY: Routledge, 2020. |
Series: Studies in medieval history and culture | Includes bibliographical references and index.
Identifiers: LCCN 2019038938 (print) | LCCN 2019038939 (ebook) |
ISBN 9781138361744 (hbk) | ISBN 9780429432491 (ebk)
Subjects: LCSH: Occultism–England–History–To 1500. |
Demonology–England–History–To 1500. | Supernatural–History–To 1500.
Classification: LCC BF1434.G7 G67 2020 (print) | LCC BF1434.G7 (ebook) |
DDC 133.40942–dc23
LC record available at https://lccn.loc.gov/2019038938
LC ebook record available at https://lccn.loc.gov/2019038939

ISBN: 978-1-138-36174-4 (hbk)
ISBN: 978-1-03-208244-8 (pbk)
ISBN: 978-0-429-43249-1 (ebk)

Typeset in Times
by Deanta Global Publishing Services, Chennai, India

For my parents

Contents

Illustrations

Figures

Table

Acknowledgements

This book has been many years in gestation. The topic ultimately originates from a PhD thesis completed at the University of Manchester under the supervision of Drs Anke Bernau and Melanie Giles. I would like to give my wholehearted thanks to Anke and Mel for their insights and encouragement over the years. Earlier versions of chapters two, three, and six have appeared previously in *Journal of Medieval History*, *English Studies* and *Social History of Medicine* respectively. I would like to thank Taylor & Francis Ltd and Oxford University Press for giving me permission to reproduce and build upon these studies in the current volume. Special acknowledgements must be given to the image digitisation team at the John Rylands Library, Manchester, and Fergus Wilde from Chetham's Library, Manchester, for their help in sourcing the images used in chapter one. Thanks also to Michael Greenwood at Routledge for his patience and enthusiasm in seeing the project to completion. Similarly, I am grateful to the anonymous peer reviewers for their helpful comments on an earlier draft of the manuscript. Any errors, of course, remain entirely my own. Ultimately, I would not have been able to complete this project without the good humour of my brother David and love and support of my parents, Chris and Margaret, to whom this book is dedicated.

Abbreviations

BL	British Library, London
BRG	Bibliotheca rerum Germanicarum
CCCC	Corpus Christi College, Cambridge
CCCM	Corpus Christianorum, Continuatio Mediaeualis
CCSL	Corpus Christianorum Series Latina
EETS	Early English Text Society
e.s	extra series
o.s	original series
MGH	Monumenta Germanica Historica
Cap	Capitularia regum Francorum
Cap. episc	Capitula episcoporum
LL	Leges (in folio)
SS	Scriptores (in folio)
PL	Patrologia Latina, ed. by J-P Migne, 221 vols. (Paris, 1841–1864)
RS	Rolls Series

Introduction

The *Chronicon de Lanercost* (c.1346) is not one of the most storied historical works produced in England in the Later Middle Ages. Adapted from a lost Franciscan chronicle of northern provenance by the Augustinian canons of Lanercost Priory, Cumbria, it is known chiefly for its insights into Anglo-Scottish relations during the political tumults of the late thirteen and early fourteenth centuries. The text itself is a typical – almost stereotypical – compilation of historical narratives, local anecdotes, and digressions on 'wonderful' or miraculous events, intended for the entertainment and edification of the reader.[1] One story in particular stands out from the rest. In the spring of 1295, a series of terrifying events was said to have befallen the village of Clydesdale in Western Scotland. A monk from nearby Paisley Abbey, excommunicated on account of the many sacrileges committed during his lifetime, died a sudden and by all accounts wretched death.[2] The grave did not keep the monk at rest for long. Soon after burial, he appeared to his former brethren, 'vexing' them in the dead of night, before proceeding to Clydesdale and attacking the household of a local knight, Duncan de Insula, members of which were rumoured to have been complicit in the monk's sins. Having assumed a bodily shape (*assumpto siquidem corpore*), and wearing a black habit, the monk used to wander the Clydesdale streets and 'settle on the highest parts of the dwellings and store houses'.[3] Whenever the men of the village attempted to stab or shoot the monk, the pitchforks and arrows that were thrust into his body immediately burnt to ashes. Equally, those who tried to physically restrain him were beaten to a bloody pulp, their limbs broken and shattered. One evening, when Sir Duncan was sitting with his household around the hearth, the dead monk suddenly appeared and started attacking Duncan and his family. The knight's son, an equally despicable character, tried to fight off the creature, but was killed in the process. The chronicler concludes with the wry comment that given the inability of the demon (*daemonem*) to harm the virtuous, it was no surprise why the young man came to such a grisly end.

The above narrative, inserted between an account of a plague that engulfs the students of Oxford and the King of France's plan to steal the relics of Thomas Becket, epitomises the vague and often tantalising nature of medieval descriptions of encounters with non-human entities. Uncertainty and ambiguity are the guiding features of such narratives. Indeed, the 'vexations' felt by the Clydesdale residents can easily apply to the modern reader: why, exactly, did the monk walk after death? Was he corporeal or incorporeal? Given that the monk's body seemed to exhibit preternatural qualities – burning as it did any weapon that was thrust into its 'flesh' – did the townsfolk believe they were encountering the ghost of the deceased or, as intimated by the Lanercost monk, a demon in his likeness? Under threat from an entity that was causing panic and distress in the local community, did the typological distinction even matter? These are questions that befuddled even medieval commentators. The author of the exemplum did not presume to know whether the monk's body was 'natural' or 'airy', mentioning only that it *seemed* 'gross and palpable' (*grosso et palpabili)* and that *something* in his likeness, a sensible illusion (*sensibili illusione*), appeared to the brethren of Paisley Abbey. *Assumpto* is a word that is also agonisingly ambiguous: did it mean that the body, described as 'damned substance' (*massae [..] damnatae*), was created specifically for the purposes of haunting – an elemental facsimile – or did the monk's spirit or demon 'assume' a cadaver that had been buried in the ground? Ultimately, it was the function of the reader to decipher the moral utility of events that, on first glance, were inexplicable to the senses. The author-compiler is certainly not above providing his own gloss, arguing that the return of the monk 'served to strike terror into sinners and foreshadow the appearance of the damned in the day of the last resurrection'.[4] Nor does he show much hesitance in insinuating that the death of the noblemen's son was a divinely-ordained punishment for the sins he committed with the monk. In recording (or even manufacturing) a tale that put specific emphasis on the dead monk's relationship to the household of Duncan de Insula, the Lanercost scribe (or his Franciscan forebearer) was able to ask questions that could not be broached directly. As will be made apparent over the course of this volume, Supernatural Encounters were narratologically unstable enough to be utilised for a variety of socio-critical effects.

The restless dead in medieval Europe: a fluid cultural text

The above story from the *Chronicon de Lanercost* is a suitably vivid introduction to the type of entity that forms the main focus of this volume: the medieval iteration of the embodied (or seemingly embodied) ghost. The fear that under certain circumstances those who suffered a 'bad' or ill-timed death could return to haunt the living is a phenomenon that can be seen across a wide chronological and geographical spectrum. From Phlegon of Tralles' tale of a lifelike dead woman, Philinnion,[5] who returned from the grave to consort with a young man named Machates (c.100s), to ethnographic accounts of the unruly dead in twenty-first-century Russia,[6] restless bodies have fascinated and repulsed in equal measure. Defined variously as a *draugr* (Scandinavia),[7] *vrykolaka*s (Greece)[8] or *upir/ vampyre* (Eastern Europe; Turkey),[9] the embodied ghost has maintained an almost universal presence in European folklore since prehistoric times, haunting the

popular imagination for thousands of years. None were more vocal in their puz-
zlement at the reappearance of the dead than the historical and religious writers
of the Middle Ages. The Lanercost chronicler was not unique amongst his peers
in devoting attention to corpses that did not stay quietly in the grave, reactions
to which ranged from tentative credulity to cool scholarly dismissal that such
things even existed. Indeed, as this current volume will demonstrate, the belief
in – or, more precisely, the *acknowledgement* of the belief in – the walking corpse
seems to have been an entrenched, if porous and malleable, socio-cultural 'text'.
To use the terminology employed by the literary theorist Brian Stock, such texts
can be understood as a shared set of dispositions; a series of assumptions, beliefs
and fears that were disseminated among a particular social grouping or 'textual
community'.[10] To quote Stock, 'we can think of a textual community as a group
that arises somewhere in the interstices between the imposition of the written
word and the articulation of a certain type of social organisation'.[11] In a similar
vein, Roland Barthes describes the text as a 'tissue of quotations drawn from the
innumerable centres of culture'; that is, an embodiment, or expression, of specific
habits and meanings.[12] Structured by the (mutable) socio-cultural environment
in which the textual community dwelt, the habitual text could find expression
in many different ways. The 'text' of the person of Christ, for example, could
be made manifest through an oral/performative experience (that is, the reception
of the Eucharist; the use of the text as a rule for one's own conduct), part of an
devotional process (the silent reading of a prayer book), or else expressed through
the medium of the visual arts (the text of Christ's perfection as evidenced through
the sacred geometry of cathedral architecture). Similarly, the text of the medieval
undead – imprecise, conflicting, but nonetheless present in the habitual repertories
of daily life – had the potential to be made manifest across a variety of experiential contexts, from chronicles and hagiographies to secular poems, satirical
invectives, medico-magical textbooks, and even in the treatment of the corpse.
Cremation, decapitation, prone burial, and deposition in liminal areas of the landscape are all key indicators that the body was considered dubious in some way.[13]
The fear of the unruly dead and coming into contact with destructive, non-human
entities are facets of a long-lived habitual tradition that can find trace in the most
unexpected and seemingly disconnected of sources.[14] Consider, for example, the
following extract from the Middle Irish hagiographical text, *Betha Cholmain Eala*
('Life of St. Colmán Ela' [d.611]), concerning a female lake monster that terrorised the lands of Fir Cell:

> And a trouble had arisen in the land at this time; to wit, there was a pestilent
> monster in Lough Ela, and no man or beast would venture to go near the
> lake for fear of it. [...] And the name of the monster was Lainn, and this was
> the nature of it – a small pointed gaping apparition, and short bushy hair,
> unwashed and unkempt, all over its head. And the monster came to land. And
> Colman said: 'If God permits, I would permit the reeds of the lake to bind
> thee for me, that I may slay thee' [...]. And these two, Cuineda and Duinecha,
> went and beheaded the monster. And they brought the head to Colman.[15]

Historians of medieval supernatural belief have given little attention to this encounter. Although identified by the author as a 'monster' (*piest*) and an 'apparition' (*fúad*), Lainn displays all the malign qualities associated with a restless corpse. She is 'pestilential' (*urcoidech*), has a dirty, cadaverous face, and presents a tangible threat to the local community. An earlier part of the text also notes that she possessed 'the form of a woman' (*ndeilb mna*). St. Colman's declaration that he wished to bind the monster in reeds before slaying it (*as ced lemsa cuilcc an locha sin dod cuilcc cengal damh fein*) recalls the archaeologically-identifiable practice of burying corpses in bogs overlain with poles to prevent them from rising.[16] Decapitation was also a common method for dealing with the dangerous dead. Without delving too deep into the hagiographic commonplace of the cleansing of polluted water sources[17] or the literary topos of the mere-dwelling hag (see, for example, the Grendelkin in *Beowulf* and the Gaelic *fuath*),[18] definite connections can be made between the figure of Lainn and the monster that harried the residents of Clydesdale. While it is true that the authors of the *Betha Cholmain Eala* and the *Chronicon de Lanercost* did not draw upon the exact same 'tissue of quotations' to construct their stories – to argue that a writer from early medieval Ireland shared the same literary outlook as a Franciscan friar from the English-Scottish border is reductive to say the least – the physicality (or apparent physicality) of the evil agent and the danger it presented to the community are placed at the forefront of each text. This is not to suggest that attitudes to the supernatural were uniform or static, but that there existed only a finite number of ways to articulate the cultural codes surrounding the traumas of corpse management and 'bad' death. As noted by Andrew Joynes, mere-dwelling monsters may represent a folkloric derivation of the corporeal ghost.[19] With due caution taken, cross-cultural analysis remains an intrinsic tool for evaluating types of entities whose presence in the historical record is spread thinly and opaquely across the extant primary material.

This said, certain regions and textual communities deliver more viable source materials than others. Germanic texts provide some of the most compelling evidence for the belief in embodied ghosts in the Middle Ages.[20] Thietmar of Merseburg's *Chronicon* (c.1018), Burchard of Worm's *Decretum* (c.1008–1012) and Caesarius of Heisterbach's *Dialogus miraculorum* (c.1220–35) have long been utilised by historians to explore prevailing social attitudes to the unruly dead as well as to trace the indefinable interstices between 'pre-Christian' and 'Christian' cultures.[21] Although written in different contexts for different pedagogical purposes and in different time periods, the stories of the undead recounted in each are connected by their ostensibly oral origins. Thietmar, bishop of Merseberg, digresses from the wider narrative of Ottonian history to describe the haunting of a cemetery in the town of Walsleben and the fate of a Deventer priest who was assaulted and immolated by dead men who invaded his church.[22] Written in the years following his election to the bishopric of Worms, Burchard's compilation of canon law is an especially valuable source for examining the tensions between official church discourse and the unorthodox, seemingly pagan beliefs of the laity. As noted by Hartmut Hoffman and Rudolf Pokorny, significant portions of the material found in book nineteen – a penitential handbook entitled *Corrector et Medicus* – draws upon older pastoral literature and canon law collections, especially Regino of Prüm's *Libri duo de synodalibus causis et disciplinis ecclesiasticis* (c.906).[23] Despite this, it has been argued that some of the more idiosyncratic errors recorded by Burchard in the canon five 'questionnaire' are a product of his own interactions with the local diocese. The *Corrector*, then, should be viewed less as an ossified literary artefact and more, in Ludger Körntgen's terms, a 'penitential exemplar';[24] that is, as a carefully-cultivated handbook that takes into account the vague and palimpsestic nature of lay belief at a time when efforts were being made to control and standardise the penitential process. It is a localised forebearer to the more universal directorates of reform that characterise the later eleventh-century church.[25] The *Corrector*'s canon five thus tells us much about the irregular practices of the Worms laity at the turn of the millennium. Two of the penances recorded by Burchard are especially revealing where the theme of this volume is concerned:

> Have you done what some women do at the instigation of the devil? When any child has died without baptism they take the corpse of the little one and place it in some secret place and transfix it with a stake, saying that if they did not do so the child would rise up and injure many? If you have done, or consented to, or believed this, you should do penance for two years on the appointed days.[26]

It was not only unbaptised babies that suffered such measures:

> Have you done what some women, filled with the boldness of the devil are wont to do? When some woman is to bear child and is not able, if when she cannot bear it she dies in her pangs, they transfix the mother and child in the grave with a stake driven into the earth. If you have done or consented to this, you should do penance for two years on the appointed days.[27]

Although Burchard does not dwell on the reasons for staking new-born infants or women who died in childbirth to the grave, the allusion to 'rising up an injuring many' is evidence enough that those who died badly demanded extra funerary lest they wreak havoc on the local community. Writing nearly 200 years after Theitmar and Burchard, the Cistercian compiler Caesarius of Heisterbach is no less vocal on the belief that unruly corpses were able to do harm to local Germanic communities. Caesarius identifies an oral source for more than half of the 747 chapters that comprised his miracle collection.[28] His account of the terror caused by the dead knight, Henricus Nodus, who emitted a sound like a 'soft bed' (*mollis lectus*) when struck with swords, is one of the most colourful tales of the restless dead included in the *Dialogus miraculorum*. The wry descriptor '*mollis lectus*', combined with statement that not a lot of time had passed since the hauntings took place (*non est diu ex quo ista contigerunt*), substantiates the commonly-held theory that Caesarius's exempla were recorded almost verbatim.[29]

The belief that ghosts were prone to physical violence is also a feature of the Scandinavian tradition of the ill-behaving dead. Detailing the history of the Danish people from their mythological origins to the turn of the thirteenth century, Saxo Grammaticus's *Gesta Danorum* (c.1190–1208) treats the text of the violent dead in a much more equivocal manner than either Burchard or the Lanercost chronicler; seen by Saxo as just one of many fantastical tales of the supernatural from the annals of northern folklore. Structurally, the *Gesta Danorum* is divided into two roughly equal parts, with books one to nine devoted to feats of pagan legend and books ten to sixteen prioritising modern documented history.[30] Book five contains an account of an angry, revived corpse that purportedly took place in the first century AD. Asvith, son of the ruler of Vik, Norway, died suddenly after a short illness. Bound by an oath of friendship, Asmund, his lifelong companion, allowed himself to be buried alive in Asvith's tomb. Sometime later Asvith's ghost (*spiritus*) returned from the hellish otherworld (*Stygii* [...] *ab infernis*) and re-entered his own dead body. Ravenous and raving, Asvith consumed the horse and dog carcasses that had been laid alongside him in the grave before turning his attention to Asmund, whose left ear was ripped off in the ensuing struggle. On being rescued from the mound by the king of Sweden, Asmund explained that he was able to quell Asvith '[by scyth[ing] off his head with my sword and thrust[ing] a stake through [his] wicked body'.[31] Variations of this topos – physical altercation with a violent corpse – can be read throughout the Icelandic Sagas, most notably *Egils saga einhenda ok Ásmundar berserkjabana* (c.1300s), where the Asmund story is retold with only slight emendations. *Grettis Saga, Eyrbyggja Saga*, and *Laxdaela Saga* contain similar accounts of reanimated *draugr* who could only be assuaged through staking, decapitation, or cremation.[32] Given the acknowledged Scandinavian influences on *Beowulf*'s narratological framework, it should come as no surprise that the act of wrestling with a violent corpse can be read (at however far a remove) in the hero's fight with the monstrous mere-walker, Grendel (ll. 750–753a),[33] an episode some scholars believe shares the same folkloric paradigm as Grettir's fight with the undead farmhand, Glamr, in *Grettis Saga*.[34] Transcribed in the thirteenth and fourteenth centuries yet detailing events that occurred during the settlement and Christianisation of Iceland (c.1000), the Sagas offer pertinent insights into the pagan history of the Scandinavian people, the processes of literary self-fashioning, and the ongoing impact of the restless corpse in a particular cultural setting.

Where the central and eastern European iterations of the walking dead are concerned, it is difficult to look past the so-called 'vampire epidemics' of the early eighteenth century.[35] Academic treatises on undecayed, masticating corpses written in the seventeenth century by such learned theologians as Heinrich Kornmann (1610), Leo Allatius (1645) and Philipp Rohr (1679) acted as a vanguard, or primer, for the more salacious accounts of *upir* and *vrykolakas* activity that began to enter western literary circles at the dawn of the Enlightenment.[36] The 1725 publication of the Austrian provisor Frombald's investigation into a series of unusual deaths in the Serbian village of Kisolova, marks the point at which the 'vampire' – or, more precisely, the literary construct of the vampire – truly became part of the western cultural lexicon.[37] The publication of the military surgeon Johann Flückinger's *Visum et Repertum* (1732) whetted the appetite for vampires still further.[38] Flückinger's treatise, a first-hand account of a purported vampire outbreak in the village of Medvegia, Serbia, complete with brief anatomical reports of ruddy 'vampiric' bodies, became a key reference point for all future writings on the subject. With contemporary historians, philosophers, travel writers, and theologians all offering insights into why the Slavic states seemed so overrun with blood-sucking and shroud-chewing corpses,[39] it is surprising that so little written data exists on the phenomenon prior to the seventeenth century. Abbot Neplach of Opatovice's *Summula chronicae tam Romanae quam Bohemicae* (c.1361) is unusual not only for being one of the few universal histories to be written in Central Europe at this time,[40] but for containing two rare accounts of the Slavic undead that can be securely dated to the medieval period. The narrative transcribed below contains much the same thematic content that would make Frombald and Flückinger's field notes the cause célèbre of the western scholarly elite nearly four centuries later:

> AD 1344: A certain woman died in Lewin [Levin, CZ] and was buried. After her burial she rose and killed many, and ran after whomever she pleased. And when she was transfixed [impaled], blood flowed as if from a living animal. She had devoured more than half of her shroud, and when it was extracted, it was covered completely in blood. When she was to be cremated, the wood could not be set alight unless, according to the instruction of some old women, it was made from the roof of a church. After she had been impaled, she always kept rising, but when she was cremated, all evil subsided.[41]

Neplach's second story is equally evocative, detailing the post-mortem activities of a shepherd name Myslata (d.1366) who terrorised the village of Blow near Cadan (Kadan, CZ) by throttling people in their sleep. On being transfixed with a stake he was heard to cry out: 'the villagers did much harm to me, but they gave me a staff to defend me from the dogs'.[42] Only after being cremated did the disturbances cease. In both cases, references to the agency of the devil are curiously absent. *Malum* ('evil') is used to describe the destructive tendencies of the woman from Lewin. Likewise, it is said that all evil subsided following the dissolution of Myslata's body (*cum fuisset crematus totum malum conquievit*). Although it possible that *malum* alludes to the workings of the devil, it is more likely that the dead were seen to walk (and kill) under their own volition. Myslata, indeed, gives voice to his own personhood. Descriptive yet allusive, Neplach's accounts ask far more questions than they answer. Recent research on the vampire has recognised the benefit of enlisting archaeological data (i.e. unwritten material texts) to gain a fuller picture of how the fear of the unruly corpse was made manifest in places where written reports are vague at best, an interdisciplinary method that is only beginning to gain a foothold in scholarship on the English undead.[43]

The contrast between Burchard and Neplach's allusivity and Saxo's forensic description of Asvith's reanimation can also be read as a function of the genre in which they were writing. Not wanting to emphasise the errors of the common folk more than necessary for the calculation of penance, Burchard's reluctance to say exactly what type of metaphysical forces caused unbaptised infants 'rise up' is entirely logical. For a pastoral teaching aid, it was sufficient only to describe the practice of staking, not propagate the sinner's rationale. Working within a milieu where the animation of the corpse through its vestigial life-force was a more likely explanation than demonic possession, Neplach's own lack of detail is nonetheless consistent with the conservative Benedictine convention of declining to provide overt meanings to inexplicable events.[44] Saxo – a learned, Latinate cleric who seems to have designed the legendary aspects of the *Gesta Danorum* as a conscious pre-figuration of later Christian history[45] – employs the appropriately Christianised topos of a spirit re-entering the defunct flesh from the 'other world', in stark contrast to the belief, as intimated in the Saga literature, that the deceased's vestigial life-force (*hugr*) remained with the body until dissolution. Adjectives relating to hell (*infernus, Stygius*) lend a diabolical and somewhat Classicised gloss to the story, obscuring the reader's comprehension as to *what* truly returned from *where*. Whether by accident (through learnt literary habit) or design (to stress Christian type), Saxo's linguistic anachronisms speak to an active authorial process. As will be discussed in more detail shortly, such formal and ontological uncertainties are just as apparent in English contexts.

The above analysis does not pretend to operate as a full overview of all extant data on the *draugr*, the Slavic vampire, or the Germanic embodied ghost, much less the Greek *vrykolakas*. Such a task is beyond the scope of this book. Instead, the selected examples highlight the myriad ways in which an enmeshed cultural text – the dangers of 'bad' death; the fear of encountering non-human entities – could be expressed in different socio-cultural arenas. More critically, the long-lived habitual belief in the vampire has shown that inherent arbitrariness of the academic distinction between the medieval and early modern worlds, a division that seeks only to highlight difference where, in certain contexts, no such schism existed.[46] Even though such social 'disruptions' as the church reforms of Pope Gregory VII (1073–1085),[47] the transition from a predominately oral to written culture during the so-called Twelfth-Century Renaissance,[48] the ratification of the doctrine of Purgatory (c.1100s–1200s), and the impact of the reformist ideals of John Wycliffe (d.1384), Jan Hus (d.1415) and, eventually, Martin Luther (d.1546), undoubtedly affected the form and function of writings on the supernatural, an awareness of the continuity of thought and action is just as important as charting its rupture. In this respect, even the generally-accepted scholarly demarcation between pagan and Christian belief can be seen as a hindrance rather than helpful. Everyday 'ways of doing' (the writing of supernatural encounters; sensory interactions with the dead) existed within and negotiated between the institutional and experiential structures in which such activities were conducted. The overt, didactic meanings ascribed to the walking dead may have depended on authorial circumstance, but the practical strategies used to manage the social and environmental fallout of 'bad' death – in literary terms, the narratological framework – belonged to an underlying perceptual schema that had persevered for generations.

The biological processes of decay are a universal function of the human body. On a purely utilitarian level, there were only certain viable methods for dealing with cadavers that, for whatever reason, did not 'perform' as expected, be it a lack of decay or a propensity to convulse post-mortem.[49] Rather than viewing long-lived reactions to the restless dead as a pagan survival,[50] it is better to see such responses as reflective of the ongoing processes of habitual re-inscription, with each new external pressure – e.g. the formulation of Purgatory; the doctrinal rejection of the false resurrection of the dead – adding to, rather than replacing, the mental repertoires of the writer and audience.[51] Habit, conscious and unconscious human agency, becomes a form of palimpsest. Tradition is active and ever-changing; mutable, not static. Thus, the conditions are met for the supernatural encounter to act as a nexus point for multiple, sometimes contradictory interpretations and meanings. As such, whilst the crux of this investigation will be devoted to written material from the Central and Late Middle Ages – roughly between c.1050–1450 – this does not mean that texts from earlier or later eras will be ignored. Habit, of course, also operates on a horizontal axis. Monastic filial networks, membership of the universal church, and medical beliefs based on shared classical precedents are three distinct but interrelated types of textual community that were not defined by geographical or national boundaries. Manuscript circulation and the dissemination of knowledge between the courts and cloisters of Western Europe led to the establishment of a pan-continental intellectual culture. On a more localised level, the pervading influence of Danelaw on the habits of daily life in post-Conquest England, especially in the North, suggests a conceptual ink, however far removed, between the English iteration of the undead corpse and the *draugr*.[52] The close socio-cultural ties that existed between the English realm and the Continent must therefore be taken into account. Simply put, an investigation into such a nebulous and wide-ranging topic as the restless dead requires synchronic flexibility as well as diachronic permeability. Although the main focus of this study will be material from the British Isles, case studies from mainland Europe will be used to augment the insular material where needed. It is to these English texts – and the myriad ways in which their authors tried to understand and articulate the agency of the undead – that we now turn.

Ambiguous ontologies and the restless dead

The overlapping cultural and religious frameworks that engendered the belief in, and prompted the transmission of, wonder stories in post-Conquest England ensured that no true consensus was ever reached regarding how the embodied ghost was defined. The terms 'supernatural' (*supernaturalis*) and 'preternatural' (*preter naturam*), though mostly interchangeable in their modern usage,[53] came to possess specific meanings by the later Middle Ages. According to the Dominican theologian Thomas Aquinas (d.1274), supernatural encounters and events occurred through the grace of God alone, operating outside the natural processes of the universe, whereas anything that was preternatural ultimately had a natural causation – 'natural' including the angelic/demonic manipulation of the environment or the human senses.[54] In practice, it was difficult to determine whether the dead reappeared, or seemed to reappear, due to an act of God (a miracle), demons (a false miracle or wonder), or hallucinations caused by an everyday dysfunction of the body (that is, without demonic or divine interference). As a result, there was considerable conceptual and linguistic slippage when it came to interpreting encounters, events, or things that deviated from the expected norm. Indeed, before the growing influence of Aristotelianism in the thirteenth century and scholastic imperative to separate the divine from the rare and unusual, *supernaturalis* and its cognate *supra naturam* were seldom used as adjectives.[55] Gervase of Tilbury (d.1228), for example, uses *preter naturam* to describe how the raising of Lazarus from the dead was *miraculous* when compared to the *natural* if seemingly unique ability of salamanders to withstand the heat of fire.[56] Where contemporary ghost encounters appeared on this continuum was open to constant speculation.

Structured by their idiosyncratic worldviews and/or context in which they were writing, learned commentators rarely used the exact same terminologies when recording strange or inexplicable events. It was difficult to establish causation when confronted with oral testimonies, written reports, or even first-hand sensory experiences that did not correspond to the author's own habitual understanding of the world. This is especially true when it came to describing encounters with the corporeal or seemingly corporeal dead. The writer of the *Chronicon de Lanercost* exemplum was unwilling to ascribe a definitive identity to the assailant, using the (perhaps figurative) descriptor *daemonem* only at the very end of the tale. Similarly, the reference to 'sensible illusion' (*sensibili illusione*) casts doubt as to the ghost's true physicality. Ontological ambiguities can be read in other Anglo-Latin texts. *Prodigium* (prodigy), *mirabilis* (marvel) and *monstrum* (monster), were the terms used in the Augustinian canon William of Newburgh's *Histora rerum Anglicarum* (c.1198) to stress that although he did not know why the dead wandered from their graves – or, indeed, by what agency – they must surely have done so for a reason, portending contemporary or future events. This said, William was in no doubt that the prodigies described in book five of the *Historia* were violent and disease-spreading cadavers, rather than vague apparitions or elemental bodies. Indeed, William's use of the descriptor *sanguisuga* ('blood-sucker') is one of the earliest extant references to the vampiric qualities of the restless corpse in the European written record.[57] Walter Map, the famed Welsh raconteur and long-suffering clerk at the Angevin royal court, may well be satirising the narratological tropes of wonder stories in his own tales of the walking dead (c.1182), but he maintains that such entities were corporeal, recounting the (supposed) assertion made by Gilbert Foliot, Bishop of Hereford, that God gave permission to the devil to 'move about in the dead corpse' (*in corpore illo mortuo se exagitet*).[58] Other churchmen were not nearly so confident in their interpretations. Geoffrey of Burton, author of the hagiographical *Vita sancte Moduenne virginis* (c.1144), describes the havoc wrought by two dead peasants who, after initially appearing in the form of a bear (*ursorum*) and a dog (*canum*), assumed the 'appearance of men' (*speciem hominem*) and wandered through the streets of Drakelow, Staffordshire, knocking on the doors of houses and calling on the inhabitants to follow them into death. Geoffrey's statement that the peasants' corpses were exhumed, decapitated, and cremated certainly indicates that the bodies themselves were seen as the cause of the complaint, with the 'evil spirit' (*malignum spiritum*) that emerged from the pyre confirming the ultimate involvement of the devil. And yet, the offhand reference to shapeshifting casts doubt as to whether Geoffrey actually believed the dead peasants rose physically from the grave. The story concludes with the observation that once the bodies had been burnt the 'phantom' sightings ceased (*cessauerunt* [...] *phantasia)*, playing into the idea that they had been devilish projections.[59] Devils, as seen previously, were not the only type of entity to mobilise or infiltrate a cadaver. The ghost stories transcribed at the turn of the fifteenth century by an anonymous monk from the Cistercian Abbey of Byland, North Yorkshire, make mention of restless corpses being activated by the spirits of the deceased, a belief that circulated alongside the equally-valid fear that shape-shifting, incorporeal ghosts haunted the towns and countryside.[60] Indeed, a contemporaneous ghost encounter said to have taken place in Newton-le-Willows, Lancashire, merely states that the spirit of a dead woman appeared to her former lover in the form of a 'dark shadow' (*umbram obscuram).*[61] The dividing line between corporeality and incorporeality, demonic and spiritual agency, was altogether blurred.

Vernacular descriptions were just as wide-ranging. Nihtgengum (night-walker) and uncuþam sidsan (strange-visitor, or enchantments) are amongst the terms used in Anglo-Saxon medical manuals to denote agents which had the potential to do physical harm, overlapping ontologically with the Old English ælfe and the demonic *incubus*. Euphemisms for the corporeal ghost, found in phrases such as 'anon after he walkyd'[62] and 'the fende ʒode into þat cors'[63] are used in tandem with proper nouns such as *spyryte* ('spirit' or 'sprite') and *fantum* (phantom) in Middle English pastoral sources. The latter two terms could also refer to ghosts that did not possess physical form. Much in the manner of the *Chronicon de Lanercost* and Newton-le-Willows exempla, some vernacular texts decline to give a clear description of the type of body encountered, specifying only that the percipients were terrified by what they saw. The following extract from the vernacular sermon collection in BL Royal 18b.xxxii (c.1400) is a perfect example of the difficulties involved in parsing the physical makeup of the assailant from linguistic evidence alone. The story itself is a translation of a tale found in the 'libro narracionum', most likely the *Alphabetum narrationum* of Arnold of Liège (c.1307). Having presided over the burial of a man who died in a state of sin, the curate of a local church was said to have taken a stroll in the churchyard '[a]nd as he com nere þe grave þer-as þe man was buried on þe toþur day be-forne, he loked up and see where was þe most horible sight þat eve he see'.[64] Perhaps not wanting to go into too salacious a detail, the sermon writer does not dwell on the 'horrible sight' that awaited the curate. The conjuration ('tell me now what þou art') and answer ('I am þat man þat was buried ʒisturdaye') do not provide useful information on the physical nature of the ghost (i.e. was it embodied or disembodied?), but the dialogue certainly encapsulates the age-old problem of discerning the true identity and motivation of non-human

agents. Influenced, of course, by the textual communities in which they were produced, poetic works from this era demonstrate a similar equivocacy as to whether
an encountered ghost was embodied or disembodied. The 'grisly goost' (l. 125)
of Guinevere's mother described in the first part of the short alliterative romance
The Awntyrs off Arthure (c.1380–1400) is a case in point. Confronted by Gawain
and Gaynor (Guinevere) in the wilderness of Tarn Wadling, the ghost certainly
seems embodied, with the poet emphasising that its body was clotted with earth,
had sunken eyes, and was being feasted upon by toads. In a further nod to the
common cultural belief in 'water hags' and the idea that dangerous bodies could
be trapped within liminal ground, the ghost reveals that it resided 'with Lucyfer'
in the depths of a forest lake, perhaps Tarn Wadling itself (l. 164).[65] But the
strange manner of Guinevere's mother appearance – the weather turns violent
as she approaches (l. 82) – combined with the demonic symbolism of toads and
the fact that her eyes glowed like coals suggest that other, more metaphysical
forces were at play (ll.105–118).[66] And yet, it is notable that after delivering
its dour pronouncements on the sins of Arthur's Court to the stupefied Gawain
and Gaynor, the ghost 'goes with gronyng sore thorgh the greves grene' (l. 327)
rather than simply vanishing; a sense of ponderous physicality that is suggestive
(but not wholly confirms) that it was more than just an apparition. To modern and
medieval readers, it remains unclear whether Guinevere's mother was a corpse
or merely had the appearance of a corpse.[67]

As a consequence of the linguistic overlap between the substantial and insubstantial dead, English language scholarship appropriated the term 'revenant'
– deriving from the French verb 'to return' (revenir) – to describe ghosts that
appeared to be fleshy, physically attacked or fed upon the living, and whose
agency was dependent on the status of the corpse, regardless of whether it was
controlled by the devil or the deceased. 'Revenant', along with the previously-
used terms 'restless dead', 'undead' and 'embodied ghost' will be employed
interchangeably throughout this study. Although slightly anachronistic, the word
'supernatural' is sufficiently ensconced in the common cultural lexicon that it
will be used (as it already has been) as a coverall term to describe anything that
in modern-day sensibilities was non-natural in occurrence. It should be reiterated that, on the whole, medieval writers did not share the tendency of modern
scholars to codify and categorise non-human entities into discreet typological or
linguistic units. The stereotypical revenant is but one component of an interrelated
ontological system that also includes airy demons, incorporeal ghosts, as well as
folkloric entities such as the English ælfe, Germanic 'masca', and the aforementioned nihtgengum. The difficulty of interpreting ambiguous sensory experiences
is the structuring principle that forges a common thread between each type of non-
human encounter. For learned religious commentators, the ability to extrapolate
the aims and intentions of the supernatural entity from the manner of its appearance and/or effect on the human body was a fundamental technique for saving
souls. Even authors who engaged with wonder stories on a base literal level, and/
or rejected the idea that ghosts and demons actually walked the earth, were well
aware of their literary value. The question as to what type of moral, satirical, or

pedagogic purpose the corporeal ghost and cognate entities were able to serve forms the main focus of this study.

Previous research and chapter breakdown

John Blair, Nancy Caciola, Ármann Jakobsson, Claude Lecouteux, Jean-Claude Schmitt and Carl Watkins are amongst the scholars whose research has done much to invigorate our understanding of the medieval belief in the restless corpse, especially in Western European contexts.[68] Such previous investigations into the 'western' revenant have tended to approach the topic as a diachronic, European-wide survey of extant narratives (e.g. Caciola; Lecouteux Schmitt),[69] or else part of a generalised exploration of supernatural beliefs in a specific socio-historical context (e.g. Watkins's focus on England in the long twelfth century; Jakobsson's work on medieval Iceland).[70] Broader still, P. G. Maxwell-Stuart, R. C. Finucane, and David Keyworth locate medieval concerns about the undead within the wider chronology of European ghost belief from Ancient Greece to the present day.[71] Working towards similarly broad requirements, Robert Bartlett's *England Under the Norman and Angevin Kings, 1075–1225*, is like-wise not able to give the revenant much more than a brief, summative mention.[72] Even such influential short-form essays as John Blair's 'The Dangerous Dead in Early Medieval England' veer towards survey. Whilst Jean-Claude Schmitt's *Ghosts in the Middle Ages* remains the tantamount urtext where contemporary investigations into the topic are concerned, the sheer scope of Schmitt's volume also necessitates a certain elision when it comes to the close, critical analysis of *individual* case studies. As a social history on the ways in which ghost and revenant narratives were reconceptualised in response to new and innovative social and religious demands (e.g. the rise of Purgatory), *Ghosts in the Middle Ages* is peerless. And yet, such a schema does not allow for chapter-long explications of single stories or texts. Only the account of Hellequin's Hunt is afforded such a luxury.[73] Ascertaining why certain authors utilised the text of the walking corpse whilst others did not is just as valid a question as exploring the base cultural habits that gave rise to such beliefs in the first place. The need to pause, take stock, and explore why, for example, one writer deemed it important to describe a walking corpse as 'pestilential' whilst another dwelt on the failure of an apo-tropaic response is a long-overdue counterpoint to the propensity, shared by most monograph-length studies, to gloss over the literariness and idiosyncrasies of individual narratives. Indeed, the neglect of close textual analysis also extends to research on poetic representations of the restless corpse. Although Corinne Saunders's *Magic and the Supernatural in Medieval English Romance* acknowl-edges the creative utility of the revenant – one of the few monographs of its type to do so – the discussion is still restricted to a few scant pages.[74] Kenneth Rooney certainly delves deep into the topic as part of his own work on late medieval 'macabre' literature – encompassing such overlapping genres as Romance, lyric, hagiography, and exemplum – but, again, breadth of material is prioritised over focus.[75] Whatever the type of source studied or methodological approach taken, close-reading exercises have been noticeably absent in previous scholarship on the undead. This is something I hope to redress.

Working, then, within the broadly chronological frameworks advocated by Caciola and Schmitt and the geographical constraints adopted by Watkins et al., this monograph does not seek to evaluate the *entire* corpus of undead encounters from England c.1050–1450; instead, each chapter will be devoted to a close reading of a particular text. The chapters, then, are designed to be read as individualised case studies, self-contained essays that do not rely on preceding material for their internal coherence. At first glance the topic of chapter one may not seem in keeping with the aims of the volume as a whole, but the tale of the Witch of Berkeley contained in William of Malmesbury's *Gesta regum Anglorum* (c.1125) is entirely structured around the fate of a damned, seemingly restless body. One of the most infamous stories in William's literary oeuvre, the Witch of Berkeley demonstrates the dangers of devoting one's life to the devil. William was one of the most sophisticated historians of his era. Thus, it should be recognised that he did not digress from the main historical narrative solely for the purposes of entertainment (although this was certainly fundamental to the function of *mirabilia* in general). As the connotation of the descriptor 'Hellish portent' (*inferno prestigio*) suggests,[76] the danger of practising illicit magic was not the only moral truth the story was designed to convey. Following a brief overview of the context of the *Gesta regum's* creation, the main part of the chapter involves a detailed explication of the Witch of Berkeley text, exploring how the manner of the witch's fate – dragged screaming from her tomb and taken to hell on the back of a demonic horse – can be read as a commentary on the expulsion of 'foreign' or otherwise unwanted elements from the body-politic. The Witch of Berkeley proved immensity popular, enjoying a long and storied circulation history. The final part of the chapter, then, involves an attempt to chart the transmission of the narrative across different contexts and media, identifying the key nexus points that transformed the Witch of Berkeley into one of the most widely-recognised witchcraft narratives of the premodern era.

Chapter two approaches William of Newburgh's *Histora rerum Anglicarum* (c.1198) with a similar emphasis on the moral utility of the restless body. The tales of the undead contained in book five of the *Historia* are well-known to modern scholarship. From Jean-Claude Schmitt and Nancy Caciola to Carl Watkins and Jacqueline Simpson, historians have devoted considerable attention to exploring the ways in which William's *mirabilia* reflect the multivalent contemporary attitudes to the undead, and how such beliefs were influenced (or not) by such theological innovations as the 'third place' of Purgatory. Much less attention has been given to the literary function of the tales themselves. Why, exactly, did William deem such stories – wholly alien to his own sensibilities – to be suitable subject matter for a chronicle of post-Conquest history? What critical function did they serve? To answer this question, I argue that a pointed connection is being made between the pestilence of the undead corpse and the social pestilence of the inveterate sinner. Beginning with a brief analysis of the scholarly concept of 'monstrousness' and exploring the wider textual and social circumstances within which the *Historia* was written, the chapter ultimately contends that the rhetoric of the dangers of contagion binds the two types of monster together. It will be seen how the pestilential nature of the undead corpse was made manifest in the violent, chaotic tendencies of William FitzOsbert (the leader of the 1196 London rebellion), the perennially-warring kings of England and France, and the figure of William Longchamp, the hated Chancellor of England.

The first two chapters explore how wonder stories were utilised by historians for sophisticated, critical effect. However, this is not to suggest that medieval writers were completely beholden to moralisation, or did not appreciate the wry, satiric possibilities offered by ghostly or demonic visitations. Chapter three, then, operates as a close reading of the undead encounters described in Distinction II of Walter Map's *De nugis curialium* (c.1182). The *De nugis* as a whole is a preeminent work of satire, at once dry and bawdy, playful and piquant. And yet, the satirical nature of Map's tales of the walking dead have mostly gone unremarked, with scholars content to take each of the narratives at surface value.[77] Following a brief overview of the twelfth-century traditions of satirical writing and the ways in which Anglo-Latin authors approached the tropes of satire and irony, the chapter examines how Map, known to his contemporaries as a liar extraordinaire, a weaver of fiction, deconstructed the base narrative conventions of the ghost encounter. As well as using the figure of the undead corpse to satirise the conventions of wonder stories and the problems of discerning inner motivation from appearance, it will be argued that the ontological ambiguity of the restless dead mirrored the equally vague and ill-defined life of the courtier.

Departing from the Latinate literature of the long twelfth century, chapter four explores how the 'text' of the restless dead was utilised in vernacular sermon collections of the later Middle Ages, giving particular emphasis to the *Liber festivalis* (*Festial*) of the Augustinian canon and prior of Lilleshall Abbey, John Mirk (c.1380s). The impact of the Fourth Lateran Council (c.1215) on the cultural conception of non-human entities cannot be underestimated. The ecclesiastical desire to codify church practice and deny the reality of 'false' bodily resurrection led – in certain textual communities at least – to the gradual disembodiment of the returning dead. This is not to suggest that belief in revenants disappeared completely. Needing to utilise the language of lay audiences to disseminate the desired pastoral message, preachers' manuals provide a tantalising glimpse into the intersection between official discourse and local beliefs concerning demons and embodied ghosts. Following a brief evaluation of the emergence of pastoral literature in the early thirteenth century, the remainder of chapter four explores why Mirk, a provincial canon writing initially for a local Shropshire audience, decided to include tales of the walking dead in his church dedication and burial sermons.

Exempla were designed to be entertaining as well as instructive. A sophisticated pastoral writer was able to tread the fine line between surface frivolity and dour moral explication. Tales that were held in particularly high regard were ripe for re-invention by secular writers. Geoffrey Chaucer was one such poet who saw the literary potential of sermon stories, the Jewish 'blood libel' narrative of the *Prioress's Tale* being the most notable example.[78] Ultimately deriving from the 'Devil and the Advocate' exemplum first recorded by the German poet Der Stricker (c.1230), Chaucer's *Friar's Tale* (c.1390s) takes the base, moral elements of the urtext – the dangers of being unable to differentiate between appearance and intent – and furnishes it with an extended dialogue between the green-clothed devil and the tale's protagonist, the avaricious Summoner, on the makeup of demonic bodies (III, ll.1447–1522). Although the dramatic irony that infuses the tale and the mercantile behaviours of the devil and the Summoner are well known in Chaucerian scholarship, little attention has been given to the specific meanings of the devil's utterances in l.1462 ('But whan us liketh we kan take us oon') and ll.1507–1508 ('and sometyme we aryse with dede bodyes in ful sondry wyse') and their relationship to the belief in the demonic infiltration (and ambulation) of the corpse. These lines provide a tantalising insight into a hitherto unstudied aspect of Chaucer's demonological knowledge. Chapter five, then, evaluates how the devil's offhand remarks about 'taking' corpses and 'arising with dead bodies' portends the Summoner's ultimate fate and exemplifies the inner/outer dissonance that permeate the poem as a whole.

The final chapter approaches the belief in the restless dead from a slightly different angle. Rather than focusing on a particular chronicle, sermon, or poem, the 'text' in this instance relates to a particular somatic experience: the nightmare phenomenon. In modern sociological and psychological research, the 'nightmare' is broadly defined as the feeling of being chocked or pressed during sleep, an experience that is sometimes accompanied by auditory or visual hallucinations and a feeling of utmost dread. Medieval physicians and theologians often disagreed as to the ultimate cause of the nocturnal assault; the former favoured a humoural explanation (that is, such attacks were viewed as sensory illusions caused by a dysfunction of the bodily spirits), while the latter argued that devils, *incubi,* were indeed able to attack the unwary as they slept. For dream theorists, the feeling of being crushed by shadowy shapes during sleep was classified as lowest kind of 'non-predictive' dream: the *visum*, or nightmare. To what extent, then, did these learned explanations reflect the lived experiences of the general populace? Ultimately, chapter six discusses the benefits of using social-scientific data on Sleep Paralysis as a viable research tool before investigating how the 'text' of the nocturnal assault was understood by medical practitioners, learned theologians, and historical commentators. Belief, of course, is highly contingent. Even social actors who belonged to the same textual community – for example, monastic inmates – did not draw upon the *exact* same tissue of quotations when determining the cause of a traumatic sensory experience. For some, the feeling of being throttled during sleep was a severe but treatable medical condition; for others, it was tantamount proof in the reality of evil spirits, embodied or otherwise. From the Old English nihtgengum to the scholastic incubus and the Slavic vampire, the nightmare experience – and the 'text' of the restless corpse in general – found many avenues of expression.

The belief in the restless dead was not just a vague cultural memory passed down through the ages, but a central (if only occasionally manifest) part of the habitual repertoires of daily life. Taken together, the following chapters highlight the potent, critical possibilities offered by the ambiguities of the supernatural encounter. For an enterprising historian, poet or religious writer, such ambiguities could yield rich literary rewards.

Notes

1 Antonia Gransden, *Historical Writing in England II: c.1307 to the Early Sixteenth Century* (London: Routledge, 1998), pp. 114–17.
2 *Chronicon de Lanercost*, ed. by Joseph Stevenson (Edinburgh, 1839), 163–64. For the English translation, see *The Chronicle of Lanercost, 1272–1346*, ed. and trans. by Herbert Maxwell (Glasgow: MacLehose, 1913), 118–19.
3 et in summitatibus domorum vel thesaurorum bladi residere
4 quod peccatoribus terrorem incutere, et damnatorum speciem in die ultimae resurrectionis valeat praemonstratare
5 Phlegon of Tralles, *Phlegon of Tralles' Book of Marvels*, ed. and trans. by William Hansen (Exeter: University of Exeter Press, 1996), p. 27.
6 Elizabeth Warner, 'Russian Peasant Beliefs and Practices concerning Death and the Supernatural Collected in Novosokol'niki Region, Pskov Province, Russia, 1995, Part I: The Restless Dead, Wizards, and Spirit Beings', *Folklore* 111 (2000), 67–90
7 N. K. Chadwick, 'Norse Ghosts (A Study in the Draugr and the Haugbúi): I and II', *Folklore* 57 (1946), 50–65, 106–27.
8 Juliet du Boulay. 'The Greek Vampire: A Study of Cyclic Symbolism in Marriage and Death', *Man*, new ser. 17 (1982), 219–38
9 For the key study on the Slavic 'vampire', the biological and environmental reasons that prompted a belief in the undead corpse, and an introduction to the restless dead in general, see Paul Barber, *Vampires, Burial and Death: Folklore and Reality* (New Haven, CT: Yale University Press, 1988). For the etymology of 'vampire' and its cognates, see Katharina M. Wilson, 'The History of the Word "Vampire"', *Journal of the History of Ideas* 46 (1985), 577–83.
10 Brian Stock, *Listening for the Text: On the Uses of the Past* (Baltimore, MD: Johns Hopkins University Press, 1990).
11 Stock, *Listening for the Text*, p. 150.
12 Roland Barthes, *Image, Music, Text*, trans. by Stephen Heath (London: Fontana, 1977), p. 146.
13 For the key research on the medieval embodied ghost, see Nancy Caciola's seminal article, 'Wraiths, Revenants and Ritual in Medieval Culture', *Past & Present* 152 (1996), 3–45 and Caciola's recent monograph, *Afterlives: The Return of the Dead in the Middle Ages* (Ithaca, NY: Cornell University Press, 2016). See also Carl. S. Watkins, *History and the Supernatural in Medieval England* (Cambridge: Cambridge University Press, 2007); John Blair, 'The Dangerous Dead in Early Medieval England,' in *Early Medieval Studies in Memory of Patrick Wormald*, ed. by Stephen Baxter et al. (Farnham: Ashgate, 2009), pp. 539–59; Jean-Claude Schmitt, *Ghosts in the Middle Ages*, trans. by T. L. Fagan (Chicago, IL: Chicago University Press, 1998); Claude Lecouteux, *The Return of the Dead: Ghosts, Ancestors, and the Transparent Veil of the Pagan Mind*, trans. by Jon E. Graham (Rochester, NY: Inner Traditions, 2009).
14 As discussed in Lecouteux, *The Return of the Dead*. For the pervasiveness of the fear of the dead in archaeological 'texts', see Anastasia Tsaliki, 'Unusual Burials and Necrophobia: An Insight into the Burial Archaeology of Fear', *in Deviant Burial in the Archaeological Record*, ed. by Eileen Murphy (Oxbow: Oxbow Books, 2008), pp. 1–16.

15 *Bethada Náem nÉrenn: Lives of Irish Saints*, 2 vols, ed. and trans. by Charles Plummer (Oxford: Clarendon, 1922), II., pp. 162–63. For the Irish text, see I, pp. 168–69.

16 Stephen Gordon, 'Dealing with the Undead in the Later Middle Ages', in *Dealing with the Dead: Mortality and Community in the Middle Ages*, ed. by Thea Tomaini (Leiden: Brill, 2018), pp. 97–128 (at p. 126). For related practices, see Kristina Jonsson, 'Burial Rods and Charcoal Graves: New Light on Old Practices', *Viking and Medieval Scandinavia* 3 (2007), pp. 43–73 (at p. 50)

17 See, for example, Peregrine Horden, 'Disease, Dragons and Saints: The Management of Epidemics in the Dark Ages', in *Epidemics and Ideas: Essays on the Historical Perception of Pestilence*, ed. by Terence Ranger and Paul Slack (Cambridge: Cambridge University Press, 1992), pp. 45–76.

18 Grendel is explicitly described as a 'mære mearcstapa' (nightmarish stalker of the marshes, l. 103), while Grendel's Mother is called a 'merewíf' (mere-wife, l.1519). In a similar situation to the monster confronted by St Colman, the Grendelkin dwell beneath dank, cheerless lake (l. 1416). See *Beowulf*, trans. by Michael Swanton (Manchester: Manchester University Press, 1997). All subsequent references to the poem will be included in parentheses in the main body of the text. For the *fuath* and similar water monsters from Celtic folklore, see Katherine M. Briggs, *The Fairies in Tradition and Literature* (London and New York: Routledge & Kegan Paul, 1967), pp. 52, 274.

19 Andrew Joynes, *Medieval Ghost Stories: An Anthology of Miracles, Marvels and Prodigies* (Woodbridge: Boydell, 2001), p. 126

20 Schmitt, *Ghosts in the Middle Ages*, pp. 12–13.

21 Caciola, *Afterlives*, pp. 113–156, 236; Schmitt, *Ghosts in the Middle Ages*, pp. 36–38, 126–33.

22 Thietmar of Merseburg, *Ottonian Germany: the Chronicon of Thietmar of Merseburg*, trans. and annotated by David A. Warner (Manchester: Manchester University Press, 2013), pp. 75–77. Caciola convincingly argues that the burning of the Utrecht priest relates to the pagan Slavic practice of offering burnt sacrifices to the Gods. See *Afterlives*, pp. 138–39.

23 Hartmut Hoffman and Rudolf Pokorny, *Das Dekret des Bischofs Burchard von Worms* (Munich, MGH, 1991).

24 Ludger Körntgen, 'Canon Law and the Practice of Penance: Burchard of Worm's Penitential, *Early Medieval Europe* 14 (2006), 103–17.

25 Greta Austin, *Shaping Church Law Around the Year 1000: The Decretum of Burchard of Worms* (Farnham: Ashgate, 2009), pp. 230–39.

26 'Fecisti quod quaedam mulieres instinctu diaboli facere solent? Cum aliquis infans sine baptismo mortuus fuerit, tollunt cadaver parvuli, et ponunt in aliquo secreto loco, et palo corpusculum ejus transfigunt, dicentes, si sic non fecissent, quod infantulus surgeret, et multos laedere posset? Si fecisti, aut consensisti, aut credidisti, duos annos per legitimas ferias debes ponitere', in Burchard of Worms, *Burchardi Vormatiensis Episcopi, Opera*, PL 140, ed. by J-P Migne (Paris, 1853), col. 974D.

27 'Fecisti quod quaedam facere solent, diaboli audacia repletae? Cum aliqua femina parere debet, et non potest, dum, parere non potest, in ipso dolore si morte obierit, in ispo sepulcro matrem cum infante palo in terram transfigunt. Si fecisti vel consensisti, duos annos per legitimas ferias debes poenitere', in Burchard of Worms, *Opera*, PL 140, cols. 974D–975A. For the English translations, see *Medieval Handbooks of Penance: A Translation of the Principal 'libri poenitentiales' and Selections from Related Documents*, ed. and trans. by John T. McNeill and Helena M. Gamer (New York: Columbia University Press, 1990), pp. 339–340.

28 Victoria Smirnova, '"And Nothing Will be Wasted": Actualization of the Past in Caesarius of Heisterbach's *Dialogus Miraculorum*', in *The Making of Memory in the Middle Ages*, ed. by Lucie Doležalová (Turnhout: Brill, 2010), pp. 253–65 (at p. 255).

29 Caesarius of Heisterbach, *Dialogus miraculorum*, dist. XII.15, in *Caesarii Heisterbacensis Monachi Ordinis Cisterciensis Dialogus Miraculorum*, ed. by Joseph

Strange, 2 vols. (Cologne: Lempertz, 1851), II, p. 327. Encounters with embodied ghosts and restless corpses can be found in books five ('On Demons'), eleven ('On Dying') and twelve ('On the Reward of the Dead'). For Caesarius's compilation as a storehouse of local belief, see Smirnova, 'And Nothing Will be Wasted', p. 257.

30 Inge Skovgaard-Petersen, 'Saxo's History of the Danes – an Interpretation', *Scandinavian Journal of History* 13 (1988), pp. 87–93.

31 'Nam ferro secui mox caput eius, Perfodique nocens stipite corpus', in Saxo Grammaticus, *Saxonis Grammatici Gesta Danorvm*, ed. by Alfred Holder (Strasburg, 1886), pp. 162–63. For the English translation, see Saxo Grammaticus, *The History of the Danes: Books I–IX*, trans. by Peter Fisher, ed. by Hilda Ellis Davidson (Cambridge: Brewer, 1979), pp. 150–151. See also Gordon, 'Dealing with the Undead', p. 106.

32 Much work has been conducted on the *draugr*. In the first instance, see Ármann Jakobsson, 'Vampires and Watchmen: Categorising the Icelandic Undead', *Journal of English and Germanic Philology* 110 (2011), 281–300; and William Sayers, 'The Alien and Alienated as Unquiet Dead in the Sagas of the Icelanders', in *Monster Theory*, ed. by Jeffrey Jerome Cohen (Minneapolis, Minnesota University Press, 1996), pp. 242–63; H. R. Ellis Davidson, 'The Restless Dead: An Icelandic Ghost Story', in *The Folklore of Ghosts*, ed. by Hilda R. Ellis Davidson and W. M. S. Russell (Cambridge: Brewer, 1981), pp. 155–75.

33 Sona þæt onfunde fyrena hyrde / þæt he ne mette middangeardes / eorþan sceatta on elran men / mundgripe maran (soon the guardian of sin found that he had not met in all of middle earth, in the regions of the world, a greater hand grip in another man).

34 A helpful overview on the relationship between Glamr and Grendel is provided in Andy Orchard, *Pride and Prodigies: Studies in the Monsters of the Beowulf-Manuscript* (Toronto, ONT: Toronto University Press, 2003), pp. 140–68.

35 The term 'epidemic' is something of a misnomer in this context. Due to changing political circumstances on the Austrian-Hungarian border with the Ottoman Empire, imperial officials and western commentators began to pay closer attention to the recently annexed Serbian borderlands, thus committing to the page tales of contagious, undead corpses that had previously only circulated locally as oral texts. Thus, while the changing social situation may have indeed precipitated more 'outbreaks' among the local populace, the epidemic itself can be read as a purely western construct. For the political context of the emergence of vampire literature in the Latin West, see the work of Michael Pickering, '"Sie Mußten in Feuer": Changing Polices within the Habsburg Monarchy on the Destruction of Vampire Bodies', in *Evil and the State: Interdisciplinary Perspectives*, ed. by Kiran Sarma and Ben Livings (Oxford: Inter-Disciplinary Press, 2013), pp. 11–29; 'Constructing the Vampire: Spirit Agency in the Anonymous *Acten-mabige und Umstansliche Relation von denen Vampiren oder Menschen-Saugern (1732)*', in *Unnatural Reproductions and Monstrosity: The Birth of the Monster in Literature, Film, and Media*, ed. by Andrea Wood and Brandy Schillace (Amherst, NY: Cambria Press, 2014), pp. 69–88. See also the first chapter of Erik Butler, *Metamorphoses of the Vampire in Literature and Film: Cultural Transformations in Europe, 1732–1933* (Woodbridge: *1933* (Rochester, NY: Camden House, 2010), pp. 27–51.

36 Heinrich Kornmann, *De Miraculis Mortuorum* (Frankfurt, 1610); Leo Allatius, *De Graecorum hodie quorundam opinationibus* (1645); Philpp Rohr, *Dissertatio Historico-Philosophica de Masticatione Mortuorum* (Leipzig, 1679).

37 Frombald, 'Copia eines Schreibens aus dem Gradisker District in Ungarn,' in *Wienerisches Diarium*, 21 July 1725, pp. 11–12.

38 Johann Flückinger, *Visum et Repertum* (Nuremburg, 1732).

39 Including, but not limited to: Michael Ranft, *Dissertatio historic-criticia des masticatione mortuorum in tumulis* (Leipzig, 1728); Johann Christian Stock, *Dissertatio physica de cadaveribus sanguisugis* (Jena, 1732); Johann Heinrich Zopf, *Dissertatio de Vampyris Serviensibus* (Duisburg, 1733); Augustin Calmet, *Dissertations Upon the*

Apparitions of Angels, Daemons, and Ghosts, and Concerning the Vampires of Hungary, Bohemia, Moravia, and Silesia (London, 1759 [first published, in French, in 1746].

40 Nora Berend, 'Historical Writing in Central Europe (Bohemia, Hungary, Poland), c. 950–1400', in *The Oxford History of Historical Writing: Volume 2: 400-1400*, ed. by Sarah Foot and Chase F. Robinson (Oxford: Oxford University Press, 2014), pp. 312–27 (at p. 324)

41 A. d. MCCCXLIV. Quedam mulier in Lewin mortua fuit et sepulta. Post sepulturam autem surgebat et multos iugulabat et post quemlibet saltabat. Et cum fuisset transfixa, fluebat sanguis sicud de animali vivo et devoraverat slogerium proprium plus quam medium, et cum extraheretur, totum fuit in sanguine. Et cum deberet cremari, non poterant ligna aliqualiter accendi nisi de tegulis ecclesie ad informacionem aliquarum vetularum. Postquam autem fuisset transfixa, adhuc semper surgebat; sed cum fuisset cremata, tunc totum malum conquievit, in Neplach of Opatovice, *Chronicon*, in *Fontes rerum Bohemicarum* III, ed. J. Emler (Prague, 1882), p. 481. This encounter is also discussed in Gordon, 'Dealing with the Undead', p. 98.

42 'multum nocuerunt michi, nam dederunt michi baculum, ut me a canibus defendam', in Neplach of Opatovice, *Chronicon*, p. 480.

43 See, for example, Tsaliki, 'Unusual Burials and Necrophobia'; Marek Polcyn and Elżbieta Gajda, 'Buried with Sickles: Early Modern Interments from Drawsko, Poland,' *Antiquity* 89 (2015), 1373–87; Tracy K. Betsinger and Amy B. Scott, 'Governing from the Grave: Vampire Burials and Social Order in Post-medieval Poland,' *Cambridge Archaeological Journal* 24 (2014), 467–76; Leszek Gardeła and Kamil Kajkowski, 'Vampires, Criminals, or Slaves? Reinterpreting 'Deviant Burials' in Early Medieval Poland,' *World Archaeology* 45 (2013), 780–96. See, also, the use of osteoarchaeological data in tracing the relationship between tuberculosis outbreaks and vampire beliefs in nineteenth-century New England: Paul S. Sledzik and Nicholas Bellantoni, 'Brief Communication: Bioarcheological and Biocultural Evidence for the New England Vampire Folk Belief', *American Journal of Physical Anthropology* 94 (1994), 269–74. For the archaeology of the restless dead in medieval England, see Stephen Gordon, 'Dealing with the Undead', and 'Disease, Sin and the Walking Dead in Medieval England, c. 1100-1350: A Note on the Documentary and Archaeological Evidence', in *Medicine, Healing and Performance*, ed. by Stephen Gordon et al. (Oxford: Oxbow, 2014), pp. 55–75; S. Mays, et al., 'A multidisciplinary study of a burnt and mutilated assemblage of human remains from a deserted Mediaeval village in England', *Journal of Archaeological Science: Reports* 16 (2017), 441–55.

44 Discussed in English contexts in Watkins, *History and the Supernatural*, p. 14.

45 Skovgaard-Petersen, 'Saxo's History of the Danes', p. 90.

46 See Brian Cummings and James Simpson, 'Introduction', in *Cultural Reformations: Medieval and Renaissance in Literary History*, ed. by Brian Cummings and James Simpson (Oxford: Oxford University Press, 2010), pp. 1–13.

47 For an overview of Pope Gregory VII's life, career, and reforms, such as the consolidation of the idea of papal infallibility and the subservience of secular lords to church authority, see H. E. J. Cowdrey's magisterial *Pope Gregory VII, 1073–1085* (Oxford: Clarendon, 1998).

48 A scholarly coverall term to describe such innovations as increased urbanisation, the rise of the mendicant orders, the development of stable nation-states, the formalisation of the school-system, new approaches to biblical exegesis (and the need to 'order' the universe in general), and the reception and circulation of Greek and Arabic texts in the Latin West. See Robert Swanson, *The Twelfth-Century Renaissance* (Manchester: Manchester University Press, 1999); Tina Stiefel, *The Intellectual Revolution in Twelfth-Century Europe* (London: Croom Helm, 1985).

49 Paul Barber describes in detail about how the processes of decomposition influenced the ways in which dangerous bodies were managed, in *Vampires, Burial and Death*, pp. 102–119; 166–77.

50 The concept of a 'pagan survival' is rejected by Carl Watkins in '"Folklore" and "Popular Religion" in Britain during the Middle Ages', *Folklore* 115 (2004), 140–50.

51 For anthropological insights into the formation of meaning in ritual contexts, see Edward L. Schieffelin, 'Performance and the Cultural Construction of Reality', *American Ethnologist*, 12 (1985), 707–24; Leo Howe, 'Risk, Ritual and Performance', *Journal of the Royal Anthropological Institute* 6 (2000), 63–79.

52 These cultural links are discussed in detail in Dawn M. Hadley, *The Northern Danelaw: Its Social Structure c. 800–1100* (London: Leicester University Press, 2000).

53 See definition two in 'preternatural, adj. and n.', *OED Online*, Oxford University Press, December 2018, www.oed.com/view/Entry/150991 [Accessed 29 January 2019].

54 See especially Ia.105, art. 7 and Ia. 110, art. 4 of the *Summa Theologiae*, in *Thomas Aquinas, Summa Theologiae, Volume 14: Divine Government (Ia. 103–109),* ed. and trans. by T. C. O' Brien (London: Blackfriars, 1975), pp. 82–85; and *Volume 15: The World Order (Ia. 110–119),* ed. and trans. by M. J. Charlesworth (London: Blackfriars, 1970), pp. 14-17. A summary of Thomas's conceptualisation of God's power can be found in Michael Goodich, *Miracles and Wonders: The Development of the Concept of Miracle, 1150–1350* (Aldershot: Ashgate, 2007), pp. 19–21.

55 Watkins, *History and the Supernatural*, p. 18. For the convoluted history of the terms 'preternatural' and 'supernatural' in theological and scientific discourse, and the demystification of the preternatural in the early modern period, see Lorraine Daston, 'Marvelous Facts and Miraculous Evidence in Early Modern Europe', *Critical Inquiry* 18 (1991), 93–124.

56 Porro miracula dicimus usitatius que preter naturam divine uirtuti ascribimus ('Now we generally call those things miracles which, being preternatural, we ascribe to divine power'), Gervase of Tilbury, *Otia Imperialia: Recreation for an Emperor*, ed. and trans. by S.E. Banks and J.W. Binns, Oxford Medieval Texts (Oxford: Clarendon, 2002), III. Preface (pp. 558–59).

57 Blair, 'The Dangerous Dead in Early Medieval England,' p. 541.

58 Walter Map, *De Nugis Curialium,* ed. and trans. by M. R. James; revised by C. N. L. Brooke and R. A. B. Mynors. Oxford: Clarendon Press 1983), distinction. ii.27 (at p. 202). All future references to the Latin text and English translation will be taken from this source, hereafter in the form of '*De nugis,* dist. ii.27.'

59 Geoffrey of Burton, *Life and Miracles of St. Modwenna,* ed. and trans. by Robert Bartlett, Oxford Medieval Texts (Oxford: Clarendon Press, 2002), pp. 196–97.

60 M. R. James, 'Twelve Medieval Ghost-Stories', *English Historical Review* 37 (1922), 413–22.

61 H. E. D. Blakiston, 'Two More Medieval Ghost Stories', *English Historical Review* 38 (1923), 85–87.

62 *The Armburgh Papers: The Brokholes Inheritance in Warwickshire, Hertfordshire and Essex c.1417–c.1453,* ed. by Christine Carpenter (Woodbridge: Boydell & Brewer, 1998), p. 62.

63 See *Mirk's Festial: A Collection of Homilies by Johannes Mirkus (John Mirk),* Part I: ed. by Theodor Erbe, EETS, e.s. 96 (London: Kegan Paul, Trench, Trübner & co, 1905), p. 295.

64 *Middle English Sermons: Edited from British Museum MS Royal 18 B xxiii,* ed. by Woodburn O. Ross, EETS o.s. 209 (London: Oxford University Press, 1940), p. 205.

65 Gordon, 'Dealing with the Undead', pp. 124–26.

66 The first section of *The Awntyrs off Arthure* was closely influenced by the prevailing literary and moralistic tradition of the Three Living and Three Dead, which emerged almost fully formed in the historical record with Baudoin de Condé's vernacular French poem, *Dit des trois morts et des trois vifs (c.*1280). In brief, the 'Three Dead' text describes how three princes (sometimes rendered as kings) encounter their dead, rotten counterparts in a forest whilst out hunting. The cadavers implore their living doppelgangers to repent their frivolous lives, using the now infamous refrain: 'as we

were, you are; what we are, you will be'. The didactic message of the poem is clear: earthly glory is transitory; death is a universal equaliser that makes no allowances for social rank or status. Building on de Condé's original, English, German, Latin, and Italian versions of the poem (and the associated visual motif) circulated widely throughout the fourteenth and fifteenth centuries. *The Awntyrs off Arthure* seems to have been especially influenced by the Middle English *De Tribus Regibus Mortuis* text. It also appears to have drawn upon another popular moralistic story from this era, the *Trentalle Sancti Gregorii*, which details an encounter between the eponymous saint and purgatorial ghost of his own mother. For the primary *Awntyrs off Arthure* text, see *Sir Gawain: Eleven Romances and Tales*, ed. by Thomas Hahn (Kalamazoo, MI: Medieval Institute Publications 1995), available online at: https://d.lib.rochester.edu/teams/text/hahn-sir-gawain-awntyrs-off-arthur [accessed 8 March 2019]. Much work has been conducted on the *The Awntyrs off Arthure* and its literary cognates, but in the first instance, see Thorlac Turville-Petre, '"Summer Sunday", "De Tribus Regibus Mortuis", and "The Awntyrs off Arthure": Three Poems in the Thirteen-Line Stanza', *The Review of English Studies*, New Ser. 25 (1974), 1–14; Christine Chism, *Alliterative Revivals* (Philadelphia, PA: University of Pennsylvania Press, 2002), pp. 237–64.

67 The majority of Arthurian scholars view the ghost as an apparition. For one of the few readings of Guinevere's mother as a decomposing corpse, see Margaret Robson, 'From Beyond the Grave: Darkness at Noon in the The Awntyrs off Arthure', in *The Spirit of Medieval Popular Romance*, ed. by Ad Putter and Jane Gilbert (Harlow: Longman, 2000), pp. 219–36.

68 See n. 13 and 32.

69 Caciola, *Afterlives*, pp. 206–53; Schmitt, *Ghosts in the Middle Ages*, pp. 61, 81–83, 147–48; Leceuteux, *The Return of the Dead.*

70 Watkins, *History and the Supernatural*, pp. 170–201; Ármann Jakobsson, *The Troll Inside You: Paranormal Activity in the Medieval North* (Santa Barbara, CA: Punctum Books, 2017).

71 R. C. Finucane, *Appearances of the Dead: A Cultural History of Ghosts* (London: Junction, 1982), pp. 49–89; P. G. Maxwell-Stuart, *A History of Phantoms, Ghouls & Other Spirits of the Dead* (Stroud: Tempus, 2006), pp. 39–78; David Keyworth, *Troublesome Corpses: Vampires & Revenants from Antiquity to Present* (Southend-on-Sea: Desert Island Books, 2007), pp. 57–78.

72 Robert Bartlett, *England Under the Norman and Angevin Kings, 1075–1225* (Oxford: Clarendon, 2000), 612–15.

73 Schmitt, *Ghosts in the Middle Ages*, pp. 93–121; See also Caciola, *Afterlives*, pp. 157–205.

74 Corinne Saunders, *Magic and the Supernatural in Medieval English Romance* (Woodbridge: Boydell & Brewer, 2010), pp. 222–25.

75 Kenneth Rooney, *Mortality and Imagination: The Life of the Dead in Medieval English Literature* (Turnhout: Brepols, 2011).

76 William of Malmesbury, *Gesta regum Anglorum: History of the English Kings, vol. 1* ed. and trans. by R. A. B. Mynors; completed by R. M. Thomson and M. Winterbottom, Oxford Medieval Texts (Clarendon: Oxford, 1998), ii. 204 (at pp. 376–77). Hereafter 'GrA'.

77 Caciola, *Afterlives*, p. 217. Jacqueline Simpson, 'Repentant Soul or Walking Corpse? Debatable Apparitions in Medieval England', *Folklore* 114 (2003), 389–402 (at p. 393).

78 The tale of a Christian boy murdered by Jews, whose crimes are revealed by the miraculous intervention of God, is a commonplace story in preachers' manuals and exemplum collections. For the indebtedness of the *Prioress's Tale* to the 'language of the pulpit', see Siegfried Wenzel, 'Chaucer and the Language of Contemporary Preaching', *Studies in Philology* 73 (1976), 138–61 (at p. 142).

Primary sources

Allatius, Leo, *De Graecorum hodie quorundam opinationibus* (Cologne, 1645).

Aquinas, Thomas, *Summa Theologiae, Volume 14: Divine Government (Ia. 103–109)*, ed. and trans. by T. C. O'Brien (London: Blackfriars, 1975).

Aquinas, Thomas, *St. Thomas Aquinas, Summa Theologiae, Volume 15: The World Order (Ia. 110–119)*, ed. and trans. by M. J. Charlesworth (London: Blackfriars, 1970).

The Armburgh Papers: The Brokholes Inheritance in Warwickshire, Hertfordshire and Essex c.1417–c.1453, ed. by Christine Carpenter (Woodbridge: Boydell & Brewer, 1998).

Bethada Náem nÉrenn: Lives of Irish Saints, 2 vols, ed. and trans. by Charles Plummer (Oxford: Clarendon, 1922).

Beowulf, ed. and trans. by Michael Swanton (Manchester: Manchester University Press, 1997).

Blakiston, H. E. D., 'Two More Medieval Ghost Stories', *English Historical Review* 38 (1923), 85–87.

Burchard of Worms, *Burchardi Vormatiensis Episcopi, Opera*, PL 140, ed. by J.-P. Migne (Paris, 1853).

Caesarius of Heisterbach, *Dialogus miraculorum*, dist. XII.15, in *Caesarii Heisterbacensis Monachi Ordinis Cisterciensis Dialogus Miraculorum*, ed. by Joseph Strange, 2 vols (Cologne: Lempertz, 1851).

Calmet, Augustin, *Dissertations Upon the Apparitions of Angels, Daemons, and Ghosts, and Concerning the Vampires of Hungary, Bohemia, Moravia, and Silesia* (London, 1759).

The Chronicle of Lanercost, 1272–1346, ed. and trans. by Herbert Maxwell (Glasgow: MacLehose, 1913).

Chronicon de Lanercost, ed. by Joseph Stevenson (Edinburgh: Bannatyne Club, 1839).

Flückinger, Johann, *Visum et Repertum* (Nuremburg, 1732).

Frombald, 'Copia eines Schreibens aus dem Gradisker District in Ungarn,' in *Wienerisches Diarium*, 21 July 1725, pp. 11–12.

Geoffrey of Burton, *Life and Miracles of St. Modwenna*, ed. and trans. by Robert Bartlett, Oxford Medieval Texts (Oxford: Clarendon Press, 2002).

Gervase of Tilbury, *Otia Imperialia: Recreation for an Emperor*, ed. and trans. by S. E. Banks and J. W. Binns, Oxford Medieval Texts (Oxford: Clarendon, 2002).

James, M. R., 'Twelve Medieval Ghost-Stories', *English Historical Review* 37 (1922), 413–22.

John Mirk, *Mirk's Festial: A Collection of Homilies by Johannes Mirkus (John Mirk)*, Part I: ed. by Theodor Erbe, EETS e.s. 96 (London: Kegan Paul, Trench, Trübner & Co., 1905).

Joynes, Andrew, *Medieval Ghost Stories: An Anthology of Miracles, Marvels and Prodigies* (Woodbridge: Boydell, 2001).

Kornmann, Heinrich, *De Miraculis Mortuorum* (Frankfurt, 1610).

Medieval Handbooks of Penance: A Translation of the Principal 'libri poenitentiales' and Selections from Related Documents, ed. and trans. by John T. McNeill and Helena M. Gamer (New York: Columbia University Press, 1990).

Middle English Sermons: Edited from British Museum MS Royal 18 B xxiii, ed. by Woodburn O. Ross, EETS o.s. 209 (London: Oxford University Press for the Early English Text Society, 1940).

Neplach of Opatovice, *Chronicon*, in *Fontes rerum Bohemicarum* III, ed. J. Emler (Prague: Museum of the Kingdom of Bohemia, 1882).

Phlegon of Tralles, *Phlegon of Tralles' Book of Marvels*, ed. and trans. by William Hansen (Exeter: University of Exeter Press, 1996).

Ranft, Michael, *Dissertatio historic-criticia des masticatione mortuorum in tumulis* (Leipzig, 1728).

Rohr, Philipp, *Dissertatio Historico-Philosophica de Masticatione Mortuorum* (Leipzig, 1679).

Saxo Grammaticus, *The History of the Danes: Books I–IX*, trans. by Peter Fisher; ed. by Hilda Ellis Davidson (Cambridge: Brewer, 1979).

Saxo Grammaticus, *Saxonis Grammatici Gesta Danorvm*, ed. by Alfred Holder (Strasburg, Trübner, 1886).

Sir Gawain: Eleven Romances and Tales, ed. by Thomas Hahn (Kalamazoo, MI: Medieval Institute Publications, 1995).

Stock, Johann Christian, *Dissertatio physica de cadaveribus sanguisugis* (Jena, 1732).

Thietmar of Merseburg, *Ottonian Germany: The Chronicon of Thietmar of Merseburg*, trans. and annotated by David A. Warner (Manchester: Manchester University Press, 2013).

Walter Map, *De Nugis Curialium*, ed. and trans. by M. R. James; revised by C. N. L. Brooke and R. A. B. Mynors, Oxford Medieval Texts (Oxford: Clarendon Press, 1983).

William of Malmesbury, *Gesta regum Anglorum*: *History of the English Kings*, vol. 1, ed. and trans. by R. A. B. Mynors; completed by R. M. Thomson and M. Winterbottom, Oxford Medieval Texts (Oxford: Clarendon, 1998).

Zopf, Johann Heinrich, *Dissertatio de Vampyris Serviensibus* (Duisburg, 1733).

Secondary sources

Austin, Greta, *Shaping Church Law Around the Year 1000: The Decretum of Burchard of Worms* (Farnham: Ashgate, 2009).

Barber, Paul, *Vampires, Burial and Death: Folklore and Reality* (New Haven, CT: Yale University Press, 1988).

Barthes, Roland, *Image, Music, Text*, trans. by Stephen Heath (London: Fontana, 1977).

Bartlett, Robert, *England Under the Norman and Angevin Kings, 1075–1225* (Oxford: Clarendon, 2000).

Blair, John, 'The Dangerous Dead in Early Medieval England', in *Early Medieval Studies in Memory of Patrick Wormald*, ed. by Stephen Baxter et al. (Farnham: Ashgate, 2009), pp. 539–59.

Berend, Nora, 'Historical Writing in Central Europe (Bohemia, Hungary, Poland), c.950–1400', in *The Oxford History of Historical Writing: Volume 2: 400–1400*, ed. by Sarah Foot and Chase F. Robinson (Oxford: Oxford University Press, 2014), pp. 312–27.

Betsinger, Tracy K. and Amy B. Scott, 'Governing from the Grave: Vampire Burials and Social Order in Post-medieval Poland', *Cambridge Archaeological Journal* 24 (2014), 467–76.

Butler, Erik, *Metamorphoses of the Vampire in Literature and Film: Cultural Transformations in Europe, 1732–1933* (Rochester, NY: Camden House, 2010).

Caciola, Nancy, 'Wraiths, Revenants and Ritual in Medieval Culture', *Past & Present* 152 (1996), 3–45.

Caciola, Nancy Mandeville, *Afterlives: The Return of the Dead in the Middle Ages* (Ithaca, NY: Cornell University Press, 2016).

Chadwick, N. K., 'Norse Ghosts (A Study in the Draugr and the Haugbúi): I and II', *Folklore* 57 (1946), 50–65, 106–27.

Chism, Christine, *Alliterative Revivals* (Philadelphia, PA: University of Pennsylvania Press, 2002).

Cowdrey, H. E. J., *Pope Gregory VII, 1073–1085* (Oxford: Clarendon, 1998).

Cummings, Brian and James Simpson, 'Introduction', in *Cultural Reformations: Medieval and Renaissance in Literary History*, ed. by Brian Cummings and James Simpson (Oxford: Oxford University Press, 2010), pp. 1–13.

Daston, Lorraine, 'Marvelous Facts and Miraculous Evidence in Early Modern Europe', *Critical Inquiry* 18 (1991), 93–124.

Du Boulay, Juliet, 'The Greek Vampire: A Study of Cyclic Symbolism in Marriage and Death', *Man*, new ser. 17 (1982), 219–38.

Ellis Davidson, H. R., 'The Restless Dead: An Icelandic Ghost Story', in *The Folklore of Ghosts*, ed. by Hilda R. Ellis Davidson and W. M. S. Russell (Cambridge: Brewer, 1981), pp. 155–75.

Finucane, R. C., *Appearances of the Dead: A Cultural History of Ghosts* (London: Junction, 1982).

Gardeła, Leszek and Kamil Kajkowski, 'Vampires, Criminals, or Slaves? Reinterpreting "Deviant Burials" in Early Medieval Poland', *World Archaeology* 45 (2013), 780–96.

Goodich, Michael, *Miracles and Wonders: The Development of the Concept of Miracle, 1150–1350* (Aldershot: Ashgate, 2007).

Gordon, Stephen, 'Dealing with the Undead in the Later Middle Ages', in *Dealing with the Dead: Mortality and Community in the Middle Ages*, ed. by Thea Tomaini (Leiden: Brill, 2018), pp. 97–128.

Gordon, Stephen, 'Disease, Sin and the Walking Dead in Medieval England, c.1100–1350: A Note on the Documentary and Archaeological Evidence', in *Medicine, Healing and Performance*, ed. by Stephen Gordon et al. (Oxford: Oxbow, 2014), pp. 55–75.

Gransden, Antonia, *Historical Writing in England II: c.1307 to the Early Sixteenth Century* (London: Routledge, 1998).

Hadley, Dawn M., *The Northern Danelaw: Its Social Structure c.800–1100* (London: Leicester University Press, 2000).

Hoffman, Hartmut and Rudolf Pokorny, *Das Dekret des Bischofs Burchard von Worms* (Munich: MGH, 1991).

Horden, Peregrine, 'Disease, Dragons and Saints: The Management of Epidemics in the Dark Ages', in *Epidemics and Ideas: Essays on the Historical Perception of Pestilence*, ed. by Terence Ranger and Paul Slack (Cambridge: Cambridge University Press, 1992), pp. 45–76.

Howe, Leo, 'Risk, Ritual and Performance', *Journal of the Royal Anthropological Institute* 6 (2000), 63–79.

Jakobsson, Ármann, *The Troll Inside You: Paranormal Activity in the Medieval North* (Santa Barbara, CA: Punctum Books, 2017).

Jakobsson, Ármann, 'Vampires and Watchmen: Categorising the Icelandic Undead', *Journal of English and Germanic Philology* 110 (2011), 281–300.

Jonsson, Kristina, 'Burial Rods and Charcoal Graves: New Light on Old Practices', *Viking and Medieval Scandinavia* 3 (2007), pp. 43–73.

Keyworth, David, *Troublesome Corpses: Vampires & Revenants from Antiquity to Present* (Southend-on-Sea: Desert Island Books, 2007).

Körntgen, Ludger, 'Canon Law and the Practice of Penance: Burchard of Worm's Penitential', *Early Medieval Europe* 14 (2006), 103–17.

Lecouteux, Claude, *The Return of the Dead: Ghosts, Ancestors, and the Transparent Veil of the Pagan Mind*, trans. by Jon E. Graham (Rochester, NY: Inner Traditions, 2009).

Maxwell-Stuart, P. G., *A History of Phantoms, Ghouls & Other Spirits of the Dead* (Stroud: Tempus, 2006).

Mays, S., R. Fryer, A. W. G. Pike, M. J. Cooper, and P. Marshall, 'A Multidisciplinary Study of a Burnt and Mutilated Assemblage of Human Remains from a Deserted Mediaeval Village in England', *Journal of Archaeological Science: Reports* 16 (2017), 441–55.

Orchard, Andy, *Pride and Prodigies: Studies in the Monsters of the Beowulf-Manuscript* (Toronto, ON: Toronto University Press, 2003).

Pickering, Michael, 'Constructing the Vampire: Spirit Agency in the Anonymous *Acten-mabige und Umstansliche Relation von denen Vampiren oder Menschen-Saugern (1732)*', in *Unnatural Reproductions and Monstrosity: The Birth of the Monster in Literature, Film, and Media*, ed. by Andrea Wood and Brandy Schillace (Amherst, NY: Cambria Press, 2014), pp. 69–88.

Pickering, Michael, '"Sie Mußten ins Feuer": Changing Polices within the Habsburg Monarchy on the Destruction of Vampire Bodies', in *Evil and the State: Interdisciplinary Perspectives*, ed. by Kiran Sarma and Ben Livings (Oxford: Inter-Disciplinary Press, 2013), pp. 11–29.

Polcyn, Marek and Elżbieta Gajda, 'Buried with Sickles: Early Modern Interments from Drawsko, Poland', *Antiquity* 89 (2015), 1373–87.

Robson, Margaret, 'From Beyond the Grave: Darkness at Noon in the The Awntyrs off Arthure', in *The Spirit of Medieval Popular Romance*, ed. by Ad Putter and Jane Gilbert (Harlow: Longman, 2000), pp. 219–36.

Rooney, Kenneth, *Mortality and Imagination: The Life of the Dead in Medieval English Literature* (Turnhout: Brepols, 2011).

Saunders, Corinne, *Magic and the Supernatural in Medieval English Romance* (Woodbridge: Boydell & Brewer, 2010).

Sayers, William, 'The Alien and Alienated as Unquiet Dead in the Sagas of the Icelanders', in *Monster Theory*, ed. by Jeffrey Jerome Cohen (Minneapolis: Minnesota University Press, 1996), pp. 242–63.

Schieffelin, Edward L., 'Performance and the Cultural Construction of Reality', *American Ethnologist* 12 (1985), 707–24.

Schmitt, Jean-Claude, *Ghosts in the Middle Ages*, trans. by T. L. Fagan (Chicago, IL: Chicago University Press, 1998).

Simpson, Jacqueline, 'Repentant Soul or Walking Corpse? Debatable Apparitions in Medieval England', *Folklore* 114 (2003), 389–402.

Skovgaard-Petersen, Inge, 'Saxo's History of the Danes – an Interpretation', *Scandinavian Journal of History* 13 (1988), 87–93.

Sledzik, Paul S. and Nicholas Bellantoni, 'Brief Communication: Bioarcheological and Biocultural Evidence for the New England Vampire Folk Belief', *American Journal of Physical Anthropology* 94 (1994), 269–74.

Smirnova, Victoria, '"And Nothing Will be Wasted": Actualization of the Past in Caesarius of Heisterbach's *Dialogus Miraculorum*', in *The Making of Memory in the Middle Ages*, ed. by Lucie Doležalová (Turnhout: Brill, 2010), pp. 253–65.

Stiefel, Tina, *The Intellectual Revolution in Twelfth-Century Europe* (London: Croom Helm, 1985).

Stock, Brian, *Listening for the Text: On the Uses of the Past* (Baltimore, MD: Johns Hopkins University Press, 1990).

Swanson, Robert, *The Twelfth-Century Renaissance* (Manchester: Manchester University Press, 1999).

Tsaliki, Anastasia, 'Unusual Burials and Necrophobia: An Insight into the Burial Archaeology of Fear', in *Deviant Burial in the Archaeological Record*, ed. by Eileen Murphy (Oxbow: Oxbow Books, 2008), pp. 1–16.

Turville-Petre, Thorlac, '"Summer Sunday", "De Tribus Regibus Mortuis", and "The Awntyrs off Arthure": Three Poems in the Thirteen-Line Stanza', *The Review of English Studies*, New Ser. 25 (1974), 1–14.

Warner, Elizabeth, 'Russian Peasant Beliefs and Practices concerning Death and the Supernatural Collected in Novosokol'niki Region, Pskov Province, Russia, 1995, Part I: The Restless Dead, Wizards, and Spirit Beings', *Folklore* 111 (2000), 67–90.

Watkins, Carl, '"Folklore" and "Popular Religion" in Britain during the Middle Ages', *Folklore* 115 (2004), 140–50.

Watkins, Carl S., *History and the Supernatural in Medieval England* (Cambridge: Cambridge University Press, 2007).

Wenzel, Siegfried, 'Chaucer and the Language of Contemporary Preaching', *Studies in Philology* 73 (1976), 138–61.

Wilson, Katharina M., 'The History of the Word "Vampire"', *Journal of the History of Ideas* 46 (1985), 577–83.

1 The Witch of Berkeley in context

Introduction

The question of how to deal with the misuse of supernatural power was one of the many Christian inheritances from the Classical world. Treatises against illicit magic and the veneration of evil spirits – formerly pagan *daemones* – formed the very bedrock of nascent theological discourse. From Tertullian's declaration that giving honour to airy demons was an affront to God,[1] to Augustine's polemics against augury,[2] astrology,[3] and the practice of divination through Holy Scripture,[4] patristic writers provided an intellectual framework through which later church-men could express their own concerns about non-normative religious practice. Indeed, the socio-spiritual danger presented by the synthesis of Classical (and Germanic) magical beliefs into Judeo-Christian thought was a key concern for early medieval law makers. Detailing and denouncing such nefarious practices as love magic, the manipulation of the weather, and the creation of medical charms, the corpus of penitential handbooks and law codes (c.600–1000) also contain numerous references to the use of demonic agents to predict the future.[5] Such condemnations should not be just read as recapitulations of old literary archetypes. The personal correspondences of St. Boniface (d.754),[6] Alcuin of York (d.804),[7] and Lanfranc (1075)[8] – to take a broad diachronic sample – betray a deep pastoral concern about contemporary interests in 'wearing amulets' (*filacteria*), 'soothsay-ings' (*auguria*), and 'casting lots' (*sortes*).

The intricacies and ambiguities of early medieval magic have been the subject of much scholarly interest in recent years.[9] Likewise, numerous studies have been conducted on the 'diabolication' of magic in the fourteenth and fifteenth centuries and the consolidation of the idea that practitioners – whether learned necroman-cers or folk healers – did not just coerce spirits to do their bidding, but formed an unholy pact with the devil.[10] It suffices to say that literature on the emergent 'witch craze' is also incredibly abundant. By contrast, scholarship on the practice of magic in the late eleventh and early twelfth centuries (c.1067–1150) is still somewhat scarce; a function, perhaps, of the dearth of primary written sources from this era.[11] Although 'magic', divination specifically, remained a cause for concern amongst educated lawmakers and churchmen,[12] it did not provoke the same level of condemnation as in earlier or later centuries, where the need to eradicate the final vestiges of paganism (early medieval) and curtail the devil's active agency (late medieval) was firmly on the agenda. Likewise, the increasing influence of Islamic astrological, alchemical, and quasi-mystical treatises in the intellectual milieu of the Latin West may explain why there was a reluctance, initially at least, to delve too deep into the profane mechanics of the diviner's art.[13] Hugh of St. Victor's *Didascalicon* (c.1127), Gratian's *Decretum* (c.1139), and Bartholomew Iscanus's *Penitential* (c.1184) drew upon earlier authoritative precedents – notably Augustine, Isidore of Seville[14] and the early tenth-century *Canon Episcopi*[15] – in their rote denunciations of magic. John of Salisbury's *Policraticus* (c.1159) includes a vivid childhood account of being coerced by a priest to divine the future using fingernails and a polished bowl, but such personal testimonies are few and far between.[16] Despite the relative lack of first-hand accounts of magical activity in the decades following the Conquest, the figure of the magical practitioner already existed as a fully-formed literary (and mental) concept, epitomised by the demonically-sired Merlin in Geoffrey of Monmouth's *Historia regum Britanniae* (c.1136).[17] Beyond the Arthurian sources, William of Malmesbury's story of the 'Witch of Berkeley' is, alongside his own retelling of the necromantic activities of Gerbert of d'Aurillac (Pope Sylvester II, d.1003), perhaps the most famous narrative of its type to emerge in the early years of the twelfth century. Included in book two of the *Gesta regum Anglorum* (c.1125), a monumental and highly influential overview of English history from 449 to 1120, the Berkeley narrative records the post-mortem fate of an inveterate soothsayer whose corpse is ripped from its tomb by demons and taken to hell on the back of a wild, demonic horse.[18] Given that the narrative is often used as a key reference point in studies of witchcraft and magic, it is surprising that no true attempts have been made to explore its literary-critical function within the *Gesta regum Anglorum*. Similarly, previous attempts to analyse the Witch of Berkeley's textual transmission and appropriation by later compilers have amounted to only a few brief sentences and footnotes.[19]

The first part of this chapter, then, will involve a close, critical analysis of the narratological elements of the extract itself, interrogating the extent to which the story – ostensibly based on first-hand testimony[20] – was shaped by classical and patristic antecedents. Particular emphasis will be given to the seeming vitality of the witch's corpse and whether this is suggestive of a pervasive local belief in the restless dead. With reference to the narrative's manuscript context, it will also be seen whether the witch's fate can be read as a piece of ironic historical criticism. Specifically, I will argue that William is making an allusive and elliptical reference to the events that led to the expulsion of Godwin of Wessex from England in 1051 and, more generally, the idea that the fracture (and subsequent re-mending) of the English state c.1066 can be reflected in a similar 'fracture' of the boundaries between the physical and metaphysical worlds. It is certainly no accident that William places the story between the political tumults of the 1040s and the Conquest of 1066. Nor is it a coincidence that Godwin stood in direct political contrast to the royal Wessex lineage represented by Matilda of Scotland, whose marriage to Henry I unified the Anglo-Saxon and Norman royal dynasties, and whose request for a more complete history of her iconic forefathers laid the foundations for the entire *Gesta regum* project.[21] As we shall see, wonder stories were not just amusing digressions from the main body of the text, but could also play an important moralistic and socio-critical function.

The final part of the chapter will involve an attempt to chart the transmission of the narrative across different contexts, genres, and media, from its initial appearance in the *Gesta regum Anglorum* and appropriation by later chroniclers and artists, to its use as an exemplum in preachers' manuals and, finally, as the basis of a ballad by the future poet laureate, Robert Southey (c.1798). Sources to be analysed include Roger of Wendover's *Flores Historiarum* (c.1220–1235), Vincent of Beauvais' *Speculum Historiale* (c. late 1240s), Arnold of Liège's *Alphabetum narrationum* (c.1307), Hartmann Schedel's *Liber Chronicarum* (1493), and Olaus Magnus's *Historia de Gentibus Septentrionalibus* (1555), amongst others. By mapping out the textual history of a single supernatural encounter from its twelfth-century origins to reformulation as an eighteenth-century folk-ballad, new, critical insights can be made into the palimpsestic nature of wonder stories.

William of Malmesbury and the Witch of Berkeley: some considerations

William of Malmesbury (c.1095–1143) is rightfully considered one of the foremost historians of the Middle Ages. A Benedictine monk from Malmesbury Abbey in Wiltshire, William developed his academic calling at an early age. After brief dalliances with Logic, medicine, and ethics, he turned his attention history writing. Using his influence as Malmesbury Abbey's precentor and librarian, he amassed an impressive collection of secular and theological manuscripts.[22] Rare foreign histories, the bedrock of his literary endeavours, were purchased at his own expense.[23] Alongside the *Gesta regum Anglorum*, William's other major works include the *Gesta pontificum Anglorum* (c.1125) – a companion piece to the *Gesta regum* that charts the ecclesiastic history of England – and the unfinished *Historia Novella* (c.1140–1143). This 'Contemporary History' was commissioned by Robert, Earl of Gloucester, and records political events from 1126 to the reign of King Stephen. Although William's primary concern was to redeem English history from its doldrums and to 'bring light to events lying concealed in the confusing mass of antiquity',[24] he seems to have developed a mid-career interest in stand-alone hagiographies and biblical exegesis. The *De miraculis beatae Virginis Mariae* (c.1135), *Liber super explanationem Lamentationum Ieremiae* (c.1130–1135), and numerous saints' lives were produced in the period between the final revision of the *Gesta pontifium* and the commissioning of the *Historia Novella*.[25] The *Gesta regum*, however, remains William's most recognised (and scrutinised) work. Divided into five books, it contains not only detailed accounts of the matters of England but also digressions into continental political events, mini-hagiographies and, of course, the occasional foray into tales of the prodigious and the supernatural.

The rehabilitation of English national identity remained a central conceit of the *Gesta regum*. Indeed, William laments that no true attempt had been made to construct an uninterrupted history of the English people since the time of Bede.[26] By seasoning his 'uncivilised' native sources with a pinch of 'Roman salt' (*exarata barbarice Romano sale condire*) – i.e. through the use of erudite, Virgilian Latin – he sought to 'mend the broken chain of our past' (*interruptam temporum seriem sarcire*) and create a historical document to rival those of his Roman forbearers.[27] As noted explicitly in the prologue to book two, the *Gesta regum* was also intended to provide moral edification through the provision of a 'pleasurable' (*iocunda*) reading experience.[28] The narratives were meant to be entertaining as well as instructive. Rather than viewing the *Gesta regum* as the work of a humourless 'proto-academic', content only with dry, didactic descriptions of a bygone age, it should be recognised that a sense of sardonic humour and irony permeates throughout.[29] Irony, the literary technique whereby the meaning of a textual unit is something other than its manifest form, was one of the most potent weapons in a historian's critical arsenal. William uses ironical inferences – specifically, allusiveness and ambiguity – to criticise the actions of contemporaries he would not otherwise be able to confront in a direct attack. See, for example, the passage relating to the historical figure of Ealhstan, bishop of Sherbourne (d.867) and his usurpation of the authority Malmesbury Abbey in the mid-ninth century:

> I would gladly praise him, had he not been carried away by human greed to lay hands on what was not his, in subjecting to his own purposes the abbey of Malmesbury. To this day we feel the grievance of his outrageous behaviour, although on his death the monastery at once recovered completely from his violence, and so remained until our own time, when it has again undergone the same ordeal.

> [quem libenter laudarem, nisi quod humana cupiditate raptatus indebita usurpavit, quando monasterium Malmesberiense suis negotiis substravit. Sentimus ad hunc diem impudentiae illius calumniam, licet locus idem statim eo mortuo omnem illam eluctatus fuerit violentiam usque ad nostrum tempus, quando in idem discrimen recidit.][30]

As Paul Hayward notes, Ealhstan seems to have been utilised as a substitute for Roger of Salisbury, one of Henry I's chief advisors who, following the death of the Abbey's chief patron and protector, Queen Matilda (d.1118), began to take control over Malmesbury's affairs.[31] Ironical distancing allows William to safely criticise Roger's actions while at the same time making clear the extent of the monks' grievances at the contemporary crisis (*idem discrimen*). The Witch of Berkeley digression may have been created for similar satiric purposes. Before this question can be answered for certain, however, it would be prudent to case a critical eye on the structure of narrative itself.

Located towards the end of book two, following an overview of the activities of Earl Godwin and his family (ii.199–200), the Witch of Berkeley (ii.204) is part of a wider textual digression that also includes an account of the life and death of Pope Gregory VI (ii.201–203), the activities of the priestly necromancer Palumbus (ii.205), the discovery of the body of the mythical Pallas (ii.206), the appearance of a monster in Normandy (ii.207), and a series of descriptions of royal English saints (ii.208–219). An evaluation of the sanctity of King Edward (ii.220–227) is the means by which William segues back into the main historical narrative, ruminating upon the political turmoil that arose following the king's death (ii.228).[32]

Noting that he heard the story from a man who witnessed the events first-hand (*qui se vidisse iuraret*), William describes how in the village of Berkeley (Gloucestershire), there once lived a woman who was 'not ignorant of the auguries of the ancients' (*augurorium veterum non inscia*). One day, whilst settling down to dinner, she was approached by a small crow that seemed to be more animated than usual. Hearing its message, she dropped the knife and her face grew pale. 'Today', she sighed, 'my plough has reached its last furrow and I shall receive a great misfortune' (*Hodie [...] ad ultimum sulcum meum pervenit aratrum; hodie audiam et accipiam grande incommodum*). Sure enough, a visitor soon appeared at her door bearing the terrible news that her son's house had collapsed and both he and his family had been killed. Taking ill, and sensing that her own death was imminent, she summoned her two surviving children – a monk and a nun – to her bedside. Admitting to be a 'servant of the demonic arts' (*daemonicis semper artibus inservii*), 'a cesspool of vice' (*vitiorum omnium sentina*), and a 'mistress of all temptations' (*illecebrarum magistra*), she confessed that their religious vocations had been the only thing protecting her against the wrath of the devil. Now that death was near, she feared for what would happen to her body – her soul long-since condemned to hell. Accordingly, she instructed her children to sew her corpse into a deer skin and lay it in a stone sarcophagus within the choir of the local monastery. The lid was to be fastened with iron and lead and the coffin itself to be bound with three heavy iron chains. Fifty masses were to be said each day and night to 'ease the viscous onslaughts of [her] adversaries' (*adversariorum excursus feroces leuigent*). Then, on the fourth day, the body was to be removed from the coffin and placed in the ground. These instructions were followed to the letter. And yet, no amount of preparation could prevent the devil from collecting his prize. For two consecutive nights, as the choir of clerks (*chori clericorum*) sung psalms around her body, demons gained access to the church and removed two of the chains. The last chain, however, remained steadfast. On the third night, a larger and more terrifying demon burst through the main entrance, shattering the door to pieces. Striding up to the coffin, the demon called to the woman by name, commanding her to rise. The woman answered that she could not, on account of the final chain. Proclaiming 'you are free' (*solveris*), the demon cut the chain as if it were not even there, kicked off the stone lid, and dragged the woman out of the church by the hand. A terrible black stallion stood waiting by the door, whinnying proudly, with pointed iron hooks protruding all the way down its back. The 'poor wretch' (*misera*) was set upon the barbs, after which she and the horse vanished along with the rest of the demonic horde. It was said that her cries for help could be heard for up to four miles away. William concludes by noting that similar occurrences can be read in the *Dialogues* of Gregory the Great and that Charles Martel's corpse was also believed to have been snatched from the grave by demons.[33]

According to Edward Peters, the inclusion of the Witch of Berkeley within a selection of stories with continental origins suggests the narrative was based on a non-native literary model and may not truly be representative of local folklore. Classical histories are, of course, the framework upon which the *Gesta regum* is based.[34] The irony of William's opening statement – that the 'truth' (*fides*) of the narrative is unshakeable – is very much apparent and thus calls into question a purely literal reading of the text.[35] The first hints of the story's classical influences can be discerned in the descriptors relating to the type of magic the woman performed. Although the *Gesta regum*'s most recent editors translate the genitive *auguriorum* into its more general medieval definition of 'soothsaying' (i.e. the interpretation of omens),[36] augury in its original, classical sense relates to the interpretation the will of the gods through the flight of birds. As noted by Livy and Ovid, the foundation of Rome was said to have been decided by an augury contest between Romulus and Remus. Romulus's observation of the flight of twelve vultures to his brother's six led to the city being founded on Palatine Hill.[37] Vultures weren't the only bird that could provide good omens. The character of Libanus in Plautus's *Asinaria* (c.200 BC) is inspired to devious action through the 'judgement' (*sententiam*) of a woodpecker, crow, and raven.[38] As evidenced by the writings of Pliny, Celsus, Servius, and Cicero, augury enjoyed a prominent position in Roman religious culture well into the time of the Empire.[39]

Despite the occasional synthesis of the 'auspicious bird' motif into early Saints' Lives,[40] on the whole Christian theologians denounced augury as a venal pursuit that involved paying homage to demons. Discussing whether the observation of auguries (*augurio*) aided the expansion of the Roman Empire, Augustine declares it 'vain' (*vano*) to believe such things and criticises the fact that these 'demonic rites' (*daemoniacis ritibus*) had once been a central part of state custom.[41] Later writers were similarly concerned about the inappropriate use of augury. In a letter directed to an anonymous English bishop (c.800), Alcuin of York notes that auguries made from 'the singing of birds and sneezing and such things are forbidden' (*Auguria quoque et avium cantus, et sternutationes et talia plurima omnino vetanda sunt*).[42] Bede, meanwhile, employs *augurium* in the broad sense of superstition.[43] The fact that the Witch of Berkeley received the information about her son's demise through the chattering of a tame crow suggests she was proficient in the interpretation of bird calls rather than soothsaying in general.[44] William's knowledge of the Roman literary canon and the narratological possibilities it offered lends credence to the theory that 'augury' was used in its strictest – i.e. classical – sense. In any case, learning of her own son's death in this manner was a suitably ironic demonstration of the witch's skill in this ancient art.

William's sources for the description of the witch's fate are much easier to fathom. His comment concerning the 'fourth book' of Gregory's *Dialogues* (*qui refert in quarto libro*) refers specifically to chapter fifty-three and the burial of the 'deceitful' (*lubricus*) Milanese churchman, Valentinus:

> The midnight following, a great noise was heard in that place, as though some body by force had been drawn out from thence: whereupon the keepers ran towards that place to see what the matter was, and when they arrived, they saw two very terrible devils, that had tied a rope about his legs, and were drawing him out of the church, himself in the meantime crying and roaring out

> [Nocte autem media in eadem ecclesia factae sunt uoces, ac si quis uiolenter ex ea repelleretur atque traheretur foras. Ad quas nimirum uoces cucurrerunt custodes, et uiderunt duos quosdam teterrimos spiritus, qui eiusdem Valentini pedes quadam ligatura strinxerant et eum ab ecclesia clamantem ac nimium vociferantem foras trahebant.][45]

Valentinus's corpse seems to retain a vestige of personhood as it is dragged from the church by demons. In another pointed parallel to the Witch of Berkeley narrative it cries and roars as it is taken. The next exemplum (ch. 54) shares a similar theme. According to Gregory, the head of the dyer's guild was buried in the church of St. Januarius in Rome, but during the night his 'spirit' (*spiritus*) was heard to cry out from the grave, 'I burn, I burn' (*ardeo, ardeo*). When the tomb was opened they found no sign of the body. Gregory is quite clear on the moral of these stories: those deemed unworthy of being buried in Holy ground will be summarily expelled from the church.

As noted by Rodney Thomson, a significant number of Frankish sources were utilised in the construction of the *Gesta regum*.[46] It is likely that William sourced his information on the fate of Charles Martel, the grandfather of Charlemagne, from Hincmar of Reims's anecdote about Bishop Eucherius of Orléans (d.743 AD), included in a letter sent to the Synod of Quierzy in 858. Hincmar, for his part, seems to have been directly influenced by Dialogues 4.54. The letter records how Eucherius experienced a vision of Charles Martel being tormented in hell. When Martel's tomb in the Cathedral of St. Denis was opened, a 'dragon' (*draco*) crawled out but the corpse was nowhere to be seen. The inside of the grave was scorched and blackened, evidence that he had been condemned to hell for the sins of confiscating church property.[47] Indeed, many churchman of the time labelled Martel a tyrant for meddling in religious affairs and filling his own coffers with church wealth.[48] William obliquely confirms Hincmar as his source by observing that Martel's fate 'was revealed to the Bishop of Orléans, and so the truth got out' *(denique illud reuelatum Aurelianensi episcopo, et per eum uulgus seminatum)*.[49] In any case, it is apparent that exempla on the sinful dead being expelled from the grave and punished by demons ultimately derived from the authority of the *Dialogues*. Interestingly, the *Deflorationes Gregorii* (Cambridge University Library MS Ii.3.20), a compilation of extracts from Gregory's works containing numerous passages from the *Dialogues*, forms one of the few extant manuscripts written in William's own hand, suggestive of his close academic connection to the material.[50] The spiritual corruption caused by secular power is a theme that also appears in Gregory's *Regula Pastoralis* (c.590), another work with which William was closely familiar.[51] If, as seems likely, William had access to a text (Hincmar) that makes tacit reference to the fate that awaited political tyrants, then it was certainly an appropriate source to utilise for his own metaphorical commentary – filtered through the precepts of Gregorian moral philosophy – on the problems of secular leaders interfering with the apparatus of the church (and disrupting divine order in general). It was a simple process, then, to adapt the base narrative components of widely-used urtext, the expulsion of sinners from the grave, to classical and early Christian templates on the dangers of augury.

And yet, to suggest that the 'Witch of Berkeley' was simply a modern reinvention of ancient archetypes is to ignore the belief in the walking dead in this era. It was argued in the previous chapter that far from being the vestigial memory of a distant pagan past, the fear of the restless corpse remained a vital part of the English habitus.[52] In the cultural upheavals following the Conquest, the historiographical traditions imported from the monastic communities of mainland Europe led to the transcription of orally-transmitted narratives and folk memories that would have otherwise been lost (History being a genre that had been neglected in England since the Viking invasions).[53] Thus, the late eleventh and early twelfth centuries witnessed the complex fusion of oral texts into revitalised literary forms, the consequence of which was that expressions (or interpretations) of the everyday habitus became much more prevalent in the written record – including, of course, tales of the walking dead. Just as in later centuries, the religious and secular works produced in the early decades of Norman rule betray a lack of consensus where the agency of the undead was concerned.[54] Simply put, did William of Malmebsury and his contemporaries believe that revenants were animated by the souls of the deceased, the vestigial life-force of the cadaver, or by the machinations of the devil? It is difficult to say whether the speech exhibited by the Witch of Berkeley's corpse – both in the grave and as it was dragged off to hell – is reflective of a native belief in the animating spirit, or if William was merely drawing inspiration from *Dialogues* 4.53 and 4.54. Certainly, contemporary English sources indicate that revenants were very much capable of speaking: see, for instance, the aforementioned exemplum from Geoffrey of Burton's *Vita sancte Moduenne Virginis* (c.1140s), in which the corpses of two peasants wandered through their former village, Drakelow, knocking on doors, shouting 'Move, quickly, move! Get going! Come!'[55] In this case, however, the active agent appears to be demonic: when the bodies were exhumed and placed on a pyre, an evil spirit in the form of a crow was said to have leapt from the flames. Similarly, Honorius of Autun's *Elucidarium* (c.1098) notes that 'the devil once spoke through serpents as he does today through possessed (dead?) men'.[56] The account of the death of sheriff Leofstan in Herman the Archdeacon's *De miraculis sancti Edmundi* (c.1090, detailing events that occurred c.1000) wryly notes that the hated tyrant was 'possessed by a demon in life, and then similarly possessed as a corpse in death' (*tum uius possessus a demone, tum itidem possidetur cadauer exanime*). Goscelin of Saint-Bertin's revision (c.1100) adds a telling gloss, explaining that while the locals believed the prefect's corpse walked as a sign of his *own* unrest (*et ipse protestans inquietudinem*), they were in actual fact being accosted by a demon in his likeness. In any case, both versions of text conclude with Leofstan's body being sewn into a calf skin and thrown into a nearby lake.[57] Given that the Witch of Berkeley asked for her body to be constrained in a similar manner, it is possible that William had access to the *De miraculis* or else shared a folkloric source with Herman.[58] Indeed, wrapping sinful bodies in deer/calf skin appears to have been a choice apotropaic strategy to prevent – or contain the damage already caused by – demonic molestation; related, perhaps, to the tradition of sewing corpses into hides for transport. Whatever the underlying motive for treating bodies in this manner, it protected the living from the dangerous miasmas that emanated from rotting flesh.[59] As will be discussed in more detail in the next chapter, restless corpses were notoriously pestilential.

If the views of Honorius of Autun, Herman the Archdeacon, and Geoffrey of Burton are indicative of English theological discourse at the turn of the twelfth century, the consensus seems to be that only demons could inhabit the dead. Goscelin overtly dismisses the notion that Leofstan walked under his own volition. Although William does not make a direct comment on the Witch of Berkeley's post-mortem agency, his opinion on such matters can clearly be detected in an earlier part of the *Gesta regum*. Discussing the death and burial of King Alfred (ii.124), he goes on to say that:

> The deluded canons maintained that the king's ghost returned to his dead body and wandered at night through their lodgings [...]. This nonsense and the like (it is believed, for example, that the corpse of a criminal after death is possessed by a demon and walks) wins credit among the English from a sort of inborn credulity

> [Mox pro deliramento canonicorum, dicentium regios manes resumpto cadauere noctibus per domos oberrare [...]. Has sane nenias sicut ceteras, ut credant nequam hominis cadauer post mortem demone agente discurrere, Angli pene innata credulitate tenent][60]

Here, William derides the belief in the walking dead as foolish in the extreme, regardless of whether the corpse was inhabited by a demon or the ghost of the deceased. Both interpretations seem to have held sway at the turn of the twelfth century, the agency of the undead being decided on a case-by-case basis, filtered through the worldview of the author/percipient and the particular 'truth' they were trying to convey. Similarly, rhetorical purpose decided whether a restless corpse signified spiritual comeuppance (e.g. the Witch of Berkeley) or mindless superstition (e.g. Alfred). The idea that the ghost (*manes*) of the Witch resided in the corpse and was able to speak and scream may not have been so foreign after all.

Clues in the text suggest that at least some level of local knowledge was used to furnish the details of the narrative. If, as mentioned earlier, it is difficult to say whether William's ostensible source witnessed the event first-hand – based on the assertion it occurred 'about the same time' as the death of Gregory VI (c.1048) – the fact remains that Berkeley village is situated only about 20 miles from Malmesbury Abbey. William was a prodigious traveller and often includes intimate local descriptions in his writings, something that is especially apparent in the *Gesta pontificum*.[61] Eyewitness reports were integral to the formation and substantiation of historical 'truth'. With this in mind, the use of the term *clericus* (clerk) rather than *monachus* (monk) to describe the churchmen who sang psalms over the coffin in the local monastery (*monasterium*) requires further explication. Whilst early historical documentation on Berkeley is problematic and unreliable, the evidence suggests that a minster church was in existence by at least the early ninth century. References to a certain 'Ælthryð abbatissa Beorclea coenobio' (Ælthryth, abbess of the convent of Berkeley) in the 1031 entry in Winchester New Minster's *Liber Vitae* is reason enough to confirm that a nunnery had been established by this time.[62] In the mid-eleventh century Berkeley itself was a small market town and had been chosen by Edward the Confessor as the location for a royal mint.[63] If Berkeley enjoyed a certain level of status in this period (1042 onwards), then the reference to the witch's 'greed' (*gulae*) may not have been taken wholesale from descriptions of classical Mediterranean witches.[64] In any case, a curious Domesday entry for the nearby village of Woodchester (1086) provides tantalising clues as to the difficulties that befell the Abbey in the mid-1040s:

> Gytha, Earl Harold's mother, held Woodchester. Earl Godwin bought it from Azor and gave it to his wife so that she could live off it while she lived at Berkeley. For she did not wish to consume anything at the manor because of the Abbey's destruction

> [Gueda mater Heraldi comitis tenuit Udecester [...]. Goduinus comes emit ab Azor et dedit suae uxori, ut inde viveret ad Berchelai maneret. Nolebat enim de ipso manerio aliquid comedere pro destructione abbaitae.][65]

William's pointed use of the term *monasterium* to describe the building in which the witch's body lay precludes the possibility that it was fully despoiled and abandoned. 'Destruction', then, refers not to the levelling of the church buildings but the expulsion of the nuns and the reduction of the Abbey to a college of secular clerks. It may even have referred to the foundation's further reduction to the status of a parochial church.[66] A salacious anecdote in Walter Map's *De Nugis Curialium* (c.1182) identifies Godwin as being responsible for sending his (unnamed) nephew to Berkeley to seduce the nuns and acquire their land for himself.[67] However, as Michael Hare notes, it is possible that Gytha and Godwin's wayward son Swein, whose earldom (1043–1047) incorporated Gloucester and who had notoriously seduced the abbess of Leominster (1046), inspired Map's story.[68] Whoever the actual instigating party, the reduction of Berkeley Abbey certainly benefited Godwin, who is noted in the *Anglo-Saxon Chronicle* C-Text as 'doing little penance for the property of God which he held belonging to many holy places'. William, for his part, mentions something similar about Godwin's dubious activities in *Gesta regum* chapter ii.196.[69]

Whilst it is true the mention of 'clerks' could refer to the priests who performed the daily services for the nuns, the allusion to the year 1048 situates the Witch of Berkeley narrative within an era when the monastery – presumed to have stood on the site currently occupied by St. Mary's parish church[70] – had been wholly secularised. William, then, undoubtedly drew upon local knowledge to augment his story with site-specific nuance. A scenario can be posited whereby William learnt of a local legend from a Berkeley priest and dressed the base elements of the story – the death of a suspected fortune-teller; a restless corpse – with the accoutrements of his classical learning. But to what end? As will be discussed in more detail below, the subtextual denunciation of secular lords who overstep their social boundaries and the dangers of moral monstrosity are themes that bind the Witch of Berkeley narrative to its specific manuscript context.

The literary function of the Witch of Berkeley

Tales of the prodigious and supernatural served a variety of functions in chronicle writing. Far from being utilised only as entertaining diversions from the main body of the historical text, accounts of monstrous births, marauding demons, and malevolent ghosts provided a platform through which the reader was invited to ruminate on their meaning and moral function.[71] The common Latin terms used to describe unusual entities, such as *prodigium* and *monstrum,* stress their role as referents. Portents were liable to appear in time of intense social discord, a material manifestation of spiritual, moral, and/or political unrest. And yet, the inherent difficulty of assigning a fixed meaning to the literal form of prodigious phenomena meant that 'wonders' could be tailored to suit the specific aims and intentions of those who decided to report them.[72] Elizabeth Freemen is correct to note that close attention should be paid to the precise terminologies used to describe wondrous happenings.[73] Translated by the *Gesta regum*'s current editors as 'infernal portent', William's term for the devilish appearances in the Witch of Berkeley, *inferno prestigio,* can also be read as 'diabolical illusion', highlighting the inherent falsity and 'unfixedness' of demonic encounters in contrast to the tangible truths ascribed to *miracula.* It would be useful, therefore, to evaluate the common themes that bind the digressions in book two, before evaluating how such themes relate to the historical circumstances into which the stories have been inserted.

As noted briefly above, the digression on the Witch of Berkeley is preceded by a semi-fictional account of the life and death of Pope Gregory VI (ii.201–203). Born John Gratian, Gregory rose to the Holy See in May 1045 after paying off the previous incumbent, his godson Benedict IX (1012–1065), who wished to abdicate the throne. However, Benedict soon reneged on his decision, causing a schism to engulf the church. Following an intervention by the Holy Roman Emperor Henry III in December 1046, Benedict and Gregory (as well as a third rival pope, Sylvester III) were forced to renounce their claims in favour of Henry's preferred candidate, Clement II. Gregory lived out his final years in exile, dying in Cologne in 1048.[74] These truths, however, William chooses to ignore, focusing instead on Gregory's attempts to reform the papacy, reassert social order in Rome, and purge the church of its undesirable elements. According to William, much blood was spilt, to the extent to which the Roman cardinals deemed Gregory unworthy of burial in St. Peter's. Gregory gave a rousing deathbed speech defending his actions, denouncing the involvement of secular 'tyrants' in church affairs, before making a final request:

> Prepare my body for burial after the fashion of my predecessors, and lay it before the church door; then make the doors fast with bolt and bar. If it is God's will that I should enter, there will be a miracle for you to acclaim; if not, you may do with my corpse whatever you have a mind to

> [Corpus meum, antecessorum more compositum, ante ianuas aecclesiae sistite; ianuae seris et repagulis dampnentur. Si Deus uoluerit ut ingrediar, applaudetis miraculo; sin minus, de cadauere meo facite quod potius uestris insederit animis'][75]

When Gregory's body was brought before St. Peter's a miraculous wind rose up and broke through the bolted doors, confirming God's will.

Thematic connections with the Witch of Berkeley narrative are immediately apparent. Both concern the crossing of thresholds, albeit from different spiritual perspectives: the witch dabbles in sin (i.e. magic), but Gregory defends against it (i.e. against secularisation); diabolical forces break down the entrance to Berkeley Abbey, whereas the bolted doors of Saint Peter's are flung open by a miracle; the witch's corpse is expelled from holy ground, while Gregory is invited by God to enter. The fates of Charles Martel and Valentinus add emphasis to the fact that Gregory, despite his ostensible sins, operated under divine sanction. Each body, then, received the dignity it deserved.[76] Concerns about the meaning of unusual bodies, cohesion, and the danger of crossing inviolate boundaries are themes that permeate into chapters ii.205–207. Indeed, William next story recalls the travails of an unnamed Roman nobleman who, not wanting to lose his engagement ring whilst playing sports, placed it on the finger of a statue of Venus. However, during the night he felt an unearthly presence in his bed and heard a voice announcing that they – he and Venus – were wed. Terrified, and unable to make love to his wife due to an invisible barrier between them, he sought the counsel of a local priest, Palumbus, who was skilled in the art of necromancy (*nigromanticis artibus instructus*). Using all the tricks of his diabolical trade, Palumbus told the man to go a crossroads at a certain time of night and hand a letter of instruction to a corpulent demon passing by in a ghostly carriage. Lamenting Palumbus's wickedness (*Deus* [...] *omnipotens, quan diu patieris nequitas Palumbi presbiteri?*) the demon nonetheless obeyed the written command and dispatched servants to wrest the ring from Venus, saving the man's marriage. Palumbus, meanwhile, hearing the demon's cry and knowing his death was near, cut off all his limbs in penance and confessed his crimes to the Pope and the people of Rome.

In a similar manner to the Witch of Berkeley, Palumbus's skill in the dark arts proves to be his undoing. His grotesque demise at his own hands is a manifest illustration of the spiritual division wrought by a lifetime of sin.[77] The irony of a demon bewailing Palumbus's wickedness lends the exemplum a dry, sardonic quality that is also apparent in the next tale concerning the discovery of the corpse of Pallas (ii.206). After noting that the lack of decay caused astonishment (*stupor*) in those who saw it – William showing his medical knowledge through a brief description of the processes of embalming[78] – he goes on to mention that a 'wonderful' ever-burning lamp discovered by Pallas's head was extinguished by an onlooker who showed the 'ingenious cunning of those up to make mischief' (*aliqui sollertius ingenium in malis habent*).[79] Eventually, the damp causes Pallas's corpse to disintegrate. Although William declines to ascribe a meaning to this wonder, he is much less reticent when commenting on the discovery of a pair of conjoined sisters in Normandy (ii.207). Sharing the same lower body, but possessing separate heads, arms, and torsos down to the navel, one of the twins died, the other carrying around her dead sister for three years 'until the heavy weight and the smell of the corpse was too much for her also' (*donec et mole ponderis et nidore cadueris ipsa quoque defecit*). This portent, says William, signifies the realms of England and Normandy, united under a single (Norman) king. Normandy, dead and almost sucked dry by taxes, is supported by England, which itself has been almost overwhelmed by the financial burden of its 'oppressors'. Acting as a counterpoint to this criticism of the monstrosity of the current English state, chapters ii.208–219 record the spiritually pure (and thus 'whole') bodies of the Anglo-Saxon royal lineage, focusing on such saints as Oswald, Kenelm, Edmund, and Mildburh, amongst many others. These saints are used as exempla to stress the sanctity of Edward the Confessor, emphasising that the current king (from a spiritual perspective at least) did not fall short of his illustrious forbearers (ii.220–227). Bodies, whether natural or unnatural, 'whole' or 'fragmented', are the base metaphor that links each wonder story together.

What, then, are we to make of these seemingly disparate set of tales? Sigbjørn Olsen Sønnesyn persuasively argues that these digressions anticipate a rupture in the English historical narrative (i.e. the Conquest of William of Normandy). Time and identity have become fractured and non-linear, circumstances which often gave rise to wonders.[80] The lack of temporal cohesion is first made apparent in the Gregory VI miracle story. Although it is curious that a historian of William's repute should including a wholly fictitious account of Gregory's death, the exemplum can be read as a deliberate manifestation of the breakdown of physical and metaphysical order. That is to say, the narrative is an *intentional* contravention of known historical fact, an ahistorical polemic against tyrants that operates as a sophisticated literary paradox: the overt 'falseness' of the narrative betrays a deep spiritual truth. Hints of temporal/historical fracture are interspersed throughout the wider textual unit: the Witch of Berkeley is skilled in the *ancient* art of augury; the Roman nobleman marries a statue of the pre-Christian deity Venus; the Roman citizens unearth the body of a man (Pallas) who belongs to the mythical past. Likewise, the monstrous portent from Normandy may have been discovered in 1048, but it resonates across time to speak to political crises in William's own time. A discussion on English sainthood is the mechanism by which the rent in time/identity is (tentatively) stitched back together before the history of the Conquest can begin.[81] The account of Edward the Confessor's prophecy (ii.226) concerning the strife that will soon overcome English lands – allegorised by the cutting in half of a green tree – lets the audience know that stability is fleeting; time/identity will soon become rent once more.[82]

Wonder stories operated on many different registers. If, on one level, the Witch of Berkeley functioned as part of a wider allusion to the rupture of the Conquest, on another it also provided an allegorical commentary on events that followed Edward the Confessor's ascension to the throne and the mechanisms by which the rupture could be healed. Portents spoke of the present (i.e. their direct manu-script context) as well as the future. The cohesive nature of good kingship and the disdain for lords who overstepped their authority (generally) and encroached on church property (specifically) are amongst the most prominent themes in William's historical writings.[83] The underlying message of the Witch of Berkeley exemplum – that fractured/sinful bodies should be expelled from the Christian community before it can be made whole again – has definite symbolic value with regards to the political fate of one of the most powerful yet divisive figures in late Anglo-Saxon England: Godwin, Earl of Wessex (c.1001–1053).

Godwin came to prominence during the reign of Cnut (r.1016–36) and served his successors, Harold Harefoot (r. 1035–40) and Harthacanut (r.1040–42), with equal distinction. Following Harthacanut's death, Godwin supported the claim of Edward the Confessor, despite having been involved in the death of Edward's brother, Alfred (1036). The alliance was cemented through Edward's marriage to Edith, Godwin's daughter (1045). Edward's relationship with his son-in-law and kingmaker was fractious to say the least, their political and familial feuds almost leading the country into civil war.[84] Whilst William lauds the saintly quali-ties of Edward (ii.220), his descriptions of the king's governance and Godwin's character are much more critical. On commenting on these so-called 'glory days' (*gloriam temporum*), he notes that:

> The monasteries at that time were emptied of monks […]. The king's sup-porters try to minimize the unpopularity resulting from these conditions by saying that the destruction of the monasteries and the corruption of the law courts came about without his knowledge through the violence of Godwin and his sons who laughed at the king's mildness

> [Monasteria tunc monachis uiduata […]. Sed harum rerum inuidiam ama-tores ipsius ita extenuare conantur: monasteriorum destructio, peruersitas iuditiorum non eius scientia sed per Goduini filiorumque eius sunt commissa uiolentiam, qui regis ridebant indulgentiam][85]

Ever careful with his sources, William includes the caveat that Edward was seen by some as being ultimately responsible for the sorry state of English monasticism in this period. However, as discussed previously, Godwin's role in the reduction of monasteries is well attested. The C-text of the *Anglo-Saxon Chronicle* makes a generalised reference to Godwin holding property belonging to the church. The Woodchester entry in the *Domesday Book* explicitly names Berkeley Abbey as one of the places that suffered under his influence, a turn of events that was given new literary life by Walter Map. Just as William rebukes Roger of Salisbury and Charles Martel for their transgressive actions against the church, so Godwin is a perfect target for satire, if not outright censure.[86]

The events that connect the Witch of Berkeley to the contemporary political narrative are first broached in chapter ii.197. From the outset William warns his readers that 'the truth of the facts is in suspense and uncertain' (*quia ueritas factorum pendet in dubio*), the first sign of the historical (and thus textual) instability that will become even more apparent with the Gregory VI exemplum. According to William, Edward retained strong links to Normandy following his many years of exile on the continent. On his ascension to the throne he appointed a Norman, Robert of Jumièges, to the bishopric of London and thereafter to the archbishopric of Canterbury (1048). Godwin and his sons opposed the influence of 'foreigners' (*aduenas*) in the realm, who for their own part, accused Godwin of insidiously usurping the king's power. William remains sceptical as to the truth of the matter, astutely noting that each side, English and Norman, is inherently biased against the other.[87] With the situation already tense, things came to a head with the death of a soldier from the retinue of Count Eustace of Boulogne, who was passing through Canterbury at this time. This led to swift reprisals by Eustace against the local population. Godwin resisted the king's orders to take further vengeance on the Canterbury residents. Accused of conspiring against the crown, Godwin and his sons were eventually outlawed and took to piracy around the English coast. The following year (1052) Godwin 'returned with peaceful intentions' and defended himself against all charges. As a consequence:

> All the Normans were branded with infamy and ejected from England. Sentence was passed on Archbishop Robert and his accomplishes for disturbing the peace of the realm by exciting the king's resentment against his subjects

> [Normannos omnes ignominiae notatos ab Anglia effugeret, prolata sententia Rotbertum archiepiscopum euisque complices quod statum regni conturbarent animum regium in prouintiales agitantes][88]

William is characteristically equivocal in his description of circumstances that almost led to civil war (*et plusquam ciuile bellum fuisset*). The anti-Norman, pro-English sentiment can be discerned in the lack of rebuke to Godwin for opposing the authority of a legitimate king.[89] The change of location of the slaying of Eustace's guardsman from Dover – as recorded in the E-text of the *Anglo-Saxon Chronicle*[90] – to Canterbury provides a pointed textual link to the much-maligned Robert of Jumièges. Nonetheless, William's interpolated account of Godwin's death in 1053 – choking on food after swearing he had never done any harm to the king – certainly alludes to the Earl's wilful, somewhat seditious nature.[91] From a base moral standpoint, William objects to those who err in the eyes of God and transgress inviolate boundaries, whatever their nationality or political allegiance may be. Spiritual and social cohesion was vital for ensuring the prosperity of the English nation. Read as a thematic counterpoint to the Gregory VI miracle story, the Witch of Berkeley operates as a direct allegory of the expulsion of 'foreign' or 'dangerous' elements from the English body-politic c.1051–1052. Whether this relates to the exile of Godwin or the purging of malign Norman influences from the state apparatus, it was up to the active reader, fuelled by their own biases and political inclinations, to piece together the textual clues. Nonetheless, it is reasonable to assume that Godwin's role in the reduction of Berkeley Abbey was at the forefront of William's mind when formulating his witchcraft exemplum, especially given his comments in chapter ii.196. Magic was a spiritually destructive practice that finds a corollary in the equally destructive actions of leaders who misuse their political power. In contemporary contexts, Roger of Salisbury's usurpation of the authority of Malmesbury Abbey was especially resonant and may have fed into William's writing process.[92] Consorting with devils and fermenting civil and ecclesiastical unrest both led to ruin. A digression on the sinful life and gruesome fate of an unrepentant augur was the perfect platform through which to express such concerns.

Whilst the despoiling of churches is reason enough to invoke the ire of a monastic historian, William's treatment of Earl Godwin must also take into account Queen Matilda's role in the conceptualisation of the *Gesta regum*. If, as Kirsten Fenton suggests, William is extolling the unification of the English and Norman peoples through his description of the marriage of Matilda to Henry I,[93] and keeping in mind Elizabeth Tyler's assertion that Matilda, as a descendent of the Wessex royal line, may have retained a certain antipathy towards the rival Godwin lineage,[94] then a symbolic dichotomy is being made between Matilda (as representative of social wholeness and continuity) and Godwin (a sower of discord and potential usurper). Indeed, Matilda's son, William Adelin, was the figure whom the *Gesta regum* declares would have fulfilled Edward the Confessor's prophecy and allowed England to 'blossom and bear fruit' had he not perished in the sinking of the White Ship (1120).[95] On a more immediate level, then, using the figures of Godwin and the Witch of Berkeley to comment upon the tumultuous political climate of the mid-eleventh century substantiates the positive character portrait of William's royal patron; that is, as someone who successfully negotiated the rupture of the Conquest.

From Malmesbury to Southey: the textual history of the Witch of Berkeley

The *Gesta regum Anglorum* circulated widely in the years following William's death, enjoyed by English and continental audiences alike. It became an influential sourcebook for compilers looking to find authoritative accounts of early English history. The Witch of Berkeley seems to have held a particular fascination for medieval and early modern writers. From its traditional role as a historically-embedded wonder story to appropriation as a preaching aid and a key text in treatises on witchcraft, it was used in a variety of different contexts. Despite the narrative's enduring popularity, it is surprising that no true attempt has been made to chart its intertextual and diachronic reception. An exploration of how the text was altered to suit a specific literary or didactic purpose can provide a telling insight into premodern – and in Robert Southey's case, modern – authorial practice. The following overview does not claim to catalogue all extant versions of the Berkeley exemplum. Such a task is beyond the remit of this chapter. Rather, it provides a long-overdue counterpoint to the scholarly propensity to cite the Witch of Berkeley as a distinct (and somewhat alienable) literary unit without full awareness of its historical typology.

Hélinand of Froidmont's *Chronicon* (c.1223) and Roger of Wendover's *Flores Historiarum* (c.1220–1235) contain the first historically identifiable appearances of the Witch of Berkeley beyond the *Gesta regum*.[96] Seemingly written independently of the other, both texts use the *Gesta regum* as their source. Hélinand's world history survives in a fragmented, incomplete state. Vincent of Beauvais, Hélinand's contemporary, notes that it became dispersed very soon after its completion.[97] The Witch of Berkeley is copied almost verbatim from the *Gesta regum*, with only minor differences in grammar, expression, and content. For instance, the authorial interjection after the woman's death – 'what availed their pious tears!' – has been conspicuously edited out.[98] Most notably, the *mulier* is described as a being an *auguratrix et malefica* ('an augur and a witch') rather than merely possessing *skills* in augury and witchcraft, whilst the final section, detailing the tale's similarity to the exempla of Gregory the Great and the vision of Eucherius of Orléans, has been pointedly omitted. Helinand also dates the narrative to 1045, rather than 1048. Roger of Wendover's version pays similarly close attention to William of Malmesbury's text, although it is a much looser transcription than that of Hélinand. As well as retaining the Gregory/Eucherius epilogue and William's authorial gloss after the witch's funerary instructions (here rendered as *Sed proh dolor! nil preces, nil lacrymae nil demum valuere catenae*), Roger also gives the story a rubric: *De quadam muliere sortilega, et ejus miserabili morte* ('concerning a certain witch, and her miserable death'). *Sortilegium* originally referred to the act of divination through the drawing of lots (*sortes*), but by the later Middle Ages had come to refer to the acts of sorcery and witchcraft in general.[99] Engaging with the text much more critically than Hélinand, Roger places the narrative in the year 852 AD, inserted between an account of the death of Burgred, King of Mercia, and the conquering of the Welsh in 853 AD. Matthew Paris, a contemporary of Roger's at the Benedictine Abbey of St. Alban's, utilised the *Flores Historiarum* as a template for his own *Chronica majora* (c.1240–1259), specifically for events prior to 1235. Somewhat confusingly for the modern scholar, Paris adopts the title *Flores Historiarum* (c.1249) for his later abridgment/summary of the *Chronica*. Both of these works include verbatim retellings of Roger's account of the Witch of Berkeley and, in keeping with their source text, continue to locate the story in the mid-ninth century.[100] As will be discussed in more detail shortly, Roger's text was the template for Robert Southey's folk-ballad, 'The Old Woman of Berkeley'.

The *Speculum Historiale* (c. late 1240s) of the aforementioned Vincent of Beauvais was particularly influential in the transmission of the Witch of Berkeley to potential new audiences. Alongside the *Speculum Naturale* and *Speculum Doctrinale*, the *Historiale* formed part of the *Speculum Maius* ('Great Mirror'), a universal encyclopaedia that took over fifteen years to compile. The *Historiale* proved to be the most popular section of Vincent's work, attested by the sheer number of extant manuscripts and printed books written in both Latin and the vernacular. Much of the *Historiale's* content was taken from Hélinand's chronicle,[101] including the Witch of Berkeley exemplum.[102] This is not to suggest that Vincent used Hélinand uncritically; rather, despite copying Hélinand's text wholesale, he notes that the story ultimately derived from 'William' (*Guillerinus*). Vincent was a discerning compiler who had close, critical knowledge of both the *Gesta regum* and the *Chronicon* but made a conscious decision to use the more condensed Hélinand version. As with Roger of Wendover, he furnishes the text with a rubric, giving emphasis to the witch's ultimate fate: *De muliere malefica a daemonibus rapta* ('concerning an evil woman carried off by demons').

The *Historiale* was not simply a storehouse of knowledge, but could be used as an active research tool for the purposes of disputation and preaching. This is something that Vincent makes abundantly clear in the *Historiale's* prologue.[103] The moralistic flavour of the Witch of Berkeley meant it was perfectly suited for inclusion in preachers' manuals as an illustrative story against the dangers of living and dying in sin. The version of the story found in the *Alphabetum narrationum* (c.1307), a collection of alphabetised and cross-referenced exempla compiled by the Dominican preacher Arnold of Liège, is taken directly from the *Historiale*.[104] Arnold's work proved immensely popular and was translated into English as the *Alphabet of Tales* (c.1400). Exempla needed to be as universal as possible to fit every audience and circumstance. Thus, in the *Alphabet of Tales*, the opening sentence says simply 'Cesarius [sic] tellis how som tyme þer was in Englond a womman þat vsid sorcerie'. No overt reference to Berkeley is given.[105] The text itself has been distilled to its base elements, with the death of the witch's son and speech to her surviving children having also been omitted. The Latin rubric, *sortilegi puniuntur*, makes it clear that the aim is not to dwell on the witch's own agency but to focus on her punishments. Joan Young Gregg argues that the *Alphabetum Narrationum* was the source for the Berkeley exemplum included in *Jacob's Well* (c.1440), an anonymous vernacular sermon story collection from Suffolk. Here, the translator reproduces the citation error made by Arnold of Liège, who misread the *Historiale's* reference to 'Guillerinus' as 'Cesarius'. Similarly, the *Jacob's Well* text makes no mention of Berkeley and completely ignores events leading up to the instructions for burial.[106] Such details may have been seen as irrelevant. The amendment to the beginning of the text emphasising that the *wycche* died unshriven speaks more directly to the pastoral concerns of the compiler.

The *Speculum Exemplorum* (c.1481) was another widely-read preaching aid that owed much to the *Historiale*. First published by Richard Pafraet (Deventer,

1481) and organised according to series of distinctions (the Witch of Berkeley appearing at dist. iv. 51),[107] later editions, such as the version produced by Johannes Major (1618), dispensed with the thematic structure and arranged the exempla in alphabetical order. Major introduces the Witch of Berkeley – the name of the town corrupted to *Berbeliam* – under the heading '*Augurium*' and helpfully provides a citation for the *Speculum Historiale* at the end of the text.[108] It would unwise, however, to suggest that pastoral appropriations of the Witch of Berkeley derived solely from Vincent of Beauvais. This is especially true in English contexts. The *Gesta regum* provides the raw materials for the version of the story found in the *Speculum Laicorum* (c.1275), an exemplum collection erroneously attributed to the Franciscan friar, John of Howden. Similarly, the *Fasciculus Morum*, a preacher's manual compiled in England in the early fourteenth-century by an anonymous Franciscan friar (c.1300), includes a namechecked version of the William of Malmesbury text as part of a wider diatribe against 'soothsayers' (*coniectores*), 'necromancers' (*nicromantici*), and other magic-wielders who conspired against the church (*qui fidem impugnant*)'. Such 'heretics', the author says, are in very real danger of excommunication.[109] A treatise on diabolical illusions ('*De Prestigio*') from Alexander Carpenter's *Destructiorum vitiorum* (c.1429) also includes a retelling of the Witch of Berkeley, ostensibly from the *Gesta regum*.[110] And yet, a closer inspection of the text suggests that Carpenter actually used the *Fasciculus Morum* as his primary source.[111] See, for instance, the descriptions of the beginning of the third night of prayer, compared below:

Destructiorum vitiorum:
Tertia vero nocte circa galli cantus horribili strepitu demonus aduenientium non
   nulla fundamenta monasterii visa sunt moueri

Fasciculus Morum:
Tercia ergo nocte circa gallicantum horribili strepitu demonum adueniencium
   nonnulla fundementa monasterii visa sunt moueri

Gesta regum:
Tertia nocte, circa gallicinium, strepitu aduenientium hostium omne monasterium
   a fundamentis moueri uisum

Other textual clues support the idea that Carpenter did not consult the *Gesta regum* directly. Both the *Destructiorum* and *Fasciculus* substitute the term *auguriorum* for a descriptor more readily attuned to the sensibilities of a lay audience (*incantationes* and *coniuracones,* respectively). Likewise, the witch's confession that she was a 'slave to the devilish arts' (*daemonicis semper artibus inservii*) is changed in both texts to the more prosaic 'soothsaying and other offences' (*sortilegia & alia maleficia*). Further similarities include the use of the word *tumulo* rather than *sarcophago* to describe the iron-shod coffin and, preceding both exempla, similarly-constructed passages detailing the delusions suffered by women who believed they danced at night with the pagan goddess Diana,[112] a tradition ultimately deriving from the influential and widely-read *Canon Episcopi* (c.900). The universality of the Witch of Berkeley's narratological structure – a sinner gets dragged to hell by demons – meant it could be used in any discursive setting, allowing for a certain degree of authorial flexibility. William of Wadington's vernacular penitential handbook *La Manuel des Pechiez* (c.1250–1270), adapted into English by Robert Mannyng as *Handlyng Synne* (c.1303),[113] versifies the story and replaces the witch with a priest's concubine. Given the extent to which the exemplum diverges from the urtext it is unclear whether Wadington or his source actually used the *Gesta regum* as a model.[114] Even so, it is notable that the narrative was included in such an early example of pastoral literature aimed primarily at the edification of the laity (as opposed to the education of the clergy).[115]

English chroniclers from the Later Middle Ages took a more direct influence from William of Malmesbury. The *Eulogium Historiarum* was compiled by an anonymous Malmesbury Abbey monk sometime in the mid-fourteenth century (c.1366), ostensibly to alleviate the tedium of the cloister.[116] Book three, which details the history of European kingship from the foundation of Rome until c.1270, includes a selection of 'portentous occurrences' (*monstra incidentia*) taken from the *Gesta regum,* intended for the edification of the reader. Rather than copying out entire sections wholesale, the compiler has shown a certain sense of discernment in the choice and presentation of exempla. Beginning with the story of the necromancer Palumbus (taken from *GrA* ii.205) and the tale concerning the discovery of Octavian's fantastical treasures (*GrA* ii.170),[117] the compiler also includes the account of a man from Rome (seemingly) transformed into an ass by two witches (*GrA* ii.171) and the testimony of the sinner 'Hotbertus' condemned to sing for a year for carousing in a German churchyard (*GrA* ii.174). It is then we find the almost verbatim retelling of the Witch of Berkeley. The digression concludes with the exhumation of Pallas (*GrA* ii.206) and the story of the cellarer from Malvern Priory admonished by the ghost of a former abbot for defrauding his dead brethren of their alms (*GrA* iii.293).[118]

The contents of the *Eulogium* were based primarily on Ranulph Higden's expansive universal history, the *Polychronicon* (c.1360), book six of which also includes an account of the Witch of Berkeley.[119] Higden makes reference to his source material, '*Willemus de Regibus libro ii*', in the main body of the text and, working directly from William, situates the story – which has been pointedly truncated – within the usual temporal/geographical framework of England in the late 1040s. The *Polychronicon* was one of the most widely-read histories of the late Middle Ages, translated into the English vernacular by John Trevisa in 1385. Trevisa's version of the Witch of Berkeley is more or less faithful to Higden's Latin original. Henry Knighton, an Augustinian canon from St. Mary of the Meadows, Leicester, drew upon Higden in the creation of his own Latin chronicle (c.1378–1396), lifting the Witch of Berkeley and the associated historical material directly from the *Polychronicon* with only a few minor amendments.[120] The version found in Robert Fabyan's vernacular *The New Chronicles of England and France* (c.1504; first printed 1516) also cites Higden as its chief source.[121]

Interest in the Witch of Berkeley did not decline with the dawning of the Reformation. Hartmann Schedel (d.1514) was another compiler who proved especially influential in the story's transmission, particularly on the continent. The brainchild of the wealthy Nuremberg merchants Sebald Schreyer (d.1520) and Sebastian

Kammermeister (d.1503), Schedel's *Liber Chronicarum* ('Nuremberg Chronicle') was one of the most ambitious universal histories ever created. Drawing its closest inspiration from Jacopo Filippo Foresti's *Supplementum chronicarum* (1483), the Latin edition was printed in the workshop of Anton Koberger between 16 March 1492 and 12 July 1493, with a vernacular edition, *Das Buch der Croniken vnnd Geschichten*, completed on 23 December 1493, having been translated into German by the Nuremberg clerk, Georg Alt. 'Unauthorised' versions of both texts were published by Johann Schönsperger, an Augsburg printer, between 1496 and 1500. The 'official' *Chronicarum* is notable for its immense size (47 x 32.4 cm) and the impressive number of woodcuts (c.1,804) interspersed throughout the volume (326-leaves in the Latin; 297 in the vernacular).[122] Situated between an overview of the life and death of the Holy Roman Emperor Henry III (r.1046–1056) and a description of the rebuilding of the Holy Sepulchre in Jerusalem (c.1048), the account of the Witch of Berkeley is unusually succinct (fol. 189v):

> There was a certain nefarious sorceress in England, and when she died, demons dragged her up in a hideous fashion while the clerics were canting [over her]. Placing her on a fearsome horse, they snatched her away through the air. Fearsome shouts were heard for nearly four miles (as they say).

> [Malefica quedam auguriatrix in anglia fuit quam mortuam demones horribiliter extraxerunt dum clerici psallerent. Et imponetes super equum terribilem per aera rapiunt. Clamones quods terribiles (ut ferunt) per quatuor ferme miliaria audiebant][123]

The brevity of the extract makes it difficult to ascertain Schedel's ultimate source, but given that some of the preceding Henry III material was taken from the *Gesta regum* (ii.192)[124] it is likely that he also consulted William of Malmesbury for the Berkeley exemplum. This said, the use of the descriptor *auguriatrix* certainly suggests a familiarity with the *Speculum Historiale,* one of the main ancillary sources consulted in the *Liber Chronicarum*'s composition. The reference to 'snatching away through the *air*' is, however, a new narratological development, one that reflects heightened contemporary concerns about the nocturnal flight of witches. Indeed, the *Malleus Maleficarum* (1487) devotes an entire chapter to the ways in which 'wicked women' were said to travel from place to place, including being transported bodily by evil spirits (*De modo quo localiter transferuntur de loco ad locum*).[125]

Ultimately, the *Chronicarum*'s influence on the literary history of the Witch of Berkeley comes not from the text itself but from the visceral and highly evocative woodcut depicting the witch – naked, fearful, and wrapped in a burial shroud – riding in the company of a gurning and seemingly hirsute demon (Figure 1.1). The skill of the woodcut's creators, Michael Wolgemut and Wilhelm Pleydenwurff, finds further expression in the incidental details that encapsulate the demon's dangerous hybridity, such as its bird-like foot and the extra face extending from the knee; physical manifestation of its depraved spiritual state.[126] Towards the bottom of the page they also saw fit to render the upturned bier on which the stone

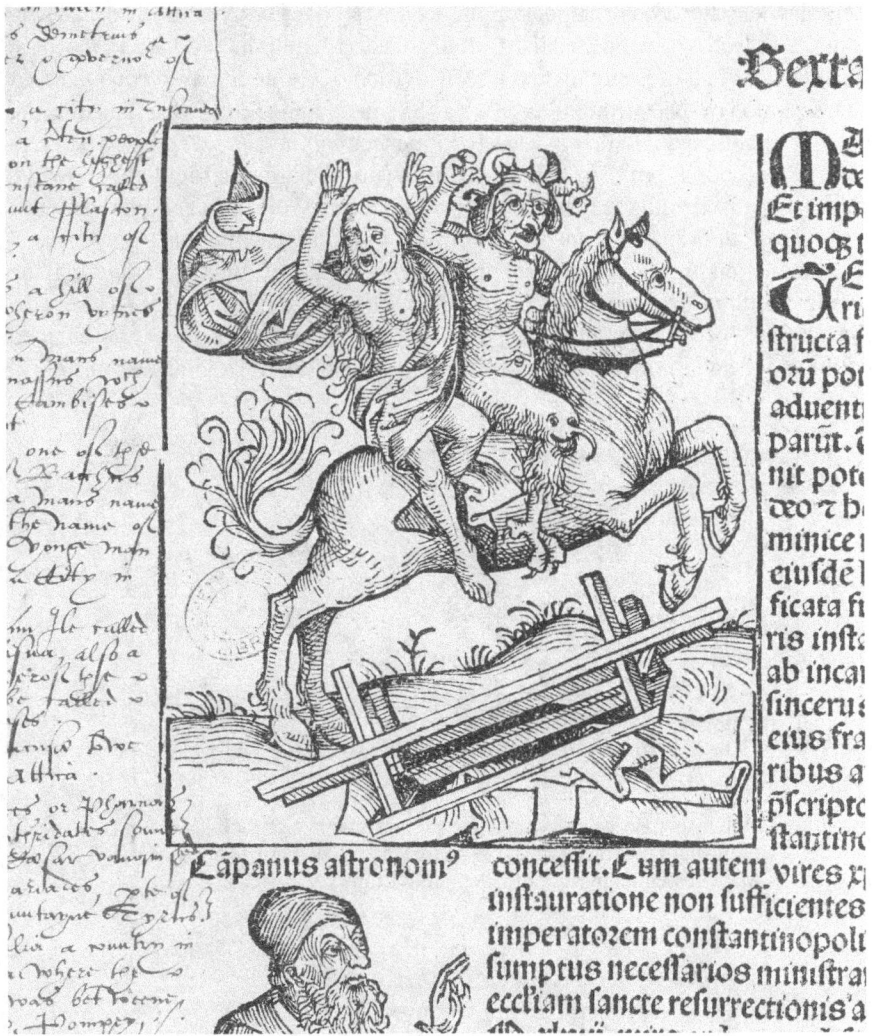

Figure 1.1 Witch of Berkeley woodcut, in Hartmann Schedel, *Liber chronicarum* (Nuremberg: Anton Koberger, for Sebald Schreyer and Sebastian Kammermeister, 1493), fol. 189v. Chetham's Library MUN I.8.2, Manchester. Photo: copyright of the University of Manchester.

coffin was placed, thus conflating the two major episodes of the narrative into one multi-temporal unit. The quarto-sized Schönsperger volumes, whilst not as extravagant as the authorised *Chronicara*, made notable attempts to recreate the original images, albeit on a smaller, less artful scale. A comparison between the 'sanctioned' and 'unsanctioned' woodcuts testifies to the differences in competency and execution (Figure 1.2).

The popularity of the *Chronicarum* meant that its depiction of the Witch of Berkeley had a profound impact on the iconography of witchcraft for decades to come.[127] Indeed, when the Swedish Catholic Olaus Magnus incorporated Vincent of Beauvais's Witch of Berkeley text into his *Historia de Gentibus Septentrionalibus* ('Description of the Northern Peoples', 1555), he included a woodcut that, despite the extra landscape detail, was clearly influenced by the *Chronicarum*. The presence of the church building and peasantry in the background highlights how the copier dispensed with the non-linear approach of the Wolgemut and Pleydenwurff exemplar – an orthodoxly medieval form of visual representation – and focused specifically on the demon's final flight from Berkeley, thus necessitating the removal of the foreground bier (Figure 1.3). The image from the 1567 Basel edition differs even further, featuring two extra demons fussing over the chained coffin and the additional flourish of the horse-bound devil wielding a pitchfork.[128]

Figure 1.2 Witch of Berkeley woodcut, in Hartmann Schedel, *Liber chronicarum* (Augsburg, Schönsperger, 1497), fol. 211v. Chetham's Library MUN 7.B.7.12, Manchester. Copyright of Chetham's Library.

Figure 1.3 Witch of Berkeley woodcut, in Olaus Magnus, *Historia de Gentibus Septentrionalibus* (Rome, 1555), p. 126. John Rylands Library SC10205C, Manchester. Copyright of the University of Manchester.

Figure 1.4 Witch of Berkeley woodcut, in Conrad Lycosthenes, *Prodigiorum ac ostentorum chronicon* (Basel, 1557), p. 378. Chetham's Library Mun 7.B.7.9, Manchester. Copyright of Chetham's Library.

Other compilers were a lot more faithful to Wolgemut and Pleydenwurf's original design. The Witch of Berkeley woodcut included in Conrad Lycosthenes's *Prodigiorum ac ostentorum chronicon* ('Chronicle of Signs and Portents', 1557), is a fair copy of the exemplar, albeit lacking the upturned bier (Figure 1.4). The associated text appears to have been modelled on, but not taken directly from, the *Chronicarum,* omitting reference to the singing clerics and noting only that the *auguratrix* was accosted by the devil, that she was taken away through the air on the back of a horse, and that her screams could be heard for up to four miles away.[129] Stephen Batman's English continuation of the *Prodigiorum, The Doome warning all men to the Judgement* (1581), dispenses with the Berkeley woodcut entirely. The text, however, is a straightforward translation of Lycosthenes's original:

Lycosthenes:
Henrico eius nominis tertio apud Romanos imperante, in Anglia uenefica quædam
    auguratrix à diabolo rapta est, quam horrendo clamore post se in equum trac-
    tam, per aëra auexit. Cuius uetule clamor ad aliquot horas per quatuor fere
    eius regionis milliaria auditus est.[130]

Batman:
When Henrie the third of that name was Emperor of Rome, in England a certain
    soothsaying Witch was caried away by the Divel, whyche being drawen after
    him uppon his horsse with a horrible crye, he caryed away up into the ayre, the
    cry of whiche old woman was heard for certaine hours almost foure miles in that
    Countrey'.[131]

Readers responded to the Witch of Berkeley woodcut in a variety of ways. A vibrant pen-and-ink rendering of the *Chronicarum* image forms part of the famed

Wickiana (MS F. 12 fol. 9r), a collection of broadsheets, jottings, and miscellaneous texts compiled over the course of thirty years by the Swiss clergyman Johann Jakob Wick (d.1588). Indeed, Wick found the Witch of Berkeley to be sufficiently interesting to not only transcribe the vernacular *Das Buch der Croniken* text beneath the drawing, but also to note down the Latin text from Lycosthenes's *Prodigiorum* on a separate leaf in the same volume (F. 12 fol. 7r).[132] By contrast, the Wigan native Thomas Gudlawe, former owner of the 'authorised' *Liber Chronicarum* held at Chetham's Library, Manchester (MUN I.8.2), did not seem to pay the image of the Witch of Berkeley much attention. Writing around 1590, Gudlawe filled the margins of his *Chronicarum* with extensive annotations and digressions, mostly taken from Latin-English dictionaries and vernacular histories, such as Batman's *The Doome*. Thus, contrary to expectations, the notes that appear next to the woodcut in the left-hand margin of fol. 189v do not comment upon the witch or her fate (Figure 1.1). They are simply a continuation of 'ph' section of the *Dictionarium historicum & poeticum* – the appendix to Thomas Cooper's *Thesaurus Linguae Romanae & Brittannicae* (1565) – carrying over from the annotations made on the previous page (fol.189r).[133]

Much in the manner of preachers, historians, and encyclopaedists, demonologists also found the tale of the Witch of Berkeley to be a useful pedagogical tool. Writing contemporaneously with Olaus Magnus and Conrad Lycosthenes, the Protestant sceptic Johann Weyer (d.1588) spent most of his academic career arguing against the efficacy of demonic influences on earth, suggesting instead that the powers attributed to witches were due to shared delusions and/or the result of Catholic credulity. The sixth book of Weyer's *De praestigiis daemonum* (first introduced in the 1568 edition) features a somewhat free transcription of the Witch of Berkeley taken from the *Speculum Historiale,* offset against an account of the life and career of the repentant magician-pope, Sylvester II.[134] Weyer is sceptical that the witch actually existed and calls the story a mere fable (*figmentum*) suitable only for entertainment (*iocis*), but he nonetheless uses it as a frame for the following chapters on the contemporary persecution of poor, delusional '*lamiae*'. The appropriation of the Witch of Berkeley as a literary shorthand to comment upon the vagaries of female agency was not just restricted to Weyer. Vincent of Beauvais is cited as the main source for the vernacular Berkeley text incorporated into playwright Thomas Heywood's *Gynaikeion* (1624).[135] Divided into nine books and drawing on a wide array of classical, medieval, and near-contemporary sources, the *Gynaikeion* is the earliest of Heywood's three prose histories of women, a collection that also includes *England's Elizabeth, Her Life and Troubles* (1631) and *The Exemplary Lives and Memorable Acts of Nine the Most Worthy Women* (1640). The account of the Witch of Berkeley is included in *Gynaikeion* book nine, which focuses primarily on the rewards and punishments given to virtuous and non-virtuous women from ancient times to the present day. Heywood's literary leanings can be discerned in the extra details that furnish the beginning of the text. The witch apparently 'lived in indifferent good opinion amongst her neighbours', was 'wonderous pleasant in companie', and had 'brought up' the crow that revealed the news of her son's demise. For a man well-versed in the requirements of the dramatic arts, the extra information regarding the witch's high social status added a further level of irony to her damnation.[136]

The literary impact of the Witch of Berkeley is not only a testament to William of Malmesbury's skill as a writer, but also to the enduring utility of the *Speculum Historiale*. Judging by the lack of reference to the tale in the extant pamphlet and broadside literature of the seventeenth and eighteenth centuries, it does not appear to have figured large in the popular imagination, especially in England. With the liturgical impact of the Reformation curtailing the Witch of Berkeley's use as a sermon story, especially in the context of advertising the efficacy of the sacraments, it owed its post-medieval existence to the continuing traditions of learned secular writing. It is ironic, then, that the Romantic poet Robert Southey (1774–1843) consulted neither the *Gesta regum* nor the *Historiale* – two of the main modes of historical transmission – when writing his 'Old Woman of Berkeley' folk ballad (c.1798). Known chiefly for his thirty-year tenure as Poet Laureate (1813–1843) and association with William Wordsworth and Samuel Coleridge as one of the Lake Poets, Southey spent the early part of his career obsessed with the composition of short Gothic ballads, influenced by the 'sublime' German style of Gothicism that was emerging at this time, particularly Gottfried August Bürger's *Lenore* (c1774).[137] According to Southey's close friend and the English translator of *Lenore*, William Taylor, such ballads were intended to be 'old in the costume of the ideas, as well as of the style and metre – in the very spirit of the superstitions of the days of yore'.[138] Southey was a prodigious writer, both in verse and prose, whose correspondences and essays provide a tantalising insight into the circumstances by which he came across and re-worked the Witch of Berkeley for his own poetic purposes.

In the preface to the sixth volume of his monumental career retrospective, *The Poetical Works Collected by Himself* (1838), Southey disputes the notion that he developed the 'Old Witch of Berkeley' in 1798 as a response to Taylor's (and another associate, Frank Sayer's) attempts to balladise the Olaus Magnus version of the text in the early 1790s.[139] Instead, he explains how he came across the story in 'Matthew of Westminster [sic]'[140] whilst visiting Hereford Cathedral library in the autumn of 1796. Smitten with the 'circumstantial details' of the text, he set about translating and versifying the Latin prose that very night, completing the first draft of the ballad during a coach ride to Abberley, Worcestershire, the following morning.[141] On 1 October 1798 Southey sent a finished copy to Taylor – to which he responded two months later with favourable comments[142] – and mentions the copyright issues surrounding the publication of the 'Old Woman' in a letter sent to his patron, C. W. Williams Wynn, on 17 December 1798.[143] Initially published under the title 'A Ballad Showing How an Old Woman Rode Double, and Who Rode Before Her' as part of Southey's *Poems: The Second Volume* (1799), it was prefaced with a transcription of the *Flores Historiarum* text and a woodcut based on the *Liber Chronicarum* (Figure 1.5).

The poem itself follows the general tenor of its source text, although Southey is not immune to adding an extra flourish when needed. As part of the witch's

Figure 1.5 Witch of Berkeley engraving, in Robert Southey, *Poems: The Second Volume,*
          2nd ed. (Bristol,1800), p. 144. John Rylands Library Unitarian Printed
          Collection N405, Manchester. Copyright of the University of Manchester.

confession to her son and daughter, reference is made to such early modern stereotypes as having 'suck'd the breath of sleeping babes / the fiends have been my slaves
/ […] nointed myself with infants fat / And feasted on rifled graves'.[144] Further inven-
tions include the detail that the witch's children remained in the church to watch
over their mother's corpse, providing the reader with an emotional tether against
the escalation of the devil's onslaughts. For Southey, Gothic tales worked best if
maintaining the same emotional perspective as those 'in the days if yore', a pointed
contrast to Coleridge, whose *The Rime of the Ancyent Marinere* (1798) betrays an
interest in the psychology of the protagonist over the danger of external agencies, a
'modern' mediation of the present-ness of the past against which the 'Old Woman
of Berkeley' was written as a form of riposte.[145] The inclusion of the source Latin
text and woodcut image encouraged the reader to identify with the historical origins
of the ballad and understand the dissonance (rather than continuity) between the past
and the present. As to the provenance of the woodcut, Southey remarks that:

> Mr Wathen, a singular and obliging person, who afterwards made a voyage to
> the East Indies, and published an account of what her saw there, traced for me
> a facsimile of a wooden cut in the Nuremberg Chronicle (which was among
> the prisoners in the Cathedral). This was put into the hands of a Bristol artist;
> and the engraving in wood which he made form it was prefixed to the Ballad
> when first published.[146]

'Mr Wathen' appears to be a reference to James Wathen (c.1751–1828), an ama-
teur Hereford artist who journeyed to India and China in 1811 and published his
memoirs of the voyage in 1814.[147] The identity of the engraver is much more difficult to decipher. The signature located in the bottom left-hand side of the picture,
'M&W Fecit', reveals only the first letter of their surname, 'M' ('the W' being

Wathen). In any case, the ballad (and the *Flores Historiarum* text) later appeared in M. G. Lewis's *Tales of Wonder* anthology (1801), only this time without the woodcut and with the title simplified to 'The Old Woman of Berkeley'.[148] Southey revised and republished the ballad many times over the years. For instance, by the time of the publication of the *Poetical Works Collected by Himself*, the stanza concerning the witch's confession of her sins had been amended to 'I have 'nointed myself with infants' fat / the fiends have been my slaves / From sleeping babies I have suck'd the breath / And breaking by charms the sleep of death / I have call'd the dead from their graves', putting greater emphasis on the act of necromancy over the more distasteful practice of necro-cannibalism.[149] The Witch of Berkeley remained a key part of Southey's imaginative lexicon until the very end of his career, despite his exasperation that his early ballads were held in higher regard than his later works. In a wry piece of meta-textual commentary, the character of Satan in another of Southey's the poems, 'The Devil's Walk' (c.1827), actively bemoans 'He [who] hath put me in ugly ballads / with libellous pictures for sale / He [who] hath scoffed at my hoofs and my horns / And has made very free with my tail'.[150] With the publication of the *Poetical Works Collected by Himself*, 'The Old Woman of Berkeley' was firmly and irrevocably canon.

That the Witch of Berkeley retained a sense of her own personhood after death is never in doubt. The description of her screams being heard up to four miles away is found in nearly all extant versions of the text, as is her pitiable response to the devil's earlier command to rise ('She said she could not on account of the chains').[151] None of the previously-mentioned authors, Southey included, saw it necessary to comment upon these facts. They were simply a given. Nor is anything said about the corpse's physical appearance. William Taylor, Southey's friend and author of the competing Witch of Berkeley folk ballad 'A Tale of Wonder' (c.1791; publ. 1803), is the only writer to truly take heed of the witch's post-mortem state. In Taylor's words, the devil removed the final chain from the coffin and found:

> […] a woman's shape,
> Her skin of ashy hue,
> With writhing limbs, and bristling hair,
> And eyes of chalk in haggard stare,
> And lips and nipples blue.
> Wringing her hands in wild affright
> She clung about the priest:
> "For this thy chalice have I quaff'd?"
> Dumb was the priest; the devil laugh'd;
> All hope of safety ceas'd.

(ll.141–150)

This scene was dramatically recreated in watercolour by the Norwich artist Edward Bell (1804), using Taylor's text as a direct inspiration.[152] Bell's depiction of a pale, desiccated corpse gripping a monk's robes in fear of the approaching devil captures the essential dynamism of the encounter and, unlike unblemished

Figure 1.6 A Tale of Wonder, watercolour, 23 × 20.6 cm. Edward Bell (1804). Credit: Wellcome Collection.

figure from the *Liber Chronicarum* woodcut, speaks to the corrupted undeadness of the Witch (Figure 1.6).

Conclusion

The Witch of Berkeley is often cited as a key text on twelfth-century witchcraft yet, ironically, it has not received much in the way of close critical attention. The aim of this chapter has been threefold: to examine the social, cultural, and literary influences on the structure of the narrative itself, to explore its moralistic function within the *Gesta regum Anglorum* and, finally, to provide a clearer understanding of its transmission into different texts, genres, and media. Informed by his considerable learning, William of Malmesbury constructed a tale that spoke at once to the authority of his classical and patristic precedents, whilst also supplying just enough local flavour to attest to the second major facet of historical truth: local eyewitness testimony. As intimated in the exemplum's gloss, Gregory the Great and Hincmar of Reims supplied the base narrative framework – sinners taken from the grave – onto which a geographical and moral immediacy was provided with the choice of Berkeley as the story's location and the oblique references to

Berkeley Abbey's reduction (specifically the use of the term '*clericus*' to describe the attending churchmen). Godwin's notoriety for pillaging churches is one of the main reasons why he is so heavily criticised in certain parts of the *Gesta regum* (see especially ii.196). By contrast, Godwin and his offspring receive only marginal censure in William's other works, such as the *Gesta pontificum* and *Vita Wulfstani*. Indeed, Wulfstan's close relationship with Harold Godwinson may have necessitated a certain amount of circumspection where the sins of the father (and brother, Swein) were concerned.[153] That is to say, different rhetorical strategies required different approaches to the 'truth'. Although Gregory's *Dialogues* is the tantamount urtext for the medieval model of the supernatural exemplum, the fate of sheriff Leofstan in the *De miraculis sancti Edmundi* provides compelling evidence that belief in restless bodies was a pervasive 'oral text' in pre- and post-Conquest England. Sewing the corpse into a deer skin, binding the tomb with chains, and hearing voices from the grave should not be read solely as an interpolation from Gregory, but reflective of everyday, unwritten fears about the vitality of dead bodies, filtered through the discursive lens of one of William's most-cited authors. Ultimately, the Witch of Berkeley was damned by her lifelong pursuit of magic. The story's moralisation on the dangers of crossing inviolate boundaries and the need to expel sinners from the body-politic meant it was perfectly suited to provide an ironic commentary on past events (the civil strife of the 1040s and early 1050s), whilst also acting as a platform through which to comment upon the ongoing resonances of Conquest. The reassertion of a sense of social cohesion through the marriage of Matilda to Henry I – Anglo-Saxon blood to Norman blood – is a rhetorical foundation expressed most notably through its obverse: the social disunity wrought by the activities of Godwin on one side (Anglo-Saxon) and Robert of Jumièges on the other (Norman). The usurpation of Malmesbury Abbey's independence by Roger of Salisbury following Matilda's death in 1118 lends a further level of meaning to the Witch of Berkeley's fate. William, as we have seen, wielded the historian's pen like a sword. Sometimes his attacks could be direct, sometimes subtle. The expulsion of the witch's body from Holy ground treads the same critical pathway as the likening of Roger to Ealhstan, the avaricious bishop of Sherbourne.[154] Defending against unwanted incursions into church affairs was one of the most hard-fought battles of William's literary career.

Perhaps more so than the *Gesta regum*, Vincent of Beauvais's *Speculum Historiale* was integral to the transmission of the Witch of Berkeley into other literary arenas, particularly preaching. The below diagram and table show the key nexus points by which the story was disseminated across different textual communities (Table 1.1). On the whole, the compilation/transcription process involved a close critical evaluation of the meaning of the source text. Roger of Wendover, for instance, deemed it narratologically necessary to include a wonder story about a dying soothsayer within the broader, formulaic framework of ninth-century royal history, perhaps as a means to re-invigorate the monastic reader and provide indirect commentary on the fate that awaited 'bad' kings. The Malmesbury monk who compiled the *Eulogium Historiarum* utilised the Witch of Berkeley in a similar way, grouping it together with a selection of other *mirabilia* from the *Gesta regum*

Table 1.1 Diagram and table showing the literary dissemination of the Witch of Berkeley

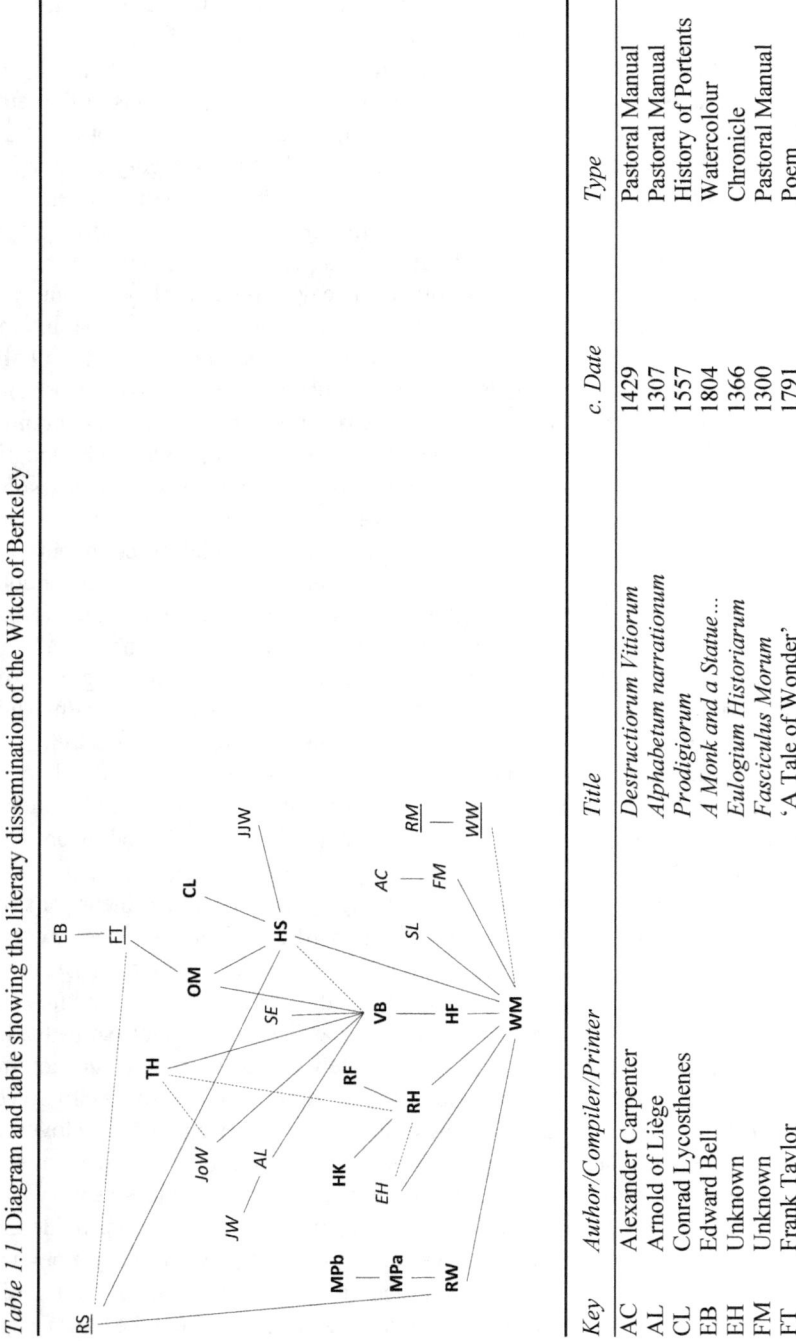

Key	Author/Compiler/Printer	Title	c. Date	Type
AC	Alexander Carpenter	*Destructiorum Vitiorum*	1429	Pastoral Manual
AL	Arnold of Liège	*Alphabetum narrationum*	1307	Pastoral Manual
CL	Conrad Lycosthenes	*Prodigiorum*	1557	History of Portents
EB	Edward Bell	*A Monk and a Statue...*	1804	Watercolour
EH	Unknown	*Eulogium Historiarum*	1366	Chronicle
FM	Unknown	*Fasciculus Morum*	1300	Pastoral Manual
FT	Frank Taylor	'A Tale of Wonder'	1791	Poem

HF	Hélinand of Froidmont,	*Chronicon*	1223	Chronicle
HS	Hartmann Schedel	*Liber Chronicarum*	1493	Chronicle and Image
JW	Unknown	*Jacob's Well*	1440	Pastoral Manual
JoW	Johann Weyer	*De praestigiis daemonum*	1568	Demonological treatise
JJW	Johann Jakob Wick	*Wickiana*	1588	Miscellany
HK	Henry Knighton	*Chronicon*	1378–96	Chronicle
MPa	Matthew Paris	*Chronica majora*	1240–1259	Chronicle
MPb	Matthew Paris	*Flores Historiarum*	1249	Chronicle
OM	Olaus Magnus	*Historia de Gentibus Septentrionalibus*	1555	History
RF	Robert Fabyan	*The New Chronicles of England and France*	1516	Chronicle
RH	Ranulph Hidgen	*Polychronicon*	1360	Chronicle
RM	Robert Mannyng	*Handlyng Synne*	1303	Verse/Pastoral Manual
RS	Robert Southey	'The Old Woman of Berkeley'	1798	Poem
RW	Roger of Wendover	*Flores Historiarum*	1220–1235	Chronicle
SE	Richard Pafraet (ed)	*Speculum Exemplorum*	1481	Pastoral Manual
SL	Unknown (John of Howden?)	*Speculum Laicorum*	1275	Pastoral Manual
TH	Thomas Heywood,	*Gynaikeion*	1624	History
VB	Vincent of Beauvais	*Speculum Historiale*	1248	Encyclopaedia
WM	William of Malmesbury	*Gesta regum Anglorum*	1125	Chronicle
WW	William of Wadington	*La Manuel des Pechiez*	1250–70	Verse/Pastoral Manual

Diagram note: **Bold** = secular and historical works; *Italics* = religious works; Underlined = poetic/verse; Unformatted = misc.

as instructive digressions from the main historical narrative. Preachers were equally as discerning in their usage. The compiler of *Jacob's Well* understood the potency of the story's message – the danger of dying in sin – and reduced the text to its base narratological framework to suit any pastoral situation. In a more sophisticated and discursive manner, the author of the *Fasciculus Morum* tied the actions of the Witch of Berkeley (and the practice of magic in general) to heresy and the sentence of excommunication. Insights can also be made into early modern reading practices and compilation strategy. Just as Thomas Heywood was aware of numerous versions of the Berkeley text yet deferred to Vincent of Beauvais, so Johan Jacob Wick's scrapbooking tendencies reveal equal knowledge of Conrad Lycosthenes's *Prodigiorum* and the vernacular *Das Buch der Croniken*, consulting both accordingly. And yet, by the end of sixteenth century the Witch of Berkeley had already begun the steady transformation from *exemplum* into historical curiosity, *figmentum*. Johann Weyer and Robert Fabyan each make allusions to the text's lack of moral substance. For Weyer, it functioned solely as a counterpoint to more serious socio-theological matters; for Fabyan, he would 'nat have shewed' the tale had it not been included in oeuvre of so many literary authorities, his editors following through on his scepticism by removing the narrative entirely from later editions of his *New Chronicles*.[155] It is not hard to see why a Romantic poet such as Robert Southey became so enamoured with the 'circumstantial details' of a text found by happenstance in Hereford Cathedral. As the echo of a distant, credulous past it made the perfect vehicle for Gothic reinvention. A story that includes a malevolent witch, talking crows, strange burial rites, and a demonic horse resonates in the imagination even today.

Notes

1 'Ceterum daemonas, id est genios, adiurare consuevimus, ut illos de hominibus exigamus, non deiearare, ut eis honorem divinitatis conferamus', Tertullian, *Apology,* 32.3, trans. by T. R. Glover, Loeb Classical Library 250 (Cambridge, MA: Harvard University Press, 1931), pp. 156–57.

2 Augustine, *De civitate Dei* IV.29, in *Opera Omnia* vol. 7, PL 41, ed. by J-P Migne (Paris, 1864), cols. 135–36.

3 Augustine, *De Doctrina Christiana* II.22, in *Opera Omnia* vol. 3, PL 34 (Paris, 1841), col. 51–52.

4 Augustine, Epistle LV. 20.37, in *Opera Omnia* vol. 2, PL 33 (Paris, 1865), col. 222.

5 See John T. McNeill and Helena M. Gamer's *Medieval Handbooks of Penance*; John T. McNeill, 'Folk-Paganism in the Penitentials', *The Journal of Religion* 13 (1933), 450–66.

6 St. Boniface, Epistle 78, in *Die Briefe des Heiligen Bonifatius und Lullus,* ed. by Michael Tangl (Berlin: Weidmannsche, 1916), p. 164.

7 Alcuin, Epistle 295, in *Monumenta Alcuiniana*, BRG 6, ed. by Phillip Jaffé (Berlin, 1873), p. 886.

8 Lanfranc, Epistle 11, in *The Letters of Lanfranc, Archbishop of Canterbury*, ed. and trans. by Helen Glover and Margaret Gibson, Oxford Medieval Texts (Oxford: Clarendon, 1979), p. 79.

9 For key introductory texts, see Valerie I. J. Flint, *The Rise of Magic in Early Medieval Europe* (Oxford: Clarendon, 1991); Bill Griffiths *Aspects of Anglo-Saxon Magic* (Hockwold-cum-Wilton: Anglo-Saxon Books, 1996).

10 Richard Kieckhefer, 'Mythologies of Witchcraft in the Fifteenth-Century', in *Magic, Ritual, and Witchcraft* 1 (2006), 79–108; Michael D. Bailey, *Fearful Spirits, Reasoned Follies: The Boundaries of Superstition in Late Medieval Europe* (Ithaca, NY: Cornell University Press, 2013).

11 For key English language investigations into magic in the long twelfth-century, see Jeffrey B. Russell, *Witchcraft in the Middle Ages* (Ithaca, NY: Cornell University Press, 1972); Edward Peters, *The Magician, the Witch and the Law* (Philadelphia, PA: University of Pennsylvania Press, 1978). Discussions on magical belief in the early years of the twelfth century are also somewhat elided in *The Routledge History of Medieval Magic*, ed. by Sophie Page and Catherine Rider (London: Routledge, 2019).

12 Bartlett, *England Under the Norman and Angevin Kings*, p. 650.

13 Peters, *The Magician*, p. 66–67; Charles Burnett, *Magic and Divination in the Middle Ages: Texts and Techniques in the Islamic and Christian Worlds* (Aldershot: Variorum, 1996).

14 'On Magic', in Isidore of Seville, *Etymologies*, ed. and trans. by Stephen A. Barney et al. (Cambridge: Cambridge University Press, 2006), VIII.ix (pp. 181–83). All subsequent English-language citations from the *Etymologies* will be taken from this edition. All Latin citations will be taken from *Isidori Hispalensis Episcopi, Etymologiarum Sive Originum Libri XX*, 2 vols. ed. by W. M. Lindsay (Oxford: Clarendon, 1911).

15 First recorded in Regino of Prüm's *Libri duo de synodalibus causis et disciplinis ecclesiasticis* (c.906), the *Canon Episcopi* was one of the most influential early medieval treatises on popular superstition. For a modern translation, see Henry C. Lea, *Materials Toward a History of Witchcraft*, Vol. 1 (New York: Yoseloff, 1957), pp. 178–80.

16 'ut in unguibus sacro nescio quo oleo aut crismate delibutis vel in exterso et leuigato corpore pelvis quod quaerebat nostro manifestaretur indicio.' ('so that we could impart the information [the priest] was seeking by means of fingernails soaked in some sort of sacred oil and/or the polished surface of a shallow bowl'), in Ioannes Saresberiensis, *Policraticus, I–IV*, CCCM 118, ed. by K.S.B. Keats-Rohan (Turnhout: Brepols, 1993), II.28 (at p. 167).

17 For the account of Merlin's inception, and the realisation that his mother had been visited by a demon in the shape of a man, see book six of Geoffrey of Monmouth, *The History of the Kings of Britain: An Edition and Translation of the De gestis Britonum (Historia Regum Britanniae)*, ed. and trans. by Michael D. Reeve (Woodbridge: Boydell & Brewer, 2007), pp. 138–39.

18 GrA, ii.204 (pp. 377–81).

19 See, for example, Russell, *Witchcraft in the Middle Ages*, p. 98; Peters, *The Magician*, p. 32; Watkins, *History and the Supernatural*, pp. 117–18; Charles Zika, *The Appearance of Witchcraft: Print and Visual Culture in Sixteenth-Century Europe* (London: Routledge, 2007), pp. 59, 206, 226–28; Corinne Saunders, *Magic and the Supernatural in Medieval English Romance* (Cambridge: Brewer, 2010), p. 98.

20 'Ego illud a tali uiro audui qui se uidesse iuraret, cui erubescerem non credere' (I have heard it from the sort of man who would swear he had seen it, and whose word I would be ashamed to impugn), GrA, ii.204 (pp. 377–78).

21 Rodney Thomson, *William of Malmesbury* (Woodbridge: Boydell, 1987), pp. 36–37.

22 Samu Niskanen, 'William of Malmesbury as Librarian: The Evidence of his Autographs', in *Discovering William of Malmesbury*, ed. by Rodney M. Thomson, Emily Dolmans and Emily A. Winkler (Woodbridge: Boydell, 2017), pp. 117–27.

23 'Itaque, cum domesticis sumptibus nonnulos exterarum gentium historicos conflassem...', GrA, ii. Prologue (p. 151).

24 'Sed ut res absconditas, quae in strue vetustatis latebant, convellerem in lucem', GrA, ii. Prologue (p. 151).

25 Thomson, *William of Malmesbury*, pp. 4–5; *William of Malmesbury: Saints' Lives: Lives of ss. Wulfstan, Dunstan, Patrick, Benignus and Indract*, ed. and trans. by M.

62 *The Witch of Berkeley in context*

Winterbottom and R. M. Thomson, Oxford Medieval Texts (Oxford: Clarendon, 2002), pp. xiv–xv.

26 GrA, i. Prologue (p. 15).

27 GrA, i. Prologue (p. 15). For William's advocation of the use of classical Latin and his own stylistic debt to Virgil, see Rodney M. Thomson, 'William of Malmesbury's Historical Vision', in *Discovering William of Malmesbury*, pp. 165–74 (at p. 171); and *William of Malmesbury*, pp. 30–31, 48.

28 For William and ethics, see Sigbjørn Olsen Sønnesyn, *William of Malmesbury and the Ethics of History* (Woodbridge: Boydell, 2012).

29 R. M. Thomson, 'Satire, Irony and Humour in William of Malmesbury', in *Rhetoric and Renewal in the Latin West 1100–1540: Essays in Honour of John O. Ward*, ed. by C. Mews, C. J. Nederman and R. M. Thomson (Turnhout: Brepols, 2003), pp. 115–27; John Gillingham, 'The Ironies of History: William of Malmesbury's Views of William II and Henry I', in *Discovering William of Malmesbury*, pp. 37–48.

30 GrA ii.108 (pp. 156–57).

31 Paul A. Hayward, 'The Importance of Being Ambiguous: Innuendo and Legerdmain in William of Malesbury's Gesta regum and Gesta pontificum Anglorum', *Anglo-Norman Studies* 33 (2011), 75–102; Matilda's patronage of Malmesbury Abbey is confirmed from prefatory letters attached to the Troyes manuscript of the *Gesta regum*, where the anonymous author, most likely William, indicates that the Queen 'ruled' over the Abbey. These letters also mention that the *Gesta regum* was begun at the Queen's behest. See Lois L. Huneycutt, *Matilda of Scotland: A Study in Medieval Queenship* (Woodbridge: Boydell, 2003), pp. 64–66; Thomson, *William of Malmesbury*, pp. 36–37.

32 Peters, *The Magician*, p. 32.

33 GrA, ii.204 (pp. 376–379).

34 Peters, *The Magician*, pp. 31–34.

35 William gives no further details as to the identity of his 'source'. If the reference to the Witch's death occurring 'around the same time' (*isdem diebus simile*) as the death of Pope Gregory VI is accurate, then the events presumably took place c.1048. If the first draft of the *Gesta regum* was completed sometime before 1118, then the man from whom William supposedly heard the tale must have been at least 75 years old. It is unlikely that his source was one of the clerks (from Berkeley Abbey?) who took part in the vigil over the woman's corpse, unless William heard the story in his youth.

36 See the entries for 'augurium', in *Dictionary of Medieval Latin from British Sources: Fascicule I A–B*, ed. by R. E. Latham (Oxford: Oxford University Press, 1975), p. 161.

37 For Rome augury, see Livy, *Ab Urbe Condita* (c.27–29BC), 1.6.3–1.7.3 and Ovid, *Fasti* (8AD), 4.807–62, in Steven J. Green, 'Malevolent Gods and Promethean Birds: Contesting Augury in Augustus's Rome', *Transactions of the American Philological Association* 139 (2009), 147–67.

38 'impetritum, inauguratumst: quovis admittunt aves, picus et cornix ab laeva, corvos, parra ab dextera, consuadent; certum herclest vostram consequi sententiam', in Plautus, Asinaria, II.1.11–13. See Plautus, Macci Plavti Comoediae, vol. 1., ed. by W. M. Lindsay, Oxford Classical Texts (Oxford: Clarendon, 1903), p. 65.

39 Flint, *Rise of Magic*, pp. 116–19.

40 Flint, *Rise of Magic*, pp. 196–99.

41 *De civitate Dei*, iv.29, PL 41, vol. 7. col. 136.

42 Alcuin, Epistle 295, p. 886.

43 Bede, *Ecclesiastical History of the English Nation, Volume I: Books 1–3*, trans. by J. E. King, Loeb Classical Library 246 (Cambridge, MA: Harvard University Press, 1930), I. 25 (at pp. 110–11).

44 The inference that the small crow was a 'favourite' suggests it may have been a familiar demon, underlining the authoritative belief that augury was a form of devil worship.

45 For the Latin, see *Sancti Gregorii Papae I, Cognomento Magni, Opera Omnia, vol. 3 PL 77,* ed. by J-P Migne (Paris, 1862), col. 416. With slight emendations on my part, the English translation has been taken from *The Dialogues of Saint Gregory, surnamed the Great,* ed. by E. G. Gardner (London: Warner, 1911), p. 247.

46 Rodney Thomson, 'William of Malmesbury's Carolingian Sources', *Journal of Medieval History* 7 (1981), 321–37.

47 Hincmar, 'Epistola Synodi Carisiacensis', in *MGH,* Cap. 2 pt. II, no. 297, ed. by Alfred Boretius and Victor Krause (Hannover, 1893), pp. 227–441 (at p. 433).

48 Paul Fouracre, *The Age of Charles Martel* (Harlow: Longman, 2000), p. 135; 'The Long Shadow of the Merovingians', in *Charlemagne: Empire and Society,* ed. by Joanna Story (Manchester: Manchester University Press, 2005), pp. 5–21 (at p. 13).

49 The *Gesta regum* includes a further reference to Charles Martel's death in a partial transcription of St Boniface's letter to King Æthelbald of Mercia (c.746): "Charles too, prince of the Franks, who overthrew many monasteries and converted the revenues of churches to his own use, was consumed by prolonged torments and died a shameful death" (Karolus quoque princeps Francorum, monasteriorum multorum euersor et aecclesiasticarum pecuniarum in usus proprios commutator, longa tortione et uerenda morte consumptus est), in GrA i.80 (pp. 116–17). Paul Fouracre argues that this interpolation is unique to the *Gesta regum* and may be William's own invention, designed to stress the terrible fate that awaited those who harmed the Church. See Fouracre, *Charles Martel,* pp. 133–35.

50 Niskanen, 'William of Malmesbury as Librarian', p. 118.

51 Book one of the *Regula Pastoralis* is especially concerned with the vice of greed. See the rubric for 1.8: De his qui præesse concupiscunt, et ad usum suæ libidinis instrumentum Apostolici sermonis arripiunt (concerning those who covet leadership, and seize on the language of the Apostles for the purposes of their own lust), in *Sancti Gregorii Papae,* vol. 3, PL 77, col.21. At least one copy of the *Regula Pastoralis* (CCCC 361, c.1000–1099) was contained in the library of Malmesbury Abbey and contains corrections in William's own hand.

52 Caciola, *Afterlives;* Roberta Gilchrist, *Medieval Lives: Archaeology and the Life Course* (Woodbridge: Boydell, 2012).

53 Catherine Cubitt, 'Folklore and Historiography: Oral Stories and the Writing of Anglo-Saxon History', in *Narrative and History in the Early Medieval West,* ed. by Elizabeth Tyler and Ross Balzaretti (Turnhout: Brepols, 2006), pp. 189–224; James Campbell, Some Twelfth-Century View of the Anglo-Saxon Past', *Perita* 3 (1984), 131–150.

54 Winston Black, 'Animated Corpses and Bodies with Power in the Scholastic Age', in *Death in Medieval Europe: Death Scripted and Death Choreographed,* ed. by Joëlle Rollo-Koster (London: Routledge, 2017), pp. 71–92 (at pp. 91–92).

55 'Promouete, citius promouete! Agite, agite et uenite!', in Geoffrey of Burton, *Life and Miracles of St Modwenna,* pp. 194–97.

56 'diabolus locutus est per serpentem, ut hodie loquitur per obsessum hominem', in Honorius of Autun, *Elucidarium,* in *Honorii Augustodunensis Opera Omnia,* PL 172 (Paris, 1854), col. 1119B.

57 Herman the Archdeacon and Goscelin of Saint-Bertin, *Miracles of St Edmund,* ed. and trans. by Tom Licence, with Lynda Lockyer, Oxford Medieval Texts (Oxford: Clarendon, 2014), pp. 12–13, 144–145.

58 *Miracles of St Edmund,* p. cxxviii.

59 For the social issues surrounding the rotting cadaver, see Danielle Westerhof, *Death and the Noble Body in Medieval England* (Woodbridge: Boydell, 2008). Other contemporary examples of bodies being sewn into animal hides can be found in Watkins, *History and the Supernatural,* p. 117, n.43.

60 GrA, ii.124 (pp. 196–197).

61 Sarah Breckenridge Wright, 'The Soil's Holy Bodies: The Art of Chorography in William of Malmesbury's *Gesta Pontificum Anglorum*', *Studies in Philology* 111 (2014), 652–79. For the viewpoint that William depended mostly on written sources for his description of places and landscapes, see Stanislav Mereminskiy, 'William of Malmesbury and Durham: The Circulation of Historical Knowledge in Early Twelfth-Century England', in *Discovering William of Malmesbury*, pp. 107–16.

62 Cited in Michael Hare, 'Anglo-Saxon Berkeley: History and Topography', *Anglo-Saxon Studies in Archaeology and History* 18 (2013), 119–56 (at p. 125); See also C. S. Taylor, 'Berkeley Minster', in *Transactions of the Bristol and Gloucestershire Archaeological Society* 19 (1894–95), 70–84.

63 Hare, 'Anglo-Saxon Berkeley', p. 139.

64 Peters, *The Magician*, p. 32.

65 *Domesday Book 15: Gloucestershire*, ed. and trans. by John S. Moore (Chichester: Fillimore, 1982), 164b.

66 Hare, 'Anglo-Saxon Berkeley', p. 128; Taylor, 'Berkeley Minster', p. 82.

67 *De nugis,* dist. v. 3 (at pp.416–19).

68 Hare, 'Anglo-Saxon Berkeley', p. 128.

69 'ac he dyde ealles to lytle dædbote of þære Godes are þe he hæfde of manegum halgum stowum'. See *The Anglo-Saxon Chronicle: An Electronic Edition* (Vol 3) < http://asc.jebbo.co.uk/c/c-L.html> [accessed 1 December 2017].

70 Some scholars believe that the Abbey was actually located at 'Oldminster', two miles north of Berkeley. However, it is possible that the name Oldminster refers to a dependent church set up to serve the peripheries of the Berkeley parish. For an overview of this argument, see Hare, 'Anglo-Saxon Berkeley', p. 143.

71 Caroline Walker Bynum, 'Wonder', *The American Historical Review* 102 (1997), 1–26.

72 Watkins, *History and the Supernatural*, pp. 223–25.

73 Elizabeth Freeman, 'Wonders, Prodigies and Marvels: Unusual Bodies and the Fear of Heresy in Ralph of Coggeshall's Chronicon Anglicanum', *Journal of Medieval History* 26 (2000), 127–143 (at p.132).

74 For an overview of these events and the strife between church and state, see Gerd Tellenbach, *Church, State, and Christian Society at the Time of the Investiture Contest,* trans. by R. F. Bennett (New York: Harvester, 1979).

75 GrA i.203 (pp. 374–377).

76 Peters, *The Magician*, p. 31.

77 It is tempting to suggest that the name Palumbus ('Wood-Pidgeon') is a lexical reference to the Witch of Berkeley's skill in augury. Alternately, it may have been intended as parody of the symbol of the Holy Spirit, the dove (*columbus*).

78 For William's medical knowledge, see Joanna Phillips, 'William of Malmesbury: Medical Historian of the Crusades', in *Discovering William of Malmesbury*, pp. 129–138.

79 GrA, ii.206 (pp. 384–385).

80 Sønnesyn, *Ethics of History*, pp. 192–93.

81 For William's belief that saints' bodies represented social integrity as opposed to sinners, whose bodies were monstrously 'open', see Robert M. Stein, 'Making History English: Cultural Identity and Historical Explanation in William of Malmesbury and Layamon's *Brut*', in *Text and Territory: Geographical Imagination in the European Middle Ages*, ed. by Sylvia Tomasch and Sealy Gilles (Philadelphia, PA: University of Pennsylvania Press, 1998), pp. 97–115 (at pp.100–102).

82 GrA. ii.226, pp. 414–15. Edward is told by the figures in his vision that the forthcoming calamities (i.e. the Conquest) can be likened to a green tree cut through the middle of the trunk. Only later would the parts be re-joined and the tree 'bloom and bear fruit' (*floribus pubescere et fructus protrudere*) as it had done in the past.

83 Sønnesyn, *Ethics of History*, pp. 155–66; Hayward, 'The Importance of Being Ambiguous', p. 10.

84 Nicholas J. Higham and Martin J. Ryan, *The Anglo-Saxon World* (New Haven, CT: Yale University Press, 2013), pp. 387–95.

85 GrA, ii.196 (pp. 350–51).

86 Sønnesyn, *Ethics of History*, p. 192.

87 GrA, ii.197–198 (pp.354–57). And yet, here William also pointedly includes a digression on Godwin's death, building upon the base facts of the *Anglo-Saxon Chronicle*. Whereas the various recessions of the *ASC* merely state that Godwin died at a feast, William adds the detail that he choked to death after swearing he had never harmed the king.

88 GrA, ii.199 (pp.360–61).

89 Sønnesyn, *Ethics of History*, p. 192.

90 Þa he com to Cantwarbyrig east þa snædde he þær 7 his menn. 7 to Dofran gewende (Then he [Eustace] came east to Canterbury, then he and his men took a meal there, and went to Dover). <http://asc.jebbo.co.uk/e/e-L.html> [accessed 25 January 2019]

91 "Sed non patiatur Deus ut istam offam transglutiam si fui conscius alicuius rei quae spectaret ad eius periculum vel tuum incommodum." Hoc dicto, offa quam in os miserat suffocatus, oculos ad mortem invertit ('May God not permit me to swallow this mouthful, if I was ever aware of having done anything designed to endanger [Edward's brother, Alfred] or hurt you'. With these words, he was choked by the food he had just put into his mouth, and turned up his eyes in death), in GrA, ii.198 (pp. 354–55).

92 Hayward, 'The Importance of Being Ambiguous', p. 95.

93 Kirsten A. Fenton, *Gender, Nation and Conquest in the Works of William of Malmesbury* (Woodbridge: Boydell and Brewer, 2008), pp. 123–26.

94 Elizabeth M. Tyler, *England in Europe: English Royal Women and Literary Patronage, c.1000–c.1150* (Toronto, ONT: University of Toronto Press, 2017), p. 215.

95 GrA v. 419 (pp. 758–59). William here is referring to Edward's allegory on the cutting of the green tree, recorded in an earlier section of the *Gesta regum* (ii.226, pp. 414–15).

96 Hélinand of Froidmont, Chronicon, in *Helinandi Frigidi Montis Monachi, Necnon Guntheri Cisterciensis, Opera Omnia*, PL 212 (Paris, 1855), col. 939D; Roger of Wendover, *Chronicon, sive Flores Historiarum* , 4 vols. ed. by Henry Coxe (London, 1841–1842), I (1841). pp. 286–88.

97 E. R. Smits, 'Helinand of Froidmont and the A-Text of Seneca's Tragedies', *Mnemosyne*, 4th ser. 36 (1983, 324–58.

98 'Sed proh nefas! nil lacrimae valuere piae'.

99 For the definition of *sortes*, see *Dictionary of Medieval Latin from British Sources: Fascicule XVI Sol-Syr*, ed. by R. K Ashdowne and D. R. Howlett (Oxford: Oxford University Press, 2013), pp. 3139–3140.

100 See Matthew Paris, *Matthæi Parisiensis, monachi Sancti Albani, Chronica majora*, vol. 1., ed. by Henry R. Luard, RS 57 (London: Longman,1872), pp. 381–383; *Flores Historiarum*, vol. 1, ed. by Henry R. Luard, RS 95 (London: Longman, 1890), pp. 420–22.

101 E. R. Smits, 'Vincent of Beauvais: A Note on the Background of the *Speculum* ', in *Vincent of Beauvais and Alexander the Great: Studies on the Speculum Maius and its Translation into Medieval Vernaculars*, ed. by W. J. Aerts, E. R. Smits, and J. B. Voorbij (Groningen: Forsten, 1996), 1–9.

102 The version consulted here is the Latin printed edition, Vincent of Beauvais, *Speculum Historiale* (Nuremberg, 1483), book 26, ch. 26.

103 Smits, 'Vincent of Beauvais' p. 6.

104 See, for example, CCCC MS 95, fol. 191r (c.1300–1400). For a modern edition of Arnold's text, see Arnoldus Leodiensis, *Alphabetum narrationum*, CCCM 160, ed. by Elisa Brilli (Turnhout: Brepols, 2015).

105 *An Alphabet of Tales: An English Translation of the Alphabetum Narrationum* EETS, o.s. 127 ed. by Mary M. Banks (London: Kegan Paul, Trench, Trübner & co, 1905), pp. 487–88.

106 *Jacob's Well, An Englisht Treatise on the Cleansing of Man's Conscience. Part I,*
     EETS, o.s. 115, ed. by Arthur Brandeis (London: Kegen Paul, Trench, Trübner &
     co, 1900), pp.186–87; Joan Young Gregg, 'The Exempla of Jacob's Well: A Study
     in the Transmission of Medieval Sermon Stories', *Traditio* 33 (1977), 359–80 (at pp.
     362, 365); Leo Carruthers, 'Where did Jacob's Well come from? The Provenance and
     Dialect of Ms Salisbury Cathedral 103', *English Studies* 71 (1990), 335–40.
107 Richard Pafraet (ed.), *Speculum Exemplorum* (Daventer, 1481), dist. iv.51.
108 Johannes Major (ed.) *Magnum Speculum Exemplorum* (Cologne, 1618), pp. 49–50.
109 *Fasciculus Morum: A Fourteenth-Century Preacher's Handbook*, ed. and trans. by
     Siegfried Wenzel (University Park, PA: Penn State University Press, 1989), Part 5,
     ch. 30 (pp. 577–85).
110 Here I have consulted the later printed edition, Alexander Carpenter, *Destructiorum
     vitiorum*, (Venice, 1578), Part 6, ch. 49 (pp.301–303).
111 As obliquely mentioned in G. R Owst, *The Destructiorum Vitiorum of Alexander
     Carpenter* (London: S. P. C. K, 1952), p. 33.
112 For a comparison between the two passages: 'Set rogo quid dicendum est de talibus
     miseriis et supersticiosis qui de nocte dixerunt se videre reginas pulcherrimas et alias
     puellas tripudiantes cum domina Dyana choreas ducentes dea paganorum, que in nos-
     tro vulgari dicitur elves', in *Fasciculus Morum*, p. 578; 'Alique sunt miserae vetulae,
     que de nocte dicunt se videre reginas pulcherrimas, & alias pullas tripudiantes & cho-
     reas ducentes cum domina Diana [...] paganorum', in *Destructiorum vitiorum*, p. 302.
113 Mannyng makes his pastoral aims explicit in ll.43-44: 'For lewde men y vndyrtoke /
     On englyssh tunge to make þys boke'. See *Robert of Brunne's Handlyng Synne, with
     the French Treatise on which it is Founded, La Manuel des Pechiez by William of
     Wadington*, ed. by F. J. Furnival (London: Roxburghe, 1862), p. 2.
114 Mannying updates Wadington's text by explaining that the story took place 'Yn þe
     tyme of Gode Edwarde [Edward I]' (ll. 7985), thus giving an approximate timeframe
     of c.1272–1307, in *Handlyng Synne*, pp. 248–53
115 Leonard E. Boyle, 'The Fourth Lateran Council and Manuals of Popular Theology', in
     The Popular Literature of Medieval England, ed. by Thomas J. Heffernan (Knoxville,
     TN: The University of Tennessee Press, 1985), pp. 30–43 (at p. 35).
116 Antonia Gransden, *History Writing in England II*, pp. 101–105.
117 In brief, William recalls a story told to him by one his brothers from Malmesbury
     who, in his youth, had joined a party in search of Octavian's treasure, supposedly bur-
     ied beneath a mountain near Rome. Arriving at an underground lake, beyond which
     stood statues made of gold, the treasure hunters were unable to cross due to the bronze
     statue of a 'rustic' (*rusticum*) that struck the water with a giant club if anyone set foot
     on the bridge. Consulting a learned scholar, who taught them the symbols for the
     unutterable name of God, which he believed had the power to overcome any barrier,
     they re-entered the mountain, only this time to be beset by devils. Finally, a Jewish
     necromancer (*nigromanticus*) entered the mountain and returned with an armful of
     treasures, including some of the dust that had the power to turn anything it touched
     into gold. The necromantic magic of the mountain proved false, however, for once
     washed with water the relics lost their golden lustre.
118 *Eulogium (historiarum sive temporis): Chronicon ab orbe condito usque ad Annum
     Domini M.CCC.LXVI.*, 3 vols. ed. by Frank Scott Haydon (London, 1858–1863), I,
     (1858), Book 3, ch.62 (pp. 400–403).
119 Ranulph Higden, *Polychronicon Ranulphi Higden Monachi Cestrensis, together with
     the English Translations of John Trevisa and of an Unknown Writer of the Fifteenth
     Century*, vol. 7. ed. by Joseph R. Lumby, RS 41 (London, 1879), Book 6, ch.25 (p.
     194).
120 Henry Knighton, *Chronicon Henrici Knighton vel Cnitthon, Monachi Leycestrensis*,
     2 vols, ed. by Joseph R. Lumby, RS 92 (London, 1889–1895), I (1889), Book 1, ch.46
     (pp. 42–43).

121 Robert Fabyan, *Prima Pars Cronecarum* (London, 1516), part 6, ch. ccxiii (fols. 133r–133v). Fabyan seems dubious as to the utility of this tale, writing that 'this wolde I nat have shewed, but that I fynde it wrytten and recorded of dyvers auctours'. Later editors agreed with this assessment: while it is retained in the 1533 edition (fol. 135r–135v), the 1542 and 1559 editions omit the story entirely.

122 Adrian Wilson, *The Making of the Nuremberg Chronicle* (Amsterdam: Israel, 1976).

123 Hartmann Schedel, *Liber Chronicorum Translation*, vol. 4, ed. by Constantine Hadvas; trans. by Michael Zellmann-Rohrer (Boston: Selim S. Nahas Press, 2012), pp. 94–95.

124 Hadvas, *Liber Chronicorum Translation*, p. 90, n. 546.

125 See Heinrich Kramer, *Malleus Maleficarum* (Nuremberg: Anton Koberger, 17th March, 1494), pa. 2, qu.1, ch. 3 (at fols. 50r–52v).

126 Bodily hybridisation as a manifestation of ontological uncertainly – sin incarnate – was a common symbolic motif in medieval art. See Jeffrey B. Russell, *Lucifer: The Devil in the Middle Ages* (Ithaca, NY: Cornell University Press, 1984), pp. 209–12.

127 Zika, *Appearance of Witchcraft*, p. 59.

128 Olaus Magnus, *Historia de Gentibus Septentrionalibus* (Rome 1555), Book 3, ch.21 (pp. 126–27); Olaus Magnus, *Historia de Gentibus* (Basel, 1567), Book 3, ch.21 (pp. 119–20). For an English translation, without the woodcut, see *A Compendious History of the Goths, Swedes & Vandals, and Other Northern Nations* (London, 1658), Book 3 ch.20 (pp. 50–51).

129 Conrad Lycosthenes, *Prodigiorum ac ostentorum chronicon* (Basel, 1557), p. 378. Interestingly, the extract is preceded by Vincent of Beauvais's transcription of the 'conjoined twins from Normandy' portent (*Historiale* book 26, ch. 38), first mentioned by William of Malmesbury (*GrA* ii.207). Here, Lycosthenes, shows a certain critical discernment of his sources, noting that while 'Vincent' (and before that 'Guillerino') places the story c.1045, 'Mathew Palmerius' (Matthew Paris) says it occurred in 1061. This is indeed its location in the *Chronica Majora* (see I, p. 530).

130 Lycosthenes, *Prodigiorum*, p. 378.

131 Stephen Batman, *The Doome warning all men to the Judgement* (London, 1581), p. 207.

132 See Zika, *Appearance of Witchcraft*, p. 204. The *Wickiana* collection has been fully digitised by its current holders, Zentralbibliothek Zürich. MS F 12 can be found at: http://doi.org/10.7891/e-manuscripta-27 [accessed 25 January 2019]

133 It must be stressed that this was not just a rote act of copying on Gudlawe's part. Conscious editorial decisions were made throughout the transcription process. The notes near the Witch of Berkeley woodcut begin with '*Phalara*, a towne in Attica' and conclude with '*Pharsalia*, a countrey in Thessalia, where the battaile was between Casar and Pompeie', but the long passages pertaining to '*Phalaris*', '*Pharao*', '*Pharisaei*', and '*Pharos*' have been pointedly omitted. See Thomas Cooper, *Dictionarium historicum & poeticum, in Thesaurus Linguae Romanae & Brittannicae (London, 1565).* The annotations at the bottom and right-hand side of fol. 189v, not pictured in figure one, form a separate textual unit and build upon the printed text's reference to Lanfranc of Canterbury, giving an overview of the history of Canterbury (bottom) and extra information on the Archbishop himself (right).

134 Johann Weyer, *De praestigiis daemonum* (Basel, 1568 [1563]), Book VI, ch.5 (pp. 583–86). Later editions separate the discussion on Sylvester II (VI.5) and the Witch of Berkeley (VI.7) into two separate chapters, interspersed by an account of the pardon and absolution of a contemporary Spanish witch, Magdalene de la Cruz (VI.6).

135 Heywood namechecks *Guillerimus* (William of Malmesbury), *Iohannes Wyerius* (Johann Weyer) and *Ranulphus* (Ranulph Hidgen) as further authorities on the tale, although it would seem he only knew of 'Guillerimus' through the reference given

at the end of the *Speculum Historiale*. See Thomas Heywood, *Gynaikeion, or Nine Books of Various History Concerning Women* (London, 1624), Book 9, pp. 443–44.

136 For an overview of the *Gynaikeion's* content and construction, see Robert Grant Martin, 'A Critical Study of Thomas Heywood's 'Gunaikeion', *Studies in Philology* 20 (1923), 160–83.

137 David Chandler, 'Southey's "German Sublimity" and Coleridge's "Dutch Attempt"', *Romanticism on the Net* 32–33 (2003–4) https://www.erudit.org/fr/revues/ron/200 3-n32-33-ron769/009257ar/ [accessed 25 January 2019].

138 *A Memoir of the Life and Writings of William Taylor*, 2 vols. ed. by J. W. Robberds (London, 1843), I, p. 235. For the literary context of gothic ballads in England, see Douglass H. Thomson and Diane Long Hoeveler, 'Shorter Gothic Fictions: Ballads and Chapbooks, Tales and Fragments', in *Romantic Gothic: An Edinburgh Companion*, ed. by Angela Wright and Dale Townshend (Edinburgh: Edinburgh University Press, 2016), pp. 147–66 (at p. 153).

139 As noted by David Chandler, William Taylor's version of the Berkeley text, entitled 'A Tale of Wonder' (c.1791) was finally published in the Norwich literary newspaper *Iris* on 29 October 1803, and re-published in *Monthly Magazine* in 1812. Intriguingly, the majority of the 180-line poem is written from the devil's perspective and diverges markedly from the source Olaus Magnus text and, indeed, all other Witch of Berkeley texts. There is also a new (and not very well-realised) conclusion in which the reanimated statue of St. Patrick (?) prevents the devil from collecting his due (ll. 161–178). Writing to Southey on 28 October 1805, Taylor agreed that the 'Old Woman of Berkeley' is superior to his own tale ('Nobody can be more completely convinced than I am of the decided superiority of the "Old Woman of Berkeley" to the "Tale of Wonder"'). Although not as widely-read as Southey's ballad, Taylor's efforts nonetheless inspired the Norwich-based artist Edward Bell (1768–1847), whose watercolour, also entitled *A Tale of Wonder* (1804), was directly influenced by the *Iris* text, specifically lines ll.86–90, concerning the priest's attempts to hold back the demon, and 136–147, the description of the corpse. Transcriptions of the aforesaid lines are included in the bottom border (see figure 1.6). See Chandler, 'Southey's German Sublimity', Appendix 2; *Memoir of the Life and Writings of William Taylor,* II, p. 106.

140 'Matthew of Westminster' is a textual ghost deriving its name from the Westminster Abbey copy of Mathew Paris's own *Flores Historiarum*.

141 Robert Southey, 'Preface', in *The Poetical Works of Robert Southey Collected by Himself, in Ten Volumes, Vol. VI: Ballads and Metrical Tales vol. 1,* ed. by Robert Southey (London, 1838), pp. xi–xvi.

142 *A Memoir of the Life and Writings of William Taylor*, I. pp. 230–37. Writing a review of Southey's *Metrical Tale, and Other Poems* (1805) for *The Annual Review*, Taylor notes that 'his Old Woman of Berkeley is the best English ballad extant', the exact same words he uses in his correspondence with Southey on 28 October 1805 (referenced in n.132). See *The Annual Review* 4 (1806), 579–81 (at p. 579).

143 *New Letters of Robert Southey, Volume One: 1792–1810*, ed. by Kenneth Curry (New York: Columbia University Press, 1965), pp. 176–78. Southey also states that he was in the process of formulating 'a very ugly ballad upon the known [...] that the Devil walks in dead bodies'. Such a ballad has, sadly, not passed down to us today.

144 Robert Southey, *Poems: The Second Volume,* 2nd ed. (Bristol, 1800), p. 151. Jan Ziarnko's etching of the Witch's Sabbath included in the 1613 edition of Pierre de Lancre's *Tableau de l'inconstance des mauvais anges et démons* ('On the Inconstancy of Witches') contains perhaps the most evocative visualisation of witches and demons feasting on the corpses of dead children. See Charles Zika, 'Cannibalism and Witchcraft in Early Modern Europe: Reading the Visual Images', in *History Workshop Journal* 44 (1997), 77–105.

145 Chandler, 'Southey's German Sublimity'.

146 Southey, 'Preface', p. xiv.
147 James Wathen, *Journal of a Voyage to Madras and China,* 2 Vols. (London, 1814).
148 Southey demanded that his poems be withdrawn from the second edition (also 1801).
    See Thomson and Hoeveler, 'Shorter Gothic Fictions', p. 154.
149 Southey, *Poetical Works*, p. 177.
150 The poem itself is a revision of an earlier work, 'The Devil's Thoughts', co-authored
    with Samuel Coleridge and first published on 6 September 1799. See Robert Southey
    and Samuel Coleridge, 'The Devil's Walk', in *Romantic Circles: A referee scholarly
    website devoted to the study of Romantic-period literature and culture*, <https://ww
    w.rc.umd.edu/editions/shelley/devil/devil.rs1860.html> [accessed 25 January 2019].
151 Qua respondente quod nequiret pro uinculis, GrA ii.204 (pp. 378–79).
152 See n. 139.
153 Of course, William is not completely silent on the topic. He admits that Harold had
    a lust for power and was not particularly pious, but that he was nonetheless devoted
    to Wulfstan, supporting him in his election to the bishopric of Worcester. See *Vita
    Wulfstani,* in *William of Malmesbury: Saints' Lives*, i. 7, 11 (at pp, 34–35, 44–45).
154 Hayward, 'The Importance of Being Ambiguous', p. 95.
155 See n. 121.

Primary sources

Alcuin, *Monumenta Alcuiniana*, BRG 6, ed. by Phillip Jaffé (Berlin: Apud Weidmannos, 1873).

A Memoir of the Life and Writings of William Taylor, 2 vols, ed. by J. W. Robberds
    (London: Murray, 1843).

The Anglo-Saxon Chronicle: An Electronic Edition (Vol 3) http://asc.jebbo.co.uk/c/c-L.
    html.

Arnold of Liège, Arnoldus Leodiensis, *Alphabetum Narrationum*, CCCM 160, ed. by Elisa
    Brilli (Turnhout: Brepols, 2015).

Arnold of Liège, *An Alphabet of Tales: An English Translation of the Alphabetum
    Narrationum*, EETS, o.s. 127, ed. by Mary M. Banks (London: Kegan Paul, Trench,
    Trübner & Co., 1905).

Augustine, *Sancti Aurelii Augustini Hipponensis episcopi Opera omnia*, PL 32–47, ed. by
    J.-P. Migne (Paris, 1841–1849).

St Boniface, *Die Briefe des Heiligen Bonifatius und Lullus*, ed. by Michael Tangl (Berlin:
    Weidmannsche, 1916).

Batman, Stephen, *The Doome Warning all Men to the Judgement* (London, 1581).

Bede, *Ecclesiastical History of the English Nation, Volume I: Books 1–3*, trans. by J. E.
    King, Loeb Classical Library 246 (Cambridge, MA: Harvard University Press, 1930).

Carpenter, Alexander, *Destructiorum Vitiorum* (Venice, 1578).

Cooper, Thomas, *Dictionarium Historicum & Poeticum*, in *Thesaurus Linguae Romanae
    & Brittanniae* (London, 1565).

Dictionary of Medieval Latin from British Sources: Fascicule I A–B, ed. by R. E. Latham
    (Oxford: Oxford University Press, 1975).

Dictionary of Medieval Latin from British Sources: Fascicule XVI Sol-Syr, ed. by R. K.
    Ashdowne and D. R. Howlett (Oxford: Oxford University Press, 2013).

Domesday Book 15: *Gloucestershire*, ed. and trans. by John S. Moore (Chichester:
    Fillimore, 1982).

*Eulogium (historiarum sive temporis): Chronicon ab orbe condito usque ad Annum Domini M.
    CCC.LXVI.*, 3 vols, ed. by Frank Scott Haydon (London: Longman, 1858–1863).

Fabyan, Robert, *Prima Pars Cronecarum* (London, 1516).

Fasciculus Morum: A Fourteenth-Century Preacher's Handbook, ed. and trans. by Siegfried Wenzel (University Park, PA: Penn State University Press, 1989).

Geoffrey of Burton, *Life and Miracles of St Modwenna*, ed. and trans. by Robert Bartlett, Oxford Medieval Texts (Oxford: Clarendon, 2002).

Geoffrey of Monmouth, *The History of the Kings of Britain: An Edition and Translation of the De gestis Britonum (Historia Regum Britanniae)*, ed. and trans. by Michael D. Reeve (Woodbridge: Boydell & Brewer, 2007).

Gregory the Great, *The Dialogues of Saint Gregory, Surnamed the Great*, ed. by E. G. Gardner (London: Warner, 1911).

Gregory the Great, *Sancti Gregorii Papae I, Cognomento Magni, Opera Omnia*, PL 75–78, ed. by J-P Migne (Paris, 1862).

Hélinand of Froidmont, *Helinandi Frigidi Montis Monachi, Necnon Guntheri Cisterciensis, Opera Omnia*, PL 212, ed. by J.-P. Migne (Paris, 1855).

Herman the Archdeacon and Goscelin of Saint-Bertin, *Miracles of St Edmund*, ed. and trans. by Tom Licence, with Lynda Lockyer, Oxford Medieval Texts (Oxford: Clarendon, 2014).

Heywood, Thomas, *Gynaikeion, or Nine Books of Various History Concerning Women* (London, 1624).

Higden, Ranulph, *Polychronicon Ranulphi Higden Monachi Cestrensis, together with the English Translations of John Trevisa and of an Unknown Writer of the Fifteenth Century*, 9 vols, ed. by C. Banington (1–2) and Joseph R. Lumby (vols. 3–9), RS 41 (London: Longman, 1865–1886).

Hincmar, 'Epistola Synodi Carisiacensis', in *MGH*, Cap2 pt. II., no. 297, ed. by Alfred Boretius and Victor Krause (Hannover, Impensis Bibliopolii Hahniani, 1883), pp. 227–441.

Honorius of Autun, *Honorii Augustodunensis Opera Omnia*, PL 172 (Paris, 1854).

Isidore of Seville, *Etymologies*, ed. and trans. by Stephen A. Barney et al. (Cambridge: Cambridge University Press, 2006).

Isidore of Seville, *Isidori Hispalensis Episcopi, Etymologiarum Sive Originum Libri XX*, 2 vols, ed. by W. M. Lindsay (Oxford: Clarendon, 1911).

Jacob's Well, An Englisht Treatise on the Cleansing of Man's Conscience. Part I, EETS, o.s. 115, ed. by Arthur Brandeis (London: Kegen Paul, Trench, Trübner & Co., 1900).

John of Salisbury, *Ioannes Saresberiensis, Policraticus, I–IV*, CCCM 118, ed. by K. S. B. Keats-Rohan (Turnhout: Brepols, 1993).

Knighton, Henry, *Chronicon Henrici Knighton vel Cnitthon, Monachi Leycestrensis*, 2 vols, ed. by Joseph R. Lumby, RS 92 (London: Longman, 1889–1895).

Kramer, Heinrich, *Malleus Maleficarum* (Nuremberg: Anton Koberger, 17th March 1494).

Lanfranc, *The Letters of Lanfranc, Archbishop of Canterbury*, ed. and trans. by Helen Glover and Margaret Gibson, Oxford Medieval Texts (Oxford: Clarendon, 1979).

Lycosthenes, Conrad, *Prodigiorum ac ostentorum chronicon* (Basel, 1557).

Major, Johannes (ed.), *Magnum Speculum Exemplorum* (Cologne, 1642).

Mannyng, Robert, *Robert of Brunne's Handlyng Synne, with the French Treatise on which it is Founded, La Manuel des Pechiez by William of Wadington*, ed. by F. J. Furnival (London: Roxburghe, 1862).

Paris, Matthew, *Flores Historiarum*, 3 vols, ed. by Henry R. Luard, RS 95 (London: Longman, 1890).

Paris, Matthew, *Matthæi Parisiensis, monachi Sancti Albani, Chronica majora*, 7 vols, ed. by Henry R. Luard, RS 57 (London: Longman, 1872–1884).

Plautus, T., *Macci Plavti Comoediae*, vol. 1., ed. by W. M. Lindsay, Oxford Classical Texts (Oxford: Clarendon, 1903).

Pafraet, Richard (ed.), *Speculum Exemplorum* (Daventer, 1481).

Roger of Wendover, *Chronicon, sive Flores Historiarum*, 4 vols, ed. by Henry Coxe (London: Sumptibus Societatis, 1841–1842).

Schedel, Hartmann, *Liber Chronicorum Translation*, vol. 4, ed. by Constantine Hadvas; trans. by Michael Zellmann-Rohrer (Boston: Selim S. Nahas Press, 2012).

Schedel, Hartmann, *Liber Chronicarum* (Augsburg: Schönsperger, 1497).

Schedel, Hartmann, *Liber Chronicarum* (Nuremberg: Anton Koberger, for Sebald Schreyer and Sebastian Kammermeister, 1493).

Southey, Robert, *New Letters of Robert Southey, Volume One: 1792–1810*, ed. by Kenneth Curry (New York: Columbia University Press, 1965).

Southey, Robert, *The Poetical Works of Robert Southey Collected by Himself, in Ten Volumes, Vol. VI: Ballads and Metrical Tales vol. 1*, ed. by Robert Southey (London: Longman, 1838).

Southey, Robert and Samuel Coleridge, 'The Devil's Walk', in *Romantic Circles: A Referee Scholarly Website Devoted to the Study of Romantic-Period Literature and Culture*, https://www.rc.umd.edu/editions/shelley/devil/devil.rs1860.html.

Tertullian, *Apology*, trans. by T. R. Glover, Loeb Classical Library 250 (Cambridge, MA: Harvard University Press, 1931).

Vincent of Beauvais, *Speculum Historiale* (Nuremberg, 1483).

Walter Map, *De Nugis Curialium*, ed. and trans. by M. R. James; revised C. N. L. Brookes and R. A. B. Mynors (Oxford: Clarendon, 1983).

Wathen, James, *Journal of a Voyage to Madras and China*, 2 vols (London: Nicholas, son, and Bentley, 1814).

Weyer, Johann, *De praestigiis daemonum* (Basel, 1568).

William of Malmesbury, *Gesta Regum Anglorum: History of the English Kings*, vol. 1, ed. and trans. by R. A. B. Mynors; completed by R. M. Thomson and M. Winterbottom, Oxford Medieval Texts (Oxford: Clarendon, 1998).

William of Malmesbury, *William of Malmesbury: Saints' Lives: Lives of ss. Wulfstan, Dunstan, Patrick, Benignus and Indract*, ed. and trans. by M. Winterbottom and R. M. Thomson, Oxford Medieval Texts (Oxford: Clarendon, 2002).

Secondary sources

Bailey, Michael D., *Fearful Spirits, Reasoned Follies: The Boundaries of Superstition in Late Medieval Europe* (Ithaca, NY: Cornell University Press, 2013).

Bartlett, Robert, *England Under the Norman and Angevin Kings, 1075–1225* (Oxford: Clarendon, 2000).

Black, Winston, 'Animated Corpses and Bodies with Power in the Scholastic Age', in *Death in Medieval Europe: Death Scripted and Death Choreographed*, ed. by Joëlle Rollo-Koster (London: Routledge, 2017), pp. 71–92.

Boyle, Leonard E., 'The Fourth Lateran Council and Manuals of Popular Theology', in *The Popular Literature of Medieval England*, ed. by Thomas J. Heffernan (Knoxville, TN: The University of Tennessee Press, 1985), pp. 30–43.

Burnett, C., *Magic and Divination in the Middle Ages: Texts and Techniques in the Islamic and Christian Worlds* (Aldershot: Ashgate, 1996).

Bynum, Caroline Walker, 'Wonder', *The American Historical Review* 102 (1997), 1–26.

Caciola, Nancy Mandeville, *Afterlives: The Return of the Dead in the Middle Ages* (Ithaca, NY: Cornell University Press, 2016).

Campbell, James, 'Some Twelfth-Century View of the Anglo-Saxon Past', *Perita* 3 (1984), 131–50.

Carruthers, Leo, 'Where Did Jacob's Well Come from? The Provenance and Dialect of Ms Salisbury Cathedral 103', *English Studies* 71 (1990), 335–40.

Chandler, David, 'Southey's "German Sublimity" and Coleridge's "Dutch Attempt"', *Romanticism on the Net* 32–33 (2003–4) https://www.erudit.org/fr/revues/ron/200 3-n32-33-ron769/009257ar/.

Cubitt, Catherine, 'Folklore and Historiography: Oral Stories and the Writing of Anglo-Saxon History', in *Narrative and History in the Early Medieval West*, ed. by Elizabeth Tyler and Ross Balzaretti (Turnhout: Brepols, 2006), pp. 189–224.

Fenton, Kirsten A., *Gender, Nation and Conquest in the Works of William of Malmesbury* (Woodbridge: Boydell and Brewer, 2008).

Flint, Valerie I. J., *The Rise of Magic in Early Medieval Europe* (Oxford: Clarendon, 1991).

Freeman, Elizabeth, 'Wonders, Prodigies and Marvels: Unusual Bodies and the Fear of Heresy in Ralph of Coggeshall's Chronicon Anglicanum', *Journal of Medieval History* 26 (2000), 127–43.

Fouracre, Paul, *The Age of Charles Martel* (Harlow: Longman, 2000).

Fouracre, Paul, 'The Long Shadow of the Merovingians', in *Charlemagne: Empire and Society*, ed. by Joanna Story (Manchester: Manchester University Press, 2005), pp. 5–21.

Gilchrist, Roberta, *Medieval Lives: Archaeology and the Life Course* (Woodbridge: Boydell, 2012).

Gillingham, John, 'The Ironies of History: William of Malmesbury's Views of William II and Henry I', in *Discovering William of Malmesbury*, ed. by Rodney M. Thomson, Emily Dolmans, and Emily A. Winkler (Woodbridge: Boydell, 2017), pp. 37–48.

Gransden, Antonia, *History Writing in England II: 1307 to the Early Sixteenth Century* (London: Routledge, 1982).

Green, Steven J., 'Malevolent Gods and Promethean Birds: Contesting Augury in Augustus's Rome', *Transactions of the American Philological Association* 139 (2009), 147–67.

Gregg, Joan Young, 'The Exempla of Jacob's Well: A Study in the Transmission of Medieval Sermon Stories', *Traditio* 33 (1977), 359–80.

Griffiths, Bill, *Aspects of Anglo-Saxon Magic* (Hockwold-cum-Wilton: Anglo-Saxon Books, 1996).

Hare, Michael. 'Anglo-Saxon Berkeley: History and Topography', *Anglo-Saxon Studies in Archaeology and History* 18 (2013), 119–56.

Hayward, Paul A., 'The Importance of Being Ambiguous: Innuendo and Legerdmain in William of Malesbury's Gesta Regum and Gesta Pontificum Anglorum', *Anglo-Norman Studies* 33 (2011), 75–102.

Higham, Nicholas J., and Martin J. Ryan, *The Anglo-Saxon World* (New Haven, CT: Yale University Press, 2013).

Huneycutt, Lois L., *Matilda of Scotland: A Study in Medieval Queenship* (Woodbridge: Boydell, 2003).

Kieckhefer, Richard, 'Mythologies of Witchcraft in the Fifteenth-Century', *Magic, Ritual, and Witchcraft* 1 (2006), 79–108.

Lea, Henry C., *Materials Toward a History of Witchcraft*, vol. 1 (New York: Yoseloff, 1957).

Martin, Robert Grant, 'A Critical Study of Thomas Heywood's "Gunaikeion", *Studies in Philology* 20 (1923), 160–83.

McNeill, John T., 'Folk-Paganism in the Penitentials', *The Journal of Religion* 13 (1933), 450–66.

McNeill, John T. and Helena M. Gamer, *Medieval Handbooks of Penance* (New York: Columbia University Press, 1990).

Mereminskiy, Stanislav, 'William of Malmesbury and Durham: The Circulation of Historical Knowledge in Early Twelfth-Century England', in *Discovering William of Malmesbury*, ed. by Rodney M. Thomson, Emily Dolmans, and Emily A. Winkler (Woodbridge: Boydell, 2017), pp. 107–16.

Niskanen, Samu, 'William of Malmesbury as Librarian: The Evidence of his Autographs', in *Discovering William of Malmesbury*, ed. by Rodney M. Thomson, Emily Dolmans, and Emily A. Winkler (Woodbridge: Boydell, 2017), pp. 117–28.

Owst, G. R., *The Destructiorum Vitiorum of Alexander Carpenter* (London: S. P. C. K, 1952).

Peters, Edward, *The Magician, the Witch and the Law* (Philadelphia, PA: University of Pennsylvania Press, 1978).

Russell, Jeffrey B., *Lucifer: The Devil in the Middle Ages* (Ithaca, NY: Cornell University Press, 1984).

Russell, Jeffrey B., *Witchcraft in the Middle Ages* (Ithaca, NY: Cornell University Press, 1972).

Phillips, Joanna, 'William of Malmesbury: Medical Historian of the Crusades', in *Discovering William of Malmesbury*, ed. by Rodney M. Thomson, Emily Dolmans, and Emily A. Winkler (Woodbridge: Boydell, 2017), pp. 129–38.

Page, Sophie and Catherine Rider (eds.), *The Routledge History of Medieval Magic* (London: Routledge, 2019).

Saunders, Corinne, *Magic and the Supernatural in Medieval English Romance* (Cambridge: Brewer, 2010).

Smits, E. R., 'Helinand of Froidmont and the A-Text of Seneca's Tragedies', *Mnemosyne*, 4th ser. 36 (1983), 324–58.

Smits, E. R. 'Vincent of Beauvais: A Note on the Background of the *Speculum*', in *Vincent of Beauvais and Alexander the Great: Studies on the Speculum Maius and Its Translation into Medieval Vernaculars*, ed. by W. J. Aerts, E. R. Smits, and J. B. Voorbij (Groningen: Forsten, 1996), pp. 1–9.

Sønnesyn, Sigbjørn Olsen, *William of Malmesbury and the Ethics of History* (Woodbridge: Boydell, 2012).

Stein, Robert M., 'Making History English: Cultural Identity and Historical Explanation in William of Malmesbury and Layamon's *Brut*', in *Text and Territory: Geographical Imagination in the European Middle Ages*, ed. by Sylvia Tomasch and Sealy Gilles (Philadelphia, PA: University of Pennsylvania Press, 1998), pp. 97–115.

Taylor, C. S., 'Berkeley Minster', in *Transactions of the Bristol and Gloucestershire Archaeological Society* 19 (1894–95), 70–84.

Taylor, William, 'Art XX: Metrical Tales, and Other Poems', *The Annual Review* 4 (1806), 579–81.

Tellenbach, Gerd, *Church, State, and Christian Society at the Time of the Investiture Contest*, trans. by R. F. Bennett (New York: Harvester, 1979).

Thomson, Douglass H. and Diane Long Hoeveler, 'Shorter Gothic Fictions: Ballads and Chapbooks, Tales and Fragments', in *Romantic Gothic: An Edinburgh Companion*, ed. by Angela Wright and Dale Townshend (Edinburgh: Edinburgh University Press, 2016), pp. 147–66.

Thomson, Rodney, *William of Malmesbury* (Woodbridge: Boydell, 1987).

Thomson, Rodney, 'William of Malmesbury's Carolingian Sources', *Journal of Medieval History* 7 (1981), 321–37.

Thomson, R. M. 'Satire, Irony and Humour in William of Malmesbury', in *Rhetoric and Renewal in the Latin West 1100–1540: Essays in Honour of John O. Ward*, ed. by C. Mews, C. J. Nederman, and R. M. Thomson (Turnhout: Brepols, 2003), pp. 115–27.

Thomson, Rodney M., 'William of Malmesbury's Historical Vision', in *Discovering William of Malmesbury*, ed. by Rodney M. Thomson, Emily Dolmans, and Emily A. Winkler (Woodbridge: Boydell, 2017), pp. 165–74.

Tyler, Elizabeth M., *England in Europe: English Royal Women and Literary Patronage, c.1000–c.1150* (Toronto, ON: University of Toronto Press, 2017).

Watkins, S. Carl, *History and the Supernatural in Medieval England* (Cambridge: Cambridge University Press, 2007).

Westerhof, Danielle, *Death and the Noble Body in Medieval England* (Woodbridge: Boydell, 2008).

Wilson, Adrian, *The Making of the Nuremberg Chronicle* (Amsterdam: Israel, 1976).

Wright, Sarah Breckenridge, 'The Soil's Holy Bodies: The Art of Chorography in William of Malmesbury's *Gesta Pontificum Anglorum*', *Studies in Philology* 111 (2014), 652–79.

Zika, Charles, *The Appearance of Witchcraft: Print and Visual Culture in Sixteenth-Century Europe* (London: Routledge, 2007).

Zika, Charles, 'Cannibalism and Witchcraft in Early Modern Europe: Reading the Visual Images', *History Workshop Journal* 44 (1997), 77–106.

2 The critical function of the walking corpse in William of Newburgh's *Historia rerum Anglicarum*

Introduction

William of Newburgh's *Historia rerum Anglicarum* ('History of English Affairs', c.1198) is one of the foremost literary artefacts of the late twelfth century.[1] Although biographical information on William is scarce,[2] much scholarship has been conducted on the origins, content, and construction of his *Historia*, with particular emphasis on the sober nature of his commentaries and purported lack of bias.[3] And yet, while William is quick to denounce the 'traditional fictions' of Geoffrey of Monmouth's *Historia rerum Britanniae* (c.1136) and advocate Bede as the model to which all writers of history should aspire,[4] attention is nonetheless given to events which, to modern sensibilities, are just as fictitious and inauthentic as the tales of King Arthur. Indeed, descriptions of animals born from rock, otherworldly banquets and green-coloured children test the twenty-first-century definition of what does, and does not, constitute 'history'.[5] But rather than seeing 'wonder' stories as mere digressions from the main body of the text, William notes that 'I call things of this nature wonderful (*mira*), not merely on account of their rarity, but because some latent meaning is attached to them'.[6] That is to say, the manifest or literal form of the marvel had the potential to reveal hidden – perhaps spiritually sensitive – truths to the active reader, and served just as important a moral function as authorial glosses on the historical narratives.

Book five of the *Historia* details a type of wonder that was touched upon briefly in the previous chapter's discussions on the post-mortem agency of the Witch of Berkeley: the walking or restless corpse.[7] Violent and pestilential, ambulatory corpses ('revenants') posed a very real threat to the cohesion of the local community. William himself declines to give an explanation for the phenomenon, content to state merely that he 'knew not by what agency' the dead wandered from their graves. Despite the lack of overt moralisation, this chapter contends that the specific placement of these narratives within the *Historia* encourages the reader to make a metaphysical connection between the activities of the revenant and the conduct of William FitzOsbert, instigator of the London riots of 1196,[8] warmongering kings,[9] and William Longchamp (d.1197), chancellor, justiciar, and bishop of Ely.[10] The first half of this chapter analyses the medieval concept of monstrousness and the cultural context of the *Historia*'s creation, and argues that learned theories of disease causation underscored the base narratology of the four revenant encounters. Following an appraisal of the unrest caused by FitzOsbert, Longchamp, and the kings of England and France, the chapter concludes by evaluating the ways in which the 'social monstrosity' of these divisive public figures was encapsulated by the destabilising and destructive tendencies of the walking corpse. Ultimately, the contagious nature of sin and the dangers of social transgression were the themes that bound the revenant narratives to the wider historical project.

Portents and monsters

According to Augustine of Hippo (d.430), 'the name "monster", we are told, evidently comes from *monstrando* ("showing"), because they show by signifying something. *Ostenta* ("sign/show") comes from *ostendendo* ("pointing out"), *portent* from *portendendo* ("portending", that is, "showing beforehand"), and "prodigy" from *porro dicant* ("foretelling the future")'.[11] Isidore of Seville (d.636) concurs, noting that

> a portent seems to have been born contrary to nature – but they are not contrary to nature, because they are created by divine will, since the nature of everything is the will of the Creator. A portent is therefore not created contrary to nature, but contrary to what is known nature. [They] are seen to indicate and predict future events.[12]

By the late twelfth century a clear terminological distinction had been made between *mirabilia* (events that were contrary to the *expected* course of nature) and *miracula* (events that had been instigated through the non-natural intervention of God). Gervase of Tilbury's *Otia Imperialia* (c.1214) offers the following definition:

> Now we generally call those things miracles (*miracula*) which, being preternatural, we ascribe to divine power, as when a virgin gives birth, when Lazarus is raised from the dead, or when diseased limbs are made whole again; while we call those things marvels which are beyond our comprehension, even though they are natural: in fact the inability to explain why a thing is so constitutes a marvel (*mirabilia*).

> [Porro miracula dicimus usitatius que preter naturam divine uirtuti ascribimus, ut cum uirgo parit, cum Lazarus resurgit, cum lapsa membra reintegrantur. Mirabilia uero dicimus que nostra cognicioni non subiacent, etiam cum sunt naturalia; sed et mirabilia constituit ignorantia reddende rationis quare sic sit][13]

Gervase also stresses that wonders were relativistic and perspectival; that is, what was marvellous to one person may have been common knowledge and unremarkable to another. Writing in his *Topographica Hibernica* (c.1188), Gerald of Wales notes that the rising and setting of the sun did not prompt feelings of awe due to the regularity of its occurrence, 'for human nature is so made that only what is unusual and infrequent excites wonder or is regarded of value'.[14] To marvel was to engage with the unknown. In sum, monstrous bodies and wondrous happenings were 'natural', albeit rare and inexplicable to the beholder, and signified something other than their own physical forms.

Deciphering the meaning of wonders was a paramount concern in the Middle Ages; however, despite the ultimate goal of *admiratio* (the act of wondering) being the attainment of *scientia* (knowledge), it was also understood that a marvel might sometimes be so unusual, so incomprehensible, as to defy any attempt at categorisation.[15] Ever equivocal, William of Newburgh advised caution when discussing the events surrounding the Green Children of Woolpit: 'the nature of those green children, who sprang from the earth, is too abstruse for the weakness of our abilities to fathom'.[16] And yet, given that medieval theories about the workings of the universe stressed the relationship between the macro- and microcosm, the physical and the moral, and if natural order was a manifestation of the oneness and wholeness of God, then disordered beings such as walking corpses had the potential to signify social and/or spiritual uncertainty – deviations from the divine norm. Medieval writers often utilised wonders to allegorise and criticise instabilities in the wider body politic.[17] Given that the four revenant narratives contained within the *Historia* were purported to have occurred in the spring of 1196, any investigation into William's use of wonders must take into account his (or his patron's) reading of the political/economic uncertainties that gripped England in the last decade of the twelfth century. While scholars such as Monika Otter and Catherine Clarke have noted that the *Historia*'s 'vampire' stories may have been used as metaphorical retellings of contemporary events, the specific reasons why William chose the walking corpse as a vehicle for historical criticism have yet to be fully explored.[18]

The *Historia rerum Anglicarum* in context

England at the turn of the thirteenth century was a country beset by instability and strife. Not only had the unseasonal rains of 1196 reduced the land to famine and given rise to pestilence – pointedly, William refers to the survivors as 'going about with pallid and cadaverous countenances, as if on the point of death'[19] – but the resumption of warfare between Richard I England and Philip II of France only added to the apocalyptic mood. Dramatic price surges and an increase in taxation – the former due to the mismanagement of the currency; the latter a function of the need to fund Richard's war efforts and, in 1192, his ransom – put a strain on the local economy and fermented resentment among the lower classes. Londoners came very close to instigating a revolt.[20] Tensions were also forming at the head of the body politic: the enmity between Count John and the office of the justiciar almost led to civil war in 1191 and 1194. Richard, meanwhile, was more concerned with his martial activities on the Continent than taking administrative control of his realm.[21] This, then, was the uncertain political climate in which Ernald, the sixth abbot of Rievaulx (1192–1199), asked William to write 'a history of memorable events which have so abundantly occurred in our times'.[22]

Founded in 1132 as a daughter house of the abbey of Clairvaux, Rievaulx, along with fellow northern Cistercian houses, Fountains (1132) and Byland (c.1147), was described by William in supremely glowing terms: 'like the triple light of our province, they blaze forth by the pre-eminence of their holy religion'.[23] Rievaulx's reputation as a financial, educational, and spiritual powerhouse can be traced to the enduring influence of its fourth abbot, Aelred (1147–1167). Born in Hexham to a father, grandfather, and great-grandfather who all enjoyed close ties with the Northumbrian church, Aelred was educated first at the cathedral school in Durham – where his uncle was a monk – and then at the royal court of David I of Scotland.[24] It has been argued that David's influence was vital in securing Aelred's entry into Rievaulx.[25] By the time he was elected to lead the community, Aelred was at the centre of a vast filial network that extended from Scotland to France, underpinned by a cultural heritage that included Bede, the hallowed library of Durham Cathedral, and a definite geographical connection to the Anglo-Saxon past. Indeed, among Aelred's many historical and spiritual tracts, his *vitae* of St. Edward and St. Ninian reveal a preoccupation with his English (Edward) and specifically Northumbrian (Ninian) lineage. The same, perhaps, can be said of his treatise, *Miracula sanctorum patrum qui in ecclesia Hagustaldensi requiescunt* ('On the Miracle of the Holy Fathers Who Rest in Hexham Church'), written in 1155.[26] He died in 1167, having overseen Rievaulx's emergence as one of the most prosperous monasteries in the kingdom. Aelred's literary legacy provides the context through which the desire for a new history of England, based on Bedan precedents, grew. With the statues of the *Carta caritatis* (the Cistercian constitution) making it difficult for Ernald or his brethren to pursue a literary career without first securing permission from the General Chapter,[27] and considering that Newburgh Priory shared a patron (the de Mowbray family) with Rievaulx's sister abbey, Byland, William, who had written his commentary of the Song of Songs at the behest of Roger of Byland, proved an ideal candidate for the task.[28]

Of the nine copies of the *Historia* to have survived to the present day, the version contained in BL Stowe MS 62 is of particular importance, being the presentation copy intended for Newburgh itself and containing corrections in William's own hand.[29] Two further manuscripts, BL MS Cotton Vespasian B VI (belonging to Osney Priory, Oxford) and Oxford, Bodleian Library, MS Rawlinson B 192 (belonging to Rufford Abbey, a daughter house of Rievaulx), are believed to be contemporaneous with the Stowe version, all three deriving from the same (hypothetical) working copy. Lambeth MS 73 (a copy of Stowe MS 62 belonging to Buildwas Abbey, a daughter of Furness) completes the list of extant *Historiae* for which a production/circulation context can be established.[30] As discussed by Anne Lawrence-Mathers, the design of Stowe MS 62 accords to the 'Northumbrian style' developed amongst the Cistercian, Augustinian, and Durham scriptoria of the era. Despite being intended for an Augustinian community, the presentation copy of the *Historia rerum Anglicarum* displays some notably Cistercian qualities, such as the lack of miniatures, the use of the 'three-lobed bud motif' for the initials, and the predominantly red, dark green, and pale blue colour scheme. Along with William's declaration that the *Historia* was commissioned by Ernald – perhaps at the behest of the wider community at Rievaulx – these stylistic traits highlight the formal and informal connections that existed between the various monastic communities of Northern England, a process that extended to the circulation of the manuscripts themselves.[31] While the lack of a library list for Newburgh Priory prohibits a discussion of the works at William's immediate disposal, the evidence suggests that he made extensive use of the collections of both Durham and Rievaulx,[32] with manuscripts from the former perhaps being made available through the library of the latter.[33] Bede's *Historia ecclesiastica* was one of the main sources consulted by William during his research, evidence from which was used to refute the existence of Arthur and Merlin and to advertise the northern traditions of history writing.[34] And yet, the fact that copies of the *Historia rerum Anglicarum* were distributed among southern Cistercian and Augustinian houses suggests that this nominally provincial project was designed to appeal to the literary interests of the wider monastic network. In an era dominated by political unrest and social upheaval, it was a history written with the conservative moral outlook of the cloister in mind. The preservation of the 'natural' order of things and the dangers of transgressing divinely-wrought boundaries were two of the main moral threads that underpinned the entire project.

Detailing events from the Norman Conquest of 1066 to the construction of Château Gaillard, Rouen, in 1198 (the abruptness of the ending suggests that this date corresponded roughly with William's death), the *Historia* is most notable for its vehement condemnation of the *Historia rerum Britanniae* and as one of two extant sources – the other is Ralph of Coggeshall's *Chronicum Anglicanum* (c.1220) – for the story of the Green Children of Woolpit.[35] And yet, despite their relative unfamiliarity to modern audiences, the revenant stories contained in book five, chapters 22 to 24, are by far the most detailed accounts of the walking dead in Anglo-Norman literature, surpassing those found in William of Malmesbury's *Gesta regum Anglorum* (c.1125), Geoffrey of Burton's *Vita sancte Moduenne virginis* (c.1144), and Walter Map's *De nugis curialium* (c.1182). Known by their sobriquets the 'Buckingham Ghost' (V. 22), the 'Berwick Ghost' (V. 23), the 'Hounds' Priest' (V. 24) and the 'Ghost of Anantis' (V. 24), William's revenants display similar attributes and agencies to the Northern European *draugr*, the Greek *vrykolakas*, and the Slavic *vampire*.[36] Indeed, while it must be reiterated that encounters with the undead reflect the authorial and experiential biases of the culture in which the attack took place – in some Norse and Breton narratives, for instance, the walking corpse is quite benign[37] – the written sources nonetheless follow a similar narratological pattern: the revenant lived or died contrary to the habits and beliefs of the community (a 'bad' death); they had a propensity to terrorise those they knew in life, either through disease, night-time chokings or physical assault;[38] the attacks became more violent and frequent over time; the offending corpse was exhumed, bound, and/or cremated to prevent the disorder from spreading further. A revenant, then, was mostly violent and uncontrollable, a threat to the very cohesion of society. It was these very attributes, the ontological instability of an entity that straddled the boundary line between life and death, that prompted William to include similar stories in his *Historia* as a warning for posterity (*ad posterorum cautelam*).[39]

Wondrous events were often employed as framing devices, their insertion into the ongoing historical narrative used to justify events which had previously occurred or else foretell events which had yet to pass.[40] While William's audience may have appreciated his tales of the undead as entertainments in and of themselves – self-referential enclosed narratives – they can also be viewed as integral components of the *Historia*'s overall framework.[41] To this end, Gabrielle Spiegel has suggested that to make sense of a chronicle, one must employ a reading technique similar to that used in the decoding of images, specifically the process whereby meanings can be generated by treading a correct mental pathway through a (seemingly) disordered textual field.[42] Just as the correct mental movement through the structure of an illumination or fresco-cycle yielded deeper layers of meaning, so the chronicle also possessed mnemonic cues and discursive patterns which, if acknowledged by the percipient, could be used to generate a more subtle understanding of the material as a whole. Stories of deviant behaviour in the context of the walking dead can add an extra moral significance to commentaries on the conduct of the living. Even if William declines to offer an overt explanation as to what his prodigies might signify, the reader, directed by their placement within the chronicle and aware of their historical context, is invited to make the connection. The active agency (or 'wandering viewpoint') of the percipient makes manifest what the written word leaves unsaid. However, before comment can be made on the meaning(s) that can be extrapolated from these wonder stories, their content and narratological elements must first be analysed.

The *Historia* and the walking dead

'Were I to write down all the instances of this kind which I have ascertained to have befallen in our times', notes William, 'the undertaking would be beyond measure laborious and troublesome'.[43] Not only is this quote suggestive of the pervading fear of the undead in twelfth-century England, a belief that may have been more common than the extant literature suggests,[44] it also forces the reader to question *why* William chose to transcribe these particular tales. The authority of his informants may well have been a factor, adding a guarantor of 'truth' to events that would seem incredulous coming from the mouths of lesser men.[45] The first such account, that of a corpse which terrorised an unnamed Buckinghamshire village, was relayed to William by the 'venerable archdeacon' (*venerabili archidiacono*) of Buckingham, Stephen de Swafeld (c.1194–c.1203). The story details the death of a man who, on the very night after his funeral (29 May 1196), returned to the marital bed and 'not only terrified [his wife] on awaking, but nearly crushed her by the insupportable weight of his body'.[46] With the revenant's attacks increasing in both frequency and intensity, the townspeople decided to take the matter to the archdeacon Stephen, who in turn consulted St. Hugh of Avalon, the bishop of

Lincoln (1186–1200). The bishop was told by his advisors that 'such things had often befallen in England', and that the usual remedy was to dig up the suspect corpse and cremate it. The bishop was unwilling to desecrate the body in such a manner; instead he ordered a scroll of absolution to be placed on the dead man's chest – an act which stopped the corpse from walking.[47]

William declines to name his source for the tale of the 'Berwick Ghost'; however, this 'noble town'(*vicus nobilis*) does rest on a main communication link to Melrose Abbey, itself the setting of a third narrative, the tale of the 'Hounds' Priest' *(Hundeprest)*, which William declares was related to him by the 'religious men' (*viris religiosis*) of that place.[48] It is possible, perhaps, that William heard an account of the Berwick ghost whilst visiting his Cistercian informants to the north, or else as second-hand information from a Rievaulx monk who once resided at Melrose. This story, then, records the fate of a wealthy man who died suddenly after leading an irreligious life. 'By the contrivance, as it is believed, of Satan' (*operatione, ut creditur, Sathanae*) the dead man emerged from his tomb at night and began terrorising the town, spreading chaos and discontent as the corpse was 'borne here and there',[49] pursued by a pack of loudly barking dogs. Fearing that the corrupted air exuded from the diseased corpse (*corruptusque aer [...] pestiferi cadaveris*) would overtake the town if no action was taken, the residents tasked 'ten young men renowned for boldness'[50] to exhume, dismember, and cremate the offending cadaver. Once this action was taken, the nightly perturbations ceased.

A similar set of motifs can be discerned in the story of the 'Hounds' Priest'. An irreligious chaplain, whose love of hunting and aristocratic pursuits earned him his unflattering nickname, died and was interred in the grounds of Melrose Abbey. However, the holy earth did not keep the corpse at rest. 'With loud groans and horrible murmurs' (*ingenti fremitu et horrendo murmure*) he rose from the grave each night and began making a nuisance of himself outside the bedchamber of his former mistress. Seeking help from the abbey, the woman was assured by one of the monks that a vigil comprising himself, a second monk and two valorous young men from the village would keep watch in the cemetery as the night drew near. Midnight passed and there was still no sign of the monster, prompting three of the party – the second monk and the two laymen – to return indoors, ostensibly to warm themselves up from the cold. It was at this moment the Devil decided to 'raise up his chosen vessel' *(illico vas proprium)* and attack the remaining monk. Unperturbed and resolute in faith, the monk, axe in hand, cleaved a hole in the chaplain's body before chasing the fiend – literary, *pestis* ('pestilence') – back to its tomb. The next morning the corpse was exhumed and found to carry a fresh, bloody wound on its torso, after which it was carried beyond the walls of the monastery and cremated.

The setting of the final story, 'a castle called Anantis' (*castellum quod Anantis dicitur*) is much more difficult to place. Alnwick in Northumbria is a possible candidate, suggesting that William's informant – an 'aged monk who lived in honour and authority in those parts' – may have belonged to the nearby abbey of Newminster in Morpeth (c.1137), a daughter house of Fountains.[51] Although the term *religioso* suggests that the testimony came from a Cistercian, further evidence, such as William's remark that 'the man from whose mouth I heard these things sorrow[ed] over the desolation of *his* parish', alludes to a pastoral connection to the local community.[52] The possibility that the use of *religioso* was a semantic error, and that the informant was a canon from the Premonstratensian priory of St. Mary's (c.1151), near Alnwick, cannot be discounted. Whatever its ultimate provenance, the 'Ghost of Anantis' tells of a man of ill-repute who, having fled the justices of York, insinuated himself within the retinue of the lord of the castle of Anantis. Marrying within the household, it was not long before he began to suspect his new wife of being unfaithful. Under the pretence of 'going on a journey from which he would not return for some days' (*finxit se longius iturum, nec rediturum nisi post dies aliquot)*, he hid in the beams of the marriage chamber where, sure enough, her adulterous activities were confirmed. Enraged, the man fell from the rafters 'and was dashed heavily on the ground' (*ad terram elisit*). So angry was he at his wife's indiscretion he failed to make confession before succumbing to his injuries. Despite being afforded a 'Christian burial' (*Christianam quidem sepulturam)*, the man's corpse nonetheless emerged from the grave each night, wandering through the streets and exuding a terrible, pestilential stench. Many townspeople succumbed to the plague (*nam tetri corporis circumactu infectus aer, hausta pestilenti universas morbis et mortibus domos replevit*). Finally, two young brothers decided to exhume the errant corpse. They found it swollen to an enormous size (*enormi corpulentia distentum*), its face suffused with blood (*facie rubenti turgentique*) and the burial shroud ripped to pieces. Realising that the corpse must be a 'blood-sucker' (*sanguisuga*), they removed the heart before burning the body on a pyre.[53] William concludes by noting that

> [when] the infernal monster (*infernali illa belua*) had thus been destroyed, the pestilence (*pestilentia*) which was rife among the people ceased, as if the air, which had been corrupted by the contagious motions (*pestilenti motu*) of the dreadful corpse, were already purified (*purgatus*) by the fire which had consumed it.[54]

Themes of deviance, pollution, and the dangers of social unrest underscore each of William's wonders. Three out of the four narratives make explicit the belief that poor Christian conduct – including dying unshriven – was the determining factor in causing the dead to rise. However, while it is true that William credits the Hounds' Priest and the Ghost of Anantis' reappearance to the work of the Devil, and although fire was a common symbol for the purgation of sin, the pestilence is described in purely natural terms. Indeed, the dissolution of the body was a pragmatic means of assuaging the physical dangers presented by the revenant and seemed to have been an entrenched local practice. Not only do the Berwick townspeople cite 'frequent examples in similar cases' whereby cremation was the only viable means of stopping the perfidious corpse,[55] similar methods of containment can also be discerned in Geoffrey of Burton's *Vita sancte Moduenne virginis*, the Icelandic family sagas, and early modern vampire narratives.[56] It should be reiterated, however, that twelfth-century cosmography allowed for no true distinction between the physical and metaphysical worlds, between the agency and intentions of man and the workings of the universe. An understanding of the holistic nature of disease causation was part of the habitual knowledge of educated churchmen.[57] While there is not enough evidence to construct an exact list of the medico-theological manuscripts used by William, practical medical manuals (catalogue no. 225) and a copy of Bernardus Silvestris's *Cosmographia* (no. 127, c.1145) were indeed available for consultation in the library at Rievaulx.[58] Haimo of Auxerre's commentary on the Pauline Epistles (no. 4, c.850s) – specifically, the explication of Paul's metaphor for the spread of spiritual corruption in 1 Cor. 5 – could also have functioned as a research tool.[59] Whether William was aware of more recent treatises on the contagiousness of sin, such as Peter the Chanter's *Verbum abbreviatium* (c.1187), is open to speculation.[60]

With these potential sources in mind, it is telling that the residents who did not succumb to illness prior to the Ghost of Anantis' cremation included William's primary source and a group of esteemed local clergymen.[61] The 'passions of the mind' were one of the 'non-natural things' which, according to medieval medical theory, affected the body's humoral balance: a deviant mental/social outlook could well have had a detrimental effect on an individual's physical wellbeing.[62] Diseased bodies were a manifestation of a person or community's deviation from the divine equilibrium and had the potential to transmit their moral/physical degradation to others. Sin, therefore, was a deciding factor in the source of (and susceptibility to) a revenant's contagion. Imbalanced humours were a manifestation of sin, just as a person or revenant's sin was made manifest through a monstrous, corrupted body.[63] *Pestilentia, pestiferi cadaveris* and *corruptusque aer* are among the terms William uses to describe how the revenant transmitted its (manifest) sin to others, its putrid stench able to destabilise the vital spirits of those already morally, and thus physically, compromised. 'Bad' death had terrible – sometimes deadly – consequences for the living. However, whilst the 'Berwick Ghost' and the 'Ghost of Anantis' are primarily concerned with the spread of pestilence, the 'Buckingham Ghost' and the 'Hounds' Priest' focus on the differences between correct and incorrect pastoral practice; the irreligious chaplain caused unrest, whereas St. Hugh of Avalon contained it.[64] William's statement in the prologue to the 'Hounds' Priest' tale, that 'we can find no evidence of [revenants] in the works of ancient authors',[65] implies that the dead may have risen in response to (or anticipation of) more recent historical developments. Thus, although the accounts can be read as literal – that is, as entertaining or terrifying diversions from the main body of the text – there were also potent symbolic meanings behind the corpses' reappearance, as testified by the reference to 'prodigies' and 'similar entities' in the narratives' chapter rubrics.[66] If one of the primary goals of *admiratio* (wonder) was *scientia* (knowledge), then knowledge of a marvel's meaning could be utilised by the historian in his role as arbiter of moral truth, the symbol becoming allegory.[67] The spread of physical and metaphysical disorder was the structuring principle that forced the monastic reader to associate the agency of the undead monster (the revenant) with the agency of the social monster (William FitzOsbert, warmongering kings and William Longchamp).

The social revenant: William FitzOsbert, warmongering kings and William Longchamp

William FitzOsbert

Information about the popular London uprising of April 1196 can be discerned in four near-contemporary manuscripts: William's *Historia rerum Anglicarum*, the *Chronicae* of Gervase of Canterbury (c.1199) and Roger of Hoveden (c.1201), and Ralph de Diceto's *Imagines historiarum* (c.1202).[68] A version of the events was later included in the *Chronica majora* of Matthew Paris (c.1240–1259).[69] Although attempts to create a prosopographic narrative for the instigator of the revolt, William FitzOsbert, are hindered by a lack of evidence about his early life,[70] a rough chronology can nonetheless be constructed using the historiographical sources, specifically William of Newburgh's *Historia*, as a template.

The youngest son of a wealthy London landowner and a veteran of the Third Crusade,[71] FitzOsbert was said to possess a rare gift for public speaking. FitzOsbert derived his sobriquet 'longbeard' (*barba prolixa*) from an impressive beard worn, so the *Historia* tells us, as a way of 'appearing conspicuous in meetings and public assemblies' *(in coetu et concione magis conspicuus appararet)*.[72] In all other respects he was contemptible and dissolute; a law student who, despite his eloquence and sharp mind, was envious, vain, and quick to hold a grudge. Indeed, having been denied an increase to his living expenses, FitzOsbert even accused his brother – the head of the family's estate – of high treason, going so far as to take the matter to the king. FitzOsbert's scorn for his social (and fiscal) betters may have prompted his decision to take up the cause of the oppressed citizens of London, proclaiming himself 'king' (*rex*) and 'saviour' (*salvator*) of the poor. Indeed, the levying of extra taxes by the city's elders had caused much consternation and anger among the lower strata of London society.[73] Despite winning up to 52,000 converts through his impassioned and eloquent public speeches, FitzOsbert's sedition did not last for long. Taking refuge in the church of St. Mary le Bow after a riot in which a member of the archbishop of Canterbury's militia was killed, FitzOsbert and his followers – including his mistress – watched as Hubert Walter, the archbishop, ordered the church to be set alight. FitzOsbert surrendered and was executed at Tyburn gallows along with nine of his most ardent followers, a fitting end 'for a pestilence and a killer' (*pestilentis et homicidae*).[74] However, much to the dismay of the city authorities, the anger that resulted from FitzOsbert's death soon coalesced into a cult. 'Fools' (*stultorum*) came from far and wide to keep vigil over the spot where he died. Seeking to denounce the beliefs of the 'idiot rabble' (*insulsa multitudo*), the authorities arrested the priest who attested to FitzOsbert's martyrdom and posted a sentry on the site of his execution. In a further indictment of the cult, the *Historia* describes how, in the moments before his death, FitzOsbert confessed to having had sex with his mistress on the altar of St. Mary le Bow and even of invoking the name of the Devil as Hubert Walter's guard closed in. Soon enough, 'the entire fabric of superstition was utterly prostrated, and popular feeling subsided'.[75] Although Gervase of Canterbury, Roger of Hoveden, and Ralph de Diceto subscribe to

William's version of the events, Roger is rather more sympathetic to the towns-folk's plight than the others.[76] As dean of St. Paul's, Ralph de Diceto was certainly affected by the civil unrest and, along with Philip of Poitiers (bishop of Durham [1196–1208], Richard I's former clerk and a close confidant of Hubert Walter), may have provided the testimony for the *Historia*'s more piquant descriptions of FitzOsbert's behaviour.[77] John Gillingham notes that if Philip had indeed been used an informant, then this may account for the lack of condemnation of Hubert Walter's encroachment into secular affairs, a boundary that William otherwise deemed inviolate.[78]

Despite this, the chaos/division caused by the breaching of natural order forms the basis for William's moralisation of the 1196 rebellion. An attentive reader, one who is able to navigate the non-linear structures of the text, can make a connection between the actions of FitzOsbert and the terrors inflicted by the walking dead. Deviant behaviour – be it in the form of public disobedience, living an irreligious life or, in the case of the revenant, dying 'badly' – was considered a great threat to social and religious order. The worshippers of FitzOsbert's cult and the townsfolk who were infected by the revenants' pestilence occupy a similar role in either story, illustrative of how 'error' has the potential to spread to others. The likening of heresy to disease was a commonly-used motif in twelfth-century moralising literature, and is something that William had used previously to great effect in the *Historia*.[79] Nowhere is this more apparent than in his descriptions of the Cathar – or *Publicani* – heresy in book two, chapter 13.

These [people] spread the *poison* of their heresy, which had originated from an unknown author in Gascony, in many regions; for such numbers are said to be *infected* with this *pestilence* throughout the extensive provinces of France, Spain, Italy, and Germany [...]. By the assistance of God, such means were adopted to counteract the *disease* that it must tremble at the idea of again entering the island.

[Hi nimirum olim ex Gasconia incerto auctore habentes originem, regioni-bus plurimis *virus* suae perfidiae infuderunt. Quippe in latissimis Galliae, Hispaniae, Italiae, Germaniaeque provinciis tam multi hac *peste infecti* esse dicuntur [...] Deo propitio, *pesti*, quae jam irrepserat, ita est obviatum, ut de cetero hanc insulam ingredi vereretur'][80]

Metaphors of infection are also used to describe the spread of the teachings of the 'False Prophet, Mohammad' (*Macometo, pseudo-propheta*):

That *pestiferous sect*, which took its beginning through the spirit of error, and of that son of perdition, as I have said, after it had *infected* many provinces through the art and arms of its author, after his death, *by the operations of Satan*, grew yet stronger, and occupied the greater part of the world.

[Sane *pestifera secta* illa, quae nimirum per spiritum erroris et filium illum perditionis, ut dictum est, initium sumpsit, cum plurimas arte et armis auctoris sui provincias *infecisset,* post mortem tamen ejus, *operatione sathanæ,* fortius invaluit, orbisque partem plurimam occupavit']⁸¹

Indeed, it is noticeable that William uses a similar phrase, 'operatione, ut creditur, Sathanae', to describe the agency of the Berwick Ghost. The use of the walking dead – that is, pestilence/sin incarnate – to allegorise FitzOsbert's insurgency highlights the extent of his transgression. Not only did the incitement of the peasantry constitute a destabilisation of the social (and thus natural) order, but FitzOsbert himself was a member of the ruling class, violating the boundary that existed between 'those who work and those who fight'. His monstrousness is compounded by his eloquence. To be schooled in law meant that FitzOsbert possessed at least some knowledge of the local tax system.⁸² The use of the phrase 'poisoned whispers' (*venenatis susurriis*) to describe the incitement of the *plebes* suggests, perhaps, that the information 'fed' to the citizens of London had been twisted to suit FitzOsbert's own agenda.⁸³ In Augustinian terms, it was an abuse of language; the semiotic system distorted to unnatural and devilish ends.⁸⁴ Social disorder was thus bound to – and exacerbated by – the contaminating effects of the monstrous tongue.⁸⁵ Such contaminations also extended to (mis)use of physical signs; the *Chronica majora*'s version of the uprising states that FitzOsbert's beard was an outward expression of his moral disdain for the clean-shaven Anglo-Norman elites.⁸⁶ William of Newburgh's own description of the beard – *prolixa* – contains similar (if not as explicit) connotations of unruliness, unkemptness and a break from social order. Further rhetorical flourishes such as he 'had horns like a lamb and tongue like a dragon' stress the combined verbal and visual distortions of the heretical body and compound FitzOsbert's monstrousness.⁸⁷

The contagiousness of entities that did not obey the constraints of social structure, either through physical appearance, action, or speech, is the principle used by William to link the peasant uprising to the tales of the undead. The actions of the revenant mirror the strife caused by the London riots. Assuaging the source of the 'error' through the use of fire ('Berwick Ghost', 'Ghost of Anantis') and submission to the authority of the church ('Buckingham Ghost', the 'Hounds' Priest') can be read as a metaphorical retelling of the burning of St. Mary le Bow, and the strategies put forward by Hubert Walter to contain FitzOsbert's pestilence. Read in this way, it is no coincidence that the concluding remarks of the revenant narratives echo those of Chapter 20 ('the contriver and fomenter of so much evil [FitzOsbert] perished at the command of justice')⁸⁸ and William reassuring his audience that the natural order had been restored.

Tyrannical kings

The moral truths that underscore the revenant narratives would be fresh in the mind of the active reader as William 'return[ed] to the regular thread of history'.⁸⁹ Chapter 25 notes a portent of a double sun that occurred on 16 June 1196, an event which seemed to ignite the 'bloodthirsty rages' of the English and French courts. Indeed, William notes with some dismay how the antagonism between Richard I and Philip II caused much hardship for the inhabitants of these countries, for 'whenever kings rage, innocent people suffer for it'.[90] Chapter 26 continues on the theme of chaos and unrest, describing how famine (*famis*), pestilence (*pestis*) and poisoned air caused by the rotting corpses of the poor (*ex pauperum mortibus aere corrupto*) began to spread over French and English lands. So many people died that even the healthy were affected, going about 'with pallid and cadaverous countenances' (*vultu pallebant, et moribundis*) as if preparing for their own demise. William concludes this chapter with the dry observation that despite the rages of disease, the aristocratic lust for war was still all the greater.

Although the physical descriptions of the walking dead can be seen as portending the 'pallid and cadaverous countenances' of those that succumbed to the 1196 famine, their agency may also provide the reader with a framework through which to interpret the devastation caused by aristocratic feuds. Perhaps again using Philip of Poitiers as his primary informant, William comments that the pestilence which blighted the land was exacerbated by the conduct of warring kings. 'Famine', he notes, 'produced by unseasonable rains, had for some years vehemently afflicted the people of France and England; but by the disputes of the kings among themselves, it now increased more than ever'.[91] According to John of Salisbury's influential political theory, set out in the *Policraticus* (c.1159), tyrants disturbed the harmony of the wider body politic. The state-as-organism metaphor of medieval political theory is an extension of the wider belief in the unity of the macro- and microcosm: the universe reflected in the structure of the human body (I Cor. 12:12).[92] Book five of the *Policraticus*, especially, uses the metaphor of a healthy, well-maintained body to demonstrate the philosophy of good secular and ecclesiastical governance.[93] An entity whose head (the ruling elite) pursued a course of action that was detrimental to the wellbeing of the rest of the organism (society) was contrary to the workings of nature and, therefore, monstrous.[94] Being based within the common milieu of cosmological theory, the conception of the body politic as read in the *Policraticus* may not have been unknown to a scholar of William's standing, despite the fact that the work itself was not widely circulated in the decades following its completion.[95] Indeed, William's use of the walking dead is a pointed application of the John of Salisbury model, illustrating the misery that could arise from a diseased and disordered body. Read in this way, the bloodshed caused by the 'raging kings' finds a perfect analogue in the Ghosts of Berwick and Anantis, whose path of destruction was just as indiscriminate. The macrocosm (monstrous kingship) and the microcosm (monstrous corpses) were inextricably linked. If, then, tyrants are like revenants who go 'here and there' (*hic illucque*) in their aimless pursuit of blood,[96] spreading pestilence and death in their wake, then on whose authority does it fall to try and put an end to their wanderings? Although William remains equivocal on this point, a closer reading of the 'Buckingham Ghost' and 'Hounds' Priest' narratives suggests that salvation, the restoration of the body politic, could come in the form of correct pastoral practice.

William Longchamp

If the need to maintain socio-spiritual order was one of the main moralistic under-tones of the *Historia*, then it is unsurprising that William displays such a deep enmity for secular-minded churchmen, specifically bishops who cared more about power and prestige than tending their flocks.[97] In a manner similar to the pas-sages relating to FitzOsbert and the warring kings, the scorn reserved for William Longchamp, the erstwhile bishop of Ely who all but ruled England in Richard I's absence on the Third Crusade, is given further emphasis by the close manu-script connection between the entry on his death (V.29) and the revenant exempla (V.22–4). Chancellor from the king's coronation in 1189, Longchamp was conse-crated bishop of Ely, became papal legate and, finally, was appointed co-justiciar with Bishop Hugh du Puiset of Durham. Following a fierce political battle with du Puiset, Longchamp was named the chief justiciar of England in the spring of 1190.[98] Longchamp's arrogance was such that he routinely ignored orders from the king, going so far as to arrest Richard's half-brother, Geoffrey, the incoming archbishop of York, following the latter's arrival at Dover in September 1191. This proved to be Longchamp's undoing. Stripped of his justiciarship, he fled to the Continent where, despite remaining in favour with Richard, he never regained the full extent of his powers. Longchamp died at Poitiers in 1197 and was bur-ied in the abbey of Le Pin. William's opinion of the bishop's demise is blunt: 'England rejoiced at his death, for the fear of him had lain like an incubus upon her [...] it was evident that he would frequently plot evil against the land which had vomited him forth as some pestilential humour'.[99] The *Historia* is not the only twelfth-century source that expresses its disdain for Longchamp and the sin of embracing secular as well as ecclesiastical lifestyles. Richard of Devizes, a monk of St. Swithun's Priory, Winchester, was particularly keen with his criticisms, describing in his *Chronicon* (c.1192) how 'William, bishop of Ely and the king's chancellor [...] made up for the shortness of his stature by his arrogance'.[100] Longchamp's chimera-like status is also acknowledged by Richard, who notes that, having been appointed chief justiciar, chancellor, and bishop of Ely, he had become 'a man with three titles and three heads' (*trinominis ille et triceps*).[101] Hugh Nonant (d.1198), bishop of Coventry, was a close friend of Prince John and one of Longchamp's more strident critics. Along with Gerald of Wales, Hugh was responsible for popularising the rumour that Longchamp's grandfather had been a runaway Beauvais serf. The 'vileness'(*nequitiam*) exhibited by the grandfather as he rose through the ranks to become chief forester of Lyons, Normandy, prefig-ured the equally unnatural career of the grandson.[102] Thus, as a low-born foreigner who had insinuated himself within the government *and* the church, and through whose actions the realm was falling into ruin, Longchamp was the very definition of monstrousness, error, and sin.

William's decision to include the account of Longchamp's death at the end of book five and his comments that the bishop was 'vomited forth as some pestilen-tial humour' (*quae illum evomueret tanquam humorem pestiferum*)[103] makes the latter's likeness with the walking dead – that is, a diseased sinful body – explicit.

As secular-minded churchmen, Longchamp and the Hounds' Priest are supremely disordered beings, neither one thing nor the other and all the more dangerous for it. Longchamp's role as justiciar-bishop almost led the country into civil war, just as the aristocratic pursuits and sexual misconduct of the Hounds' Priest had dire consequences for the inhabitants of Melrose. As intimated in the 'Buckingham Ghost' narrative, recourse to good, uncorrupted churchmen was the only way to make these epidemics cease. St. Hugh of Avalon is the model used by William to illustrate how a true – that is, ideal – member of the clergy should behave.[104] With Hugh mindful not to overstep his authority in the secular/political sphere, he is one of the few churchmen in the *Historia* to escape William's wrath.[105] His 'venerability' (*venerabili*) and attention to the spiritual wellbeing of his people are qualities which make him the exact opposite of the chimera Longchamp. Gerald of Wales' *Vita sancti Hugonis* (c.1210), written to advertise Hugh's saintliness and the burgeoning cult that had begun to form around his tomb, highlights the bishop's pious nature, his dedication towards caring for the dead and, pointedly, his scorn for ecclesiastics who neglected their offices for the sake of worldly business.[106] Similarly, the *Magna vita sancti Hugonis* of Adam of Eynsham (c.1212) records that Hugh did not countenance the appointment of courtiers to high ecclesiastical offices and was unafraid to scold Henry II for interfering in church matters.[107] The intrigues of the court were a spiritual detriment to the churchman, just as secular appointees were unsuitable for the task of serving the will of God. To overstep either boundary was unacceptable. As an exemplar of good conduct, it is not surprising that Hugh plays such a prominent role in assuaging the Buckingham Ghost; the revenant (the proxy chancellor) taking the opposite role, as an epitome of bad conduct.[108] References to the 'crushing' of the Buckingham widow and the incubus-like qualities of Longchamp ('*incubuerat*'), merely solidify the connection between the two types of monster.[109] The use of a feminine pronoun (*illam*) to personify the 'smothered' English nation allows for Longchamp's agency to be read against the Buckingham widow's violent, undead husband – underscoring the trauma of being subject to a social monster's thrall.[110]

Conclusion: William of Newburgh and the uses of the walking corpse

Encounters with the walking dead were rare, inexplicable, and contrary to expected course of nature – the very definition of a 'wonder'. However, the insertion of the revenant stories within book five of the *Historia* was not simply a means of diverting the audience's attention away from the main historical narrative. When considered in the context of the chronicle as a whole, they could be read as allegorical commentaries on other deviant and destructive events in recent history. William was not unique among contemporary historians in using *mirabilia* to provide a subtextual reading of current, rather than abstractly moralistic, concerns. The Cistercian monk Ralph of Coggeshall, in his continuation of the *Chronicon Anglicanum* (c.1220), appropriates six wonders – all disfigured or 'unnatural' bodies – as part of a wider historical discussion on the threat that Catharism posed to the cohesion of the church.[111] Non-monastic works such as Gerald of Wales's *Topographia Hibernica* were more overt in their use of wonders in socio-political discourse. Gerald specifically links the prevalence of monstrous births in Ireland to the sinfulness and marginality of its people.[112] Such physical and metaphysical disorders were also liable to infect outsiders with whom the native population came into contact: 'foreigners coming to this country almost inevitably are contaminated (*corrumpunt*) by this inborn vice of the country [treachery]; a vice that is most contagious (*contagiosissimo*)'.[113] According to Gerald, the monstrosity of the Irish made the conquest of their lands an inherently just pursuit. The moral diseases that infected *Hibernia* could only be healed through complete subservience to the political centre (that is, the English crown).

William of Newburgh's assertion that he merely transcribed what was recounted to him may indeed hold true but, like Gerald of Wales and Ralph of Coggeshall, this did not stop him from utilising such stories in a pointed, critical manner. Revenants, as supremely disordered bodies, were co-opted to signify chaos and unrest in the wider body politic and warn of the eschatological dangers of transgression.[114] By virtue of their textual placement, the 'heresy' of William Longbeard and the resumption of war between England and France are diagnosed as particularly destructive and sinful events. The disparities between bishops who tended their flock (St. Hugh of Avalon) and those who promoted ruin (the Hounds' Priest; William Longchamp) are also signified through the prism of the undead corpse. For a provincial, nominally Cistercian audience, FitzOsbert's rebellion and Richard I's continental campaigns were events that contrasted sharply with their own beliefs regarding the 'natural' order of things. The disdain felt for William Longchamp – who in life epitomised the unnatural mix of the secular and spiritual – was the culmination of William of Newburgh's chronicle-wide attack on worldly churchmen. Who better, then, to recast as pestilential, destructive monsters?

As the revenant's manifest form revealed unsaid truths about the body politic, so the specific linguistic motifs used to describe the wonder also helped structure the reader's interpretation of historical events. Moral equivalences between the conduct of the walking corpse and the tumults of the late twelfth century were encouraged through the deliberate use of medico-theological terminologies to describe each type of disordered body. References to 'infection', 'pestilence', and 'poison' permeate the descriptions of the revenant, just as they describe the activities of William Longbeard and William Longchamp (and, indeed, the spread of Catharism and Islam). Utilising common literary *topoi* regarding sin/disease causation, William of Newburgh invites his monastic readership to meditate on the literary function of portents, forcing them to question his prefatory statement that history writing 'does not impose upon me any research into profound matters or mystical exposition'.[115] Correct reading practice – comprehension of the seemingly incomprehensible wonder – reveals the irony of William's claim. It would be wrong, then, to view the tales of the undead as mere folkloric residues, stories with no critical import. A closer investigation into form and function of the revenant narratives in the *Historia rerum Anglicarum* allows for a more nuanced understanding of the themes of the wider historical text.

Notes

A version of this chapter was published previously as: 'Social Monsters and the Walking Dead in William of Newburgh's *Historia Rerum Anglicarum*' *Journal of Medieval History* 41 (2015), 446–65. Reproduced by permission of Taylor & Francis Ltd. http://www.tandfonline.com

1 William of Newburgh, *Historia rerum Anglicarum*, in *Chronicles of the Reigns of Stephen, Henry II., and Richard I*, ed. by Richard Howlett, 2 vols, RS 82 (London: Longman, 1884–5), I, pp. 1–408; II, pp. 409–500. For the English translations of the *Historia* consulted in this chapter, and elsewhere in the volume, see 'The History of William of Newburgh', in *The Church Historians of England*, vol. IV, pt. 2, ed. by Joseph Stevenson (London: Seeleys, 1856), pp. 395–672. All references to the *Historia* are hereafter are cited as 'Newburgh', followed by the book number and chapter. The page numbers are taken from the Howlett Edition.

2 H. E. Salter attempted to construct a biography based on the 'William of Newburgh' mentioned in the cartulary of Osney Abbey, Oxfordshire: see 'William of Newburgh', *English Historical Review* 22 (1907), 510–14. According to Salter, William was born in Bridlington in 1135/6 and moved to Newburgh at a young age to receive his education. He married a local heiress, Emma de Peri, when he was around 25 to 30 years old, before retiring to the Augustinian priory of Newburgh in the 1180s. This interpretation has been refuted by Antonia Gransden, amongst others: it is much more likely that William spent his entire life in the cloister: see Antonia Gransden, *Historical Writing in England c.550– c.1307* (London: Routledge, 1974), p. 264.

3 Works that have been attributed to William's authorship include the *Historia* (c.1198) a commentary on the Song of Songs (c.1196), and three exegetical sermons on Luke 11: 27, the Trinity, and the Martyrdom of St. Alban. See Richard Sharpe, *A Handlist of the Latin Writers of Great Britain and Ireland Before 1540*, Publications of the *Journal of Medieval Latin*, 1 (Turnhout: Brepols, 1997), p. 794. For key works on the *Historia*, see Nancy F. Partner, *Serious Entertainments: The Writing of History in Twelfth-Century England* (Chicago, IL: University of Chicago Press, 1977), pp. 51–113; Anne Lawrence-Mathers, 'William of Newburgh and the Northumbrian Construction of English History', *Journal of Medieval History* 33 (2007), 339–57; Peter Biller, 'William of Newburgh and the Cathars', in *Life and Thought in the Northern Church c.1100–c.1700*, ed. by Diana Wood, Studies in Church History 12 (Woodbridge: Boydell, 1999), pp. 11–30; Monika Otter, *Inventiones: Fiction and Referentiality in Twelfth-Century English Historical Writing* (Chapel Hill, NC: The University of North Carolina Press, 1996), pp. 93–128.

4 Newburgh, Preface (p. 12).

5 Newburgh, I. 27–28 (pp. 82–87).

6 'Mira vero hujusmodi dicimus, non tantum propter raritatem, sed etiam quia occultam habent rationem', Newburgh, I. 28 (pp. 84–85).

7 Newburgh, V. 22–24 (pp. 474–82).

8 Newburgh, V. 20–21 (pp. 466–73)

9 Newburgh, V. 25–6 (pp. 482–85)

10 Newburgh, V. 29 (pp. 489–90).

11 'Monstra sane dicta perhibent a monstrando, quod aliquid significando demonstrent, et ostenta ab ostendendo, et portenta a portendendo, id est praeostendendo, et prodigia, quod porro dicant, id est future praedicant', Augustine, *De civitate Dei, Libri XI–XXII*, ed. by Alphonse Kalb, *Aurelii Augustini Opera* 14.2., CCSL 48 (Turnhout:

Brepols, 1965), XXI. 8 (at p. 773). For the English translation, see Augustine, *City of God,* trans. by Henry Bettinson (Harmondsworth: Penguin, 1984), pp. 982–83.

12 'Portentum ergo fit non contra naturam, sed contra quam est nota natura. Portenta autem et ostenta, monstra atque prodigia ideo nuncupantur, quod portendere atque ostendere, monstrare ac praedicare aliqua futura videntur.' Isidore of Seville, *Etymologies,* XI.iii.2.

13 Gervase of Tilbury, *Otia Imperialia: Recreation for an Emperor,* ed. and trans. by S. E. Banks and J. W. Binns, Oxford Medieval Texts (Oxford: Clarendon, 2002), III. Preface (pp. 558–59).

14 'Sic enim composita est humana natura, ut nihil praeter inusitatum, et raro contingens, vel pretiosum ducat vel admirandum'. Gerald of Wales, *Topographia Hibernica* (hereafter GW, *TH*), in *Giraldus Cambrensis Opera,* 8 vols., ed. by J. S Brewer, J. F. Dimock, and G. F. Warner, RS 21 (London: Longman, 1861–1891), V (1867), dist. I. 15 (at p. 49). For the English translation, see Gerald of Wales, *The History and Topography of Ireland,* ed. and trans. by John J. O' Meara (Harmondsworth: Penguin, 1982), p. 42.

15 Bynum, 'Wonder', pp. 1–26; Carl S. Watkins, 'Memories of the Marvelous in the Anglo-Norman Realm', in *Medieval Memories: Men, Women and the Past, 700–1300,* ed. by Elizabeth Van Houts (Harlow: Pearson, 2001), pp. 92–112.

16 'Porro puerorum illorum viridium, qui de terra emersisse dicuntur, abstrusior ratio est, quam utique nostri sensus tenuitas non sufficit indagare.' Newburgh, I. 28 (p. 87).

17 Otter, *Inventiones,* pp. 102–3.

18 Otter, *Inventiones,* p. 103; Catherine A. M. Clarke, 'Signs and Wonders: Writing Trauma in Twelfth-Century England', *Reading Medieval Studies* 35 (2009), 55–77 (at p. 69).

19 'et vultu pallebant, et moribundis similes incedebant, tanquam continuo morituri', Newburgh, V. 26 (p. 485).

20 Paul Latimer, 'The English Inflation of 1180–1220 Reconsidered', *Past and Present,* 171 (2001), 3–29 (at p. 14); Christopher N. L. Brooke, *London 800–1216: The Shaping of a City* (London: Secker & Warburg, 1975), p. 48.

21 Ralph V. Turner and Richard R. Heiser, *The Reign of Richard Lionheart: Ruler of the Angevin Empire, 1189–1199* (Harlow: Longman, 2000), pp. 225–40.

22 'quae nostris temporibus copiosius provenerunt': Newburgh, Prefatory Epistle (p. 3).

23 'Et tanquam tria nostrae provincae lumina, sacrae religionis praerogativa refulgent.' Newburgh, I. 15 (p. 53).

24 Marsha Dutton, 'The Conversion and Vocation of Aelred of Rievaulx: a Historical Hypothesis', in *England in the Twelfth Century: Proceedings of the 1988 Harlaxton Symposium,* ed. by Daniel Williams, Harlaxton Medieval Studies 5 (Woodbridge: Boydell, 1990), pp. 31–49 (pp. 34–35).

25 For a biography of Aelred, see Aelred Squire, *Aelred of Rievaulx: A Study* (London: S. P. C. K., 1969).

26 Squire, *Aelred of Rievaulx,* pp. 112–15.

27 See the statute that 'no abbot, monk, or novice is permitted to compose books, except by permission of the general chapter', in Elizabeth Freeman, *Narratives of a New Order: Cistercian Historical Writing in England, 1150–1220* (Turnhout: Brepols, 2002), p. 91.

28 Freeman, Narratives of a New Order, pp. 91–97.

29 The MS contains a Newburgh 'ex libris'.

30 Newburgh, pp. xlii–xliii. Other versions include Dublin, Trinity College, MS E. 4. 21 (c.1300); BL Add. MS 24981 (fourteenth century); CCCC MS 262 (thirteenth century); Oxford, Bodleian Library, MS Digby 101 (fourteenth century), and BL MS Royal 13 B IX (fifteenth century).

31 Anne Lawrence, 'A Northern English School? Patterns of Production and Collection of Manuscripts in the Augustinian Houses of Yorkshire in the Twelfth and Thirteenth

Centuries', in *Yorkshire Monasticism: Archaeology, Art and Architecture, from the 7th to 16th Centuries*, ed. by Lawrence Hoey (Leeds: Maney, 1995), pp. 145–53; Anne Lawrence-Mathers, *Manuscripts in Northumbria in the Eleventh and Twelfth Centuries* (Woodbridge: Brewer, 2003), pp. 207–8.

32 Fortuitously, two twelfth-century library catalogues from Rievaulx (c.1190–1200) survive in Cambridge Jesus College MS 34 fols. 1–5r and 5v–6. For the manuscripts attributed to Durham, see Neil R. Ker, *Medieval Libraries of Great Britain: a List of Surviving Books*. 2nd edn. (London: Royal Historical Society, 1964), pp. 60–76.

33 Anne Mathers-Lawrence, 'The Augustinian Canons in Northumbria: Region, Tradition and Textuality in a Colonizing Order', in *The Regular Canons in the Medieval British Isles*, ed. by Janet E. Burton and Karen Stöber (Turnhout: Brepols, 2012), pp. 59–78 (pp.72–75).

34 Lawrence-Mathers, 'William of Newburgh', p. 344.

35 Jeffrey J. Cohen, 'Green Children From Another World, or the Archipelago of England', in *Cultural Diversity in the British Middle Ages*, ed. by Jeffrey J. Cohen (Basingstoke: Palgrave Macmillan, 2008), pp. 75–94.

36 Paul Barber, *Vampires, Burial, and Death*; William Sayers, 'The Alien and the Alienated', pp. 242–63; Julie Du Boulay, 'The Greek Vampire', 219–38.

37 For the benign *draugr*, see Chadwick, 'Norse Ghosts I, p. 61. For an early fifteenth-century sermon story concerning a Breton baker who returned from the grave to knead bread with his family, see Schmitt, *Ghosts in the Middle Ages*, pp. 147–48.

38 For a closer analysis of the relationship between the nightmare experience and the revenant, see chapter six.

39 Newburgh V. 24 (p. 477).

40 Freeman, 'Wonders, Prodigies and Marvels', 127–43.

41 Chris Given-Wilson, *Chronicles: The Writing of History in Medieval England* (London: Hambledon, 2004), p. 22; Otter, *Inventiones*, p. 128.

42 Gabrielle Spiegel, *The Past as Text: The Theory and Practice of Medieval Historiography* (Baltimore, MD: Johns Hopkins University Press, 1997), pp. 99–110. For the reading of images, see Michael Camille, 'Some Visual Implications of Medieval Literacy and Illiteracy', *Art History,* 8 (1985), 26–49.

43 'Porro si velim omnia hujusmodi scibere quae nostris contigisse temporibus comperi, nimis operosum simul et onerosum erit.', Newburgh V. 24 (p. 477).

44 Gordon, 'Dealing with the Undead', p.128.

45 Watkins, 'Memories of the Marvellous', p. 97.

46 'excitatem non solum terruit verum etiam paene obruit importabili sui pondere super-jacto'. Newburgh V. 22 (p. 474).

47 'fuere qui dicerent talia saepius in Anglia contigisse […] corpore effosso et con-cremato'. Newburgh, V. 22 (p. 475). Although, as Carl Watkins states, the use of absolution scrolls to quell the undead may have been an innovation born out of the increasing acceptance of the Purgatory – that is, the walking corpse was seen more a purgatorial spirit than a demon-in-disguise – archaeological evidence for the absolution of morally-suspect corpses can be traced back to at least the eleventh century. See, for example, the lead cross placed in the coffin of Godfrey, Bishop of Chichester (d. 1088), which was inscribed with a papal absolution for Geoffrey's (unnamed) sins. Hugh's decision to contain the revenant with a written prayer thus built upon an already established practice. Elisabeth Okasha, 'The Lead Cross of Bishop Godfrey of Chichester', *Sussex Archaeological Collections* 134 (1996), 63–69; Watkins, *History and the Supernatural*, pp. 180–92.

48 Newburgh, V. 24 (p. 479).

49 'huc illucque ferebatur'. Newburgh V. 23 (p. 476).

50 decem juvenes audacia insignes'. Newburgh, V. 23 (p. 476).

51 'sene religioso, qui clarus et potens in partibus illis exstiterat'. Newburgh V. 24 (p. 479).

52   'hanc nimirum suae desolationem parrochiae dolens vir ille, ex cujus haec ore accepi.' Newburgh, V. 24 (p. 481). My italics.

53   Newburgh, V. 24 (p. 482).

54   'Porro infernali illa belua sic deleta, pestilentia quoque quae grassabatur in populo conquievit, tanquam igne illo, qui dirum cadaver absumpserat, aer jam esset purgatus, qui ejus fuerat pestilenti motu corruptus'. Newburgh V. 24 (p. 482).

55   'consimili clarebat exemplis': Newburgh V. 23 (p. 476).

56   For the decapitation of the suspected revenants and the burning of their hearts, see Geoffrey of Burton, *Life and Miracles of St Modwenna*, pp. 196–97. For the cremation of the troublesome *draugr*, see the story of Hrapp's ghost in *Laxdaela Saga*, ed. and trans. by A. C. Press, 2nd ed. (London: Dent, 1906), p. 78. See also Barber, *Vampires, Burial, and Death*, pp. 6–7, 11–13.

57   Susan R. Kramer, 'Understanding Contagion: The Contaminating Effects of Another's Sin', in *History in the Comic Mode: Medieval Communities and the Matter of the Person*, ed. by Rachel Fulton and Bruce Holsinger (New York: Columbia University Press, 2007), pp. 145–57 (at p. 151).

58   For a modern translation of the *Cosmographia*, see the version by Winthrop Wetherbee (New York and London: Columbia University Press, 1973). The catalogue numbers have been taken from the first, longer version of the Rievaulx catalogue, see David N. Bell, *The Libraries of the Cistercians, Gilbertines and Premonstratensians* (London: British Library, 1992), p. 109 (no. 127) and p. 121 (no. 225).

59   'Only a tiny amount of yeast corrupts the whole mass of flour' (Sicut modicum fermentum omnem massam farinae conspersam corrumpit), in Haimo of Auxerre, *Haymonis Halberstatensis Episcopi, Opera*, vol. 2, PL 117, ed. by J.-P. Migne (Paris, 1852), col. 536B; Bell, *Libraries*, p. 90 (no. 4).

60   As Peter states, 'the sins of the community reside in individuals, and the sins of an individual can affect everyone' (et peccatum universalitatis spargitur in singulos, et peccatum unius redundat in plures). Peter the Chanter, *Petri Cantoris Verbum abbreviatum*, PL 205, ed. by J-P. Migne (Paris, 1855), col. 535D.

61   'The man from whose mouth I heard these things, sorrowing over this desolation of his parish, applied himself to summon a meeting of wise and religious men [so] that they might impart healthful (*salubre*) counsel in so great a dilemma, and refresh the spirits of the miserable remnant of the people.' (hanc nimirum suae desolationem parrochiae dolens vir ille, ex cujus haec ore accepi, in sacra dominica, quae Palmarum dicitur, viros sapientes et religiosos accersire studuit, qui in tanto discrimine salubre darent concilium, et consolatione vel modica miseras plebis reliquias recrearent). Newburgh, V. 24 (p. 481).

62   The six 'non-natural things' were defined as the moral, social, and environmental properties that existed outside of the body, the qualities of which affected the balance of the humours. Air and environment, food and drink, sleep and wakefulness, motion and rest, evacuation and repletion, and the passions of the mind, needed to be carefully monitored to maintain a patient's health. For an overview of the mid- to late-twelfth century understanding of contagion, see Kramer, 'Understanding Contagion', p. 148.

63   For the relationship between sin and disease, see R. I. Moore, 'Heresy as Disease', in *The Concept of Heresy in the Middle Ages (11th–13th c.): Proceedings of the International Conference, Louvain, May 13–16, 1973*, ed. by W. Lourdaux and D. Verhelst (Leuven: Martinus Nijhoff, 1976), pp. 1–11; Richard Palmer 'In Bad Odour: Smell and its Significance in Medicine from Antiquity to the Seventeenth Century', in *Medicine and the Five Senses*, ed. by W. F. Bynum and Roy Porter (Cambridge: Cambridge University Press, 1993), pp. 61–68.

64   A discussion of how the theological innovations emerging from Paris influenced Hugh's decision to absolve rather than cremate the corpse is discussed in more detail in chapter four. For an overview of this argument see Watkins, *History and the Supernatural*, pp. 186–88.

65 'Cum nihil tale in libris veterum reperiatur'. Newburgh, V. 24 (p. 477). Indeed, William had access to a vast array of 'ancient' histories in the Rievaulx library, including the *Chronicon* of Eusebius of Caeserea (catalogue no. 112, c.325) and the *Historia* of Hegesippus (no. 113 c.180). See Bell, *Libraries*, p. 106.

66 'De prodigio mortui post sepulturam oberrantis' (Newburgh, V. 22, p. 474), 'de re consimili quae accidit apud Berewic' (V. 23, p. 476), 'De quibusdam prodigiosis' (V. 24, p. 477).

67 Freeman, 'Wonders, Prodigies and Marvels', p. 142.

68 Modern translations of all four accounts can be found in R. C. Van Caenegem, *English Lawsuits from William I to Richard II*, vol. 2, *Henry II and Richard I (nos. 347–665)*, Publications of the Seldon Society 107 (London: Selden Society, 1991), pp. 687–94.

69 Matthew Paris, *Matthæi Parisiensis, monachi Sancti Albani, Chronica majora*, vol. 2., ed. by Henry R. Luard, RS 57 (London: Longman, 1874), pp. 418–19.

70 G. W. S. Barrow, 'The Bearded Revolutionary': the Story of a Twelfth-Century London Student in Revolt', *History Today* 19 (1969), 679–87; John McEwen, 'William FitzOsbert and the Crisis of 1196 in London', *Florilegium* 21 (2004), 18–42; Alan Cooper, '1190, William Longbeard, and the Crisis of Angevin England', in *Christians and Jews in Angevin England*, ed. by Sarah Rees Jones and Sethina Watson (Woodbridge: Boydell, 2013), pp. 91–105.

71 Roger of Hoveden, Gesta regis Henrici Secundi Benedicti abbatis: The chronicle of the reigns of Henry II and Richard I, A.D. 1169–1192, known commonly under the name of Benedict of Peterborough, 2 vols. ed. by William Stubbs, RS 51 (London: Longman, 1867), II. p. 116.

72 Newburgh, V. 20 (p. 466).

73 Barrow, 'Bearded Revolutionary', p. 679.

74 Newburgh V. 20 (p. 471). Indeed, FitzOsbert's execution was the first such recorded at Tyburn. See R. E. Zachrisson, 'Marylebone: Tyburn: Holborn', *Modern Language Review* 12 (1917), 146–56.

75 'tota illa concinnatae superstitionis machina funditus concidit, et popularis opino conquievit', Newburgh, V. 21 (p. 473).

76 Roger notes the following: 'In the same year strife originated amongst the citizens of London, for not inconsiderable aids were imposed because of the King's imprisonment [...] and in order to spare their own purses the rich wanted the poor to pay for everything', in Van Caenegem, *English Lawsuits*, p. 693. If Roger's personal enmity against Hubert Walter can account for his less than severe tone, then Gervase's loyalties to his archbishop may well explain his own vehemence against FitzOsbert, and, indeed, his reluctance to name the person who ordered the destruction of St Mary le Bow. For an overview of this argument, see John Gillingham, 'The Historian as Judge: William of Newburgh and Hubert Walter', *The English Historical Review* 119 (2004), 1275–87 (at p. 1282).

77 Gillingham, 'Historian as Judge', p. 1285.

78 Gillingham, 'Historian as Judge', p. 1286.

79 Moore, 'Heresy and Disease', pp. 2, 10. For the likening of rebellion to madness and rabies, see Daniel Power, '"La rage méchante des traîtres prit feu": le discours sur la révolte sous les rois Plantagenêt (1144–1224)', in *La trahison au moyen âge: De la monstruosité au crime politique (Ve-XVe siècle)*, ed. by Maïté Billoré and Myriam Soria (Rennes: Presses universitaires de Rennes, 2009), pp. 53–65.

80 Newburgh II.13 (p. 132). Italics my emphasis.

81 Newburgh, V. 14 (p. 454). Italics my emphasis.

82 It can be theorised that FitzOsbert derived his ideas about proportional (and just) taxation of the poor from his experiences on the Third Crusade, specifically the tax levy imposed in Jerusalem in response to the threat posed by Saladin. William of Tyre late twelfth-century chronicle notes that one should give 'one besant for every hundred besants which they own, or its equivalent either on things in their possession or on

credits owning to them. From revenues also they shall give two besants for every hundred besants.' See William of Tyre, *A History of the Deeds Done Beyond the Sea*, vol. 2, ed. and trans. by E. A. Babcock and A. C. Frey (New York: Columbia University Press, 1943), XXII.23 (at p. 487).

83 Newburgh, V. 20 (p. 468).

84 Eric Jager, *The Tempter's Voice: Language and the Fall in Medieval Literature* (Ithaca, NY: Cornell University Press, 1993), pp. 96–97.

85 Tim W. Machan, 'Language and Society in Twelfth-Century England', in *Placing Middle English in Context*, ed. by Irma Taavitsainen et al. (Berlin: De Gruyter, 2000), p. 43–65 (at p. 49); Sandy Bardsley, *Venomous Tongues: Speech and Gender in Late Medieval England* (Philadelphia, PA: University of Pennsylvania Press, 2006), pp. 42–44.

86 Matthew Paris, *Chronica majora*, II, p. 418; Pauline Stafford, 'The Meaning of Hair in the Anglo-Norman World: Masculinity, Reform and National Identity', in *Saints, Scholars and Politicians: Gender as a Tool in Medieval Studies*, ed. by Mathilde van Dijk and Renée Nip (Turnhout: Brepols, 2005), pp. 153–71 (at p. 159).

87 'habensque cornua similia agni loqueretur ut draco', Newburgh, V. 20 (p. 469).

88 'tantorum incentor artifexque malorum dictante justitia periit', Newburgh, V. 20 (p. 471).

89 'ad historiae ordinem redeamus', Newburgh, V. 24 (p. 482).

90 'cruentus [...] furor [...] quicquid enim delirant reges, innoxiae plectuntur plebes', Newburgh, V. 25 (pp. 483–84).

91 'et quidam fames intempestivis edita imbribus, per annos jam aliquot Galliae Angliaeque populos vehementer attriverat, sed regibus inter se debacchantibus plus solito invaluit', Newburgh, V. 26 (p. 484).

92 I Cor. 12:12: 'Sicut enim corpus unum est, et membra habet multa, omnia autem membra corporis cum sint multa, unum tamen corpus sunt: ita et Christu' (For as the body is one and has many members, but all the members of that one body, being many, are one body, so also is Christ). See Tilman Struve, 'The Importance of the Organism in the Political Theory of John of Salisbury', in *The World of John of Salisbury*, ed. by Michael Wilks, Studies in Church History, Subsidia 3 (Oxford: Blackwell, 1984), pp. 303–17.

93 John of Salisbury, *Policraticus: Of the Frivolities of Courtiers and the Footprints of Philosophers*, ed. and trans. by Cary J. Nederman (Cambridge: Cambridge University Press, 1990), V (at pp. 65–102).

94 Cary J. Nederman and Catherine Campbell, 'Priests, Kings, and Tyrants: Spiritual and Temporal Power in John of Salisbury's *Policraticus*', *Speculum*, 66 (1991), 572–90.

95 Ilya Danes, 'The Earliest Use of John of Salisbury's *Policraticus*: Third Family Bestiaries', *Viator,* 44 (2013) 107–18 (at p. 107).

96 Newburgh V. 23 (p. 476).

97 Gillingham, 'Historian as Judge', p. 1276.

98 For Longchamp's political career, see Turner and Heiser, *Reign of Richard Lionheart*, pp. 110–30.

99 'Laetata est Anglia in morte ejus, quia incubuerat timor est super illiam [...] manifestum erat, quod terrae, quae illum evomuerat tanquam humorem pestiferum erebro machinaretur malum': Newburgh, V. 29 (p. 490).

100 'Willelmus Eliensis episcopus et regis cancellarius [...] corporis brevitatem animo recompensans', Richard of Devizes, *The Chronicle of Richard of Devizes of the Time of King Richard the First*, ed. and trans. by John T. Appleby (London: Nelson, 1963), p. 9.

101 Devizes, *Chronicle*, p. 13.

102 Quote concerning Longchamp's grandfather are taken from Gerald of Wales's *de vita Galfridi* and cited in David Balfour, 'The Origins of the Longchamp Family', *Medieval Prosopopography* 18 (1997), 73–92 (at p. 80).

103 Newburgh V. 29 (p. 490).
104 Given-Wilson, *Chronicles*, pp. 2–3.
105 See William's criticisms of Hubert, the Archbishop of Canterbury (IV. 35), Hugh
     Nonant, Bishop of Coventry (IV. 36) and the abbot of Caen (V. 19). Given that Philip
     of Poitiers was one of William's main sources for contemporary political events
     (including, perhaps, the death of Longchamp), it is perhaps not surprising that this
     most worldly of churchman escapes rebuke.
106 Specifically, Hugh upbraids Hugh Nonant for reciting rather than singing the mass
     after being summoned by the king. See Chapter 6 of Gerald of Wales, *The Life of
     Saint Hugh of Avalon, Bishop of Lincoln 1186-1200*, ed. and trans. by R. M. Loomis
     (New York: Garland, 1985), pp. 19–25.
107 'Lectis vero episcopus petitoriis sibi destinatis, "non", inquit "aulicis, sed potius
     ecclesiasticis, ecclesiastica oportet beneficia conferri personis: quarum possessores
     non palatio, aut fisco, sive scaccario, sed ut docet scriptura, altario convenit deser-
     vire."' See Adam of Eynsham, *Magna vita sancti Hugonis: The Life of Saint Hugh of
     Lincoln*, 2 vols., ed. and trans. by Decina L. Douie and Dom Hugh Farmer (London:
     Nelson, 1961–1962), I (1961), III.9, (at p. 115).
108 Although it is true that the contents of *vitae* accord to certain rules of the genre,
     and that the activities of Hugh of Avalon may be based on authoritative models, it
     should be reiterated that William of Newburgh was writing a history of England, not
     advertising the glory and virtue of a saint. Hugh was still alive during the *Histora*'s
     composition. The accurate representation of the facts was one of the main principles
     of historical truthfulness. If Stephen de Swafeld was indeed William's main inform-
     ant, it can be inferred that he was merely recounting his own experience of one of the
     more colourful petitions Hugh had to deal with over the course of his church career.
     It is doubtful that William interpolated Hugh's role in the narrative. The reverence
     shown to the corpse and the reluctance to get involved in secular affairs may not
     be entirely constructed devices. For the strategies involved in promoting a saint's
     cult, see Thomas J. Heffernan, *Sacred Biography: Saints and Their Biography in the
     Middle Ages* (Oxford: Oxford University Press, 1988).
109 Newburgh, V. 29 (p. 490).
110 Newburgh, V. 22 (p. 474).
111 See Freeman, 'Wonders, Prodigies and Marvels', pp. 127–43.
112 GW, *TH*, dist. III.35 (pp. 181–82).
113 'adeo, inquam, bonos mores corrumpunt colloquia parva, ut hoc vitio patriae tanquam
     innato et contagiosissimo etiam alienigenae huc advecti fere inevitabiliter involvan-
     tur', GW, *TH*, dist. III.24 (at p.168).
114 Freeman, Narratives of a New Order, p. 211.
115 'non altis scrutandis, mysticisque rimandis insistere': Newburgh, Prefatory Epistle (p. 4).

Primary sources

Adam of Eynsham, *Magna Vita Sancti Hugonis: The Life of Saint Hugh of Lincoln*, 2
    vols, ed. and trans. by Decina L. Douie and Dom Hugh Farmer (London: Nelson,
    1961–1962).
Augustine, *City of God*, trans. by Henry Bettinson (Harmondsworth: Penguin, 1984).
Augustine, *De civitate Dei, Libri XI–XXII*, ed. by Alphonse Kalb, *Aurelii Augustini Opera*
    14.2. CCSL 48 (Turnhout: Brepols, 1965).
Bernardus Silvestris, *The Cosmographia of Bernardus Silvestris*, ed. and trans. by Winthrop
    Wetherbee (New York and London: Columbia University Press, 1973).
Geoffrey of Burton, *Life and Miracles of St Modwenna*, ed. and trans. by Robert Bartlett,
    Oxford Medieval Texts (Oxford: Clarendon Press, 2002).

Gerald of Wales, *Giraldus Cambrensis Opera*, 8 vols, ed. by J. S Brewer, J. F. Dimock, and G. F. Warner, RS 21 (London: Longman, 1861–1891).

Gerald of Wales, *The History and Topography of Ireland*, ed. and trans. by John J. O'Meara (Harmondsworth: Penguin, 1982).

Gerald of Wales, *The Life of Saint Hugh of Avalon, Bishop of Lincoln 1186–1200*, ed. and trans. by R. M. Loomis (New York: Garland, 1985).

Gervase of Tilbury, *Otia Imperialia: Recreation for an Emperor*, ed. and trans. by S. E. Banks and J. W. Binns, Oxford Medieval Texts (Oxford: Clarendon, 2002).

Haimo of Auxerre, *Haymonis Halberstatensis Episcopi, Opera*, PL 117, ed. by J.-P. Migne (Paris, 1852).

Isidore of Seville, *Etymologies*, ed. and trans. by Stephen A. Barney et al. (Cambridge: Cambridge University Press, 2006).

Isidore of Seville, *Isidori Hispalensis Episcopi, Etymologiarum Sive Originum Libri XX*, 2 vols, ed. by W. M. Lindsay (Oxford: Clarendon, 1911).

John of Salisbury, *Policraticus: Of the Frivolities of Courtiers and the Footprints of Philosophers*, ed. and trans. Cary J. Nederman (Cambridge: Cambridge University Press, 1990).

Laxdaela Saga, ed. and trans. by A. C. Press, 2nd ed. (London: Dent, 1906).

Paris, Matthew, *Matthæi Parisiensis, monachi Sancti Albani, Chronica majora*, 7 vols, ed. by Henry R. Luard, RS 57 (London: Longman, 1872–1884).

Peter the Chanter, *Petri Cantoris Verbum Abbreviatum*, PL 205, ed. by J.-P. Migne (Paris, 1855).

Richard of Devizes, *The Chronicle of Richard of Devizes of the Time of King Richard the First*, ed. and trans. by John T. Appleby (London: Nelson, 1963).

Roger of Hoveden, *Gesta Regis Henrici Secundi Benedicti Abbatis: The Chronicle of the Reigns of Henry II and Richard I, A.D1169–1192, Known Commonly under the Name of Benedict of Peterborough*, 2 vols, ed. by William Stubbs, RS 51 (London: Longman, 1867).

Van Caenegem, R. C., *English Lawsuits from William I to Richard II, vol. 2, Henry II and Richard I (nos. 347–665)*, Publications of the Seldon Society 107 (London: Selden Society, 1991).

William of Newburgh, 'Historia Rerum Anglicarum', in *Chronicles of the Reigns of Stephen, Henry II., and Richard I*, 2 vols, ed. by Richard Howlett, RS 82 (London: Longman, 1884–5).

William of Newburgh, 'The History of William of Newburgh', in *The Church Historians of England*, vol. IV, pt. 2, ed. by Joseph Stevenson (London: Seeleys, 1856).

William of Tyre, *A History of the Deeds Done Beyond the Sea*, vol. 2, ed. and trans. by E. A. Babcock and A. C. Frey (New York: Columbia University Press, 1943).

Secondary sources

Balfour, David, 'The Origins of the Longchamp Family', *Medieval Prospopography* 18 (1997), 73–92.

Barber, Paul, *Vampires, Burial, and Death: Folklore and Reality* (New Haven, CT: Yale University Press, 1988).

Bardsley, Sandy, *Venomous Tongues: Speech and Gender in Late Medieval England* (Philadelphia, PA: University of Pennsylvania Press, 2006).

Barrow, G. W. S., 'The Bearded Revolutionary': The Story of a Twelfth-Century London Student in Revolt', *History Today* 19 (1969), 679–87.

Bell, David N., *The Libraries of the Cistercians, Gilbertines and Premonstratensians* (London: British Library, 1992).

Biller, Peter, 'William of Newburgh and the Cathars', in *Life and Thought in the Northern Church c.1100–c.1700*, ed. by Diana Wood (Woodbridge: Boydell, 1999), pp. 11–30.

Brooke, Christopher N. L., *London 800–1216: The Shaping of a City* (London: Secker & Warburg, 1975).

Bynum, Caroline W., 'Wonder', *American Historical Review* 102 (1997), 1–26.

Camille, Michael, 'Some Visual Implications of Medieval Literacy and Illiteracy', *Art History* 8 (1985), 26–49.

Chadwick, N. K., 'Norse Ghosts (a Study in the Draugr and the Haugbui)', *Folklore* 57 (1946), 50–65.

Clarke, Catherine A. M., 'Signs and Wonders: Writing Trauma in Twelfth-Century England', *Reading Medieval Studies* 35 (2009), 55–77.

Cohen, Jeffrey J., 'Green Children from Another World, or the Archipelago of England', in *Cultural Diversity in the British Middle Ages*, ed. by Jeffrey J. Cohen (Basingstoke: Palgrave Macmillan, 2008), pp. 75–94.

Cooper, Alan, '1190, William Longbeard, and the Crisis of Angevin England', in *Christians and Jews in Angevin England*, ed. by Sarah Rees Jones and Sethina Watson (Woodbridge: Boydell, 2013), pp. 91–105.

Danes, Ilya, 'The Earliest Use of John of Salisbury's *Policraticus*: Third Family Bestiaries', *Viator* 44 (2013), 107–18.

Du Boulay, Julie, 'The Greek Vampire: A Study of Cyclic Symbolism in Marriage and Death', *Man*, new ser. 17 (1982), 219–38.

Dutton, Marsha, 'The Conversion and Vocation of Aelred of Rievaulx: A Historical Hypothesis', in *England in the Twelfth Century: Proceedings of the 1988 Harlaxton Symposium*, ed. by Daniel Williams, Harlaxton Medieval Studies 5 (Woodbridge: Boydell, 1990), pp. 31–49.

Freeman, Elizabeth, *Narratives of a New Order: Cistercian Historical Writing in England, 1150–1220* (Turnhout: Brepols, 2002).

Freeman, Elizabeth, 'Wonders, Prodigies and Marvels: Unusual Bodies and the Fear of Heresy in Ralph of Coggeshall's *Chronicon Anglicanum*', *Journal of Medieval History* 26 (2000), 127–43.

Heffernan, Thomas J., *Sacred Biography: Saints and Their Biography in the Middle Ages* (Oxford: Oxford University Press, 1988).

Gillingham, John, 'The Historian as Judge: William of Newburgh and Hubert Walter', *The English Historical Review* 119 (2004), 1275–87.

Given-Wilson, Chris, *Chronicles: The Writing of History in Medieval England* (London: Hambledon, 2004).

Gordon, Stephen, 'Dealing with the Undead in the Later Middle Ages', in *Dealing with the Dead: Mortality and Community in the Middle Ages*, ed. by Thea Tomaini (Leiden: Brill, 2018), pp. 97–128.

Gransden, Antonia, *Historical Writing in England c.550–c.1307* (London: Routledge, 1974).

Jager, Eric, *The Tempter's Voice: Language and the Fall in Medieval Literature* (Ithaca, NY: Cornell University Press, 1993).

Ker, Neil R., *Medieval Libraries of Great Britain: A List of Surviving Books*, 2nd ed. (London: Royal Historical Society, 1964).

Kramer, Susan R., 'Understanding Contagion: The Contaminating Effects of Another's Sin', in *History in the Comic Mode: Medieval Communities and the Matter of the*

Person, ed. by Rachel Fulton and Bruce Holsinger (New York: Columbia University Press, 2007), pp. 145–57.

Latimer, Paul, 'The English Inflation of 1180–1220 Reconsidered', *Past and Present*, 171 (2001), 3–29.

Lawrence, Anne, 'A Northern English School? Patterns of Production and Collection of Manuscripts in the Augustinian Houses of Yorkshire in the Twelfth and Thirteenth Centuries', in *Yorkshire Monasticism: Archaeology, Art and Architecture, from the 7th to 16th Centuries*, ed. by Lawrence Hoey (Leeds: Maney, 1995), pp. 145–53.

Lawrence-Mathers, Anne, *Manuscripts in Northumbria in the Eleventh and Twelfth Centuries* (Woodbridge: Brewer, 2003).

Lawrence-Mathers, Anne, 'William of Newburgh and the Northumbrian Construction of English History', *Journal of Medieval History* 33 (2007), 339–57.

Machan, Tim W., 'Language and Society in Twelfth-Century England', in *Placing Middle English in Context*, ed. by Irma Taavitsainen et al. (Berlin: De Gruyter, 2000), pp. 43–65.

Mathers-Lawrence, Anne, 'The Augustinian Canons in Northumbria: Region, Tradition and Textuality in a Colonizing Order', in *The Regular Canons in the Medieval British Isles*, ed. by Janet E. Burton and Karen Stöber (Turnhout: Brepols, 2012), pp. 59–78.

McEwen, John, 'William FitzOsbert and the Crisis of 1196 in London', *Florilegium* 21 (2004), 18–42.

Moore, R. I., 'Heresy as Disease', in *The Concept of Heresy in the Middle Ages (11th–13th c.): Proceedings of the International Conference*, Louvain, May 13–16, 1973, ed. by W. Lourdaux and D. Verhelst (Leuven: Martinus Nijhoff, 1976), pp. 1–11.

Nederman, Cary and Catherine Campbell, 'Priests, Kings, and Tyrants: Spiritual and Temporal Power in John of Salisbury's *Policraticus*', *Speculum* 66 (1991), 572–90.

Okasha, Elisabeth, 'The Lead Cross of Bishop Godfrey of Chichester', *Sussex Archaeological Collections* 134 (1996), 63–69.

Otter, Monika, *Inventiones: Fiction and Referentiality in Twelfth-Century English Historical Writing* (Chapel Hill, NC: The University of North Carolina Press, 1996).

Palmer, Richard, 'In Bad Odour: Smell and its Significance in Medicine from Antiquity to the Seventeenth Century', in *Medicine and the Five Senses*, ed. by W. F. Bynum and Roy Porter (Cambridge: Cambridge University Press, 1993), pp. 61–68.

Partner, Nancy F., *Serious Entertainments: The Writing of History in Twelfth-Century England* (Chicago IL: University of Chicago Press, 1977).

Power, Daniel, '"La rage méchante des traîtres prit feu": le discours sur la révolte sous les rois Plantagenêt (1144–1224)', in *La trahison au moyen âge: De la monstruosité au crime politique (Ve-XVe siècle)*, ed. by Maïté Billoré and Myriam Soria (Rennes: Presses universitaires de Rennes, 2009), pp. 53–65.

Salter, H. E., 'William of Newburgh', *English Historical Review* 22 (1907), 510–14.

Sayers, William, 'The Alien and the Alienated as Unquiet Dead in the Sagas of the Icelanders', in *Monster Theory: Reading Culture*, ed. by Jeffrey J. Cohen (Minneapolis, MN: University of Minnesota Press, 1996), pp. 242–63.

Schmitt, Jean-Claude, *Ghosts in the Middle Ages*, trans. by T. L. Fagan (Chicago, IL: Chicago University Press, 1998).

Sharpe, Richard, *A Handlist of the Latin Writers of Great Britain and Ireland Before 1540*, Publications of the Journal of Medieval Latin 1 (Turnhout: Brepols, 1997).

Simpson, Jacqueline, 'Repentant Soul or Walking Corpse? Debatable Apparitions in Medieval England', *Folklore* 114 (2003), 389–402.

Spiegel, Gabrielle, *The Past as Text: The Theory and Practice of Medieval Historiography* (Baltimore, MD: Johns Hopkins University Press, 1997).

Squire, Aelred, *Aelred of Rievaulx: A Study* (London: S. P. C. K., 1969).

Stafford, Pauline, 'The Meaning of Hair in the Anglo-Norman World: Masculinity, Reform and National Identity', in *Saints, Scholars and Politicians: Gender as a Tool in Medieval Studies*, ed. by Mathilde van Dijk and Renée Nip (Turnhout: Brepols, 2005), pp. 153–71.

Struve, Tilman, 'The Importance of the Organism in the Political Theory of John of Salisbury', in *The World of John of Salisbury*, ed. by Michael Wilks, Studies in Church History, Subsidia 3 (Oxford: Blackwell, 1984), pp. 303–17.

Turner, Ralph V. and Richard R. Heiser, *The Reign of Richard Lionheart: Ruler of the Angevin Empire, 1189–1199* (Harlow: Longman, 2000).

Watkins, Carl S., *History and the Supernatural in Medieval England* (Cambridge: Cambridge University Press, 2007).

Watkins, Carl S., 'Memories of the Marvelous in the Anglo-Norman Realm', in *Medieval Memories: Men, Women and the Past, 700–1300*, ed. by Elizabeth Van Houts (Edinburgh: Pearson, 2001), pp. 92–112.

Zachrisson, R. E., 'Marylebone: Tyburn: Holborn', *Modern Language Review* 12 (1917), 146–56.

3 Satirising the undead
Walter Map and the ambiguation of wonder

Introduction

The *De nugis curialium* ('Courtiers' Trifles'), the only surviving work that can be accurately attributed to the courtier and cleric Walter Map (c.1140–1210), is a testament to its author's contemporary reputation as a raconteur, parodist and wit. Gerald of Wales (c.1146–1223), a close acquaintance of Map, remarks that his fellow Welshman was famous for his urbane speech and eloquence.[1] The poet Hugh of Rhuddlan (c.1190) insists that Map, much like himself, was a skilled proponent of 'the art of lying'.[2] Eloquence and ambiguity are certainly terms that can be applied to the contents of the *De nugis*. Contained within this seemingly ramshackle collection of anecdotes, asides and invectives is a selection of 'wonder' stories that remain as puzzling to the modern reader as they must have been to Map's own audience. It is surprising, therefore, that the prodigies described in Distinction II, chapters, 27, 28, and 30 (corpses that rose from the grave to cause consternation among the living) have not generated much in the way of academic debate, especially given the current interest in the subversive and satirical nature of Map's 'trifles' (*nugae*).[3] Likewise, previous studies into corporeal ghosts have given Map's contributions to the topic only a marginal consideration. The question of how a famed satirist, known in equal measure for his earthy invectives and dense literary allusions, approached the topic of the walking corpse has yet to be fully answered.

The aims of this chapter, then, are twofold: to analyse the ironical and satirical function of Map's 'prodigies' and discuss their relationship to the wider textual tradition of medieval revenant encounters. The belief that the dead could rise from the grave to terrorise the living was certainly not an alien concept to the local populaces of twelfth-century England. As noted in the previous chapter, William of Newburgh's *Historia rerum Anglicarum* (c.1198) includes a grudging admission that 'it would not be easy to believe that the corpses of the dead should sally (I know not by what agency) from their graves [...] did not frequent examples, occurring in our own times, suffice to establish this fact, to the truth of which there is abundant testimony'.[4] William of Malmesbury's *Gesta regum Anglorum* (c.1125) and *Gesta pontificum Anglorum* (c.1125), and Geoffrey of Burton's *Vita*

sancte Moduenne virginis (c.1144) are amongst other works that provide a tantalising glimpse into the habitual fear of restless corpses in this era.

Thus, the first part of this chapter will provide a brief overview of the traditions
of satire that influenced Map's own contributions to the genre, before analysing
the socio-cultural context in which the various fragments of the *De nugis* were
composed, with specific emphasis on the literary trope of the 'miseries of the
courtier' (*miseriae curialium*). Following an appraisal of the main discursive elements in twelfth-century accounts of the undead, the crux of the investigation will
explicate the ways in which Map deconstructed the genre tropes inherent in such
stories, inverting the expectations of the audience and opening up new, hitherto
unrealised meanings in the text. Above all, by highlighting the conceptual link
that exists between 'disordered', monstrous entities (the revenant) and disordered,
monstrous literature (satire, irony),[5] it will be demonstrated that the walking dead
were the perfect vehicle through which to critique, mock, and disassemble the
truths of life in the royal court.

Satire in twelfth century England: some considerations

According to Quintilian (d.100 AD) satire was a specifically Roman invention
(*satura quidem tota nostra est*),[6] the ultimate aim of which was the correction of
society through the mockery of vice and the ridicule of folly.[7] Isidore of Seville
(d.636) classified satire as a sub-section of comedy, noting in his *Etymologies*
that 'they [the satirists] do not refrain from describing any very wicked person, or
from censuring the wrongdoings and morals of anyone. They are pictured naked
because by them individual faults are laid bare'.[8] Irony was one of the sharpest
weapons in the satirists' arsenal. Quintilian defined the meaning of ironic statements as being 'the opposite of what is said. (*contrarium ei quod dicitur*)'.[9] Cicero
(d.43 BC) takes a more nuanced reading of the trope, suggesting instead that 'irony
too gives pleasure, when your words differ from your thoughts [...] what you
think differing contentiously from what you say'.[10] That is, irony is said to occur
when the meaning of the written or spoken text is *other than*, rather than *opposite
of*, its literal form. The sense of multiplicity, the potential for many different interpretations (or 'truths') to be read into the ironic statement, makes it the perfect
vehicle for subtle satirical invective.

The works of the foremost Roman satirists, Horace (d.8 AD), Persius (d.62 AD),
and Juvenal (d.150 AD), were widely circulated in the educational establishments
of twelfth-century Europe.[11] School curricula took advantage of the literal (to use
Isidorian terminology, the 'nude') aspects of the genre, teaching base moral les-
sons to grammarians who had yet to master an understanding of the more spirit-
ually-inclined poets.[12] Indeed, one of the two surviving manuscripts of William
of Conches's *Glosae in Iuvenalem* (c.1150), an evaluation of the moral and literary implications of the *Satires*, seems to have been based on a lecture given by
William at Chartres.[13] The *accessus* of the second extant copy of William's *Glosae*
– written, it has been suggested, by one of William's own students – revisits the
popular tradition that satire and *satyr* were etymologically connected. However,

whereas Isidore notes that the term could have derived from either saturitas (full-ness), satura (diversity), *or* the satyrs – 'who are not punished for things said in drunkenness[14] – William's student gives only one possible explanation:

> It is possible 'satire' is derived from 'satiri', that is, from peasants [who, when feasting, would] pour out abuse, chiming together in ungainly fash-ion, as harsh and rough as befits the peasantry. And these types of outburst anticipated satire, because the craftiest of farmers, those with most skill and artistry, later fashioned verse intended to reprehend.[15]

Satire, then, was seen as coarse and playful, diverse and multiple in its usage. Its primary function was to attack moral and social wrongdoings, often under the cloak of irony. A skilled satirist with a sophisticated sense of the ironic could use his words to incisive comic effect.

Twelfth century attempts at satire, based on the precedents set by Horace (gentle, witty) and Juvenal (harsh, abrasive), continued the classical tradition of criticising the iniquities of everyday life. Rodney M. Thomson detects a distinct satirical edge to William of Malmesbury's denouncements of avaricious bishops and papal intrigue in his *Gesta pontificum Anglorum*.[16] Likewise, the pervading theme of the virtue of secularity evident in Geoffrey of Monmouth's *Historia regum Britanniae* (c.1136) has been read as a subtle, satirical swipe at the increas-ing power base of the celibate clergy.[17] The anonymous 'Archpoet' (c.1130–1165), Hugh of Orléans (c.1090–1160), Johannes de Hauvilla (d.1200s) Walter of Châtillon (d.1190s), and Nigel Wireker (d.1200) are among other twelfth-century authors whose criticisms took the form of satire. Indeed, Wireker's *Speculum Stultorum*, which charts the escapades of the ass, Brunellus, is an especially well-realised example of the genre. From the flattery of merchants and the vainglorious pursuit of knowledge, to the pomposity of church edicts and the hypocrisy of the monastic orders, no secular or ecclesiastical profession is spared. The humour and whimsy of Wireker's 'Mirror of Fools' ensured its popularity for many cen-turies to come.[18] Johannes de Hauvilla's *Architrenius* (c.1184) which details the pilgrimage of the eponymous 'Archweeper' to consult the wisdom of Nature, was another satire which enjoyed circulation in the late twelfth century. Like Nigel Wireker, Johannes de Hauvilla was especially critical of the Parisian schools and the vanity and wretchedness of the 'new men' who studied therein – a theme which will be discussed in more detail in a later part of this chapter.[19]

And yet, this is not to suggest that all medieval attempts at satire had a corrective function. Ben Parsons has noted the negative connotations that could be attached to the genre. The resemblance of satire and satyr (a disruptive monster, a beast), as mentioned above, betrays something of the dangers associated with excessive 'playfulness'. Defamatory or insulting remarks may have been used for no other purpose than the art of criticism itself.[20] Irony was just as much a tool for ambigu-ating and obscuring meaning, playing with convention, as it was for the revelation of truth.[21] Menippean satire, deriving its name from the philosopher Menippus of Gadara (d.260 BC) *is* a satiric genre that, in contrast to the moralistic worldviews espoused by Juvenal and Horace, rejects the notion of an ideal truth or order in things.[22] A mixture of literary styles, 'high' and 'low' language, exaggeration, mockery, and the deconstruction of established tropes characterise the Menippean satirist. The verse-prose structure of Boethius's *De consolatione philosophiae* (c.524) has been noted to possess a mixed Menippean style.[23] Although it has been suggested that the High Middle Ages did not produce any notable examples of – in the words of Mikhail Bakhtin – 'carnivalesque' satire, Richard of Devizes's *Chronicon* (c.1192) demonstrates some explicitly Menippean qualities, especially with regard to its parodic description of Winchester's Jews, rejecting the common notion of Judaism as a foreign entity within the English realm and questioning instead the moral integrity of the Christian body-politic.[24] The manipulation of linguistic and literary forms in order to negate comprehension and subvert the expectations of the audience is something that also characterises the *De nugis curialium*.[25] As Hugh of Rhuddlan notes with none-too-disguised admiration, Walter Map was one of the greatest proponents of this *mentir l'art*.

Walter Map and the *De nugis curialium*

Biographical details on Walter Map's life and career are scarce. Much of the information that survives to the present day is taken directly from the *De nugis curialium*. According to Map, he was born in the Welsh Marches, just south of Hereford, (c.1135) and claimed Welsh descent (*'Compatriote nostri Walenses'*).[26] It is probable that he received his initial education at the Abbey of St. Peter's in Gloucester, before continuing his studies in Paris. Map also intimates that whist in Paris he was instructed by Gerard la Pucelle, the future Bishop of Coventry.[27] After completing his studies in Theology and Canon Law, he entered the service of the bishop of London, Gilbert Foliot (c.1160s), and was made a canon of St. Paul's. By the early 1170s Map had taken up a position as a clerk in Henry II's court, where he remained until accepting the chancellorship of Lincoln (c.1186) and, later, the archdeaconship of Oxford (c.1197). Map died on 1st April 1209 or 1210, having enjoyed a varied and not unsuccessful career.

As noted above, references to Map's reputation and literary output can be discerned in the writings of his contemporaries, Gerald of Wales and Hugh of Rhuddlan. Gerald, it seems, enjoyed a close relationship with Map, devoting an entire chapter of his *Speculum Ecclesiae* (c.1216) to his friend's witticisms (*facetis*) against the religious orders.[28] It was a topic that found its most fruitful literary manifestation in dist. i.24–25 of the *De nugis*.[29] Map's disdain for the hypocrisy of the Cistercians was widely known and most likely originated in a tithing dispute between Flaxley Abbey and the church of Westbury-on-Severn, Gloucestershire, which Map owned as a benefice. An *Invective* (c.1197–1210) by the subprior of St. Frideswide, Oxford, highlights the dedication with which Map pursued his grudge:

[This is] an invective of Master Bothewald, canon and subprior of the Church of St. Frideswide, against Walter Map Archdeacon of Oxford, who, both

in youth and in old age, says derisory things, in verse and prose, about the
spread of the White Monks.[30]

A quote attributed to the 'eloquent Walter Map' (*eloquio clarus, W. Mapus*) can
also be found in the dedicatory letter to King John in Gerald of Wales's *Expugnatio
Hibernica* (c. 1210):

> You, Master Gerald, have written and are still writing much, and I have spo-
> ken many things (*et nos multa diximus*). You have uttered writings and I
> words (*verba*). Your writings are far more praiseworthy and lasting that my
> words; yet because mine are easy to follow and in the vernacular, while yours
> are in Latin which is understood by fewer folk, I have carried off reasonably
> reward while you and your distinguished writings have not been adequately
> rewarded; because learned and gracious princes have long since vanished
> from the world.[31]

It has been argued that the *verba* to which Map is referring are vernacular – perhaps orally-composed – romances. The reference to speaking about 'many things'
alludes to literary interests that extend beyond romance and into the less rarefied
realms of storytelling.[32] Hugh of Rhuddlan's quip in the *Ipomedon* (c. 1180) about
Map being a master in the art of lying provides further evidence of his fame as a
weaver of fiction.[33] And yet, despite suggestions that Map composed a prose cycle
of Lancelot, the only work that can be accurately attributed to his authorship is the
De nugis curialium which, ironically, does not find any mention in the historical
record.[34] It is generally believed, however, that some of Map's *nugae*, including the diatribe against the religious orders,[35] the story of *Sadius and Galo*[36] and
the anti-marriage tract, *Dissuasio Valerii*,[37] may have circulated separately before
being collected together by a later copyist, or even Map himself. The fact that the
only extant copy of the *De nugis* survives in a single fourteenth century miscellany, MS. Bodley 851 (c. 1375–1440), hinders any attempt to ascertain how Map
intended his *nugae* to be structured. Indeed, it has even been suggested the given
title – *De nugis curialium* – was an interpolation by a later copyist.

   Although the copy of the *De nugis* from Bodley 851 seems to have been collated from a series of fragments (20 in total) and does not represent a finished
work,[38] the collection of *nugae* can be read as more than just 'an untidy legacy
of an untidy mind', the haphazard jottings of witty asides and anecdotes.[39] Most
of the fragments of the *De nugis* were composed between 1180 and 1183, during
Map's employment at the royal court. Joshua Byron Smith argues against the theory that the *De nugis* was intentionally piecemeal, theorising instead that the five
main Distinctions in fact represents a series of *separate* texts frozen in a state of
revision, inexpertly welded together during the processes of textual transmission.
For Smith, each Distinction is united by a single theme (dist. i: direct satire; dist.
ii: a treatise on miracles and wonders; dist. iii: romance; dist. iv: chapters united
by their 'exemplariness'; dist. v: imbalance between modernity and antiquity),
with Distinctions I and II and two being revisions of Distinctions IV and V.[40]

However, it should be stressed that the structural ambiguities of Bodley 851 do not detract from the 'planned waywardness', the Menippean interlacing of different modes of storytelling, that characterises Map's writing.[41] Indeed, the fluidity with which the fragments of the *De nugis* navigate between style and genre can be read as a microcosmic manifestation of a courtier's own fluid and unbound identity, a testament to Map's skills as an orator and a pointed expression of his chaotic and often vexing life as a courtier. For Map, the court's hellishness derived from its inherent mutability:

> I do know however that the court is not time; but temporal it is, changeable and various, space-bound and wandering, never continuing in one state. [The court] is constant only in its inconsistency
>
> [Scio tamen quod curia non est tempus; temporalis quidem est, mutabilis et uaria, localis et erratica, nunquam in eodem statu permanens [...] ut sola sit mobilitate stabilis][42]

According to Map, only the host of legendary King Herla – fated to roam the earth until such time a dog, a gift from a pygmy king, alighted from his horse – rivals that of Henry II's for ceaseless and maddening movement. Map wryly suggests that the lack of recent sightings of Herla is due to Henry II taking on his predecessor's mantle as the preeminent restless king.[43] Indeed, the first main 'fragment' (dist. i.1–12) does not hold back in its criticisms of the unquiet (*inquietas*) and variable (*tumultus*) nature of court life.

An exact definition of *curialis* ('courtier') as it was used by twelfth-century authors is difficult to ascertain. Ralph V. Turner notes that such men, ostensibly learned administrators, could fulfil a variety of roles for the crown: royal advisors, copyists, witnesses to charters, attachés to foreign dignitaries, justices of the peace.[44] Educated in the secular Parisian schools that Nigel Wireker and Johannes de Hauvilla found so distasteful, courtiers came from a range of social-economic backgrounds. These 'men raised from the dust', chosen for their ability and ambition rather than their birth-right, are paradigmatic examples of the increase in social mobility that was occurring in this period.[45] Flattery and obsequiousness were as valuable as administrative competency in the acquisition of social status, with royal favourites expected to gain large benefices for their service. A skilful courtier was 'all things to all men', hiding their true intentions behind a mask of affability.[46] Thus, the fluid, uncertain status of the *curialis* and the creation of a social grouping that did not correspond to the known patterns of those who worked (peasants), prayed (clergy) and fought (nobles), threatened to overhaul the established structures of secular and religious life. Nigel Wireker's tract *Contra Curiales et Officiales Clericos,* dedicated to William Longchamp on the latter's elevation to the chancellorship (1190), is demonstrative of the concern shared by conservative churchmen: that the destabilisation of social order was also a destabilisation divine order.[47] Secular commentators such as John of Salisbury tended to focus on the ways in which the behaviour of courtiers effected good and bad governance. Salisbury's influential political treatise, the *Politcraticus* (c.1159) uses the established metaphor of the body-politic to rebuke those whose pride, vanity and hypocrisy inhibited the workings of the court.[48] Herbert of Bosham's *Vita* of Thomas Becket (c.1184) meanwhile, notes that Becket engaged in 'courtiers trifles (*nugis curialibus*), empty and vain pursuits' so that he would stand out from the crowd, with the implication that vanity and moral lassitude were the means by which courtiers advanced their social status.[49] For Johannes de Hauvilla, vanity, the careful curation of surface appearance, was just another manifestation of the courter's dangerous hypocrisy:

> [For courtiers] lurking hatred wears a face of peace, and the poison / of fraud disguises itself in the thin cloak of friendship / A human countenance hides inhuman thoughts (ll. 325–27).

> [Pacis habent vultus odii secreta, venenum / Fraudis amiciciam tenui mentitur amictu / Occultit immanes animos clemencia vultus][50]

Likewise, the French poet and diplomat Peter of Blois (d.1211), whose career included employment in the courts of William II of Sicily and Henry II of England, knew from experience the deceitful ways of the *curialis*: treachery and corruption lurked at every turn, the envy of others could lead to one's own downfall.[51] An eleven stanza poetic dialogue ascribed to Peter echoes Map's sentiments in comparing the 'miseries of courtiers' (*miseriae curialium*) to a form of damnation: 'if you want to be swallowed up in the lasting torment of death and the marsh of hell, then put your trust in princes and their sons – salvation is not to be found there (ll. 68–78)'.[52]

Just as the movements and ambiguous status of the 'new men' threatened the established structures of feudal society, so the ironic, Menippean use of words subverted the semiotic structures of language. Map's dexterity with words and the inherent ironies of courtly and worldly life (that is, the dissonances between appearance and intention; the lack of stability), were each forms of ambiguation. The *De nugis curialium* expertly connects these two manifestations of monstrousness together.[53] Whatever the intended organisation of the five Distinctions, the content of the *De nugis* is appropriately mixed: wonder stories, historical narratives and observations of court life intermingle with prose romances, invectives against religious orders, and autobiographical anecdotes. Map himself acknowledges the unrefined, unstructured nature of his work, stating in a somewhat Isidorian fashion that 'I set before you a whole forest and timberyard [...] every reader must cut into shape the rough material that is here'.[54] It stands at the opposite end of the spectrum to the divine order demonstrated by the 'ideal' courtiers' manual, the *Politcraticus*; a manifestation of the untruthful, contingent world that the *curialis,* and humankind in general, actually inhabited.[55]

The playfulness displayed with regard to the mixture of genre styles extends to the makeup of the individual *nugae* themselves. Siân Echard, for example, has noted that the romance narrative, *Sadius and Galo,* manipulates the 'genre markers [in order] to unsettle an audience and encourage it to question the literary codes by which it understands and creates literary meaning'.[56] In other words, the expected tropes of chivalric literature are inverted. While the tale seems to be an ostensible riff on the 'Gawain and Bran de Lis' digression in *Perceval* (c.1181),[57] given Map's reputation, the reader is unsure whether the events depicted – the lusting of the queen after Galo, the use of a frame story, the identity swap – are to be read as parodies of known literary formulas.[58] The difficult cognitive processes involved in the explication of this 'trifle' are made even more taxing by its curious narrative details. For example, Sadius's intimation of Galo's impotence ('my Galo, who though he could extort every favour from women, confesses, to me alone, that he cannot') provokes uncertainly in readers more accustomed to the ideal of a chivalric lover.[59] These structural 'disruptions' force the creation of new, unstable discourses. From the distorted text an array of possible new meanings is created in the mind of the reader.[60] Such is the contingent nature of irony and the function of Menippean-style satire.[61]

Despite frequent attempts to categorise the *Dissuasio Valerii* as a reflection of Map's misogynistic attitudes towards women,[62] a critical reading of the text reveals that it too operates in a way that undermines its literal form. Ralph Hanna and Warren Smith speculate that Map's highly rhetorical language and refusal to authorise the text – hence leading it to be ascribed a classical provenance – was a satire on the contemporary preoccupation with the 'authority' of the ancients.[63] Map tacitly admits his intentions in dist. iv. 5: 'I changed our names for those of dead men in the title, for I knew that it would be popular: had I not done so, my book, like myself, would have been thrown aside'.[64] The 'hoax' proved successful; the *Dissuasio* (c.1177) was 'greedily seized upon, eagerly copied, and read with vast amusement',[65] as the 131 surviving manuscript copies testify. Indeed, Peter of Blois's own attempts at an anti-marriage satire (Epistle 79) seems to have been especially influenced by the *Dissuasio*. By removing key textual markers such as the name of the author – one of the main trees in the 'timberyard' – what may ostensibly seem like an attack on women can also be read as an attack on the tastes (or lack thereof) of Map's audience and a commentary on the precarious nature of 'active' reading. Its antifeminism is a cypher that should not be taken at face value.

Likewise, the mistakes in the *De nugis's* historical narratives can be seen less as the work of an unskilled scholar and more another attempt at textual 'knotting' or disruption. For someone whose learning and competency led to him being a royal representative at the Third Lateran Council,[66] Map's versions of the histories of Byzantium, France, and Britain are conspicuous by their inaccuracy.[67] The account of 'Andronius, Emperor of Constantinople', for example, rewrites the Byzantine family dynasty,[68] while the creation of the New Forest is erroneously credited to William II ('which he had himself taken away from God and men to devote it to beasts and sport with hounds').[69] Further dissonances can be discerned in the inclusion of historically-incorrect information from a *chanson de geste* on the life of Louis the Pius.[70] The boundary between fact and fiction, truth and untruth, are altogether blurred, making the task of reading these *nugae* an incredibly – and intentionally – difficult process.

As *Sadius and Galo* and the *Dissuasio* force a re-evaluation of the known 'truths' about romances and the concept of authorship, and the historical narratives subvert the formulas of chronicle writing, so the revenant narratives in Distinction II can be read as a play on the conventions of 'wonder' stories. 'Wonders' form an integral part of the *De nugis curialium*. The most famous narrative concerns the 'eternal wanderings' (*infinito circuitus*) of the ancient British king, Herla.[71] Other notable *nugae* include a talking severed head, the capture of fairy women, dances of the dead, and an encounter with a centaur. It is notable, however, that the rubric *prodigio* ('monster', 'portent') is used only with regard to the tales of ambulatory corpses, with 'apparitions' (*aparicionibus*) and 'wonder' (*mirabile*) being used to describe the other types of unusual entity. Although, as Joshua Byron Smith notes,[72] the rubrics are likely to be marginal notes mistakenly interpolated into the text by a later scribe, the monstrous and *meaningful* nature of the walking dead has nonetheless been highlighted by making them semantically – and codicologically – distinct from the wider collection of marvels. Before an examination of the revenant stories in the *De nugis* can commence, it would be prudent to first reiterate the literary tradition of wonders as understood by a twelfth-century audience.

'Moral' revenants in twelfth-century literature

To building upon the points made in the previous two chapters, 'wonder' is a general term for an event which was beyond the ability of the human mind to truly comprehend. *Miracula* (the suspension of the natural order through the will of God) can be differentiated from *mirabilia* (occurrences that may not have been divinely wrought, but which were 'marvellous' because they had a *reason* that could not yet be understood. One of the main goals of *admiratio* (wonder) was to explicate the ambiguity of the marvel and arrive at a true, moral reading. However, it was also accepted that a 'wonder' may be so strange and horrifying that its true meaning may never be discovered.[73] Nonetheless, if, according to cosmological theory, the order of the universe (God) could be detected in all its manifest forms, then disordered beings, such as monsters, may be reflective of social, environmental, and/or political uncertainties – deviance from the divine norm.[74] As such, medieval historiographers and hagiographers often stressed the truthfulness of such narratives, intimating that they were no mere fables, but portents, warnings to posterity, that had actually occurred and which had the potential to signify other deviations in the body-politic. Gerald of Wales invited the readers of the *Topographia Hibernica* (c.1188) to make a connection between the proliferation of monsters in Ireland and the godlessness and marginality of the island's inhabitants.[75] In a similar way, the marvellous events described in Gervase of Tillbury's *Otia Imperialia* (c.1214) were not only collated for entertainment purposes, but also provided moral edification for the book's patron, the Holy Roman Emperor Otto IV. Where the didactic quality of the exemplum is obscure, Gervase furnishes Otto with his own interpretation.[76] Thus, it was the role of the reader to evaluate the moral and/or spiritual truths that underlay the supposed literal (historical) event. The meaning of the text was sometimes other than its literal form. In some respects, monsters were inherently and ontologically ironic.

Examples of a particular type of prodigy, the ambulatory corpse, may not be as representative in the extant literary corpus as fairy wives or monstrous births, but the extant evidence reveals quite a lot of 'cultural facts' about the pervasive belief in the walking dead in post-Conquest England. Hagiographies are a prime source of evidence in this regard. As noted briefly in chapter one, Goscelin of Saint-Bertin's revision of the *De miraculis sancti Edmundi* (c.1090) describes how the corpse of a local sheriff, Leofstan, was deposited in a swamp to stop him troubling (*inquietare*) the local community in death just as he had done so in life.[77] Likewise, the *Vita et Miracula S. Kenelmi* (c.1070s) reveals the sinfulness of the saint's sister, Cweonthryth, through the revelation that her body 'could not stay buried in either the church or the forecourt nor in the cemetery, but that a brilliantly shining child appeared before a certain man, and gave instructions that she should be thrown into some remote gully'.[78]

The traditional function of wonders in hagiographical writing was to extol the miraculous nature of the saint and provide a warning for the fate of those who sinned against the patron church. Indeed, not only was Leofstan a cruel and wicked man, but, crucially, he also failed to show due reverence to St. Edmund. Geoffrey of Burton's own revenant story – pointedly inserted between chapters on St. Modwenna's role in the miraculous release of bonds from the bodies of penitents (ch. 46) and the healing of the infirm (ch. 48) – is similarly structured around the dangers of provoking the ire of the holy dead. Setting the scene with a note on the punishment meted out to a royal official, Ælfwine of Hopwas, who was compelled to gouge out his own eye after defaming Modwenna's cult, Geoffrey recalls how, c.1090, two peasants from Stapenhill village renounced their fealty to Burton Abbey, Modwenna's resting place, and entered the service of the secular lord Roger de Poitevin in nearby Drakelow. Angry at the betrayal, Abbot Geoffrey Malaterra petitioned Modwenna for help. Divine justice was immediate. The peasants were 'suddenly struck down dead' and duly buried in Stapenhill cemetery.[79] However, that very evening their corpses rose out of their graves and trod the same path to Drakelow as they had taken in life, carrying their coffins on their backs. The following night they took to knocking on doors and calling out to their victims, shouting '*Promouete, citius promouete! Agite, agite et uenite!*' (Move, quickly, move! Get going! Come!). Soon after, all but three of the villagers succumbed to a plague. To contain the epidemic, the peasants' corpses were exhumed, decapitated, and their heads placed between their legs, after which their hearts were removed and burnt to ash. Indeed, 'when [their hearts] had been burnt up, they cracked with a great sound and everyone there saw an evil spirit in the form of a crow fly from the flames'.[80] Only then, and with Roger healing the schism by issuing a humble apology to the abbot for meddling in church affairs, did the revenant sightings cease.

The *Gesta regum Anglorum* (c.1125) is notable for William of Malmesbury's equivocal attitude to the subject of restless corpses. Not only does he dismiss the idea that the ghost of King Alfred returned to his body each night – deeming it 'nonsense' (*nenias*) – he reserves particular scorn for those who claimed that 'the corpse of a criminal after death is possessed by a demon and walks'.[81] And yet, the sense of incredulity that can be read in the critique of Alfred's wanderings does not extend to the description of the vital corpse of the Witch of Berkeley. Questioning the post-mortem agency of the witch served no rhetorical purpose. Nor does William's disdain about the folk belief in Alfred's ghost prevent him from mentioning, without critical comment, the tradition surrounding the death of a former bishop of Malmesbury, Brihtwold (d.1010s) in the *Gesta pontificum Anglorum* (c.1125). Brihtwold, it seems, died during a drinking bout. William notes that strange ghostly shapes began tormenting the wardens of the churchyard where the bishop was buried, until Brihtwold's body was exhumed and reburied in marshland some distance from the monastery, whereupon a toxic stench emerged from the bog and spread over the surrounding countryside.[82] To William, the circumstance surrounding Brihtwold's death were an 'unpleasant' (*injocundus*) topic of discussion, useful only as a point of contrast for the following chapter's description of the miracles that occurred at the tomb of another former bishop of Malmesbury, Aldhelm (d.709).

William of Newburgh's *Historia rerum Anglicarum* (c.1198) is of course the most detailed extant source where the twelfth-century belief in the walking dead is concerned. Out of the four narratives included in book five, three involve the cremation of the troublesome corpse (Berwick, Melrose, 'Anant'), while the other concludes with the deceased being granted absolution (Buckinghamshire). As noted previously, William's narratives seem to focus on the disease and destruction wrought by the violent, pestilential dead. Considering that they were pointedly inserted between an account of the London rebellion of William FitzOsbert ('Longbeard') (V.21) and the resumption of warfare between England and France (V.25), whilst anticipating the death of the hated Chancellor of England, William Longchamp (V.29), it has been argued they were employed as inverted framing devices, structural markers, to criticise warmongers and social malcontents. FitzOsbert, Longchamp, and the royal courts were acting like revenants in that they too were destabilising the body-politic through their wild and destructive movements. Indeed, by calling FitzOsbert a 'pestilence and killer' (*pestilentis et homicidae*),[83] William is forcing the audience to make an implicit connection between the rebellious Londoners and the 'contagious motions' (*pestilenti motu*) of the wandering corpse.[84] The codicological placement of *mirabilia* was just as critical for the formation of a 'correct' moral reading as the structure of the narratives themselves.

Although most English tales of the undead ostensibly derived from oral sources – a truth William of Newburgh was especially keen to impart – they were nonetheless constrained by literary and moralistic convention: (a) living and dying in a manner that contradicted the prevailing social norms of the community condemned the sinner's corpse to walk after death; (b) the monstrous and destabilising nature of the revenant was made manifest through corrupted air and pestilential vapours; (c) only a dramatic method of assuagement could contain the corpse and bring order to the world once more. Ultimately, the gross physicality of the revenant signified something about its own metaphysical state or the metaphysical state of others. As suggested above, the moralising impetus attached to *mirabilia* invited the reader to look beyond the narrative's literal form and, having been directed by their own habitual knowledge and the story's manuscript context, arrive at the 'true', intended reading. The pestilence (and sin) of Brihtwold's corpse is physically and metaphysically opposed to curative properties attached to Aldhelm's; the afterlife of Drakelow peasants is all the more terrifying due to the story's insertion between accounts of Modwenna's benevolence towards the sick and penitent. For a master of the art of lying, revenant stories provided an ideal platform through which to ambiguate meanings (create falsehood; 'lie') and parody the tropes of historiographic and hagiographic writing. If an analogy can indeed be made between monstrous, ambiguous words (irony) and monstrous, ambiguous bodies (*prodigium;* the *curialis*) then the revenant, as a signifier of *something other* and an entity trapped between life and death, is the perfect tool for satire. It is the very manifestation of the breakdown of socio-linguistic order.[85]

'Amoral' revenants: an ironic subversion of genre

The *De nugis curialium* records three encounters with the walking dead. Located at the end of Distinction II, following an appraisal of the manners, folklore and history of the Welsh (dist. ii.20–26), the first revenant narrative details, somewhat appropriately, the problems caused by the corpse of an irreligious Welshman.

> I know of a strange portent [*prodigium*] that occurred in Wales. William Laudun, an English Knight, strong of body and of proved valour came to Gilbert Foliot, then bishop of Hereford [1148–63], now of London, and said: 'My Lord, I come to you for advice. A Welshman of evil life died of late unchristianly enough in my village, and straightaway after four nights took to coming back every night to the village, and will not desist from summoning singly and by name his fellow villagers, who upon being called at once fall sick and die within three days, so that now there are very few of them left'. The bishop, marvelling, said: 'Peradventure the Lord has given power to the evil angel of that lost soul to move about in the dead corpse. However, let the body be exhumed, cut the next through with a spade, and sprinkle the body and the grave well with holy water, and replace it'. When this was done, the survivors were none the less plagued by the former illusion. So, one night when the summoner had now left but few alive, he called William himself, citing him thrice. He, however, bold and quick as he was, and awake to the situation, darted out with his sword drawn, and chases the demon, who fled, up to the grave, and there, as he fell into it, clave his head to the neck. From that hour the ravages of the wandering pestilence ceased, and did no more hurt either to William himself or to anyone else. The true facts of his death I know, but not the explanation [cause].[86]

Map does not dwell on the implications of the Welshmen's return, for he immediately recounts the story of the Bishop of Worcester's inability to quell a revenant that had been trapped in an orchard:

> I know too that in the time of Roger, Bishop of Worcester [1164–79], a man, reported to have died unchristianly, for a month or more wandered about in his shroud both at night and also in open day, till the whole population of the neighbourhood laid siege to him in an orchard, and there he remained exposed to view, it is said, for three days. I know further that this Roger ordered a cross to be laid upon the grave of the wretch, and the man himself to be let go. When, followed by the people, he came to the grave, he started back, apparently at sight of the cross, and ran in another direction. Whereupon they wisely removed the cross: he sank into the grave, the earth closed over him, the cross was laid upon it and he remained quiet.[87]

Map punctuates the second and third revenant narratives with an extract from Turpin of Reims's 'Gests of Charlemagne' concerning a knight from the Frankish king's army who, on his deathbed, asked a cleric to distribute all his worldly goods to the poor. Although the cleric nominally agreed to his friend's request, he was reluctant to part with the knight's warhorse. After being visited three times by the knight's spirit in his sleep, imploring him to bequeath the horse to the needy, the cleric was still unprepared to give up his prize. Finally, the knight's ghost appeared (*aparuit*) whilst the cleric was awake and condemned his former friend to be carried off into the air by demons (*demonibus rapieris in aera*). Despite the best efforts of Charlemagne and his retinue, the doomed *clericus* was duly snatched away by a band of howling spirits. His broken body was found four days later, dashed against some nearby rocks.[88]

Following this, the next 'trifle' details the plight of a northern nobleman who confronted the corpse of his late father:

> A knight of Northumberland was seated alone in his house after dinner in summer about the tenth hour, and lo, his father, who had died long before, approached him clad in a foul burial shroud. He thought the appearance was the devil and drove it back from the threshold, but his father said: 'Dearest son, fear not. I am your father and I bring you no ill; but call the priest and you shall learn the reason for my coming.' He was summoned, and a crowd ran to the spot; when falling at his feet the ghost said: 'I am that wretch whom long since you excommunicated unnamed, with many more, for unrighteous withholding of tithes; but the common prayers of the church and the alms of the faithful by God's grace so helped me that I was permitted to ask for absolution.' So being absolved he went, with a great train of people following, to his grave and sank into it, and closed it over him of his own accord. This new case has introduced a new subject of discussion into the book of divinity.[89]

Distinction II culminates with a seemingly-unfinished story about a seneschal of France, and a warning by Map that it is up to the reader to provide meaning to 'what has gone before'.[90] Although a cursory reading would suggest that the revenant narratives contain the same tropes and conventions as other stories of this type, a closer examination reveals quite a few 'disruptions' in the text.

With regards to the first tale, the descriptions of the revenant's 'evil life' *(maleficus)* and method of assuagement are remarkably orthodox, recalling the fate of the Drakelow peasants in the *Vita sancte Moduenne virginis* and the cuckolded husband in the *Historia rerum Anglicarum's* 'Anantis' narrative. It does not surprise the reader that the Welshman's sinful, unfortified body was open to abuse and ambulation by the devil. If a moral causation could be ascribed to the contagion, then Map's suggestion that the village had been almost completely depleted by the 'wandering pestilence' *(pestis erratice)* is telling. In keeping with contemporary medical and theological discourse, Map may be intimating that the pestilence given off by the revenant could only affect those who were already predisposed to be affected, those who were already weak of faith, 'open', or corrupt in some way. With the depravity of the Welsh being a commonplace trope in twelfth-century chronicles and *vitae*, Map's decision to augment dist. ii.20, 23, and 26 with allusions to the barbarousness of his 'compatriots' invites an orthodox explication of dist. ii.27. John of Salisbury,[91] Theobald of Bec (d.1161), William of Newburgh (d.1198),[92] and Hubert Walter (d.1205),[93] are among the twelfth-century churchmen whose literary outputs included criticisms of the mores of the Welsh. Bec's observation that 'the people of the country are rude and untamed; they live like beasts and despise the word of life, and though they nominally profess Christ, they deny him in their life and ways' is an example of a *topos* that also permeates the *De nugis*.[94] 'See how foolish and unreasonable is the wrath of these Welsh and how swift they are to shed blood', Map pointedly tells his audience in the final sentence of dist. ii.26.[95]

As suggested above, the codicological placement of 'wonder' stories played an important role in the explication of their moral truth. As the tale of King Herla was intended to illuminate the hellish nature of Henry II's court in *De nugis* in Distinction I, so the damned, pestilential status of the Welsh revenant structured the readers' interpretation of its kinsmen in dist. ii.20–26. In both cases *mirabilia* are being enlisted for the criticism of vice. And yet, as intimated in dist. ii.32 ('I set before you a whole forest and timberyard'), Map may have intentionally obscured the meaning of this 'trifle', the truth(s) of which had to be actively pieced together by his audience.[96] Given the sense of ambiguity and multiplicity that pervades the *De nugis*, the Menippean urge to break down order, the narrative may also have been intended as a parody of such a conventional reading: a satire on a satire.

The Welsh, considered by the Anglo-Norman elite as being a liminal race on the very bounds of the civilised world, were the source of much consternation to the crown in the late twelfth century.[97] A village that was located in the Marches was considered susceptible to all manner of deviant, indigenous influence.[98] It is certainly no coincidence that William Laudun, a knight of 'proven valour' (*audacie probate*) who ultimately answered to the crown, was one of the few people who was able to resist the Welshman's call.[99] As a courtier in Henry II's court during the king's more turbulent suppressions of the native Britons, Map may have been allegorising events he himself had witnessed or, perhaps, was parodying court fears about perfidious Welshmen in times of ostensible non-aggression.[100] Either way, the failure of Gilbert Foliot's advice subverts and ironises the belief that the church could mediate between the two nations. The Archbishop of Canterbury, Hubert Walter, made just such a claim in his declaration that the authority of his See was the only thing keeping the Welsh hordes in check.[101] Map's manipulation of genre tropes forces the reader to accept the (untruthful?) possibility that the sickness and sinfulness of the Welsh – or, more widely, those who conspired against the interests of the sovereign realm – could only be stopped via the sword. Indeed, court fears that the semi-autonomous Marcher Lords would make truces with the enemy and circumscribe royal authority shows how pervasive this sickness could be.[102] Loyal servants of the realm, like William Laudun, were able to resist the overtures of the Welsh. The fact that Map himself came from the Herefordshire Marches and was in the service of the crown lends another level of irony – a self-critical edge – to the 'trifle'. Vexed by the hellish nature of the court and the monstrosity of those who worked there (including, perhaps, himself), Map may be making a grim joke in describing how 'Laudun' cleaved the head of the revenant, the proxy *curialis*, in two. Read in this way, Map's referral to the revenant as a 'prodigy' (*prodigium*), an entity with a single moral or spiritual meaning, can ultimately be rejected as a lie, a truth deconstructed. Guided by the careful rearrangement of genre codes, the audience is given the opportunity to disassociate themselves from a conventional reading of the narrative (that is, as a moralistic attack on the depravity of the Welsh). Not only was a revenant encounter the perfect vehicle for satirising the political and social tensions occurring in the borderlands and the royal court at this time but, in the hands of a master of the art of lying, a purveyor of untruth, it could also be used to parody one of the main features of historiographic writing: the *mirabilia*-as-portent.

Criticisms of poor practice, the conventions of history writing, court paranoia, and the author's own cultural identity are all equally valid readings. References to 'unchristian Welshmen' (*maleficus Walensis*), 'pestilence' (*pestis*) and 'evil angels' (*angelo* [...] *malo*) provide a vague schema for the passage's interpretation. The ambiguities of the story – 'the true facts of his death I know, but not the explanation'[103] – encourages the reader to find his or her own explanation. As Map himself states, again using the metaphor of the cultural re-fashioning of unrealised natural matter, 'I bring you the game, it is for you to make dainty dishes of it' (*Venetor uester sum: fera uobis affero, fercula faciatis*).[104]

The inability of William Laudun to assuage the revenant using the advice given by the Bishop of Hereford would have undoubtedly confounded the expectations of the reader. Spiritual matters were, after all, the purview of the church. Dist. ii.28 maintains a connection to the preceding chapter through a similar vein of anti-authoritarian satire. As Gilbert Foliot's advice did nothing to prevent the Welshman's corpse from spreading its pestilence, so the initial actions of the

Bishop of Worcester also resulted in failure. Repelled by the cross that was placed in the empty grave, the corpse, seemingly inhabited by an 'evil angel', ran off in a different direction. Roger's loyalty to Thomas Becket during the latter's quarrel with Henry II may account for the bishop's struggle to quell the revenant: a gentle rebuke of his role in the schism between church and state.[105] Further disruptions can be discerned in the agency of the revenant itself. Instead of causing terror and consternation to the townsfolk, it is treated as nothing more than a figure of curiosity. A playful, almost comic mood pervades this *nugae*: whereas literary convention dictates that the revenant be 'bound', decapitated, or put to flame, the Worcester prodigy is merely trapped in an orchard before being chased back to its grave. As the *mirabilia* from the *Vita sancte Moduenne virginis* and the *Historia rerum Anglicarm* attest, this is the opposite of how 'conventional' revenants should behave. Indeed, Geoffrey of Burton describes how 'men were living in terror of the phantom dead men' and their lethal scourge.[106] William of Newburgh's 'Ghost of Anant' narrative is even more explicit on the threat posed by the undead: 'the atmosphere, poisoned by the vagaries of this foul carcass, filled every house with disease and death by its pestiferous breath [...] those of its inhabitants who had escaped destruction migrated to other parts of the country, lest they too should die'.[107] Death, disease, and destruction do not seem to follow the Worcester revenant, nor do the townsfolk show much fear about having a walking corpse in their midst. Whereas the diseased corpses from Drakelow are dismembered and cremated, Sheriff Leofstan and Bishop Brihtwold are thrown into unconsecrated ground, and the irreligious Welshmen from dist. ii.27 has its head cleaved in two, no such action is taken against the Worcester revenant. The narrative codes have been disrupted.

The structure and content of the third revenant narrative, however, seems to take its thematic cues from the preceding story, dist. ii.29. Both concern the return of the named dead (the former incorporeal, the latter corporeal) who plead with the percipient to undertake a task on their behalf, and detail the terrible fates of those who covet wealth. The unorthodox revelation that the corpse of the knight's father was 'permitted [by God] to ask for absolution' (*liceat absolucionem petere*) would have been very much apparent to Map's audience. The conception of Purgatory, a 'third place' between life and death was, at the end of the twelfth-century, only just gaining wider theological acceptance. As noted by Robert Easting, the earliest usage of the noun *purgatorium*, a *place* of fire where venial sins were punished before the soul ascended to heaven, can be traced back to the 1150s.[108] Although belief in a 'third place' and the possibility that the dead could ask for suffrage had been a part of the Christian worldview since the time of Gregory the Great (d.604),[109] the doctrine only began to cohere during the twelfth-century reform of the church and the popularisation of the Benedictine funeral liturgy (specifically, the ritual efficacy of praying for the dead). Peter the Venerable's *De Miraculis* (c.1135–1149), written in part to defend Cluny Abbey's doctrinal standpoint that suffrage can indeed save souls,[110] contains numerous examples of ghostly visitations, not all of them agreeing upon where, exactly, purgatorial punishments took place. Peter's exemplum concerning the (disembodied) ghost of a Spanish servant, Sancho, persists with the notion, popularised by Gregory, that such spirits endured their punishments on earth, 'in the place [they] committed' (*ubi deliqui-mus*) their sins[111]. Compare this story with Peter's account of the apparition of the secular magnate, Bernard le Gros who, somewhat ambiguously, was 'allowed to come back' (*venire permissus*) to ask for forgiveness for his economic transgressions against Cluny.[112] By contrast, a dialogue between a clerk and the 'spirit' (*spiritus*) of a girl written in a twelfth-century hand and included in Lambeth Palace MS 1213 (c.1300), consolidates the idea that purgatory is a distinct place of torment, from which the spirits of the deceased could return to earth to ask for prayer.[113] This new subject of discussion (to use Map's phraseology) further ambiguated the identity of the walking corpse which, for educated churchmen at least, had hitherto been read as a demon-in-disguise.[114]

De nugis dist. ii.30 contains further Menippean qualities. The revelation that the Knight's father was excommunicated for withholding tithes invites the reader to associate the corpse's damned state with the activities of Map's most hated of adversaries, the Cistercians. Among the main criticisms aimed at the White Monks was their hypocrisy.[115] The *Incidencia de monachia* (dist. i.25), a digression on monasticism that circulated as a separate text before its inclusion in the *De nugis* (and which may have been the 'derisory' prose work alluded to by subprior Bothewald), is an unambiguous riposte to the Cistercians' desire for economic domination: 'They have their hands open to the poor, but very little open', proclaims Map, who also admonishes their compulsion to 'seize and declare [lands] to be their own property' and 'take away tithes'. The razing of villages and the condemnation of their former inhabitants to a life of suffering and destitution is an ironic reflection of the Cistercians' own desire to live in exile.[116] The socially-disruptive tendencies of the White Monks were a particularly resonant subject for Map, who uses the derogatory term 'Hebrews' throughout the *Incidencia de monachia* to highlight the dissonance between the Cistercians' ostensible vow of poverty and the inner, rapacious truth – that is, to be all surface and no substance.[117] A non-linear reading of the *De nugis* enjoins the audience to make a connection between the iniquities described in dist. i.24–25 and the covetousness that condemned the Knight's father in dist. ii.30. On one level of irony, then, this final 'trifle' would seem to operate as a part of Map's ongoing satire against the Cistercians, a wry appropriation of the language of theological innovation for the continuation of his lifelong feud. Monstrousness and ontological instability permeate the figures of the White Monk and the revenant.[118] The overt orthodox reading, the efficacy of post-mortem prayer for the salvation of the soul, has again been disrupted.

In a similar manner to how Map structured *Sadius* and *Galo,* the *Dissuasio*, and the above-mentioned historical narratives, Distinction II's walking corpse *nugae* are conventional enough to seduce the expectations of the reader. On a surface level they operate according to the expected norms of a wonder story. Unchristian activity led to the reanimation of the sinner's body; apotropaic strategies were needed to assuage the troublesome dead. However, mindful of the admonition that these tales are mere 'timber', raw material, to be cultivated how the reader saw fit,[119] a closer analysis of the texts reveals the ways in which Map, toying with his audience, adds extra 'trees' to the expected narrative formulae. The unchristian Welshman from dist. ii.27 can be inscribed with multiple – and not always moral – meanings. Excesses of ambiguity and irony can also be read in the following chapter, dist. ii.28, which destabilises the stereotype of the undead corpse as an entity that invokes panic and fear. The revelation that the corpse of the knight's father in dist. ii.30 was, in fact, permitted to ask for suffrage, is a narratological element that completely destabilises how the restless corpse should be read, impacting on the reader's initial interpretation of the agency of the Marcher and Worcester revenants. The extract from the 'Gests of Charlemagne' – that is to say, chapter seven of the *Historia Karoli Magni et Rotholandi* by Pseudo-Turpin (c.1110)[120] – is used as a structuring device in this regard. On a further discursive level, the reference to the squandering of alms in dist. ii.29 and the withholding of tithes in dist. ii.30 provokes an association, however subtle, between the fate of Charlemagne's cleric, the damned state of the Northumberland corpse, and the covetous activities of the Cistercians. Above all, the metaphysical connection between the monstrous corpse and the monstrous 'new man' is the principle that binds the tales of the undead to the rest of Map's oeuvre, especially the anti-court satires of Distinction I. The audience, then, is lost in a cognitive maze of possible moral (corrective) and amoral (Menippean, relativist) readings. 'Mixedness' is a theme that permeates the *De nugis curialium* as a whole.

Conclusion

The aim of this chapter, then, has been to examine the relationship between the medieval conception of irony and the tales of the walking dead in the *De nugis curialium*. As a clerk educated in the secular Parisian schools, Map was well-versed in the conventions of classical satire, whether it be the corrective, 'nude' writings of Horace and Juvenal or the more destabilising elements of the Menippean School. According to Map, the court was hell incarnate, its wanderings mirroring that of the phantom king, Herla. A courtier's life could never correspond to the ideals taught by the *Policraticus*. The intrigues of court were as vexing and chaotic as the movements of a walking corpse. Map, I contend, uses the trope of the revenant encounter to satirise the reality of court life and, on a deeper level, the literary function of ambiguity itself.[121] Walking corpses (and monsters in general) are the ultimate irony: their potential to signify anything meant that they could also signify nothing.[122] The reversals and double-meanings present in Map's *nugae* parody the idea of sinfulness/disorder that the corpse's literal form – its rotten, diseased body – symbolised in the historiographic tradition. A singular, moral reading becomes unattainable; multiple, contingent readings are instead taken from the text. Indeed, the overarching themes of fluidity, mixture, and the dissonance between 'outer' and 'inner' can be readily discerned in Map's descriptions of the *prodigium*: the revenant was at once a 'demon-in-disguise' (dist. ii.27), a pitiable figure of mockery (dist. ii.28), and a vessel for a purgatorial spirit (dist. ii.30). The inclusion of an extract pertaining to the dangers of *disembodied* ghosts (dist. ii.29) further destabilises the ontology of the restless dead. The motivations of revenants, courtiers, and the White Monks were *something other* than their literal form. In sum, the unstable, disruptive identity of the walking corpse made it conceptually similar to the hypocritical Cistercians and the monstrous 'new men'. These are the focus of Map's (if not the active reader's) ironical concern.[123]

Although unfinished at the time of Walter Map's death, the *De nugis curialium* represents an insight into one of the most idiosyncratic minds of the late twelfth century. His appropriation of the trope of the walking dead shows that he was adept at deconstructing the conventions of wonder stories as he was romance (*Sadius and Galo*), misogyny (the *Dissuasio*) and monastic foundation texts (the 'origin' of the Cistercians in dist. i.24). Whether to amuse or critique, slander or praise, the *De nugis* can be read as more than just an 'untidy legacy of an untidy mind'.[124] The 'artfully-unstructured legacy of an incisive mind' would be much more exact.

Notes

A version of this chapter was published previously as: Stephen Gordon, 'Monstrous Words, Monstrous Bodies: Irony and the Walking Dead in Walter Map's *De Nugis Curialium*', *English Studies* 96 (2015), 379–402. Reproduced by permission of Taylor & Francis Ltd. http://www.tandfonline.com

1 Gerald of Wales, 'Dedicatory Letter to King John', *Expugnatio Hibernica* [hereafter GW, *EH*], ed. and trans. by A. B. Scott and F. X. Martin (Dublin: Royal Irish Academy 1978), p. 264. (ll.154–56).

2 Hugh of Rhuddlan notes in his Anglo-Norman romance, the *Ipomedon (*c.1180s), that 'sul ne sais pas de mentir l'art, / Walter Map reset ben sa part' (I am not the only one who knows the art of lying; Walter Map also knows well his share of it [ll. 7183−84]). Translation from Neil Cartlidge, 'Masters in the Art of Lying? The Literary Relationship between Hugh of Rhuddian and Walter Map', *The Modern Language Review*, 106 (2011), 1–16 (at. p.1).

3 English-language scholarship on the *De Nugis Curialium* has seen an upturn in recent years. See, in the first instance, Joshua Bryon Smith, *Walter Map and the Matter of Britain* (Philadelphia, PA: University of Pennsylvania Press, 2017). See also Robert Levine, 'How to Read Walter Map,' *Mittellateinisches Jahrbuch*, 23 (1988), 91–105; Siân Echard, 'Map's Metafiction: Author, Narrative and Reader in De Nugis Curialium,' *Exemplaria*, 8 (1996), 287–314; Otter, *Inventiones*, pp. 93–128; R. R. Edwards, 'Walter Map: Authorship and the Space of Writing,' *New Literary History*, 38 (2007), 273–92.

4 Newburgh, V. 24 (p. 477).

5 Ben Parsons, '"A Riotous Spray of Words": Rethinking the Medieval Theory of Satire', *Exemplaria* 21 (2009), 105−28 (at p. 116).

6 Quintilian, *The Orator's Education: Books 9–10,* ed. and trans. by Donald A. Russell, Loeb Classical Library 127 (Cambridge, MA: Harvard University Press, 2001), 10. 1. 93 (at pp. 302–03).

7 Ronald E Pepin, *Literature of Satire in the Twelfth Century: A Neglected Mediaeval Genre* (Lampeter: Edwin Mellen Press, 1988), p. 2.

8 'nec vitabatur eis pessimum quemque describere, nec cuilibet peccata moresque reprehendere. Vnde et nudi pinguntur, eo quod per eos vitia singula denudentur', Isidore of Seville, *Etymologies*, VIII.vii. 7.

9   Quintilian, 9. 2. 44 (at pp. 58–59).

10 'Urbana etiam dissimulatio est, cum alia dicuntur ac sentias [...] cum aliter sentias ac loquare', in Cicero, *De Oratore: Books 1–2*, ed. and trans. by E. W. Sutton and H. Rackham, Loeb Classical Library 348 (Cambridge, MA: Harvard University Press, 1942), II. lxvii.269 (at pp. 402–03).

11 For an overview of the (re)emergence of satire in the twelfth-century, see Rodney M. Thomson, 'The Origins of Latin Satire in Twelfth-Century Europe', *Mittellateinisches Jarhbuch* 13 (1978), 73–83.

12 Vincent Gillespie, 'From the Twelfth-Century to c.14500, in *Cambridge History of Literary Criticism. Vol. 2: The Middle Ages*, ed. by Alastair Minnis and Ian Johnson (Cambridge: Cambridge University Press, 2005), pp. 145–235 (at pp. 223–34).

13 William of Conches, *Glosae in Iuvenalem*, ed. by Bradford L. Wilson (Paris: J. Vrin, 1980), p. 28.

14 'qui inulta habent ea quae per vinolentiam dicuntur', Isidore of Seville, *Etymologies of Isidore of Seville*, VIII.vii. 9.

15 'Potest et satira dici a satiris, id est ab agrestibus dicta est [...] fundebant convicia non bene consona pro discretione rusticana. Et huius modi convicia predicta sunt satire, id est agregestes callidores autem in artem redigerunt et metrice ceperunt reprehendere.' Cited in Parsons, 'A Riotous Spray of Words', p. 110.

16 Thomson, 'Satire, Irony, and Humour in William of Malmesbury', p.117.

17 Valerie I. J., Flint, 'The *Historia Regum Brittanniae* of Geoffrey of Monmouth: Parody and its Purpose. A Suggestion', *Speculum* 54 (1979), 447–68 (at p. 467).

18 Nigel de Longchamps [Wireker], *Speculum Stultorum*, ed. by John H. Mozley and Robert R. Raymo (Berkeley, CA: Univ. of California Press, 1960). For an analysis, see Pepin, *Literature of Satire in the Twelfth Century*, pp. 117–57.

19 Ralph V. Turner, 'Toward a Definition of the Curialis: Educated Court Cleric, Courtier, Administrator, or 'New Man'?', *Medieval Prosopography* 15 (1994), 3–35.

20 Parsons, 'A Riotous Spray of Words', pp. 115. 124.

21 For irony as an 'unstable', contingent text, see Linda Hutcheon, *Irony's Edge: The Theory and Politics of Irony* (London: Routledge, 1994), p. 33.

22 For Mikhail Bakhtin's discussion of carnivalesque/Menippean literature, see *Problems of Dostoevsky's Poetics*, ed and trans. by Caryl Emerson (Manchester: Manchester University Press, 1984), pp. 112–23.

23 W. Scott Blanchard, *Scholars' Bedlam: Menippean Satire in the Renaissance* (Lewisburg, PA: Bucknell University Press, 1995), pp. 14–41.

24 Heather Blurton, 'Richard of Devizes's *Cronicon*, Menippean Satire, and the Jews of Winchester', *Exemplaria* 22 (2010), 265–84.

25 Echard, 'Map's Metafiction', p. 306.

26 *De nugis*, dist. ii. 20 (pp. 182–83).

27 *De nugis*, dist. ii. 7 (pp. 142–43).

28 Gerald of Wales, *Speculum Ecclesiae* (Henceforth GW, *SE*), in *Giraldus Cambrensis Opera*, 8 vols., ed. by J. S Brewer, J. F. Dimock, and G. F. Warner, RS 21 (London: Longman, 1861–1891), IV (1873), dist. III. 14 (at pp. 219–23).

29 For scholarship on Map's disdain for the Cistercians, see Stephen Gordon, 'Parody, Sarcasm, and Invective in the *Nugae* of Walter Map', *Journal of English and Germanic Philology* 116 (2017), 82–107; Margaret Sinex, 'Echoic Irony in Walter Map's Satire against the Cistercians', *Comparative Literature* 54 (2002), 275–90; John Aberth, 'Walter Map and his Criticisms of the Cistercian Order: The Welsh Evidence', *Transactions of the Honourable Society of Cymmrodorion* 88 (1988), 29–35.

30 'Invectio magistri W. Bothewald canonici et supprioris ecclesiae sanctae Frideswide contra Walterum Mat. Archidiaconum Oxoniae; qui tam in juvenute quam in senectute, quaedam derisoria dicere consuevit et metrice et prosaice, de monachis albis, ad eorundem diffa[ma]tionem', included in Thomas Wright, *The Latin Poems Commonly*

Attributed to Walter Mapes (London: Camden Society, 1841), pp. xxxv. One of the 'derisory' tales may include a version of anecdote given about Bernard of Clairvaux in *De nugis*, dist. i. 24 (pp.80–81). Whilst in the company of his friend and patron, Gilbert Foliot, Map overhears a Cistercian talking about Bernard's failed attempt to heal a dead child by throwing himself on the body. Ever quick-witted, Map retorts that 'I have heard before now of a monk throwing himself upon a boy, but when the monk got up, the boy promptly got up too', much to the White Monk's annoyance. ('Nunquam enim audiui quod aliquis monachus super puerum incubuisset, quin statim post ipsum surrexisset puer'.)

31 'Multa, magister Giralde, scripsistis, et multum adhuc scribitis; et nos multa diximus. Vos scripta dedistis, et nos verba. Et quamquam scripta vestra longe laudabiliora sint et longeviora quam dicta nostra, quia tamen hec aperta, communi quippe idiomate prolata, illa vero, quia Latina, paucioribus evidencia, nos de dictis nostris fructum aliquem reportavimus, vos autem de scriptis egregiis, principibus litteratis nimirum et largis obsoletes olim et ab orbe sublatis, Dignam minime retribucionem consequi potuistis', in GW, *EH*, ll.157–65. English translation from *De nugis*, p. xxii.

32 *De nugis,* p. xxii.

33 Cartlidge, 'Masters in the Art of Lying', p. 5.

34 Pepin, 'Walter Map and Yale MS 229', pp. 15–17.

35 *De nugis*, dist. i. 25 (pp.85–113).

36 *De nugis*, dist. iii. 2 (pp.210–47).

37 *De nugis*, dist. iv. 3 (pp.288–311).

38 James Hinton, 'Walter Map's *de Nugis Curialium*: Its Plan and Composition.' *PMLA* 32 (1917), 81–132 (at p.125).

39 *De nugis,* p. xxx.

40 See Stephen Gordon, review of *Walter Map and the Matter of Britain,* by Joshua Byron Smith, *Journal of English and Germanic Philology* 118 (2019), 458–60.

41 Smith, *Walter Map and the Matter of Britain*, pp. 37–39, 52.

42 *De nugis,* dist. i. 1 (pp.2–3).

43 *De nugis,* dist. i. 11 (pp.30–31).

44 Turner, *Men raised from the Dust*, p. 14.

45 Turner, *Men Raised from the Dust*, p. 21.

46 C. Stephen Jaeger, *The Origins of Courtliness: Civilizing Trends and the Formation of Courtly Ideals, 939–1210* (Philadelphia, PA: University of Pennsylvania Press, 1985), pp. 54–66.

47 *Anglo-Latin Satirical Poets and Epigrammatists of the Twelfth-Century*, 2 vols., ed. by Thomas Wright (London: Longman, 1872), I, p. 153; Turner, 'Toward a Definition of the Curialis', p. 10.

48 John of Salisbury, *Policraticus: Of the Frivolities of Courtiers and the Footprints of Philosophers,* ed. and trans. by Cary J. Nederman (Cambridge: Cambridge University Press, 1990), III. 3–9 (at pp. 17–22)

49 Herbert of Bosham, *Vita Thomae*, in *Materials for the History of Thomas Becket, Archbishop of Canterbury (Canonised by Pope Alexander III, AD 1173),* 7 vols., ed. by James C. Robertson, RS 67 (London: Longman, 1875–1885), III (1877), p. 165.

50 Johannes de Hauvilla, *Architrenius,* ed. and trans. by Winthrop Wetherbee (Cambridge: Cambridge University Press, 1994), iv. 13 (p. 106).

51 See especially Peter of Blois, Epistle 14, in, Lena Wahlgren, *The Letter Collections of Peter of Blois: Studies in the Manuscript Tradition* (Gothenburg: Acta Universitatis Gothoburgensis, 1993), pp. 140–65

52 'Quid te iuvat vivere si vis vitam perdere? In anime dispendio nulla est estimacio: si vis ut te perhennibus absorbeant suppliciis mors et inferna palus, confidas in principibus et in eorum filiis, in quibus non est salus', transcribed in Jaeger, *The Origins of Courtliness*, pp. 58–59.

53 Otter, *Inventiones,* p.117.
54 'Siluam uobis materiam [...]. Singuli lectores appositam ruditatem exculpant', *De nugis,* dist. ii. 32 (pp. 208–09). Isidore of Seville remarks upon the close conceptual relationship between 'matter' (*materia*) and 'wood' (also *materia*), hence the appropriate metaphor of the *nugae* as a forest, unrealised matter, just waiting to be shaped into cohesion by the reader. See *Etymologies,* XIII.iii.1.
55 Some scholars have suggested the Map was explicitly parodying John of Salisbury's work. See Otter, *Inventiones,* p. 117.
56 Echard, 'Map's Metafiction', p. 306.
57 For a comparison between the two stories, see R. E. Bennett, 'Walter Map's Sadius and Galo', *Speculum* 16 (1941), 34–56.
58 In brief, the episode records how Galo, a knight in the Asian court, was lusted after by the queen. His comrade, Sadius, nephew of the King, tries to negate these unwanted advances and confesses to the queen that Galo is impotent. The queen, however, sends a maidservant to test Galo's condition; upon returning from his bedchamber (Galo having rejected her advances), the maidservant is beaten by the queen in a jealous rage. Later, at a banquet for the king, the queen demands that Galo confess his innermost thoughts, hoping to expose his love for the maidservant. Instead, Galo recounts how, the year before, he journeyed into an unknown land and entered into a contract to fight the giant, Rivius. However, he confesses that he finds Rivius too formidable and will shirk his responsibility. Sadius, wishing to help his friend, dresses up in Galo's armour while, at the same time, Galo dresses up in Sadius' armour and goes on to face Rivius before Sadius can intervene. The queen abuses Sadius (dressed as Galo), while praising Galo (dressed as Sadius). Eventually the giant is defeated, the correct identities are revealed, and the queen's shame is complete. See *De nugis,* dist. iii. 2.
59 Echard, 'Map's Metafiction', p. 309.
60 Edwards, 'Authorship and the Space of Writing', p. 282.
61 Hutcheon, *Irony's Edge,* p. 64.
62 See, for example, Levine, 'How to Read Walter Map', p. 98.
63 Ralph Hanna III and Warren S. Smith., 'Walter as Valerius: Classical and Christian in the *Dissuasio*', in *Satiric Advice on Women and Marriage: From Plautus to Chaucer,* ed. by Warren S. Smith (Ann Arbor, MI: University of Michigan Press, 2005), pp. 210–21 (at. p 218).
64 'Nomina nostra nominibus mortuorum in titulo mutaui; sciebam enim hoc placere. Sin autem, abiecissent illam, ut me,' *De nugis,* dist. iv. 5 (pp. 312–13).
65 'auide rapitur, transcribitur intente, plena iocunditate legitur', *De nugis,* dist. iv. 5 (pp. 312–13).
66 *De nugis,* dist. i. 31 (pp.124–25).
67 A. G. Rigg, *A History of Anglo-Latin Literature 1066–1422* (Cambridge: Cambridge University Press, 1992), p. 91.
68 *De nugis,* dist. ii.18 (pp.174–75, n.2).
69 'quam ipse Deo et hominibus abstulerat u team dicaret feris et canum lusibus', in *De nugis,* dist. v. 6 (pp. 466–67)
70 *De nugis,* dist. v. 5 (pp. 440–41)
71 *De nugis,* dist. i. 11 (pp. 26–27).
72 Smith, *Walter Map and the Matter of Britain,* pp. 175–76.
73 Caroline W. Bynum, *Metamorphosis and Identity* (New York: Zone Books, 2005), pp. 39, 71.
74 For the base tenants of twelfth-century cosmological theory and the belief that the micro- and macrocosm were inextricably linked, see the *Cosmographia* (c. 1147) of Bernardus Silvestris.
75 GW, *TH,* Dist. III. 35 (pp. 181–82).
76 See, for example, Gervase's lengthy discourse on the meaning of ghost encounters in the *Otia Imperialia,* III. 103 (at pp. 759–89).

77 Goscelin of Saint-Bertin, *Miracles of St Edmund*, pp. 144–45.
78 'Quam ferunt nec in ecclesia nec in atrio nec in campo sepultam posse teneri, sed quendam infantem lucidissimum apparentem cuidam iussisseque in quodam profundo semoto proici,' in *Three Eleventh-Century Saints' Lives: Vita S. Birini, Vita et miracula S. Kenelmi, and Vita S. Rumwoldi*, ed. by Rosalind C. Love, Oxford Medieval Texts (Oxford: Clarendon Press, 1996), pp. 71–72.
79 'Subita morte ambo perculsi sunt', in Geoffrey of Burton, *Life and Miracles of St Modwenna*, pp. 194–95.
80 'Que tandem cremata et ueluti multum coacta cum maximo sonitu uix ad ultimum crepuerunt et confestim malignum spiritum tanquam coruum uolantem de ignibus uniuersi qui aderant uisibiliter conspexerunt'
81 Ut credant nequam hominis cadauer post mortem demone agente discurrere, in GrA, ii.124 (pp. 196–97).
82 Donec cadaver suffossum longe a monasterio paludi profundae immerserint; unde aliquotiens teter odor emergens sevam vicinis exhalat mefitim, in William of Malmesbury, *De Gestis Pontificum Anglorum Libri Auinque*, ed. by N. E. S. A. Hamilton (London, 1870), V. 258 (at pp. 411–12). See also *The Deeds of the Bishops of England*, ed. and trans. by David Preest (Woodbridge: Boydell, 2002), p. 281. Herafter 'GpA'.
83 Newburgh V. 20 (p. 471).
84 Newburgh, V. 24 (p. 482).
85 Parsons, 'A Riotous Spray of Words', p. 116.
86 *De nugis*, dist. ii. 27 (pp. 202–05).
87 *De nugis*, dist. ii. 28 (pp. 204–05).
88 *De nugis*, dist. ii. 29 (pp. 204–07).
89 De nugis, dist. ii. 30 (pp. 206–07).
90 *De nugis*, dist. ii. 31 and 32 (pp. 206–09).
91 John of Salisbury, *Policraticus*, IV. 6.
92 '[Wales], after its own nature, produces men of savage manners, bold and faithless, greedy of the blood of others, and prodigal of their own; ever on the watch for rapine, and hostile to the English, as if by a natural instinct.' (Gignit autem pro sui natura homines moribus barbaros, audaces, et infidos, alieni sanguinis avidos, et proprii prodigos, rapinis semper inhiantes, et tanquam transfuso a natura odio genti Anglorum infestos). Newburgh II. 5 (p. 107). See also the Preface and II. 8.
93 Hubert Walter's letter to the incumbent pope, describing how the Welsh claim dominion over England is based on to their ancient bloodline, is included in Gerald of Wales, *De Invectionibus* [Hereafter GW, *I*]. in *Giraldi Cambrensis Opera*, vol. 3, ed. by J. S. Brewer, RS 21 (London: Longman, 1863), Dist. I. 1, (at p. 15)
94 'Gens enim rudis et indomita bestiali more uiuens aspernatur uerbum uitae et Christum nomine tenus profitentes uita et moribus diffitentur'. See Theobald's letter to the pope (no. 87) in *The Letters of John of Salisbury, Vol. 1: The Early Letters (1153–1161)*, ed. by W. J. Miller, W. J. and H. E. Butler; revised by C. N. L. Brooke, Oxford Medieval Texts (Oxford: Clarendon Press, 1986), p. 135.
95 Ecce quam stulta quamque iniusta est ira Walensium, et quam in sanguine[m] proni sunt
96 Echard, 'Map's Metafiction', p. 313.
97 John Gillingham, *The English in the Twelfth Century: Imperialism, National Identity and Political Values* (Woodbridge: Boydell, 2000), pp. 59–68.
98 A March is defined as a frontier between two countries. The allusion to English jurisdiction in Map's village suggests that the revenant attack occurred in a Marcher settlement. For relevant scholarship on the topic, see Max Lieberman, *The Medieval March of Wales: The Creation and Perception of a Frontier, 1066–1283* (Cambridge: Cambridge University Press, 2010); Brock W. Holden, *Lords of the Central Marches, English Aristocracy and Frontier Society, 1087–1265* (Oxford: Oxford University

Press, 2004); R. R., Davies, 'Kings, Lords and Liberties in the March of Wales, 1066–1272', *Transactions of the Royal Historical Society*, Fifth Ser. 29 (1979), 41–61.

99 Davies, 'Kings, Lords and Liberties', pp. 53–55.

100 Although the narrative takes place during Gilbert Foliot's tenure at Hereford (1148–63) and may have been related to Map by bishop himself, it was transcribed around 1180, a time when Henry II enjoyed an uneasy peace with Rhys ap Gruffydd, the Lord of South Wales. See Hinton, 'Walter Map's *de Nugis Curialium*', p. 106.

101 GW, *I.* (p. 15).

102 Davies, Kings, Lords and Liberties', p. 56.

103 'Huius rei uerum tenorem scimus, causam nescimus'.

104 *De nugis,* dist. ii. 32 (pp. 208–09).

105 It is difficult to ascertain the nature of Walter's relationship with Roger, and whether he gleaned the base details of the story from the bishop himself. Whilst records indicate that on 19 March 1177 Roger oversaw a property dispute in which a certain 'Waltero Mapp' was a witness, it is unknown whether this remains the sum of their personal interaction. See Mary G., Cheney, *Roger, Bishop of Worcester 1164–1179* (Oxford: Clarendon Press, 1980), pp. 260–61.

106 Geoffrey of Burton, *Life and Miracles of St Modwenna,* pp. 196–97.

107 Newburgh V. 24. See chapter two of this volume.

108 Robert Easting, 'Dialogue Between a Clerk and the Spirit of a Girl de purgatorio (1153): A Medieval Ghost Story', in *Mediaevistik* 20 (2007), 163–83 (at p. 168). Easting's assertion is in contrast to findings of Jacques le Goff, who asserts that the word *purgatorium* was first used in Peter Comestor's *De Sacramentis* (c. 1170). See Jacques Le Goff, *The Birth of Purgatory,* trans. by Arthur Goldhammer (London: Scolar Press, 1984), p. 157.

109 See, for example, the narrative in Gregory's *Dialogues* (IV.55) concerning the ghost of the 'ruler' (*dominus*) of the public baths in city of Centumcellis, condemned to haunt his former place of work on account of his sins, from which he was released through the prayers of a priest, in Gregory the Great, *Sancti Gregorii Papae I,* PL 77, col. 417. For an overview of the Patristic discussions on the fate of the soul between death and the Last Judgement, see R. R. Atwell, 'From Augustine to Gregory the Great: An Evaluation of the Emergence of the Doctrine of Purgatory.' *Journal of Ecclesiastical History* 38 (1987), 173–86.

110 Schmitt, *Ghosts in the Middle Ages,* pp.76–77.

111 Peter the Venerable, 'De Miraculis Libri Duo', in *Petri Venerabilis Abbatis Cluniacensis Noni Opera Omnia,* PL 189, ed. by J-P Migne (Paris, 1854), I.28 (at col 905).

112 Peter the Venerable, 'De Miraculis Libri Duo' PL 189, I.11, (at col. 875)

113 Easting, 'Dialogue Between a Clerk and the Spirit of a Girl', p. 180.

114 See Newburgh, V.22, where St. Hugh of Lincoln uses this innovative theological outlook to grant the Buckingham Ghost absolution rather than consign it to the flame.

115 Map was particularly critical of Bernard of Clairvaux, questioning his sanctity and ability to perform miracles. One memorable anecdote, ostensibly from Map's fellow clerk, John Platena, concerns the abbot's supposed exorcism of a madman in Montpellier. However, following the ritual, the madman began throwing stones at Bernard and chased him through the city streets. The madman, so Map says, was gentle and kind to everyone expert hypocrites. Bernard's failure on two occasions to bring the dead back to life is also cited as evidence of his hypocrisy and presumptuousness. These failures of grace, Map deadpans, 'did not add to his reputation' (et famam eius non secundans), in *De nugis,* dist. i. 24 (pp. 80–81).

116 'Quos horum apprehendit inuasio, exilium sibi sciant imminere perpetum' (Those upon whom comes an invasion of Cistercians may be sure that they are doomed to a lasting exile'), *De nugis,* dist. i. 25 (pp. 94–95).

117 For a full overview of this argument, see Gordon, 'Parody, Sarcasm and Invective', pp. 95–105.

118   Sinex, 'Echoic Irony', p. 277.

119   *De nugis,* dist. ii. 32 (pp. 208–09).

120   The *Historia Karoli Magni et Rotholandi* is a chronicle ostensibly written by one of Charlemagne's contemporaries, Turpin, Archbishop of Reims (d.800) but it seems to have actually been composed in the early twelfth century. Map's *nugae* is a drastic reinvention of chapter seven's narrative on the death of a knight named Romaricus while Charlemagne's army is camped near the city of Bayonne, south west France. In the longer, original version of the story, the cleric does not keep his friend's horse, but sells it and keeps the money for himself. Here, Romaricus' ghost appears as a dream vision (*'extasi'*) only once, lamenting that he suffers terrible torments on account of the misappropriation of his alms and warns the cleric that he, too, shall receive the same punishment. Sure enough, the next morning the cleric is seized by a pack of howling demons and carried off into the air whilst still alive. His body was found twelve days later in a desert near Navarre, dashed to pieces on a rocky outcrop – a clear example to others who would also wilfully withhold alms. See *Turpini historia Karoli magni et Rotholandi*, ed. by. Ferdinand Castets (Montpellier, 1880), pp. 10–11.

121   Otter, *Inventiones,* p. 127.

122   Parsons, 'A Riotous Spray of Words', p. 116.

123   Echard, 'Map's Metafiction', p. 312.

124   *De nugis,* p. xxx.

Primary sources

Anglo-Latin Satirical Poets and Epigrammatists of the Twelfth-Century, 2 vols, ed. by Thomas Wright (London: Longman, 1872).

Bernardus Silvestris, *Cosmographia*, ed. and trans. by Winthrop Wetherbee (New York: Columbia University Press, 1973).

Cicero, *De Oratore: Books 1–2*, ed. and trans. by E. W. Sutton and H. Rackham, Loeb Classical Library 348 (Cambridge, MA: Harvard University Press, 1942).

Gerald of Wales, *Giraldi Cambrensis opera*, 8 vols, ed. by J. S. Brewer (Vols. 1–4). J. F. Dimock, (Vols. 5–7) and G. F. Warner, (Vol. 8), RS 21 (London: Longman, 1861–1891).

Gerald of Wales, *Expugnatio Hibernica*, ed. and trans. by A. B. Scott and F. X. Martin (Dublin: Royal Irish Academy, 1978).

Geoffrey of Burton, *Life and Miracles of St. Modwenna*, ed. and trans. by Robert Bartlett, Oxford Medieval Texts (Oxford: Clarendon Press, 2002).

Gervase of Tilbury, *Otia Imperialia: Recreations for an Emperor*, ed. and trans. by S. E. Banks and J. W. Binns, Oxford Medieval Texts (Oxford: Clarendon Press, 2002).

Gregory the Great, *Sancti Gregorii Papae I, Cognomento Magni, Opera Omnia*, vol. 3, PL 77, ed. by J.-P. Migne (Paris, 1862).

Herbert of Bosham, *Vita Thomae*, in *Materials for the History of Thomas Becket, Archbishop of Canterbury (Canonised by Pope Alexander III, ad 1173)*, 7 vols, ed. by James C. Robertson, RS 67 (London: Longman, 1875–1885).

Herman the Archdeacon and Goscelin of Saint-Bertin, *Miracles of St Edmund*, ed. and trans. by Tom Licence, with Lynda Lockyer, Oxford Medieval Texts (Oxford: Clarendon, 2014).

Isidore of Seville, *The Etymologies of Isidore of Seville*, ed. by Stephen A. Barney (Cambridge: Cambridge University Press, 2006).

Johannes de Hauvilla, *Architrenius*, ed. and trans. by Winthrop Wetherbee (Cambridge: Cambridge University Press, 1994).

John of Salisbury, *Policraticus: Of the Frivolities of Courtiers and the Footprints of Philosophers*, ed. and trans. by Cary J. Nederman (Cambridge: Cambridge University Press, 1990).

The Letters of John of Salisbury, Vol. 1: The Early Letters (1153–1161), ed. by W. J. Miller and H. E. Butler; revised by C. N. L. Brooke, Oxford Medieval Texts (Oxford: Clarendon Press, 1986).

Nigel de Longchamps, *Speculum Stultorum*, ed. by John H. Mozley and Robert R. Raymo (Berkeley, CA: University of California Press, 1960).

Peter the Venerable, *Petri Venerabilis Abbatis Cluniacensis Noni Opera Omnia*, PL 189, ed. by J.-P. Migne (Paris, 1854).

Pseudo-Turpin, *Turpini historia Karoli magni et Rotholandi*, ed. by Ferdinand Castets (Paris, Maisonneuve et cie, 1880).

Quintilian, *The Orator's Education*, ed. and trans. by Donald A. Russell, Loeb Classical Library 127 (Cambridge, MA: Harvard University Press, 2001).

Three Eleventh-Century Saints' Lives: Vita S. Birini, Vita et miracula S. Kenelmi, and Vita S. Rumwoldi, ed. by Rosalind C. Love, Oxford Medieval Texts (Oxford: Clarendon Press, 1996).

Walter Map, *De Nugis Curialium*, ed. and trans. by M. R. James; revised by C. N. L. Brooke and R. A. B. Mynors (Oxford: Clarendon Press, 1983).

William of Conches, *Glosae in Iuvenalem*, ed. by Bradford L. Wilson (Paris: J. Vrin, 1980).

William of Malmesbury, *Gesta Pontificum Anglorum*, ed. and trans. by David Preest (Woodbridge: Boydell, 2002).

William of Malmesbury, *Gesta Regum Anglorum: History of the English Kings*, vol. 1, ed. and trans. R. A. B. Mynors; completed by R. M. Thomson and M. Winterbottom, Oxford Medieval Texts (Clarendon: Oxford, 1998).

William of Newburgh, 'Historia rerum Anglicarum', in *Chronicles of the Reigns of Stephen, Henry II., and Richard I*, 2 vols, ed. by Richard Howlett, RS 82 (London: Longman, 1884–5).

William of Newburgh, 'Historia rerum Anglicarum', in *The Church Historians of England*, vol. IV, pt. 2, ed. by Joseph Stevenson (London: Seeleys, 1856), pp. 395–672.

Secondary sources

Aberth, John, 'Walter Map and His Criticisms of the Cistercian Order: The Welsh Evidence', *Transactions of the Honourable Society of Cymmrodorion* 88 (1988), 29–35.

Atwell, R. R., 'From Augustine to Gregory the Great: An Evaluation of the Emergence of the Doctrine of Purgatory', *Journal of Ecclesiastical History* 38 (1987), 173–86.

Bakhtin, Mikhail, *Problems of Dostoevsky's Poetics*, ed. and trans. by Caryl Emerson (Manchester: Manchester University Press, 1984).

Bennett, R. E., 'Walter Map's Sadius and Galo', *Speculum* 16 (1941), 34–56.

Blurton, Heather, 'Richard of Devizes's *Cronicon*, Mennipean Satire, and the Jews of Winchester', *Exemplaria* 22 (2010), 265–84.

Bynum, Caroline W., *Metamorphosis and Identity* (New York: Zone Books, 2005).

Cartlidge, Neil, 'Masters in the Art of Lying? The Literary Relationship Between Hugh of Rhuddian and Walter Map', *Modern Language Review* 106 (2011), 1–16.

Cheney, Mary G., *Roger, Bishop of Worcester 1164–1179* (Oxford: Clarendon Press, 1980).

Davies, R. R., 'Kings, Lords and Liberties in the March of Wales, 1066–1272', *Transactions of the Royal Historical Society*, 5th ser. 29 (1979), 41–61.

Easting, Robert, 'Dialogue Between a Clerk and the Spirit of a Girl de purgatorio (1153): A Medieval Ghost Story', *Mediaevistik* 20 (2007), 163–83.

Echard, Siân, 'Map's Metafiction: Narrative and Reader in *de Nugis Curialium*', *Exemplaria* 8 (1996), 287–314.

Edwards, Robert R., 'Walter Map: Authorship and the Space of Writing', *New Literary History* 38 (2007), 273–92.

Flint, Valerie I. J., 'The *Historia Regum Brittanniae* of Geoffrey of Monmouth: Parody and its Purpose. A Suggestion', *Speculum* 54 (1979), 447–68.

Gillespie, Vincent, 'From the Twelfth-Century to *c*.14500', in *Cambridge History of Literary Criticism, Vol. 2: The Middle Ages*, ed. by Alastair Minnis and Ian Johnson (Cambridge: Cambridge University Press, 2005), pp. 145–235.

Gillingham, John, *The English in the Twelfth Century: Imperialism, National Identity and Political Values* (Woodbridge: Boydell, 2000).

Gordon, Stephen, 'Parody, Sarcasm, and Invective in the *Nugae* of Walter Map', *Journal of English and Germanic Philology* 116 (2017), 82–107.

Gordon, Stephen, *Review of Walter Map and the Matter of Britain*, ed. by Joshua Byron Smith, *Journal of English and Germanic Philology* 118 (2019), 458–60.

Hanna III, Ralph and Warren S. Smith, 'Walter as Valerius: Classical and Christian in the *Dissuasio*', in *Satiric Advice on Women and Marriage: From Plautus to Chaucer*, ed. by Warren S. Smith (Ann Arbor, MI: University of Michigan Press, 2005), pp. 210–21.

Hinton, James, 'Walter Map's *de Nugis Curialium*: Its Plan and Composition', *PMLA* 32 (1917), 81–132.

Holden, Brock W., *Lords of the Central Marches, English Aristocracy and Frontier Society, 1087–1265* (Oxford: Oxford University Press, 2004).

Hutcheon, Linda, *Irony's Edge: The Theory and Politics of Irony* (London: Routledge, 1994).

Jaeger, C. Stephen, *The Origins of Courtliness: Civilizing Trends and the Formation of Courtly Ideals, 939–1210* (Philadelphia, PA: University of Pennsylvania Press, 1985).

Le Goff, Jacques, *The Birth of Purgatory*, trans. by Arthur Goldhammer (London: Scolar Press, 1984).

Levine, Robert, 'How to Read Walter Map', *Mittellateinisches Jahrbuch* 23 (1988), 91–105.

Lieberman, Max, *The Medieval March of Wales: The Creation and Perception of a Frontier, 1066–1283* (Cambridge: Cambridge University Press, 2010).

Otter, Monika, *Inventiones: Fiction and Referentiality in Twelfth-Century English Historical Writing* (Chapel Hill, NC: The University of North Carolina Press, 1996).

Parsons, Ben, '"A Riotous Spray of Words": Rethinking the Medieval Theory of Satire', *Exemplaria* 21 (2009), 105–28.

Pepin, Ronald E., *Literature of Satire in the Twelfth Century: A Neglected Mediaeval Genre* (Lampeter: Edwin Mellen Press, 1988).

Pepin, Ronald E., 'Walter Map and Yale MS 229', in *Essays on the Lancelot of Yale 229*, ed. by Elizabeth M. Whittingham, (Turnhout: Brepols, 2007), pp. 15–17.

Rigg, A. G., *A History of Anglo-Latin Literature 1066–1422* (Cambridge: Cambridge University Press, 1992).

Schmitt, Jean-Claude, *Ghosts in the Middle Ages*, trans. by Teresa Lavender Fagan (Chicago, IL: Chicago University Press, 1998).

Scott Blanchard, W., *Scholars' Bedlam: Menippean Satire in the Renaissance* (Lewisburg, PA: Bucknell University Press, 1995).

Sinex, Margaret, 'Echoic Irony in Walter Map's Satire Against the Cistercians', *Comparative Literature* 54 (2002), 275–90.

Smith, Joshua Bryon, *Walter Map and the Matter of Britain* (Philadelphia, PA: University of Pennsylvania Press, 2017).

Swanson, Robert, *The Twelfth-Century Renaissance* (Manchester: Manchester University Press, 1999).

Thomson, Rodney M., 'Satire, Irony, and Humour in William of Malmesbury', in *Rhetoric and Renewal in the Latin West, 1100–1450: Essays in Honour of John O. Ward*, ed. by Constant J. Mews, Cary J. Nederman, and Rodney M. Thomson (Turnhout: Brepols, 2003), pp. 115–27.

Thomson, Rodney M., 'The Origins of Latin Satire in Twelfth-Century Europe', *Mittellateinisches Jarhbuch* 13 (1978), 73–83.

Turner, Ralph V., *Men Raised from the Dust: Administrative Service and Upward Mobility in Angevin England* (Philadelphia, PA: University of Pennsylvania Press, 1988).

Turner, Ralph V., 'Toward a Definition of the Curialis: Educated Court Cleric, Courtier, Administrator, or "New Man"?', *Medieval Prosopography* 15 (1994), 3–35.

Wahlgren, Lena, *The Letter Collections of Peter of Blois: Studies in the Manuscript Tradition* (Gotëborg: Acta Universitatis Gothoburgensis, 1993).

4   Between demons and the undead

Preaching practice and local belief in the
sermons of John Mirk

Introduction

The development of the belief in Purgatory as a distinct, bounded place where the
souls of the middling dead were shorn of accumulated sin was just one of many
theological innovations that emerged from the Parisian schools in the late twelfth
century.[1] As revealed in the story of the Buckinghamshire revenant from William
of Newburgh's *Historia regum Anglicarum* (c.1198), the difficulty of codifying
the restless corpse was a function of the new interpretative frameworks that could
be drawn upon by secular and religious commentators.[2] For learned churchmen
of the late twelfth and early thirteenth centuries, no longer was it a case of simply assigning a demonic causation to rumours of a corpse rising from the grave.
Devilish indiscretion may have indeed been the most viable interpretation but, as
illustrated by Hugh of Lincoln's reticence when confronted with the details of the
Buckinghamshire haunting, the possibility that the deceased's soul inhabited the
body could not be discounted in light of the emerging pastoral theology.[3] Indeed,
if insubstantial ghosts were able to return from their purgatorial torments to ask
for prayer – as seen previously in the ghost story found in Lambeth MS 1213
(c.1153)[4] – it took only a small mental leap on Hugh's part to accept that souls
of the dead could utilise their own bodies for similar ends.[5] In these doctrinally
fluid environs, the reformulation of the ghost as purely the *incorporeal* soul of the
deceased had yet to be fully (and rigorously) clericalised.

And yet, it would be a mistake to assume that the top-down re-conceptuali-
sation of the mechanics of the afterlife represented a uniform and unproblem-
atic enterprise on the part of the theological innovators. According to William
of Malmesbury, the credulous English already accepted the possibility that
corpses could be mobilised by a non-diabolical agency.[6] Similarly, Goscelin of
Saint-Bertin's account of the death of sheriff Leofstan makes reference to his
corpse walking under its own volition,[7] related, perhaps, to the belief – consolidated by Gregory the Great[8] and expressed by Orderic Vitalis[9] and Peter the
Venerable,[10] amongst others – that the sinful dead endured their punishments on
earth. Contrary to the expectation of his advisors, Hugh's innovation involved
granting the corpse absolution, a turn of events that would have been unusual
but not completely unfathomable to earlier, more conservative churchmen,

especially if the lead absolution cross placed in the grave of Godfrey, Bishop of Chichester (d.1088), can be taken as representative of everyday practice. Even so, the novelty of a cadaver *asking* for suffrage (ostensibly) surprised even such courtly sophisticates as Walter Map.[11] The gradual disembodiment of the ghost following the acceptance of the doctrine of Purgatory (fully ratified at the Council of Lyon in 1274) may well have reflected the general, learned consensus that only demons could inhabit the corpse, but this did not fully dispel the belief that, on rare occasions and for whatever reason, the souls of the deceased were permitted to enter, or remain trapped within, their own rotting cadavers.[12] Despite efforts to the contrary, multivalent attitudes to supernatural encounters endured.

Although the socio-political issues and doctrinal deficiencies that prompted the desire for reform in this period are too wide-ranging to go into much detail here,[13] it suffices to say that the early thirteenth century was a time when the combat of heresy and the provision of correct pastoral care occupied a central concern for the religious elites, particularly the incumbent pope, Innocent III (r.1198–1216). As noted by Ronald J. Stansbury, the meaning of the phrase 'pastoral care', the care of souls, (*cura animarum*), is not always easy to define. At an essential level it related to the correct administration of the sacraments (for example, the reception of the Eucharist; penance; the anointing of the sick) and the need to disseminate orthodox moral teachings to the laity, such as the Seven Deadly Sins, the Ten Commandments, and the Seven Virtues and Vices.[14] The decrees issued at the Fourth Lateran Council of 1215 should not be treated as a wholesale schism from what had gone before, but the culmination of an inexorable, decades-long drive to reform morals, ratify canon law, and codify pastoral practice across the entirety of Latin Christendom. This, indeed, was the agenda set out by Innocent III in the *Vineam Domini*, a papal letter issued on 19 April 1213 to summon church leaders to Lateran IV.[15] Out of the seventy canons issued at the Council, canon ten is perhaps the most important where the dissemination of church teachings was concerned:

> Among the various things that are conducive to the salvation of the Christian people, the nourishment of God's word is recognised to be especially necessary [...]. We therefore decree by this general constitution that bishops are to appoint suitable men to carry out with profit this duty of sacred preaching, men who are powerful in word and deed [...].We therefore order that there be appointed in cathedral and other conventual churches suitable whom the bishops may have as coadjutors and co-operators not only in the office of preaching but also in hearing confessions and enjoining penances and in other matters which are conducive to the salvation of souls.[16]

The art of preaching was, of course, hardly a new phenomenon and can be traced back to Augustine's *Sermones ad Populum* and book four of *De Doctrina Christiana*.[17] Prior to the early thirteenth century sermons had generally been delivered in Latin to clerical or monastic audiences, focusing mainly on biblical exegesis and the intricacies of doctrine. The delivery of 'university sermons' was similarly treated as an exercise in academic and rhetorical prowess.[18] Through the efforts of such practical theologians as Peter the Chanter (d.1197), Maurice de Sully (d.1196) and Alain of Lille (d.1202), learned sermons began to be used as models to teach the uneducated clergy in the base tenets of moral and doctrinal thought, to be thereafter relayed to the priests' own congregations.[19] Popular (as opposed to strictly clerical) preaching also developed in response to the unsanctioned and insidious activities of the Waldensian and Cathar heretics and, on a wider political level, as a way to secure secular support for the Crusades in the Holy Land, one of the central concerns of Innocent III's papacy. Thus, the pastoral programmes instigated by Lateran IV opened up new avenues through which the various precepts of the church could be disseminated to all levels of society. The spread of the Franciscan (1209) and Dominican Orders (1216) and the ratification of their ability to hear confession in 1227 fed into the newfound impetus to educate and inform the growing urban masses, especially the need to confess one's sins at least once a year lest suffer the pains of excommunication (Lateran IV, Canon 21).[20] Tales of supernatural encounters, hitherto the purview of monastic miracle collections, hagiographies and chronicles, found new literary life as exempla for the masses. As expressed most notably by the Dominican preacher Stephen of Bourbon (c.1250–1261), the beauty of the exemplum resided in its ability to impress itself upon the memory of the listener,[21] couching complex theological truths in an easily digestible, entertaining, and emotionally resonant form. With churchmen needing to attune to the sensibilities of the lay audience in order to successfully disseminate the desired pastoral message, preachers' manuals provide a tantalising glimpse into the intersection between office discourse and local beliefs concerning ghosts, witches, and demons. Sermons could not truly be effective if the illustrative exempla were alien to the everyday experiences and expectations of the laity. As noted briefly in chapter one, exempla collections such as the *Liber Exemplorum* (c.1275–79), *Speculum Laicorum* (c.1275) and *Alphabetum narrationum* (c.1307) offered up vast repositories of edifying tales of the supernatural to be utilised how a preacher saw fit. Weighty, discursive handbooks such as the *Fasciculus Morum* (c.1300) and *Destructiorum vitiorum* (c.1429) also demonstrate how stories of malevolent demons and contrite spirits could add flavour to the pastoral programme.

It is not the intention of this chapter to provide a full overview of the use of supernatural narratives in the context of preaching, nor chart the socio-cultural history of pastoral care in the years following Lateran IV. Leonard Boyle's impressive body of work on *pastoralia* is required study in this regard.[22] In keeping with the emphasis on the close reading of individual texts, the aim instead is to analyse the extent to which habitual belief in restless corpses was made manifest a specific English-language sermon collection: the *Festial* of John Mirk, canon (and later prior) of the Augustinian Abbey of Lilleshall in Shropshire. Written during the late 1380s, the *Festial* represents one of the most widely read vernacular preaching aids of the fifteenth and early sixteenth centuries. A chronological collection of sermons covering the full liturgical year, the original recensions of the *Festial* ('Group A') retain a distinctly local flavour, with the later recensions ('Group B') dividing the material into separate sections for the *temporale* (sermons based on Sundays and moveable holidays) and *sanctorale* (sermons based on saints' days), becoming more 'learned' in the process. William Caxton utilised a copy of the 'Group B' text as the template for the first printed edition of the *Festial*, published in 1483. Some 'Group A' manuscripts, such as the oldest and most cohesive version of the text, BL MS. Claudius A. II (c.1400), include extra, appendicised sermons and notes not included in the *Festial* proper.[23] Although the content of the *Festial* is based primarily on Jean Beleth's *Summa de ecclesiasticis officiis* (c.1162) and Jacobus de Voragine's *Legenda Aurea* (c.1260), the references to the restless dead found in the 'Dedication of a Church' sermon (*De dedicacione ecclesie*) and the additional burial sermon (*In die sepulture alicuius Mortui*) find no analogue in the wider literary record and appear wholly unique to Mirk. The dedication sermon features the tale of a thief from Lilleshall village, condemned to roam after death until granted absolution by the local abbot, while the burial sermon describes how a demon entered the corpse of a man who had died violently and unshriven, causing mischief in the deceased's name until conjured to depart by a local anchorite. Strangely, given the amount of scholarship conducted on Mirk's output in recent years,[24] neither sermon has prompted much in the way of close critical attention.[25] Following a brief overview of the context of the *Festial*'s creation and the traditions of pastoral instruction in the late fourteenth century, the main part of this chapter will be devoted to analysing how, and why, Mirk utilised these specific supernatural narratives in the formulation of his pastoral project. Rather than reflecting a theological insecurity about the ontology of the restless dead, it will be argued that the choice to render the mobilising agent as either a devil or spirit of the deceased tied into the specific didactic message each sermon was trying to convey. The local ghost stories transcribed by the anonymous Byland Abbey Monk (c.1400) and contemporaneous sermon collections such as the *Speculum sacerdotale* (c.1400) will be consulted to provide a further sense of historical and literary context. The question to be asked is simple: what moral statement could a restless body convey that an insubstantial ghost or airy demon could not?

The *Festial*: background and context

Lilleshall Abbey was founded c.1145–1148 by canons from Dorchester Abbey, Oxfordshire, belonging to the rigorous Arrouaisian branch of the Augustinian Order. Originally granted a charter of land in Lizard Grange, Shropshire, by the local lord, Philip of Beaumais (c.1144), the canons subsequently moved to nearby Donnington before finally settling at Lilleshall. The endowment was provided by Philip's brother, Richard of Beaumais, dean of the collegiate church of St. Alkmund's in Shrewsbury and holder of the prebend at Lilleshall. The college at St. Alkmund's was subsequently reduced and its properties transferred to the canons from the new colony. Conceived from its inception as a royal foundation

– deriving, ultimately, from the tradition that St. Alkmund's was founded by King Alfred's Daughter, Æthelflæd – Lilleshall does not seem to have enjoyed a particularly storied or impactful history.[26] Little is known about the contents of the abbey's library or the intellectual pastimes of its canons. Whilst the surviving Lilleshall cartulary (BL Add. MS 50121) mostly contains information on the administrative and financial workings of the Abbey from the thirteenth to the sixteenth centuries, it also includes a few tantalising paragraphs on early English history, based on a chronicle compiled at nearby Haughmond Abbey (CCCC MS 433, c.1294) and written in a fourteenth-century hand.[27] The content of the paragraphs also indicates that the writer was familiar with Peter of Ickham's *Compilatio de gestis Britonum et Anglorum*, an annotated copy of which, CCCC MS 339 (c.1300), was likely housed at Lilleshall. Indeed, at the very end of CCCC MS 339, written in Latin, an anonymous scribe provides brief details on Richard II's accession to the throne, his stay at 'Lilleshull' from 24–26 January 1398 on his way to the Shrewsbury Parliament, and John of Gaunt's convalescence at the Abbey following the Parliament's completion. Other high-status individuals who received the monks' hospitality are also given mention (fols. 47r-47v [91r-91v]).[28] The intimacy of the marginal notes is proof enough that the annotator was resident at Lilleshall and witnessed these events first-hand. The connection of CCCC MS 339 to Lilleshall suggests that the provision for secular reading must surely have existed in some form. It is to the detriment of historical scholarship that the wider intellectual pursuits of the monks can now only be approached at a remove.

Mirk, it seems, spent his entire life at Lilleshall. Alongside the *Festial*, two more pastoral handbooks circulated in his name. The first, the vernacular *Instructions for Parish Priests*, is a 1934-line text written in easy-to-memorise rhyming couplets and translated from a Latin 'pars oculi' (likely the *Oculus Sacerdotis* of William of Pagula, c.1328). The second, the Latin *Manuale Sacerdotis*, differed from the *Instructions* in being addressed to a specific member of the local clergy, 'Johannis de S, vicario de A', and containing much more explicit exhortations about the correct conduct of a parish priest.[29] The colophon to the copy of the *Festal* found in BL MS. Claudius A. II (fol. 125v) confirms Mirk's residence as a canon a Lilleshall: 'Per fratrem Iohannem Mirkus compositus, canonicum regularem monasterii de Lulshull'[30] The colophon to the *Instructions for Parish Priests* found in the same manuscript uses almost the exact same formula (fol. 154v):

> Explicit tractatus qui dicitur pars oculi, de latino in anglicum translatus per fratrem Iohannem myrcus, canonicum regularem Monasterij de Lylleshul, cuius anime propicietur deus! Amen[31]

The address to 'Johannis de S' that prefaces most of the extant copies of the *Manuale Sacerdotis* notes Mirk's status as prior – Iohannes, dictus prior de Lylleshull' – providing clear typological evidence that the *Manuale* was written at a later date than either the *Festial* or the *Instructions*.[32] If, as noted by Alan

Fletcher, 'Johannis de S' can be identified with John Sotton, who became vicar of St. Alkmund's, Shrewsbury, on 24 January 1414,[33] and taking into account Susan Powell's suggestion that the *Festial* was written just prior to 1390,[34] then Mirk seems to have enjoyed a literary career spanning almost thirty years.

Pastoral care in late fourteenth-century England still felt the resonance of the Fourth Lateran Council. The intellectual and literary background to Mirk's outputs can ultimately be traced to the decrees issued at 1281 Lambeth Council instigated by the Archbishop of Canterbury, John Pecham (d.1292). Canon nine, which often circulated separately under its incipit, *Ignorantia Sacerdotum*, argued that the Fourteen Articles of Faith, the Ten Commandments, the Precepts of the Gospel, the Seven Works of Mercy, the Seven Deadly Sins, the Seven Virtues and the Seven Sacraments should be preached to the laity at least four times a year, constituting the very minimum knowledge that a Christian should possess.[35] Pechan's decrees proved especially influential, and was later used as the basis for the more expansive *Lay Folks' Catechism* (c.1357), drawn up in Latin by the Archbishop of York, John Thoresby, and later translated into English by the Benedictine monk, John Gaytrick.[36] Other works influenced the *Ignorantia Sacerdotum* include the previously-mentioned *Oculus Sacerdotis* of William of Pagula (c.1328). Divided into three parts – the Pars Oculi (on confessional practice), Dextera Pars (on moral teachings), and Sinistra Pars (on pastoral theology) – the *Oculus Sacerdotis* was subsequently refined by John de Burgh as the *Pupilla oculi* (c.1370–1388).[37] Mirk utilised both the 'Pars Oculi' (as he himself exclaims) and the 'Dextra Pars' for the main content of the *Instructions*.[38] Originality and scholastic intricacy was not at the forefront of the compilers' minds when creating such texts. As practical handbooks intended for everyday use, it would be illogical to include material that could not be understood by those for whom the work was intended. By versifying his *Instructions*, Mirk provides an effective mnemonic aid for digesting and reproducing the precepts contained within, ensuring that the reader (and listener) stayed within the bounds of orthodoxy. Priests needed to know how to interrogate the sins of a parishioner, how to perform the sacraments, how to recite specific prayers. They needed advice on how to deal with the more mundane, day-to-day aspects of clerical life; for example, what to do if an insect falls into the chalice (*Instructions*, ll.1825–1834) or what to wear whilst visiting the sick (*Instructions*, ll. 1845–1848). The sermons contained in the *Festial* were designed to be similarly comprehensible, both to the priests and their audience.

The *Festial* was, by some margin, the most coherent vernacular sermon collection produced in the later Middle Ages. According to the analysis carried out by Beth Allison Barr, the 'fullest' extant version of the *Festial* comprises 110 exempla from seventy-four sermons, including some duplications.[39] Since the first sermon for Lent, and the sermons for the Assumption of the Virgin, the Life of Nero, and Maundy Thursday did not form part of the original *Temporale/Sanctorale* programme, and discounting also the presence of six 'additional' notes/sermons, the original *Festial* manuscript likely contained sixty-four sermons in total.[40] Mirk's rationale for the project survives even if the urtext does not. The Preface to the text from BL Cotton Claudius A.ii cites that the lack of clerical education as the motivating factor. It is a statement worth repeating in full:

> By myne owne febul lettrure Y fele how yt faruth by othur that bene in the same degre that hauen charge of soulus and bene holdyn to teche hore pare-schonus of all the principale festus that cometh in the ʒere schewyng home what the seyntus soffreden and dedun for Goddus loue, so that thay schuldon haue the more deuocion in Goddus seyntys and wyth the better wylle com to the chyrche to serue God and pray to holy seyntys of here help. But for mony excuson ham by defaute of bokus and sympulnys of letture therfore in helpe of suche mene clerkus as I am my selff I haue drawe this treti sewyng owt of *Legenda Aurea* wyth more addyng to, so he that hathe lust to study therein he schal fynde redy of alle the principale festis of the ʒere a schort sermon nedful for hym to techyn and othur for to lerne. And for this treti speketh alle of festis i wolle and pray that it be called a *Festial*, the whyche begynnyth the forme Sonday of the Advent in worschup of God [and] of alle [the] seyntis that be wryten there in. Explicit prefacio incipit liber qui vocatur festial. In dei nomine. Amen'[41]

As a man of letters, it was Mirk's religious duty to provide unschooled church-men with readymade vernacular sermons for all the major feast days of the year, or else bring his readers back from the pitfalls of unorthodox thinking if, perhaps, 'defaute of bokus' can read as the neglect of *orthodox* books and the dangers of flirting with Lollardy.[42] The full 'A' text does not differentiate between the *temporale* and *sanctorale*. Such distinctions would have caused unnecessary con-fusion for an unlettered priest. Prizing the utility of chronological order, Mirk intermingles the sermons for the moveable feast days with those for the fixed saints' days, beginning with Advent Sunday (27 November to 3 December) and concluding with the feast of St. Katherine (25 November). With the anniversary of a church's dedication liable to occur throughout the year, the dedication for a church sermon is logically included at the very end of the handbook. The sermons for the Sts. Alkmund (19 March) and Winifred (21 June), omitted from the 'B' texts, attest to the fact that the *Festial* was originally conceived as a guide for local priests. Indeed, it has been argued quite convincingly that the Alkmund sermon – and, perhaps, the *Festial* as a whole – was written for use at St. Alkmund's in Shrewsbury. The references to the church's mythical founder, Æthelflæd ('qwene of þys March of Wales') and St. Alkmund's itself ('þus he was made patron of þis chirch') make the connection explicit. St. Alkmund's, of course, had longstand-ing historical links with Lilleshall and was held as a vicarage by the canons.[43] The idea that the *Festial* was written for a *specific* parish priest – Phillip de Lawlye was the vicar of St. Alkmund's in the 1380s[44] – is tempered slightly by the dedica-tion sermon not being included within the wider framework of the calendar. As noted above, its role as the final sermon makes sense if the *Festial* served a vari-ety of churches. However, with the feast of St. Alkmund already out of sequence in both BL Cotton Claudius A.ii and Bodleian Gough Eccl. Top. 4 – located as it is between the feasts of St. Bartholomew (24 August) and the Nativity of the Virgin (8 September) – the structure of the urtext remains purely hypothetical. The St. Winifred sermon isn't so closely associated with a particular place of worship. The fact that the saint's relics were interred in Shrewsbury Abbey in 1138 and a significant portion of the sermon deals with her martyrdom and translation does not itself suggest a direct link with the town. The 'narracio' detailing three men who were bitten by a spider, one of whom was cured by St. Winifred, is prefaced by the statement '[in] þe towne of Schorosbury', not a clarification one would make if writing *directly* for a priest of St. Alkmund's. Mirk does, however, mention that a disfigured man from 'Erkaleton' named Adam was cured of his impairment after visiting St. Winifred's shrine. The present-day villages of Child's Ercall and High Ercall, only 17 and 9 miles distant from Shrewsbury, are viable candidates for Erkalton ('Erkal toune' in Cotton Claudius A.ii). The naming of such an obscure village without clarification as to its whereabouts speaks to the audience's knowledge that it was located close by. As such, a connection to St. Alkmund's may still be feasible.[45] Either way, these weren't the only sermons to balance literary authority with reference to local history or recent events. Amongst the many authoritative statements on the spiritual and practical importance of the church building contained in the *De dedicacione ecclesie* sermon, Mirk recalls a revenant encounter in the vicinity of Lilleshall that he himself may have witnessed. As a central part of the 'language of the marketplace',[46] tales on the restless dead – especially those close to home – offered a credible, emotionally-charged framework through which to hold the parishioners' attention.

Prayers for the undead: exploring the Festial's *De dedicacione ecclesie* sermon

Research on the form and function of church dedication rituals is unusually scarce. Ruth Horie's *Perceptions of Ecclesia* (2006) remains the most detailed exploration of the subject in late medieval contexts.[47] Churches, of course, needed to be consecrated by a bishop before worship could commence. The ritual built upon Jewish precedents and by the eleventh century had been more or less standardised in the official guidebook for roman liturgy, the *Pontificale*.[48] As a general rule, the rite began at dawn, with the bishop, clergy, and congregation gathering outside the front door of the church whilst a single deacon remained inside. Following the lighting of twelve candles around the church perimeter and the blessing of holy water mixed with salt, the bishop embarked on three circuits of the building, casting aspersions on the walls whilst the attending clergy recited the appropriate responsories and versicles. After each circuit the bishop knocked on the front door and repeated the words of psalm 24: 7 ('Lift up your heads, you gates, be lifted up, you ancient doors, that the King of glory may come'),[49] which were answered by the deacon with the first part of psalm 24: 10 ('Who is this king of glory?').[50] The third circuit culminated with the rest of the verse ('The Lord Almighty, he is the king of glory') being completed by both the bishop and attending clergy.[51] On entering the church, the bishop again recited the appropriate antiphon – usually deriving from Luke 19: 5–6[52] – and made his way to the middle of the building, using his staff to trace the Greek and Latin alphabets on the floor in the form of a cross. The altar, the interior walls, and pavement were then blessed in sequence with a mixture of holy water, ashes, salt, and wine (a substance known as 'Gregorian Water') using a hyssop branch. Incense was burned upon the altar before being anointed with oil and chrism. It is at this point that the relics (if indeed the church possessed such artefacts) were to be taken into the building. After this, the bishop delivered his address and sermon.[53] Next, the relics were interred and sealed within the altar, alongside a consecrated Host, grains of incense, and/or other sacred objects. The rite concluded with a Mass. A feast was held on the anniversary of the dedication, often representing the most popular holiday of the liturgical year.[54]

The liturgical writer Durandus of Mende devotes an entire chapter of the *Rationale divinorum officiorum* (c.1286) to discussing the symbolism of the church dedication ritual.[55] At a fundamental level it represented nothing less than the purging of evil from the body of the 'material temple', understood as a physical analogue to the 'spiritual temple' of the soul and a microcosm of the 'universal temple' of the church. The expulsion of sin and the sanctification of the body (in its widest context) was a metaphor employed by almost all dedication rite exegetists and sermon writers, from Augustine to Bernard of Clairvaux and beyond.[56] Indeed, Durandus mentions quite explicitly 'that the water, by whose aspersions the church is consecrated, signifies Baptism, since in a certain manner the church itself is baptised',[57] building upon his earlier assertion that 'the house must be dedicated; the soul must be sanctified'.[58] Themes of repentance and rebirth permeate the dedication liturgy. The antiphons, versicles, psalms and hymns were specifically chosen to stress the act of humility and purification. The act of purification is demonstrated most notably by the Rite of Blessing of Salt and Water, recited by the bishop prior to the aspersion of the church interior. This ritual, a longstanding aspect of church liturgy, explicitly calls for the casting out of demons., The exorcism of the salt from the version of the dedication ritual found in the *Pontificalis* of the bishop of Exeter, Edmund Lacey (d.1455), for example, commands that 'all the delusions of the devil, his cunning and deceit, be driven far from the place where you are sprinkled, and let all the unclean spirits be repulsed by Him'.[59] Durandus of Mende confirms that one of the main reasons for the triple baptism of the church interior/exterior was to ensure the expulsion of unclean spirits.[60] The church building as purified body – once stained with sin, now fully cleansed – certainly influenced the choice of exempla when it came to constructing an appropriate sermon.

Mirk's dedication sermon is a finely-honed bricolage of liturgical, historical, and folkloric sources. Its structure was influenced most notably by Jacobus de Voragine's own *De dedication ecclesiae*[61] sermon and the *De officio mortuorum* chapter from Jean Beleth's *Summa de ecclesiasticis officiis*,[62] the treatise that formed the basis for Durandus of Mende's *Rationale divinorum officiorum*. The sermon itself is arranged according to a simple tripartite structure, a framework that was used throughout the *Festial* and which speaks to the preference for practicality over scholastic nuance.[63] Following an exhortation to the 'Goode men and woymen' of the congregation, Mirk begins by explaining that there were three main reasons why the 'chyrche ys hallowed' (i.e. consecrated): to be cleansed of sin; to act as an appropriate place for praying; and to function as a place for burying the dead. The first part of the sermon – the church as a place ordained for people to come together and worship God without being harried by the devil – namechecks the 'Legenda Aurea' and 'Saynt Gregory' as the source for the first 'narracio', concerning a pig-shaped demon seen exiting an unnamed church following the culmination of the dedication ritual and the deposition of the saints' relics. The demon tried to re-enter the church on three consecutive nights, causing much noise and terror but ultimately to no avail. Here, Mirk distils the original narrative (deriving from book three, chapter thirty of Gregory's *Dialogues* and repeated in Jacobus de Voragine's dedication sermon), omitting such unnecessary details as the fact that it was an Arian church being sanctified and that the relics belonged to Sts. Sebastian and Agatha.[64] The next part of the sermon, concerning the church as an appropriate place of prayer, begins by addressing the audience directly ('I hope þat ȝe all prayen well at hom yn your houses') before explaining how, just as one would go to a friend's home to speak to him, it is better to speak to God in his own house. Mindful that 'mony of you wyttuþe noght how ȝe schull pray to God', Mirk then provides a helpful overview of the various things one should pray for, such as God's compassion, being thankful that Christ died on the cross, and for the forgiveness of one's sins. Idle chatter ('jangling') by the congregation was a fundamental concern of sermon writers.[65] Mirk was no exception. Deploring the harm caused by 'spekyng of vanyte and of oþer fylthe', he illustrates the danger of gossiping during church with the exemplum of the writing-demon, Tutivillus (here unnamed).[66] Mirk again distils the narrative down to its most salient points, noting how, during Mass, a deacon observed a demon sitting on the shoulders of two gossiping women, writing their words down on a roll 'als fast as he myght'. At the deacon's behest, the bishop approached the two women after Mass and casually asked them how they had occupied themselves during the service. 'The Pater Noster', came the reply. The bishop then commanded the demon to read back what he had written on the parchment. Hearing this, the women fell to the floor and begged for mercy.[67] It is unclear where Mirk sources his version of the Tutivillus tale, which existed in two main versions: a) the sack-carrying demon collecting Latin words misspoken by the clergy; b) the demon writing down the idle gossip of the parishioners. 'I rede þat' is the phrase used by Mirk at the beginning of the story, suggesting a literary rather than oral source. The 'b' text was popularised in the *Sermones vulgares* of Jacques de Vitry (d.1240) and thereafter became part of the common repertoire of sermon writers, sculptures, and artists.[68] Given the location of Mirk's *fende* – perched between the shoulders of the two women – it is possible he was inspired by the version of the tale included in Robert Mannyng's *Handlyng Synne* (c.1303), who is similarly precise about the demon's proximity to his charges: 'Betwyx hem to y say a fende [...] Pryuyly be hynde here bake'

((1, ll. 9280, 9283). According to Margaret Jennings, Mannyng's account represents the most 'complete' early version of the text.[69]

It is immediately after this exemplum that Mirk expounds on the third main reason for consecrating the church: to provide an appropriate place to bury the dead. 'Seynt [sic] Ion Belet' is quoted almost verbatim in the initial overview of the pseudo-history of burial practice, specifically the statement that rich men were buried on the top and bottom of mountains and that poor men were buried in their homes. Amending Beleth's wording slightly, Mirk notes that due to the overriding stench of the rotting cadavers, the 'holy fadyrs' insisted that the dead should instead be buried in churchyards.[70] Burial in consecrated ground benefitted the dead for two fundamental reasons: it enabled them to receive the prayers of the faithful and also ensured that 'þe bodyes of þe ded schuld lye þer wythout trauelyng oþir vexyng of þe fende'. That is, burial in hallowed ground prevented the corpse from being moved and infiltrated by the devil. Such a sentiment is repeated in Mirk's burial sermon (to be discussed shortly) and the 'Officiorum Mortuorum' sermon from the *Speculum Sacerdotale* (c.1425), a vernacular sermon collection that also originated in the West Midlands and which may have been influenced by the *Festial*.[71]

Not everyone was protected by hallowed ground. Quoting from Beleth, Mirk argues that only the defenders of the church were afforded such luxury, and that there have been occasions when unworthy bodies were cast out of the grave leaving their burial clothes behind. This leads Mirk into a 'narracio', taken from Beleth but originally from Gregory's *Dialogues* (IV.52), concerning a church-warden who, at the behest of an angel, went to the bishop and commanded him to exhume the body of a sinner he had buried within in the church, lest he himself die within thirty days. The bishop ignored the warning and died soon after. Mirk obviously saw utility in this tale, for it is re-used in the 'Burial Notes' sermon (*Qui Sunt Sepeliendi in Cimiterio*), only with the warden substituted for the more impressive figure of a 'holy man'.[72] Mirk namechecks the allusive 'Gestes of Fraunce' as the source of his next narrative concerning the dragon that emerged from Charles Martel's burnt, blackened tomb, evidence he had been transported to hell on account of his sins against the church. Mirk was not unknown to misidentify his sources[73] and the title 'Gestes of Fraunce' is ambiguous enough to make a true source difficult to pin down. The lack of reference to Martel's *fiery* grave in the version recounted by Ranulph Higden suggests Mirk did not consult the *Polychronicion* for this particular exemplum,[74] despite professing his knowledge of Higden in the *Festial*'s St. Matthew sermon.[75] William of Malmesbury's account of Martel's fate, mentioned in the epilogue to the Witch of Berkeley narrative, does not mention a dragon, only that the king was snatched from the grave by evil spirits (*malignis spiritibus*). It is possible that Mirk knew the tale from Hincmar's original, or more likely from a continuation of the *Historia regum Francorum monasterii sancti dionysii*. (c.1118–1137),[76] French versions of which indeed circulated under the rubric 'geste de france'. Another hypothetical source – again predicated on Mirk's knowledge of vernacular French – is the *Chronique rimée*, a versified history of the kings of France from prehistory to the thirteenth century composed by Phillippe Mouskes, bishop of Tournai (c.1272). Mouskes also makes mention of Eucherius (here rendered as 'Eustere', l. 1936), the dragon ('S'en issi volant dragons' l. 1954) and the blackened tomb ('Tout ausi noir comme la poit', l.1958).[77] Regardless of the narrative's provenance, Mirk concludes with the unequivocal statement that 'buryyng yn holy plas helpyþe not hom þat byn worthy to be dampned'.[78]

With the miraculous expulsion of the sinful dead from holy ground established by recourse to liturgical authority (Beleth) and historical precedent, the next part of Mirk's sermon builds upon the narrative logic of the movement of unworthy corpses to focus on a topic that was mostly elided in universal church discourse but was undoubtedly a concern for local audiences: the rationale for the ambulation of the worthy dead. To quote Mirk's explanation in full:

> Also þer ben mony þat walketh aftyr þat þay ben ded and buryet yn holy plase; but þat is of no wexyng of þe fend, but of grace of God, forto gete horn som helpe of som synne þat þay ben gylty yn, and may not haue no rest, tyll þat synne be holpen. As hit fell bysyde þe abbay of Lulsull by þre men þat hadden stolen an ox of þe abbot, and he had made a sentens þerfor; then two of þilke wern schryuen and asked mercy, but þe þryd deyd and was not asoy-let. Wherfor his spyryte ʒede nyghtes and soo feeryd þe parysch þat aftyr þe sonne going downe þer dyrst no man go out of his yn. Then, as þe prest, Syr Thomas Wodward, þat þen was parysche prest, ther he toke Godys body, and ʒede toward a seke woman at þe sonne goyng don. And þen come þis spyryte, and mete hym, and told hym who he was and why he ʒede, and prayed hym forto take his wyfe, and go to þe abbot of Lulsull, and help pat he wer asoylet, and er he myʒt haue no rest. And soo he come to Lulsull, and made þe mon asoylet, and þen he had rest.[79]

Mirk does not take issue with the idea that corpses were able to walk after death. If judging by the wording of the exemplum it appears to have been a common occurrence. He questions only the belief that bodies buried in holy ground were susceptible to the machinations of the devil. The need to clarify that corpses did not walk due to the 'wexyng of þe fend' suggests, perhaps, that the opposite was deemed true in minds of his audience. Such beliefs may have even been shared by the clerics themselves. Mirk's own burial sermon contains a commonplace reference to the sprinkling of holy water on the body to ensure 'þat fyndys schal haue no pouste ('power') in hys graue'.[80] This does not mean that Mirk was confused or contradictory in his reasoning, only that a specific discursive standpoint was needed to suit a particular pastoral situation. In this instance, the ability of post-mortem prayer to relieve the suffering of the unshriven took precedence over the equally valid belief that dangerously 'open' bodies needed extra spiritual protection.

Unlike the other exempla used in the dedication sermon, the walking corpse narrative has a distinctively folkloric flavour and likely derived from an oral source. Not only was the theft of oxen perpetrated against an unnamed Abbot of Lilleshall (perhaps William of Peplow 1353–1369; Roger Norris 1369–1375, or

William of Peynton, 1375–1398),[81] but it appears that the dead thief was also a resident of Lilleshall village, if the fact that he haunted the parish streets presupposes he was buried in the local churchyard of St. Michael's. The parish priest at the time is also named: Sir Thomas Wodward. Although it is clear from the narrative context that Mirk is discussing embodied ghosts – the introductory statement that 'mony [...] walketh aftyr þat þay ben ded' is somewhat unambiguous on this point – the descriptor *spyryte* ('spirit', or life-force) still lends a sense of uncertainty as to the true physicality of the assailant, even if the narratology of the encounter echoes the writings of William of Newburgh and Geoffrey of Burton, et al. A more neutral term such as *cors*, used elsewhere in the *Festial*, did not instil the same sense of moral contrast as *spyryte* does to *fende*. The use of *spyryte*, the spirit of the deceased, more effectively stresses the identity of the mobilising agent.

The twelve ghost stories transcribed by an anonymous monk from Byland Abbey, North Yorkshire, at the turn of the fifteenth century provide further evidence that Mirk's 'repentant corpse' exemplum was not just a literary commonplace employed for didactic convenience. Written on blank leaves in a late twelfth-century miscellany containing several works of Cicero and theological tracts by Honorius of Autun and Ivo of Chartes (BL Royal 15 A. XX), the tales lack any form of over moralisation or uniform rhetorical structure. As admitted by the Monk himself, they represent the unfiltered gossip and folklore of the local community (*'dicitur, referunt aliqui'*).[82] Story III finds certain narratological affinities with Mirk's own tale. It professes to detail the post-mortem activities of Robert, son of Robert de Boltby, who lived in the village of Kilburn about two miles west from Byland. Robert's corpse, it seems, had a habit (*solebat*) of leaving its grave at night and causing distress to the local townsfolk. The corpse wandered aimlessly through the village streets (*egredi)*, accompanied by a pack of barking dogs – a topos also employed by William of Newburgh. It was noted that Robert often stood at the walls, doors, and windows of the neighboring houses, as if trying to grab the attention of those inside. One night, two young men managed to accost the corpse in the cemetery. One of the men, Robert Foxton, pinned it to the 'kirkestile' (the church gate) and commanded the other fetch the parish priest, who arrived as quickly as he could. Conjured to speak, the corpse groaned from the bottom of its 'bowels' (*interioribus visceribus*) as it confessed its many misdeeds.[83] Absolved of sin, and with the priest charging all those present not reveal the contents of the confession to anyone else, Robert of Kilburn was finally able to rest. The Monk concludes by idly speculating on what caused the corpse to rise – Robert was rumoured to have been an accessory to murder – but decides that it is best not to dwell on such matters.

The post-mortem remittance of sin was the motivating factor in nine of the twelve stories recorded by the Byland Monk. Of the three that do not mentioned absolution, the disposal of the restless corpse of James Tankerley in Story IV betrays a greater concern for the safety of the community than the salvation of the deceased's soul. Similarly, Story V, concerning a woman who carried a 'spirit' made of phantom flesh (*non solida sed fantastica*), does not specify the ghost's intentions. The narrative about a necromancer being unable to scry the location of a penitent who received absolution from a priest contains no reference to the restless dead at all (Story X). *Spirituum* is nonetheless the most commonly term used to describe such entities. Whilst the vagueness of language makes the ontology of the Byland Monk's ghosts unclear, explicit references to shapeshifting (Stories I, II, VIII) is evidence enough that some ghosts were disembodied and merely assumed their apparent forms. The verbs 'carried' (*cepit*) 'seized' (*comprehendit*) and 'wrestled' (*luctabatur*) assign a sense of physicality, if not complete corporeality, to at least some of the assailants (see Stories V and VI). The statements that James Tankereley 'walked' (*egredi*) from his tomb in Byland Abbey's chapterhouse is unambiguous (Story IV). Likewise, the dead sister of the landowner Adam de Lond (d.1361) is not only physically seized (*comprehensa*) on the roadside (Story XII), but her intransigent brother states that he does not care if she 'walks for all eternity' (*ambulaueris imperpetuum*).⁸⁴ Interestingly, neither James Tankerley nor Adam de Lond's sister are described as being 'spirits'. Given that their method of movement betrays physical footfall – *egredi, ambulare* – they may be unequivocally read as walking corpses. And yet, the rubric to Story III, '*De spiritu Roberti filii Roberti de Boltebi de Killeburne comprehenso in cimiterio*', suggests that 'spirit' did not solely refer to insubstantial or quasi-embodied ghosts but could also relate the identity of the activating agent, if, like Robert of Kilburn, the ghost was trapped within the bowels of the corpse. The designation of the undead was wholly ill-defined, lacking experiential and typological certainty. The fact that Mirk uses *spyryte* does not invalidate the reading that the Lilleshall ghost was corporeal. It is a choice that stresses the non-diabolical agency of the thief's corpse.

Mirk did not record the haunting of Lilleshall village for posterity's sake. Nor did he intend to provide scurrilous entertainment for his audience. The absolution of a walking, repentant corpse was entirely appropriate subject matter for a dedication sermon. There is a clear symbolic connection between the sanctification of the church building (the material temple) and the absolution of a soul that was also stained with sin (the spiritual temple). Both acts involved the purification of the body. The 'Dedication of the Church' sermon from the *Speculum sacerdote*, while not as lengthy or discursive as the *Festial's*, is much more explicit on the metaphysical equivalency that exists between the soul, flesh, and stone, remarking that 'owith ye to be holy in herte and in body þat ye may be the temples of God', a statement justified with reference to 1 Cor. 3: 17 (*Templum* [enim] *Dei sanctum est, quod estis vos*).⁸⁵ Mirk's revenant story also provides an appropriate thematic counterpoint to the earlier exempla on the expulsion of the pig-demon and the forcible removal of those 'worthy to be damned'. Whether it was apparent to the congregation or not, the decrease in the severity of sin recorded in the three main exempla – from devilish (the pig-demon in the church building), to mortal (Charles Martel), to venial (Lilleshall thief) – mirrors the gradual process by which the bishop fortified and cleansed the structure of the church, from its baser, outlying layers (the aspersion of the exterior walls and churchyard) to the most holy inner sanctum (the sanctification of the altar). To worship without hindrance, pray properly, and die well: these are the truths Mirk is trying to convey about the importance of the church and churchyard. The final sentence succeeds in the tricky task of tying all three strands of the argument together:

> Now pray ȝe to allmyghty God, as all goodnes and grace ys wyth hym, to ȝeue you grace of þe Holy Gost yn holy chyrche hym to worschyp here, þat ȝe may come to þe rest þat he boȝt you to. Amen.

Correct devotional practices in a sanctified place of worship ensured that the listener achieved perpetual succour and restfulness in death.

Exorcising demons: exploring Mirk's *In die sepulture alicuius Mortui* sermon

The reality of Purgatory, the benefits of post-mortem prayer, and importance of the funerary rite are the three main themes that underlie the late medieval burial sermon.[86] Burial and memorial sermons written for high-status individuals – such as Thomas Beauchamp, Earl of Warwick, (d.1401) – were also likely to include allegorical commentaries on the deceased's life, virtues, and career.[87] As a template for local parish priests, Mirk's burial sermon does not include reference to any named individuals, nor does it delve into sophisticated exegesis on the philosophy of material and spiritual death. It does, however, reflect Mirk's propensity to combine material from literary authorities with emotionally-resonant exempla that cater to the sensibilities of the local Shropshire audience.

Written in the same easy style that characterises the sermons in the *Festial* proper (brisk, with no preamble or protheme),[88] the burial sermon begins with the declaration that the corpse is brought into the church for three fundamental reasons. The first, simply, is to demonstrate that the deceased was devoted to the church and loved God. Just as a mother would not reject a child, so the church would not reject those that wished to be saved.[89] Mirk follows standard rhetorical practice in invoking the visceral imagery of rot and decay as part of the second reason why the corpse is brought into the church: to be buried in sanctified ground. On death, the flesh 'begyraiuth to stynke and turne to foulest careyn' and thus needs to be 'hud in þe erth þat is halowod'.[90] The deathbed ritual itself goes unmentioned. By contrast, the 'Officium Mortuorum' sermon from the *Speculum sacerdotale* is explicit on the processes involved in the transference of the body from the deathbed, to the church, to the grave. Based on the writings of Jean Beleth,[91] the sermon argues that the dying man or woman should ideally be lain on a bed of ashes in the manner of St. Martin of Tours, with the Passion being recited to ensure the deceased approached death in the appropriate state of mind (with the implicit assumption that dying 'badly' would leave the soul vulnerable to molestation by the devil). Anointed, washed, and wrapped in a burial shroud, the body would then be carried to the church for the funeral Mass, accompanied by the ringing of bells: two for a man, three for a woman, and 'for as many tymes has he hadde ordres' for a member of the clergy. If the deceased's secular or religious status did not allow for burial in the church building itself, a second funerary procession – comprising pallbearers of the deceased's social station – carried the body to the graveyard. It was here that the corpse was removed from the coffin, blessed by the priest, and deposited in the ground.[92]

Mirk is concerned only with interrogating the meaning of the funerary rite once the body reached its final resting place. The act of deposition formed the most public part of the death performance (as opposed to the more private environs of the deathbed itself) and required a synopsis of its main components so that the audience – the mourners – did not misread the situation when the funeral Mass finished and they proceeded to the burial ground. Mirk's overview omits some of the traditional details found in the *Speculum sacerdotale* and Beleth, such as the placement of ivy (iuy; *hedera*) and laurel (lorey; *laurus*) in the grave to signify everlasting life, and the inclusion of charcoal (coles; *carbones*) to highlight that the ground had ceased to be used for common purposes.[93] His choices should be read less as a rote regurgitation of liturgical authority – an accusation that can be laid at the author of the *Speculum sacerdotale* – and more a representation of the actual schema of a late fourteenth-century West Midlands burial. Indeed, Mirk notes simply that the white burial shroud signified contrition; alignment on the east-west axis ensured that the deceased was ready to rise come the Last Judgement; a memorial cross at the deceased's head showed that he or she had been saved by Christ's Passion; the placement of broken staff next to the corpse symbolised that the deceased had a long, arduous journey to salvation ('mote nede take bettur and worse, as he hath deseruyth').[94] Intriguingly, Mirk also mentions that a 'cros of a wax-candul' should be placed on the deceased's breast, evidence that he or she died showing charity to God and man (the corporal and spiritual works of mercy). Such a provision was not unique to England. An eleventh-century liturgical handbook from Northern Italy also makes reference to the placement of a wax cross on the breast (*pectus*) of the deceased as one of the final acts the funerary ritual.[95] As mentioned previously with regards to the lead absolution cross found in the grave of Godfrey of Chichester (d.1088), it is likely that the placement of crosses in the grave also had an apotropaic function, employed to assuage residual sin and prevent the devil from harrying the corpse.[96] Walter Map's *nugae* concerning the walking corpse from Worcester includes a pointed reference to a cross being placed on the grave to ensure the 'wretch' (*miseri*) stayed in the ground.[97] The function of Mirk's wax cross may well be multivalent, acting both as a sign of charity and an apotropaic device depending on the viewpoint of the percipient, but there is nothing ambiguous about the reasons for the sprinkling of holy water in the grave. The devil, warns Mirk, has no 'pouste' (power) over bodies protected in such a manner. Indeed, evil spirits are eager to brutalise corpses that have not received the full benefit of the sacraments, as is shown in the subsequent exemplum:

I fynde þat þer wer þre bretheren at debate in a toune and weron slayne all þre; but þe too haddon all þer rythus, and þe þrydde was not hosullud, and so weron beried togydur in þe church. Þan com a fend and toke þis cors þat was not anoylud, and ȝode into itte and so forth into þe toun, and makud many cryes be þe which men weron sore agaste; and dured þus a long tyme. Þan was þer an ankur in þat toun in þe chyrch, þat was in hys preyeres before mydnythe, and seygh þe fende come be lythe of þe mone leke an ape; and whan he com to þe graue, anone, þe corse arose, and he ȝode into hytte, and so forth in hys iurney, as he was wonte. Ðan, whan he come aȝeyne, þis ankur coniured þis fende, in þe vertu of hym þat dyod on þe cros for mankynde, þat he schulde tellyn hym, why he hadde such power in þat cors rather þan in any othur. Þan sayde he: 'For þis was not annoylid, þerfore I haue power in þis cors; bot þe soule is saffe. Wherefore I go not þus for harme of hys soule, but to maken oþur to synnon on hym and to demon hym oþur þan he is, so þat I may putton þat aȝeynus hym in þe day of dome, and say how þei demod here neyghburres othur þan þei schulde done, aȝeynus Goddys commaundement. Þan þis ankur charged hym be þe uertu of Goddys passion to leue of, and no more tempton Goddus pepul, and so sesud. Þis is þe secunde cause why fis cors is browthe to chyrch[98]

Three brothers were killed in a brawl in an unnamed town. Two of the brothers received the appropriate deathbed sacraments but the third did not. As such, a fiend was able to take control of his corpse and wreak havoc amongst the local community. One day, an anchorite saw the demon in 'the shape of an ape' approach the dead man's grave, enter the corpse, and set forth into town. When the fiend returned to the graveyard, the anchorite conjured it to speak, asking why it had so much power over this particular body. It replied that it was able to enter the cadaver due to it not having been anointed at death. The devil confessed that whilst the deceased's soul was safe it wanted to make mischief in his name so that the body's misdeeds would count against him at the Last Judgement. Hearing this, the anchorite commanded the demon to depart.

Mirk was not the only sermon writer to stress the metaphysical importance of exorcising the corpse at the graveside. Beleth's provision that holy water was an anathema to demons, and that such evil entities were known to otherwise 'rage'[99] in dead bodies, is rendered by the author of the *Speculum sacerdotale* as 'deuilles vsen to schewe wodenes in the bodies of dede for to do hem schame in here deþ that they myȝt noȝt do them in here lyfe'.[100] 'Wodenes' meaning either 'raving' or 'frenzy', is a direct translation of Beleth's *des[a]euire*, attesting to the unwillingness of the anonymous author to deviate too far from the source material. Mirk uses Beleth in a much more sophisticated manner, putting the devilish desire to 'shame' the dead into the mouth of the demonically-activated corpse ('to demon hym oþur þan he is'). Indeed, the entire exemplum is an indirect manifestation of the instruction, recorded by Beleth and Durandus, that those who died in a fight were not permitted burial in holy ground lest they received absolution, as repeated by Mirk himself in his Burial Notes ('And he þat dyeth in iustes, bot he ask a preste ere he dye, he schal not ben byried in sentuary').[101] An exemplum about a demonically-activated body was the perfect vehicle through which to convey one of the base tenets of the burial liturgy and illustrates, in graphic terms, the means by which a demon 'raged' within a corpse. It is tempting to speculate that the use of violent death as a framing device was an oblique way to highlight the type of behaviour seen as most damaging to the salvation of the soul, especially in light on the evidence from medieval coroners' rolls.[102]

References to the demonically-activated dead are not as prevalent in the later Middle Ages as in earlier centuries, although this not to suggest such beliefs were not current. A letter written by a member of the prominent Armburgh family from Warwickshire, containing a brief account of the untimely death of the parliamentarian and lawyer, Richard Baynard (d.1434), does not mention outright that dying without communion and confession caused a demon to enter Baynard's body, but the description of his corpse causing 'harm' in the local community is certainly suggestive:

> [A]nd with inneafter as he went a hunting with my lady Bergeveny sodenly felle downe and dyed with owte howsill and shrifte and anon after he walkyd and yit doth and hath don moche harme as it is openly noysed and knowen in the contre there a boute.[103]

The use of the present-tense singular 'doth' and 'hath' intimates that the whole affair had yet to be resolved at the time of writing. As a brief, gossipy aside in a longer correspondence concerning a family inheritance dispute, it is not surprising that the author (perhaps the main claimant, Joan Armburgh) does not dwell on the agency behind Baynard's harmful corpse. Didactic texts were not so oblique. John Bromyard's influential preaching aid, the *Summa predicantium* (c.1352), includes a sardonic exemplum about a man who fakes his death, sat up on the bier, and was subsequently killed by his terrified servant, aiming to chase the devil away from the corpse.[104] In pseudo-literary contexts, the prose history of the Marcher Lord Fouke Fitz Waryn (d.1256), based on a lost thirteenth-century verse romance, describes the death of the legendary giant Gogmagog, whose body was subsequently inhabited and mobilised by the devil ('e un espirit del deble meyntenant entra la cors Geogmagog e vynt et ces parties').[105] The Byland Abbey Monk does not record any ghosts that are specifically identified as evils spirits. Shape-shifting, one of the fundamental attributes of a number of the entities recorded by the Monk, is an ability usually associated with airy demons, who, as will be discussed in more detail in chapter five, were able to cause hallucinations in the minds of their human victims and/or manipulate the elements to better trap their prey. The spirit of the excommunicate encountered by the tailor 'Snawball' (Snoweshull)[106] in Story II certainly displays these qualities. Appearing to the tailor in the form of a raven, dog, she-goat and, finally, a rotting corpse 'like one of the kings in pictures' (*ad instar vnius regis mortui depicti*),[107] the ghost was ultimately conjured using the techniques employed by necromancers to raise demons, with Snawball creating a magic circle on which he placed holy relics and inscribed the names of God.[108] Vernacular exempla collections from the *Alphabet of Tales* to *Jacob's Well* similarly act as repositories for stories on the demonic infiltration of 'open' bodies. Ultimately, there was nothing unorthodox about an unshriven corpse being used as the devil's plaything.

The remainder of Mirk's burial sermon is relatively straightforward and concerns the third main reason for burial in the church: to receive the benefits of the sacraments and post-mortem prayer. Mirk quotes the same 'Ion Belete' passage used in the church dedication sermon, concerning how the stench of rotting flesh forced people to bury their loved ones 'otwyth þe toun' rather than in their homes, and that rich men used to bury their dead in/on mountains. Mirk adds the extra detail that the souls of the deceased often appeared to their friends and family, complaining that they received no succour in death. Thus, the bishops created churchyards to help the dead achieve salvation. Mirk then highlights the prayer cycles and sacraments that were considered the most useful to souls trapped in Purgatory – the Mass, of course, being the most beneficial service of all – before concluding with an exemplum, given without source, detailing intercessory powers of the Virgin. The story is framed as testimony given by a 'spryte' to an unnamed prior, concerning what happens to the soul immediately after death. If the soul leaves the body having received all the appropriate deathbed rituals, it is protected by Mary against the hordes of awaiting demons. As the 'emperace of helle', with 'power oure alle [the] fyndys' she is able to command all evil spirits to depart and grant succour to those in need of protection.

The sermon concludes by reiterating that there were three main reasons for bringing the corpse to the church to be buried (to show devotion to God; to gain protection from demons; to receive the benefits of intercession). With demons ready to ensnare the soul and abuse the body at a moment's notice, the statement that 'vche man and womman þat is wyse, make hym redy þerto, for alle we schul dyon and we wyte note how sone' was a warning that those present at the funeral Mass could not afford not take lightly.

Conclusion

Scant biographical information exists on John Mirk. His sermon collection and pastoral handbooks provide a tantalising glimpse into the emotional outlook and professional life of a workaday provincial canon. Lilleshall Abbey was not an especially prosperous establishment and in the mid-fourteenth century suffered from severe financial mismanagement at the hands of Abbot John (resigned 1330). Similarly, due to its prime location near the main road from Stafford to Shrewsbury the burden of offering hospitality to travellers often left the canons in a state of near destitution.[109] Nor did the Abbey hold any political power. In many respects it exemplified any number of low-level monastic foundations that interspersed the English landscape. Although the contents of the Lilleshall library have been lost to history, an analysis of Mirk's literary influences allows for a tentative appraisal of the types of material that may have been available for study. Jean Beleth's *Summa de ecclesiasticis officiis*, William of Pagula's *Oculus Sacerdotis* and, perhaps, Robert Mannyng's *Handlyng Synne* formed part of the hypothetical liturgical catalogue. Jacobus de Voragine's *Legenda*

Aurea, the *Vita Patrum,*[110] Gregory the Great's *Dialogues* and Bede's *Historia Ecclesiastica,* all invoked at some point in the *Festial,* were also likely to have been kept at Lilleshall.[111] Secular history was perhaps represented by the chronicle of John Ickham, Ranulph Hidgen's *Polychronicon,* a vernacular continuation of the *Historia regum Francorum monasterii sancti dionysii* and, potentially, the rather more exotic *Chronique rimée* of Philippe Mouskes. It may not have been the most prestigious of monasteries, but it was certainly not intellectually impoverished.

By the early thirteenth century narratives on the restless dead had ceased to be the purview of Latinate clerks and churchmen, finding new literary life as sermon stories to educate the laity in the base tenets of Christian practice. Mirk's *De dedicacione ecclesie* sermon elaborated upon the spiritual importance of the church building and churchyard in an unambiguous and straightforward manner. The need to illustrate the consequences of incorrect behaviour was a defining feature of sermon stories, both for Mirk and the wider community of pastoral writers. Fear was one of the prime instigators of behavioural change. If, as has been speculated, the *Festial* was first written for the congregation of St. Alkmund's in Shrewsbury, then the post-mortem wanderings of the Lilleshall thief were geographically immediate enough to remind the audience that suffering (and walking) after death was not merely a fate reserved for others, a quirk of history, but could affect anyone from the local community. Stories with a distinct local provenance had a much greater emotional impact than material consciously regurgitated from older, more abstract sources, especially when it came to the provisions for 'dying well'.

The importance of receiving the appropriate deathbed sacraments is likewise the central theme of the walking corpse exemplum from Mirk's *In die sepulture alicuius Mortui* sermon. Unlike the story of the Lilleshall thief, which stresses that fiends are not able to infiltrate the bodies of venial sinners, here the corpse of the unshriven brother is clearly mobilised by an airy demon – one that occasionally takes the form of an ape. With the exemplum located immediately after the discussion of the symbolism of the burial rite and the statement that corpses needed to be protected from the 'rage' of evil spirts, Mirk downplays the interpretation of the revenant as a soul in need of suffrage in favour of exemplifying the worst-case scenario for leaving the body spiritually 'open'. Whilst the base message of both exempla is ostensibly the same – do not die unshriven; protect the sanctity of the corpse – the topic is approached in entirely different ways. Far from being a habitual residue that the post-Lateran IV church was unable to fully eradicate, the topos of the restless corpse remained a vital part of pastoral teachings on deathbed performance and burial practice, even taking into account the proliferation of the belief in the disembodied, purgatorial spirit. Progressive theological treatises (such as William of Auvergne's *De universo,* c.1249) that denied the ability of demons or spirits to mobilise the corpse did not meet the emotional expectations of the laity. Mirk well understood the social logic and moral utility of the walking dead, presenting his audience with manifest examples of 'bad death' that they were not liable to forget.

Notes

1 Le Goff, *The Birth of Purgatory,* pp. 165–67.
2 For an overview of this cultural shift and its manifestation in the changing narratological framework of ghost narratives, see chapter five, 'Imagining the Dead', in Watkins, *History and the Supernatural,* pp. 170–201.
3 Watkins, *History and the Supernatural,* pp. 187–90.
4 The ghost of the girl, Cecilia, explicitly mentions that she is a prisoner (*captiva*) in purgatory, in Easting, 'Dialogue Between a Clerk and the Spirit of a Girl', p. 168.
5 The influence of the theologian William de Montibus (d.1213) on Hugh's decision to absolve the Buckingham revenant cannot be underestimated. As a contemporary of Peter Comestor at Paris, William was very much concerned with the practical applications of speculative theology. Indeed, William's treatises on pastoral care (*Pastoralia*) and the elimination of doctrinal error (*Errorum Eliminatio*) reflect his preoccupation with disseminating new – and 'correct' – modes of thought among the general populace. On becoming chancellor of Lincoln's school in 1194, William was tasked by Hugh with educating the next generation of churchmen in the reforms emerging from Paris. As such, Hugh's response to the news that a revenant was terrorising the Buckingham village can also be read as an expression of the intellectual climate of his inner circle: the absolution of an errant corpse was the application of theory (the reality of the *purgatorium*; the benefits of post-mortem prayer) in an everyday, practical context. For the life and works of William de Montibus, see Joseph Goering, *William de Montibus (c.1140–1213): The Schools and the Literature of Pastoral Care* (Toronto, Ont: Pontifical Institute of Medieval Studies, 1992); Hugh MacKinnon, 'William de Montibus: A Medieval Teacher', in *Essays in Medieval History Presented to Bertie Wilkinson,* ed. by T. A Sandquist and M. R. Powicke (Toronto, Ont: Toronto University Press, 1969), pp. 32–45.
6 GrA ii.124 (pp. 196–97).
7 Goscelin of Saint-Bertin, *Miracles of St Edmund,* pp. 144–45.
8 See the previous chapter's discussion of the ghost that haunted the public baths in city of Centumcellis, in Gregory the Great, *Sancti Gregorii Papae I, PL 77,* col. 417.
9 See book eight, chapter seventeen of Orderic's *Historia Ecclesiastica* (c.1133–1135) and the account of the priest Walchelin's encounter with Hellequins's Hunt, the army of the dead, that was said to have occurred on January 1 1091 near the village of *Bonneval,* Northern France. The Hunt was a pervasive folkloric motif, utilised to satiric effect by Walter Map in his nugae on the wanderings of 'King Herla'. For a full explication of Orderic's exemplum, see Schmitt, *Ghosts in the Middle Ages,* pp. 93–121.
10 See Peter's story concerning the ghost of the Spanish servant, Sancho (himself part of the retinue of a ghostly army), who tells his interlocutor and former master, Pedro d'Englebert, that he hopes to be purged of his sins in the place where he committed them in life, in Peter the Venerable, 'De Miraculis Libri Duo', PL 189, I. 28 (at col 905).
11 Watkins, *History and the Supernatural,* p. 187.
12 Schmitt, *Ghosts in the Middle Ages,* pp. 147–48.
13 For an overview, see Giles Constable, *The Reformation of the Twelfth-Century* (Cambridge: Cambridge University Press, 1996).
14 Ronald J. Stanbury, 'Preaching and Pastoral Care in the Middle Ages', in *A Companion to Pastoral Care in the Late Middle Ages (1200–1500),* ed. by Ronald J. Stanbury (Leiden: Brill, 2010), pp. 23–39.
15 Innocent III, *Romani Pontificis Opera Omnia, vol. 3,* PL 216, ed. by J-P Migne (Paris, 1855), col. 829.
16 'Inter caetera quae ad salutem spectant populi christiani pabulum verbi Dei permaxime sibi noscitur esse necessarium [...]. Generali constitutione sancimus, ut episcopi

viros idoneos ad sanctae praedicationis officium salubriter exequendum assumant, potentes in opera et sermone […]. Unde praecipimus tam in cathedralibus quam in aliis conventualibus ecclesiis viros idoneos ordinari, quos episcopi possint coadiutores et cooperatores habere, non solum in praedicationis officio verum etiam in audiendis confessionibus et poenitentiis iniungendis ac caeteris, quae ad salute pertinent animarum', in *Decrees of the Ecumenical Councils, Volume One: Nicaea to Lateran V*, ed. by Norman P. Tanner (London: Sheed & Ward and Georgetown University Press, 1990), pp. 239–40.

17 Discussed in Peter Scanlon, *Augustine's Theology on Preaching* (Lanham, Fortress Press 2014).

18 Phyllis Roberts, 'Sermons and Preaching in/and the Medieval University', in *Medieval Education*, ed. by Ronald B. Begley and Joseph, W. Koterski (New York, NY: Fordham University Press, 2005), pp. 83–98.

19 Stanbury, 'Preaching and Pastoral Care', p. 26.

20 'Omnis utriusque sexus fidelis, postquam ad annos discretionis pervenerit, omnia sua solus peccata confiteatur fideliter, saltem semel in anno proprio sacerdoti, et iniunctam sibi poenitentiam studeat pro viribus adimplere […] alioquin et vivens ab ingressu ecclesiae arceatur et moriens christiana careat sepultura' (All the faithful of either sex , after they have reached the age of discernment, should individually confess all their sins in a faithful manner to their own priest at least once a year, and let them take care to do what they can to perform the penance imposed on them […] otherwise they shall be barred from entering a church during their lifetime and they shall be denied a Christian burial in death), in Tanner, *Decrees of the Ecumenical Councils I*, p. 245.

21 'Maxime ualent exempla, que maxime erudiunt simplicum hominum ruditatum, et faciliorem et longiorem ingerunt et imprimunt in memoria tenacitatem', in Stephen of Bourbon, *Tractatus de diversis materiis predicabilibus*, ed. by Jacques Berlioz and Jean-Luc Eichenlaub, CCCM 124 (Turnhout: Brepols, 2002), pp. 3–4.

22 See the essays collated in Leonard E. Boyle, *Pastoral Care, Clerical Education and Canon Law, 1200–1400* (London: Variorum, 1981).

23 The first modern edition of the *Festial* was completed by Theodor Erbe, deriving from Bodleian Library MS Gough Ecclesiastical Topography 4 (c.1415–1433), and which also includes the additional sermons from BL MS. Claudius A. II. A two-volume edition of the BL MS. Claudius A. II text has recently been edited by Susan Powell: *John Mirk's Festial,,edited from the British Library MS. Claudius A. II*, 2 vols, EETS o.s. 335 (Oxford: Oxford University Press, 2009). All quotes from the *Festial* have been take from the Erbe edition unless otherwise stated.

24 Susan Powell and Alan J. Fletcher remain two of the most notable scholars on John Mirk. See especially the following works by Susan Powell, 'John Mirk's *Festial* and the Pastoral Programme', *Leeds Studies in English*, n.s. 22, (1991), 85–102; 'A New 'Dating of John Mirk's *Festial'*, *Notes and Queries* 29 (1982), pp. 487–89; 'The *Festial*: The Priest and His Parish', in *The Parish in Late Medieval England: Proceedings of the 2002 Harlaxton Symposium*, ed. by Clive Burgess and Eamon Duffy, Harlaxton Medieval Studies 14 (Donington, Tyas, 2006), pp. 160–76. See also Alan J. Fletcher, 'John Mirk and the Lollards', *Medium Ævum* 56 (1987), 217–24.

25 Mirk's burial sermon is mentioned briefly in Susan Powell and Alan J. Fletcher, 'In die sepulture seu Trigintali: the Late Medieval Funeral and Memorial Sermon', *Leeds Studies in English*, n.s. 12, (1981), 195–228. Kenneth Rooney gives a cursory analysis of this sermon's revenant story in *Mortality and Imagination*, pp. 116–117.

26 See Robert W. Eyton, 'The Monasteries of Shropshire: Their Origin and Founders – Lilleshall Abbey', *The Archaeological Journal* 12 (1855), 229–37; M. J. Angold, G. C. Baugh, Marjorie M. Chibnall, D. C. Cox, D. T. W. Price, Margaret Tomlinson and B. S. Trinder, 'Houses of Augustinian Canons: Abbey of Lilleshall', in *A History of*

the County of Shropshire: Volume 2, ed. by A. T. Gaydon and R. B. Pugh (London: Victoria County History, 1973), pp. 70–80; *British History Online* <http://www.brit ish-history.ac.uk/vch/salop/vol2/pp70-80> [accessed 3 October 2018].

27 *The Cartulary of Lilleshall Abbey*, ed. by Una Rees (Shrewsbury: Shropshire Archaeological and Historical Society, 1997), p. 160.

28 Angold et al, 'Lilleshall', p. 76; Powell, 'The Priest and his Parish', p. 175. For a partial transcription of the note on Richard II's visit, see *A Descriptive Catalogue of the Manuscripts in the Library of Corpus Christi College, Cambridge, Volume II: nos. 251–538*, ed. by M. R. James (Cambridge: Cambridge University Press, 1912), p. 172. CCCC MS 39 is a miscellany that also contains Richard of Devizes' *Chronicon* and the *Annales Wintonienses*. The folio numbers the square brackets are taken from the 'full' manuscript foliation as digitised on: https://parker.stanford.edu/parker/catal og/gs070yh9296 [accessed 20 October 2018].

29 See the exemplary study by Susan Powell, 'John to John: The Manuale Sacerdotis and the Daily Life of a Parish Priest', in *Recording Medieval Lives: Proceedings of the 2005 Harlaxton Symposium*, ed. by Julia Hoffey and Virginia Davis, Harlaxton Medieval Studies 17 (Donington: Tyas, 2009), pp. 112–29 (at p. 114).

30 Cited in Powell, 'John to John', p. 113 (n. 9).

31 John Mirk, *Instructions for Parish Priests: Edited from Claudius A. II*, ed. by Edward Peacock, EETS o.s. 31; rev. by F. J. Furnivall (London: Kegan Paul, Trench, Trübner & co, 1902 [1868]), p. 60.

32 Cited in Powell, 'John to John', p. 115 (at n. 17).

33 Fletcher, 'John Mirk and the Lollards', p. 222.

34 A supposition taken from a close analysis of the *Festial*'s Quinquagesima sermon (i.e. the Sunday before the beginning of Lent), which makes unique reference to the plenary indulgences granted to pilgrims who visit Rome every fifteenth year, a degree inaugurated by Clement VI in 1350. This provision was revoked by Urban VI in 1389, who instead reduced the timespan to every thirty-three years, hence the *Festial*'s *terminus ante quem*. See 'Powell', 'Dating of the *Festial*', p. 488.

35 F. W. Powicke and C. R. Cheney, *Councils and Synods, with other documents related to the English Church*, 2 vols (Oxford: Clarendon, 1964), II, p. 2, pp. 886–918 (at p. 901).

36 *The Lay Folks' Catechism*, ed. by Thomas Frederick Simmons and Henry Edward Nolloth, EETS o.s 118 (London: Kegan Paul, Trench, Trübner & co, 1901).

37 Richard Helmholz, 'John de Burgh (fl.1370–1398)', in *Ecclesiastical Law Journal* 18 (2016), 67–72.

38 L. E. Boyle, 'The "Oculus Sacerdotis" and Some Other Works of William of Pagula: The Alexander Prize Essay', *Transactions of the Royal Historical Society* 5, 5th ser. (1955), 81–110 (at pp. 83, 86, 89)

39 See Appendix II in Beth Allison Barr, *The Pastoral Care of Women in Late Medieval England* (Woodbridge: Boydell, 2008), pp. 125–34.

40 As discussed in detail by Powell, *John Mirk's Festial*, I, p. xxix.

41 Powell, *John Mirk's Festial*, I, p. 3. Powell's transcription does not include the full explicit, which can be found at the *Manuscripts of the West Midlands: A Catalogue of Vernacular Manuscript Books of the English West Midlands, c.1300–c.1475 database*: https://www.dhi.ac.uk/mwm/browse?type=ms&id=52&titleid=4 [accessed 26 January 2019].

42 Alan J. Fletcher, 'Unnoticed Sermons from John Mirk's Festial', *Speculum* 55 (1980), 514–22 (at p. 515).

43 In full: 'Wherfor a qwene of þys March of Wales þat was cosyn to Saynt Alkmunde let make þys chirch yn þe worschip of God and Saynt Alkmunde, and þus he was made patron of þis chirch', Erbe, *Festial*, p. 244. See also Fletcher, 'John Mirk and the Lollards', p. 221.

44 Powell, 'The Priest and His Parish', p. 164.

45 For the St Winifred sermon, see Beth Allison Barr, 'Medieval Sermons and Audience Appeal after the Black Death', in *History Compass* 16 (2018), 1–8 [e12478].

46 Watkins, *History and the Supernatural*, p. 231.

47 Ruth Horie, *Perceptions of Ecclesia: Church and Soul in Medieval Dedication Sermons* (Turnhout: Brepols, 2006). See also Lee Bowen, 'The Tropology of Medieval Dedication Rites', *Speculum*16 (1941), 469–79. For the early medieval rite, see Brian V. Repsher, *The Rite of Church Dedication in the Early Medieval Era* (Lewiston, NY; Lampeter; Edwin Mellen Press, 1998).

48 Horie, *Perceptions of Ecclesia*, p. 2.

49 Attollite portas, principes, vestras, et elevamini, portae aeternales, et introibit rex gloriae.

50 Quis est iste rex gloriae?

51 Dominus virtutum ipse est rex gloriae.

52 'Zacchaeus, come down immediately. I must stay at your house today', So he came down at once and welcomed him gladly ('Zachaee, festinans descende: quia hodie in domo tua oportet me manere'. Et festinans descendit, et excepit illum gaudens).

53 Horie, *Perceptions of Ecclesia*, p. 7.

54 Horie, *Perceptions of Ecclesia*, pp. 3–8, 171–74.

55 For an English translation, see *The Rationale divinorum officiorum* of *William Durand of Mende (A New Translation of the Prologue and Book One)*, ed. and trans. by Timothy M. Thibodeau (New York: Columbia University Press, 2007), I. 6 (pp. 60–76). For the full Latin text, see *Rationale divinorum officiorum: Accedit aliud Divinorum officiorum rationale a Joanne Beletho* (Naples: Dura, 1859).

56 Horie, *Perceptions of Ecclesia*, pp. 21–34.

57 Manifestum quidem est quod haec aqua cujus aspersione Ecclesia consecratur, baptismum significat, quia quodammodo ipsa Ecclesia baptizatur, Durandus, *Rationale*, I.6.9.

58 Domus igitur dedicanda est, anima sanctificana, Durandus, *Rationale*, I.6. 7

59 Ut effugiat atque discedat ab eo loco in quo aspersum fueris, omnis fantasia, et nequiea, vel versutia diabolice fraudis, omnisque spiritus immundus adjuratus per eum, in *Liber Pontificalis of Edmund Lacy, Bishop of Exeter*, ed. by Ralph Barnes (Exeter, 1847), p. 13.

60 Durandus, *Rationale*, I. 6.11.

61 Jacobus de Voragine, *The Golden Legend: Readings of the Saints*, ed. and trans. by William Granger Ryan; introduction by Eamon Duffy (Princeton, NJ: Princeton University Press, 2012), pp. 771–81. For the Latin, see Jacobi a Voragine, *Legenda Aurea, vulgo Historia Lombardica dicta*, ed. by Th. Graesse (Dresden & Leipzig, 1846), pp. 845–57.

62 Iohannis Beleth, *Summa de ecclesiasticis officiis*, ed. by Heriberto Douteil, CCCM 41A (Turnhout: Brepols, 1976), ch. 159 (at pp. 303–10)

63 Powell, 'The Priest and his Parish', pp.165–66.

64 Erbe, *Festial*, p. 278.

65 See Susan E. Phillips, '*Janglynge in cherche*: Gossip and the *Exemplum*', in *Hands of the Tongue: Essays on Deviant Speech*, ed. by Edwin D. Craun (Kalamazoo, MI: Medieval Institute Publications, 2007), pp. 61–94.

66 Margaret Jennings, 'Tutivillus: The Literary Career of the Recording Demon', *Studies in Philology* 74, no. 5 Texts and Studies (1977), 1–96; Kathy Cawsey, 'Tutivillus and the "Kyrkchaterars": Strategies of Control in the Middle Ages', *Studies in Philology* 102 (2005), 434–51.

67 Erbe, *Festial*, p. 280.

68 Jacques de Vitry, *The Exempla: Or the Illustrative Stories from the Sermones Vulgares of Jacques de Vitry*, ed. by Thomas Frederick Crane (London: Nutt, 1890), no. CCXXXIX (p 100).

69 Jennings, 'Tutivillus', p. 28. See Robert Mannyng, *Handlyng Synne*, p. 287.

70 Beleth, *Summa de ecclesiasticis officiis*, p. 306.
71 *Speculum Sacerdotale: Edited from British Museum MS Additional 36791*, ed. by Edward H. Weatherly, EETS, o.s. 200 (London: Oxford University Press, 1936)
72 Erbe, *Festial*, p. 298.
73 Powell, 'The Priest and his Parish', p. 166.
74 Ranulph Higden, *Polychronicon Ranulphi Higden Monachi Cestrensis, together with the English Translations of John Trevisa and of an Unknown Writer of the Fifteenth Century*, vol 6. ed. by Joseph R. Lumby, RS 41 (London: Longman, 1876), Book 5, ch.23 (pp. 198–201); Powell, 'The Priest and his Parish, p. 166, n. 42.
75 Erbe, *Festial*, p. 81.
76 'Qui pergentes ad locum ubi corpus eius humatum fuerat, sepulchrumque eius aperientes, subito visus est draco exisse; et totum iliud sepulchrum inventum est interius denigratum, ac si fuisset exustum', in *Historia regum Francorum monasterii sancti dionysii*, in *MGH*, SS 9, ed. by Georg Waitz (Hannover, 1851), pp. 395–406 (at p. 399); Gregory Fedorenko, 'The Language of Authority? The Source Texts for the Dual Chronicles of the "Anonymous of Béthune" (fl. *c.* 1220) and the Evolution of Old French Prose Historiography', in *Authority and Gender in Medieval and Renaissance Chronicles*, ed. by Juliana Dresvina and Nicholas Sparks (Newcastle: Cambridge Scholars, 2012), pp. 202–30 (at p. 211).
77 Philippe Mouskes, *Chronique rimée de Philippe Mouskes*, 2 vols, ed. by Frédéric de Reiffenberg (Brussels 1836–1838), I (1836). pp. 80–81.
78 Mirk's Burial Notes, again based primarily on Beleth, provide a thorough list of those considered unworthy of being buried in sanctified ground, including excommunicates, thieves who died during the practice of their craft, adulterers, the unbaptised children of women who died in childbirth (the women are nonetheless afforded a churchyard burial), those that incited brawls (lest they ask for confession before dying), lechers returning from brothels, and intentional suicides. See Erbe, *Festial*, pp. 297–99.
79 Erbe, *Festial*, p. 281.
80 Erbe, *Festial*, p. 295.
81 For a full list of the Abbots of Lilleshall, from foundation to dissolution, see *The Cartulary of Lilleshall Abbey*, p. xx.
82 James, 'Twelve Medieval Ghost-Stories', 413–22; for the English translation of these tales, see A. J. Grant, 'Twelve Medieval Ghost Stories', *The Yorkshire Archaeological Journal* 27 (1924), 363–79. See also Schmitt, *Ghosts in the Middle Ages*, pp. 142–47; Maik Hildebrandt, 'Medieval Ghosts: The Stories of the Monk of Byland', in *Ghosts – or the (Nearly) Invisible: Spectral Phenomenon in Literature and the Media*, ed. by Maria Fleischhack and Elmar Schenkel (Frankfurt: Peter Lang, 2016), pp. 13–23.
83 Quo coniurato loquebatur in interioribus visceribus et non cum lingua sed quasi in vacuo dolio ('On being conjured he spoke in the inside of his bowels, and not with his tongue, but as it were an empty cask').
84 Adam de Lond (or de London) is a name that recurs frequently in the Yorkshire legal documents of the mid fourteenth century and is the most easily identifiable of all the characters mentioned by the Byland Monk. He appears to have been a tenant in Ampleforth by 1316, is mentioned in a 1332 rent agreement in the Cartulary of Byland Abbey, and had died by 1361, providing a rough *terminus post quem* for Story XII. The incipit to the tale records that the account was given by 'old men' (*antiquorum*) about 'old Adam de Lond' (*veteris Ade de Lond*), indicating that the events took place late in Adam's life, relayed much later by witnesses to the whole affair. See James, 'Twelve Medieval Ghost-Stories', p. 422; *The Cartulary of Byland Abbey*, ed. by Janet Burton, The Publications of the Surtees Society 208 (Woodridge: Boydell, 2004), pp. 2–3.
85 *Speculum Sacerdotale,* p. 164.
86 Powell and Fletcher, 'The Late Medieval Funeral and Memorial Sermon', p. 200.

87 Patrick. J. Horner, 'A Sermon on the Anniversary of the Death of Thomas Beauchamp', *Traditio* 34 (1974), 381–401. See also David L. D'Avery, 'Sermons on the Dead before 1350', *Studi Medievali* 31, 3rd ser. (1990), 207–23.

88 For an overview of the structural complexity of more academic sermons, as relayed in scholastic preaching manuals, see Siegfried Wenzel, *Medieval Artes Praedicandi: A Synthesis of Scholastic Sermon Structure* (Toronto, ONT: University of Toronto Press, 2015), especially pp. 45–86.

89 Erbe, *Festial*, p. 294.

90 Powell and Fletcher, 'The Late Medieval Funeral and Memorial Sermon', p. 202.

91 Ch, 61 'De ipsa celebratione officii', in Beleth, *Summa de Ecclesiasticis Officiis,* pp. 313–19.

92 *Speculum Sacerdotale,* pp. 233–34. See also Christopher Daniell, *Death and Burial in Medieval England: 1066–1550* (London: Routledge, 1997). For an overview of the high status funerary ritual and its visualisation in the form of manuscript illuminations, see Roger S. Wieck, *Painted Prayers: The Medieval Book of Hours in Medieval and Renaissance Art* (New York: George Braziller, 1997), pp, 117–31.

93 *Speculum Sacerdotale,* p.235; Beleth, *Summa de Ecclesiasticis Officiis*, p. 319.

94 In some contexts it has been that argued the placement of poles within the burial matrix represented a strategy for keeping the restless dead either physically or symbolically transfixed to the grave. See Kristiana Jonsson, 'Burial Rods and Charcoal Graves', p. 50; Gordon, 'Dealing with the Undead, p. 126.

95 Istam crucem quam hic uides factam omni christiano quando mortuus fuerit de cera ita debes facere et ponere super pectus eius et dum sepelitur corpus crucem de cera super eum ponatur et sepulchro recondatur, in Dom C. Lambot, *North Italian Services of the Eleventh Century,* Henry Bradshaw Society 67 (London: Harrison and Sons, 1961), p. 62.

96 Wax crosses also formed one of the main tools of the catholic exorcism ritual. See, for example, one of the most widely circulated exorcism manuals of the premodern era, Pietro Antonio Stampa, *Fuga satanae* (Como, 1597).

97 *De nugis,* dist. ii.28 (pp. 204–5).

98 Erbe, *Festial*, p. 295.

99 Aqua benedicta, ne ad corpus demones accedant, qui multem timent aqua benedictam. Solent namque deseuire dyaboli sepius in corporibus mortuorum, ut quod non potuerunt in uita, faciant saltem post morte', in Beleth, *Summa de ecclesiasticis officiis*, p. 318.

100 *Speculum Sacerdotale,* pp. 234–35.

101 Erbe, *Festial,* p. 298.

102 For an overview of deaths caused by violent crime in the later Middle Ages, see Barbara A. Hanawalt, 'Violent Death in Fourteenth- and Early Fifteenth-Century England', *Comparative Studies in Society and History* 18 (1976), 297–320; R. F. Hunniset, *The Medieval Coroner* (Cambridge: Cambridge University Press, 1961).

103 *The Armburgh Papers*, p. 62.

104 John Bromyard, *Summa predicantium* (Venice, 1586), I, xxvii, fol. 84v.

105 *Fouke le Fitz Waryn, ed. by E. J Hathaway, P. T. Ricketts, C. A Robson, and A. D. Wilshere, Anglo-Norman Texts Society 26–28 (Oxford, Blackwell, 1975),* p. 4.

106 Previous investigations into this story have been altogether silent on the unusualness of the victim's name, with no comment as to whether 'Snawball' represented a nickname, family name, or even first name. It is possible that the Byland Monk's 'Snawball' belonged to the local de Snoweshull family. A certain 'Ricardo de Snoweshull' is mentioned in the Cartulary of Byland Abbey as witness to a tithing agreement between the Abbey and Newburgh Priory, on 21 July 1334 (no. 734). *The Cartulary of Byland Abbey*, p. 271.

107 This, of course, refers to the popular Three Living and Three Dead motif found in church fresco cycles and as devotional images in the Office of the Dead prayer

cycle from Books of Hours. For the visual tradition of this motif, see the work of Ashby Kinch, *Imago Mortis: The Mediating Image of Death in Late Middle English Culture* (Leiden: Brill, 2013), and 'Image, Ideology, and Form: The Middle English "Three Dead Kings" in Its Iconographic Context', *The Chaucer Review* 43 (2008), 48–81.

108 The creation of magic, protective circles was an integral component of learned necromancy. Sermon stories on the danger of demonic conjuration can be found in such contemporary manuals as the *Alphabet of Tales* (c.1400). One of Arnold's exempla (no. 561), ultimately taken from Caesarius of Heisterbach, concerns an unnamed knight who asked a local necromancer, Philip, to conjure demons for his amusement. The experiment almost went awry, with the knight almost being snatched away by the devil. The moral, of course, is that curiosity in this branch of the forbidden arts can only lead to damnation. See Arnold of Liège, *An Alphabet of Tales*, pp. 375–76. For the history of necromancy, see Richard Kieckhefer, *Magic in the Middle Ages* (Cambridge: Cambridge University Press, 1989), pp. 151–75.

109 *The Cartulary of Lilleshall Abbey*, p. xvii.

110 The *Vita Patrum* is a collection of hagiographies of the desert fathers consulted by Mirk in the writing of the 'Death of Nero' sermon. Erbe, *Festial*, p. 194.

111 'Seynt bede' is namechecked in the Advent Sunday sermon, where Mirk provides a brief overview of the *Historia Ecclesiastica's* account of the Vision of Dryhthelm, detailing Dryhthelm's tour of the afterlife in the company of an angelic guide. Erbe, *Festial*, p. 5.

Primary sources

Arnold of Liège, *An Alphabet of Tales: An English Translation of the Alphabetum Narrationum, Part II, I–Z*, EETS o.s. 127, ed. by Mary M. Banks (London: Kegan Paul, Trench, Trübner & Co., 1905).

The Cartulary of Byland Abbey, ed. by Janet Burton, The Publications of the Surteees Society 208 (Woodridge: Boydell, 2004).

The Cartulary of Lilleshall Abbey, ed. by Una Rees (Shrewsbury: Shropshire Archaeological and Historical Society, 1997).

Decrees of the Ecumenical Councils, Volume One: Nicaea to Lateran V, ed. by Norman P. Tanner (London: Sheed & Ward and Georgetown University Press, 1990).

Fouke le Fitz Waryn, ed. by E. J. Hathaway, P. T. Ricketts, C. A. Robson, and A. D. Wilshere, *Anglo-Norman Texts Society 26–28* (Oxford: Blackwell, 1975).

Grant, A. J., 'Twelve Medieval Ghost Stories', *The Yorkshire Archaeological Journal* 27 (1924), 363–79.

Gregory the Great, *Sancti Gregorii Papae I, Cognomento Magni, Opera Omnia*, 3 vols, PL 77, ed. by J-P Migne (Paris, 1862).

Herman the Archdeacon and Goscelin of Saint-Bertin, *Miracles of St. Edmund*, ed. and trans. by Tom Licence, with Lynda Lockyer, Oxford Medieval Texts (Oxford: Clarendon, 2014).

Historia regum Francorum monasterii sancti dionysii, in *MGH*, SS 9, ed. by Georg Waitz (Hannover, Impensis Bibliopolii Hahniani, 1851), pp. 395–406.

Innocent III, *Romani Pontificis Opera Omnia*, 3 vols, PL 216, ed. by J-P Migne (Paris, 1855).

Iohannis Beleth, *Summa de ecclesiasticis officiis*, ed. by Heriberto Douteil, CCCM 41A (Turnhout: Brepols, 1976).

Jacobi a Voragine, *Legenda Aurea, vulgo Historia Lombardica dicta*, ed. by Th. Graesse (Dresden & Leipzig: Impensis Librariae Arnoldianae, 1846).

Jacobus de Voragine, *The Golden Legend: Readings of the Saints*, ed. and trans. by William Granger Ryan; introduction by Eamon Duffy (Princeton, NJ: Princeton University Press, 2012).

Jacques de Vitry, *The Exempla: Or the Illustrative Stories from the Sermones Vulgares of Jacques de Vitry*, ed. by Thomas Frederick Crane (London: Nutt, 1890), no. CCXXXIX, p. 100.

James, M. R., 'Twelve Medieval Ghost-Stories', *English Historical Review* 37 (1922), 413–22.

John Bromyard, *Summa predicantium* (Venice, 1586).

John Mirk, *Instructions for Parish Priests: Edited from Claudius A. II*, ed. by Edward Peacock, EETS o.s. 31; rev. by F. J. Furnivall (London: Kegan Paul, Trench, Trübner & Co., 1902 [1868]).

John Mirk, *John Mirk's Festial, Edited from the British Library MS. Claudius A. II*, 2 vols, ed. by Susan Powell, EETS Society o.s. 335 (Oxford: Oxford University Press, 2009).

John Mirk, *Mirk's Festial: A Collection of Homilies by Johannes Mirkus (John Mirk)*, Part I, ed. by Theodor Erbe, EETS e.s. 96 (London: Kegan Paul, Trench, Trübner & Co., 1905).

Lambot, Dom C., *North Italian Services of the Eleventh Century*, Henry Bradshaw Society 67 (London: Harrison and Sons, 1961).

The Lay Folks' Catechism, ed. by Thomas Frederick Simmons and Henry Edward Nolloth, EETS o.s. 118 (London: Kegan Paul, Trench, Trübner & Co., 1901).

Liber Pontificalis of Edmund Lacy, Bishop of Exeter, ed. by Ralph Barnes (Exeter: Roberts, 1847).

Peter the Venerable, *Petri Venerabilis Abbatis Cluniacensis Noni Opera Omnia*, PL 189, ed. by J.-P. Migne (Paris, 1854).

Philippe Mouskes, *Chronique rimée de Philippe Mouskes*, 2 vols, ed. by Frédéric de Reiffenberg (Brussels: Hayez, 1836–1838).

Powicke F. W. and C. R. Cheney, *Councils and Synods, with Other Documents Related to the English Church*, 2 vols (Oxford: Clarendon, 1964).

Ranulph Higden, *Polychronicon Ranulphi Higden Monachi Cestrensis, together with the English Translations of John Trevisa and of an Unknown Writer of the Fifteenth Century*, 9 vols, ed. by C. Banington (1–2) and Joseph R. Lumby (vols. 3–9), RS 41 (London: Longman, 1865–1886).

Robert Mannyng, *Robert of Brunne's Handlyng Synne, with the French Treatise on Which it is Founded, La Manuel des Pechiez by William of Wadington*, ed. by F. J. Furnival (London: Roxburghe, 1862).

Speculum Sacerdotale: Edited from British Museum MS Additional 36791, ed. by Edward H. Weatherly, EETS, o.s. 200 (London: Oxford University Press, 1936).

Stampa, Pietro Antonio, *Fuga satanae* (Como, 1597).

Stephen of Bourbon, *Tractatus de diversis materiis predicabilibus*, ed. by Jacques Berlioz and Jean-Luc Eichenlaub, CCCM 124 (Turnhout: Brepols, 2002).

Walter Map, *De Nugis Curialium*, ed. and trans. M. R. James; revised C. N. L. Brooke and R. A. B. Mynors (Oxford: Clarendon, 1983).

William Durandus, *Rationale divinorum officiorum: Accedit aliud Divinorum officiorum rationale a Joanne Beletho* (Naples: Dura, 1859).

William Durandus, *The Rationale Divinorum Officiorum of William Durand of Mende (A New Translation of the Prologue and Book One)*, ed. and trans. by Timothy M. Thibodeau (New York: Columbia University Press, 2007).

William of Malmesbury, *Gesta regum Anglorum: History of the English Kings*, 1 vol, ed. and trans. by R. A. B. Mynors; completed by R. M. Thomson and M. Winterbottom (Clarendon: Oxford, 1998).

Secondary sources

A Descriptive Catalogue of the Manuscripts in the Library of Corpus Christi College, Cambridge, Volume II: nos. 251–538, ed. by M. R. James (Cambridge: Cambridge University Press, 1912).

Angold, M. J., G. C. Baugh, Marjorie M. Chibnall, D. C. Cox, D. T. W. Price, Margaret Tomlinson, and B. S. Trinder, 'Houses of Augustinian Canons: Abbey of Lilleshall', in *A History of the County of Shropshire: Volume 2*, ed. by A. T. Gaydon and R. B. Pugh (London: Victoria County History, 1973), pp. 70–80.

Barr, Beth Allison, 'Medieval Sermons and Audience Appeal after the Black Death', *History Compass* 16 (2018), 1–8 [e12478].

Barr, Beth Allison, *The Pastoral Care of Women in Late Medieval England* (Woodbridge: Boydell, 2008).

Bowen, Lee, 'The Tropology of Medieval Dedication Rites', *Speculum* 16 (1941), 469–79.

Boyle, Leonard E., *Pastoral Care, Clerical Education and Canon Law, 1200–1400* (London: Variorum, 1981).

Boyle, Leonard E., 'The "Oculus Sacerdotis" and Some Other Works of William of Pagula: The Alexander Prize Essay', *Transactions of the Royal Historical Society* 5, 5th ser. (1955), 81–110.

Cawsey, Kathy, 'Tutivillus and the "Kyrkchaterars": Strategies of Control in the Middle Ages', *Studies in Philology* 102 (2005), 434–51.

Constable, Giles, *The Reformation of the Twelfth-Century* (Cambridge: Cambridge University Press, 1996).

D'Avery, David L., 'Sermons on the Dead before 1350', *Studi Medievali* 31, 3rd ser. (1990), 207–23.

Daniell, Christopher, *Death and Burial in Medieval England: 1066–1550* (London: Routledge, 1997).

Easting, Robert, 'Dialogue Between a Clerk and the Spirit of a Girl de purgatorio (1153): A Medieval Ghost Story', *Mediaevistik* 20 (2007), 163–83.

Eyton, Robert W., 'The Monasteries of Shropshire: Their Origin and Founders – Lilleshall Abbey', *The Archaeological Journal* 12 (1855), 229–37.

Fedorenko, Gregory, 'The Language of Authority? The Source Texts for the Dual Chronicles of the "Anonymous of Béthune" (fl. *c*.1220) and the Evolution of Old French Prose Historiography', in *Authority and Gender in Medieval and Renaissance Chronicles*, ed. by Juliana Dresvina and Nicholas Sparks (Newcastle: Cambridge Scholars, 2012), pp. 202–30.

Fletcher, Alan J., 'John Mirk and the Lollards', *Medium Ævum* 56 (1987), 217–24.

Fletcher, Alan J., 'Unnoticed Sermons from John Mirk's Festial', *Speculum* 55 (1980), 514–22.

Goering, Joseph, *William de Montibus (c.1140–1213): The Schools and the Literature of Pastoral Care* (Toronto, ON: Pontifical Institute of Medieval Studies, 1992).

Gordon, Stephen, 'Dealing with the Undead in the Later Middle Ages', in *Dealing with the Dead: Mortality and Community in the Middle Ages*, ed. by Thea Tomaini (Leiden: Brill, 2018), pp. 97–128.

Hanawalt, Barbara A., 'Violent Death in Fourteenth- and Early Fifteenth-Century England', *Comparative Studies in Society and History* 18 (1976), 297–320.

Helmholz, Richard, 'John de Burgh (fl.1370–1398)', *Ecclesiastical Law Journal* 18 (2016), 67–72.

Hildebrandt, Maik, 'Medieval Ghosts: The Stories of the Monk of Byland', in *Ghosts – or the (Nearly) Invisible: Spectral Phenomenon in Literature and the Media*, ed. by Maria Fleischhack and Elmar Schenkel (Frankfurt: Peter Lang, 2016), pp. 13–23.

Horie, Ruth, *Perceptions of Ecclesia: Church and Soul in Medieval Dedication Sermons* (Turnhout: Brepols, 2006).

Horner, Patrick J., 'A Sermon on the Anniversary of the Death of Thomas Beauchamp', *Traditio* 34 (1974), 381–401.

Hunniset, R. F., *The Medieval Coroner* (Cambridge: Cambridge University Press, 1961).

Jennings, Margaret, 'Tutivillus: The Literary Career of the Recording Demon', *Studies in Philology* 74, no. 5 Texts and Studies (1977), 1–96.

Jonsson, Kristiana, 'Burial Rods and Charcoal Graves: New Light on Old Burial Practices', *Viking and Medieval Scandinavia* 3 (2007), 43–73.

Kieckhefer, Richard, *Magic in the Middle Ages* (Cambridge: Cambridge University Press, 1989).

Kinch, Ashby, 'Image, Ideology, and Form: The Middle English "Three Dead Kings" in Its Iconographic Context', *The Chaucer Review* 43 (2008), 48–81.

Kinch, Ashby, *Imago Mortis: The Mediating Image of Death in Late Middle English Culture* (Leiden: Brill, 2013).

Le Goff, Jacques, *The Birth of Purgatory*, trans. by Arthur Goldhammer (London: Scolar Press, 1984).

MacKinnon, Hugh, 'William de Montibus: A Medieval Teacher', in *Essays in Medieval History Presented to Bertie Wilkinson*, ed. by T. A Sandquist and M. R. Powicke (Toronto, ON: Toronto University Press, 1969), pp. 32–45.

Phillips, Susan E., 'Janglynge in cherche: Gossip and the Exemplum', in *Hands of the Tongue: Essays on Deviant Speech*, ed. by Edwin D. Craun (Kalamazoo, MI: Medieval Institute Publications, 2007), pp. 61–94.

Powell, Susan, 'A New Dating of John Mirk's *Festial*', *Notes and Queries* 29 (1982), 487–89.

Powell, Susan, 'John Mirk's *Festial* and the Pastoral Programme', *Leeds Studies in English*, n.s. 22, (1991), 85–102.

Powell, Susan, 'John to John: The Manuale Sacerdotis and the Daily Life of a Parish Priest', in *Recording Medieval Lives: Proceedings of the 2005 Harlaxton Symposium*, ed. by Julia Hoffey and Virginia Davis, Harlaxton, Medieval Studies 17 (Donington: Tyas, 2009), pp. 112–29.

Powell, Susan, 'The *Festial*: The Priest and His Parish', in *The Parish in Late Medieval England: Proceedings of the 2002 Harlaxton Symposium*, ed. by Clive Burgess and Eamon Duffy, Harlaxton Medieval Studies 14 (Donington: Tyas, 2006), 160–76.

Powell, Susan and Alan, J. Fletcher, 'In die sepulture seu Trigintali: The Late Medieval Funeral and Memorial Sermon', *Leeds Studies in English*, n.s. 12, (1981), 195–228.

Repsher, Brian V., *The Rite of Church Dedication in the Early Medieval Era* (Lewiston, NY; Lampeter: Edwin Mellen Press, 1998).

Roberts, Phyllis, 'Sermons and Preaching in/and the Medieval University', in *Medieval Education*, ed. by Ronald B. Begley and W. Koterski Joseph (New York, NY: Fordham University Press, 2005), pp. 83–98.

Rooney, Kenneth, *Mortality and Imagination: The Life of the Dead in Medieval English Literature* (Turnhout: Brepols, 2011).

Scanlon, Peter, *Augustine's Theology on Preaching* (Lanham: Fortress Press, 2014).

Schmitt, Jean-Claude, *Ghosts in the Middle Ages*, trans. by Teresa Lavender Fagan (Chicago, IL: Chicago University Press, 1998).

Stanbury, Ronald J., 'Preaching and Pastoral Care in the Middle Ages', in *A Companion to Pastoral Care in the Late Middle Ages (1100–1500)*, ed. by Ronald J. Stanbury (Leiden: Brill, 2010), pp. 23–39.

Watkins, Carl S., *History and the Supernatural in Medieval England* (Cambridge: Cambridge University Press, 2007).

Wenzel, Siegfried, *Medieval Artes Praedicandi: A Synthesis of Scholastic Sermon Structure* (Toronto, ON: University of Toronto Press, 2015).

Wieck, Roger S., *Painted Prayers: The Medieval Book of Hours in Medieval and Renaissance Art* (New York: George Braziller, 1997).

5 'But whan us liketh we kan take us oon'

Vain surfaces and walking corpses in Chaucer's *Friar's Tale*

Introduction

At this point in the investigation it should be apparent that demonically- and spiritually-activated corpses were a vital part of medieval viewpoints on life after death. With chapters one, two, and three arguing that the entrenched nature of such beliefs made the revenant a powerful critical tool, chapter four highlighted how the gradual disembodiment of the dead following the Fourth Lateran Council (1215) did not fully preclude the fear that cadavers, under whatever agency, were able to walk after death. The local character of the *De dedicacione ecclesie* sermon from John Mirk's *Festial* (c.1380s) and the twelve ghost stories transcribed by the anonymous Byland Abbey Monk (c.1400) provide ample evidence that belief in ambulatory corpses was still very much alive in the fourteenth century, even if the ontology of the encountered being was sometimes hard to pin down: was it an embodied ghost, a shape-shifting spirit with the appearance of physicality, or something in-between? Such questions formed part of the underlying framework of church writings on – and dealings with – the supernatural. In any case, moralistic accounts of rampaging corpses, wily demons, and purgatorial spirits traded on their ability to engage with the sensibilities of their audience, whether to provoke the listener (or reader) into correcting their own modes of behaviour, or add flesh to the theological bones of some deeper spiritual truth. The need to adequately prepare oneself for death and avoid the machinations of the devil was the fundamental reason why churchmen such as John Mirk included cautionary tales of the supernatural in their pastoral handbooks. On occasion the dividing line between religious exemplum and literary artefact was so fine as to be almost non-existent. This is especially true where Chaucer's *Friar's Tale* is concerned. One of the most unheralded yet sophisticated narratives from the *Canterbury Tales*,[1] the *Friar's Tale* utilises the narratological framework of a popular exemplum, 'The Devil and the Advocate', to create a story that at once maintains the base meaning of the urtext – the dangers of avarice; the difference between outer appearance and inner *entente* – and supplies it with a newfound satirical edge. Forming the middle part of an intertextual triad with the *Wife of Bath's Prologue* and *Tale* (III, ll. 1–1264) and the *Summoner's Prologue* and *Tale* (III, ll. 1665–2294) – a group known in modern editions as 'Fragment III' – the *Friar's Tale,* along with the

Prologue (III, ll. 1265–1664), ostensibly functions as a rebuke to Friar Huberd's primary antagonist, the pilgrim-Summoner, whose counterpart in the tale is so beholden to greed – all surface profit, no moral awareness – that he damns himself not only through eager companionship with a devil-in-disguise, but his inability to discern between unintended '(outer') and heartfelt ('inner') oath-making. Chaucer's genius lies in using the exemplum, a literary genre especially designed to explicate moral truths, to add an ironic flourish to Huberd's diatribe against the Summoner's 'literal' reading of the world.

Although the dramatic irony and mercantile themes that permeate the *Friar's Tale* are well known in Chaucerian scholarship,[2] little attention has been paid to the demonological dialogue between the devil and the Summoner (III, ll. 1447–1522), specifically lines 1462 ('But whan us liketh we kan take us oon') and 1507–1508 ('Somtyme we feyne, and sometyme we aryse / with dede bodyes in ful sondry wyse') and their relationship to the belief in the demonic infiltration (and ambulation) of the corpse.[3] These lines, spoken by the devil-yeoman, provide a tantalising glimpse into a hitherto understudied aspect of Chaucer's theological knowledge. Thus, the first part of the chapter begins with a brief overview of the literary context of the *Friar's Tale's* creation and an overview of it most salient features, before undertaking a close, critical analysis of lines 1447–1522, arguing that Chaucer not only utilises Vincent of Beauvais and Thomas Aquinas in his discussion of demons, but also draws from the broad cultural sediments of local revenant belief. As we shall see, the problems of trying to discern the identity of spirits (*discretio spirituum*),[4] signposted in the *Friar's Tale* by reference to the conjuring of Samuel (III ll. 1510–1512), correlate perfectly with the tale's overarching emphasis on deceptive surfaces and inner truths. In this way, I aim to challenge the assumption shared by most Chaucerian scholars that the yeoman is an airy, shape-shifting demon, modulating its elemental form to better ensnare the hapless Summoner.[5] The intentional ambiguity of the text ensures that the reader does not know exactly what type of body the Summoner encounters on the road to Mabely's house – is it airy, made of flesh, or perhaps an airy 'mask' concealing a putrid cadaver? The Summoner's exclamation that his companion has a 'mannes shap' (III, l. 1458) is only a surface, subjective appraisal of the situation. The juxtaposition at the start of the discourse, where the devil first speaks of 'taking' bodies (l. 1462) before turning its attention to the fooling of the human senses (l. 1463), is a subtle indicator that we, the reader, should not take the interpretation of the yeoman's body as a pure elemental illusion as absolute.

The final part of the chapter, then, explores how the belief in the demonic usurpation of the corpse – i.e. the outer human shell mobilised by a malign, hidden agency – reinforces the theme of dissonance between outward appearance and *entente*[6] and, indeed, acts as a further avenue for commenting upon the mechanisms of spiritual and material economics.[7] The Summoner's corruption of his own office through thievery and extortion (III. ll. 1350–1360) and the devil's gleeful reception of souls given in earnest (III, l. 1430) are two aspects of the same interrelated system of physical and metaphysical exchange. Ultimately, it will be shown that the devil's penchant for taking 'dede bodyes' (l. 1508) adds an extra ironic nuance to the mercantile themes that permeate the *Friar's Tale* and the *Canterbury Tales* as a whole.

The *Friar's Tale*: an overview

Circulating orally as a Northern European folk tale before being committed to the page, 'The Devil and the Advocate' first appears in the written record as an exemplum composed in High Middle German by the Austrian poet and moralist, Der Stricker (c.1230). The story itself is relatively straightforward: an avaricious judge meets the devil on the road to market. The devil explains that he has been given permission to take anything that has been offered to him in earnest. Over the course of their journey the devil demurs when he hears curses offered in his name, as they have not been said with true conviction. At the market, the judge is condemned to hell by an old woman from whom he stole a cow and forced into a life of poverty. The woman's curse is heartfelt and the devil gladly takes his gift.[8] A near-contemporaneous Latin version of the tale can be found in Caesarius of Hesiterbach's *Libri octo miraculorum* (c.1240).[9] The oral origins of the story are obliquely confirmed by Caesarius, who states that he first heard of it 'a few years ago from a certain Cistercian Abbot in the diocese of Bremen'.[10] Whilst the Der Stricker exemplum identifies the protagonist as a *rihtaere* (secular judge), Larry D. Benson and Theodore M. Anderson argue that Caesarius's use of *advocatus* refers not to a lawyer – the common translation of the term – but to an ecclesiastical official responsible for the management of church estates, including the collection of fines. It is tempting to theorise that Chaucer worked directly from Caesarius, changing the Germanic *advocatus* to the closest English equivalent, the summoner (that is, a low-level official charged with delivering citations to the local ecclesiastical court).[11] But, as noted by Peter Nicholson, it is just as likely that Chaucer was influenced by the later English branch of the Latin 'Advocate' tradition, which put emphasis on the protagonist's obliviousness to the danger presented by the devil. Indeed, the exempla found in British Library MSS Add. 38654 (1300–1350), Cotton Cleopatra D VIII c.1400), and Harley 4894 (c.1401) contain narratolgoical elements that are easily identifiable in the *Friar's Tale*. The version from Harley 4894, forming part of a collection of sermon stories by the prior of Finchale, Robert Rypon (1350-1422), echoes the terminology of the *Canterbury Tales* in calling the protagonist a 'bailiff' (*ballivo*).[12] Rather than trying to uncover the exact source for the *Friar's Tale*, it suffices to say that there existed in the late fourteenth century a broad corpus of oral and written texts for moralists and secular poets to re-invent at their own discretion.

Out of the thirty or so iterations of 'The Devil and the Advocate' to survive to the present day, Chaucer's re-imagining is undoubtedly the most sophisticated.[13] Following a tense standoff between the pilgrim-Summoner and Huberd in the *Wife of Bath's Prologue* (III, ll. 829–849) and *Friar's Prologue*, with the former promising to pay back ('quitten')[14] the Friar's insults in kind (III. l. 1292), the *Tale* begins by establishing the 'fictional' Summoner as the agent of an unscrupulous archdeacon who lived in Huberd's own part of the country (III. l. 1301).[15]

With the *General Prologue* describing Huberd as being 'the beste beggar in his house' (I l. 252) and a man possessed of extremely elegant language (I l. 211), it is appropriate that the first section contains a deliciously ekphrastic description of the Summoner's many and varied sins (III l. 1301–1374). This Summoner, it is said, was an inveterate thief, giving the archdeacon only half of what he actually collected in fines. As well as cultivating a wide network of spies and threatening people with excommunication should they not pay a bribe, he also employed prostitutes to sleep with unwitting men, whereupon he would present them with a forged summons, exact a hefty fine and, under the pretence of friendliness, quietly expunge the whole affair from the ecclesiastical records.[16] Thus from the very start the Summoner is described as being a creature of profit, on the prowl for material wealth.

The Summoner-as-predator motif (III. ll. 1369–1374) is an irony that is picked up at the beginning of the narrative proper. On his way to deliver a bogus summons to an old widow, Mabely, he encounters a green-coated yeoman in the glade of a forest, carrying a bow and arrow and wearing a hat trimmed with sable – the very image of an expert hunter.[17] Identifying themselves as bailiffs, they swear allegiance as brothers and compare strategies for extorting the maximum amount of profit from their victims (III. ll. 1424–1444). Only after the Summoner (ironically) invokes St. James and asks for his companion's name does the yeoman finally admit that he is, in fact, a devil, out to ensnare whatever men will give him. Here follows the demonological discourse – to be discussed in more detail shortly – that concludes with the Summoner wilfully ignoring the warning signs about the devil's true intentions and reiterating his pledge to his newfound brother. Arriving at a nearby town they encounter a cart stuck in the mud, the carter whipping and yelling obscenities at his horses:

> "The feend", quod he, "you fecche, body and bones
>
> As ferforthly as evere were ye foled,
>
> So muche wo as I have with yow tholed!
>
> The devel have al, bothe hors and cart and hey!" (III, ll. 1544–1547)

The Summoner asks the devil why he does not simply take what has been offered him. The devil replies that he cannot, for 'it is nat his entente, trust me weel' (III, ll. 1556). Sure enough, when the is cart finally extricated from the bog, the carter reneges on the curse, giving thanks to God, Jesus and, appropriately enough, St. Loy (Eligius), the patron saint of farriers and horses.[18]

Leaving the town behind, the pair eventually arrive at the old widow's cottage. Chiding the devil's inability to 'wynne thy cost' (III. l. 1580) in this place, the Summoner knocks on the widow's gate, explaining that he has a writ of summons to be ignored on the pain of excommunication. The widow angrily contests the charge, and is equally adamant that she cannot pay the twelve pence bribe to see 'thee acquite' (III. l. 1599). It is here that the Summoner makes his fatal mistake and becomes the agent of his own downfall. Swearing that 'the foule feend me feche / If I th'excuse, though thou shul be split' (III. l, 1610–1611), he also vows by St. Anne, the patron saint of grandmothers,[19] to confiscate the widow's frying pan as payment for an earlier (falsified) crime of adultery. Hearing this, the widow utters her faithful curse: 'Unto the devel blak and rough of hewe / Yeve I thy body and my panne also!' (III. ll. 1621–1622). The devil, who up until this point has been a silent bystander, asks the widow, kindly and by name, to confirm her intent. Yes, she replies, 'The Devel [...] so fecche hym er he deye / And panne and al, but he wol hym repente' (III. ll. 1628–1629). But the Summoner does not repent, vowing instead to take every last thing the widow owns. Hearing this, the devil summarily drags his 'brother' body and soul to hell. The *Tale* concludes with a pointedly formulaic (yet ironic) gloss on the preceding story, warning both the pilgrims and the reader against succumbing to the wiles of 'the temptour Sathanas' (III, l. 1655).[20]

The *Friar's Tale*, then, operated on various levels of discourse and in different moral registers.[21] From a socio-critical standpoint it can be read as a broad satire on the perceived corruption of archdeacons and summoners.[22] The procedures for enforcing spiritual correction on a rural village level were often subject to abuse. Incomes generated through fines were considerable. Indeed, the historical evidence suggests that the propensity for summoners to issue spurious citations was not just an exaggeration on Chaucer's part. A parliamentary petition dating to 1378, for example, denounces the extortions made by summoners for no reason other than their own avarice:

> The said summoners make their summons to divers people maliciously as they are going along in their carts through the fields, and elsewhere, and accuse them of various wrongful crimes, and they force poor people to pay a fine called the Bishope Almois; or alternately the said summoner summons them 20 or 21 leagues away to two places on one day, to the great hurt, impoverishment, and oppression of the said poor Commons.[23]

As detailed by Paul Hahn and Richard W. Kaeuper, the fourteenth-century court rolls also include references to the threat of excommunication on the non-payment of fines, numerous falsified allegations of adultery, and even the citation of entire villages by one vindictive archdeacon. While it would be incorrect to suggest that *all* summoners were corrupt, for the reader to understand and take pleasure in the *Friar's Tales* exaggerations – that is, for the satire to work – it must resonate within the broader cultural belief that extortion and blackmail did indeed take place.[24] Summoners were seen to vex and harry the common folk much in the manner of demons (and demonically-activated bodies), an irony that Chaucer was all too ready to exploit.

Irony, as mentioned previously, was one the sharpest tools in a satirist's arsenal. It is something that the *Friar's Tale* displays in abundance. The fact that the Summoner is tasked to bring sinners to justice while at the same time being the most dissolute sinner of all ('a theef, and eek a somnour, and a baude', III. l. 1354) needs no elaboration. Neither it difficult to trace the irony of the Summoner sating his lust for money through the prosecution of real or imagined sex crimes, crimes that formed his (and his archdeacon's) primary source of income ('but certes, lecchours dide he grettest wo', III, l. 1310). The character portrait of the pilgrim-Summoner in the *General Prologue* adds a further dimension to the stereotype that summoners as a whole were driven by material and monetary excess.[25] Not only is the pilgrim-Summoner described as being 'lecherous as a sparwe' (I, l. 626), but he was also a drunkard (I, l. 649), pimped his concubine in exchange for wine (I. l. 650), and circumvented the penalties of excommunication by punishing his customers 'in [their] purs' instead. Indeed, his sardonic appraisal that '[the] purs is the ercedekenes helle' (I, l. 658)[26] acts as tacit confirmation that the spiritual and material exchange networks had been completely destabilised. Sin was a valuable commodity. In the debased social network that Chaucer crafts for the pilgrim-Summoner, theological truths have become bastardised, damnation secularised, providing further proof that the archdeaconries – and by proxy their field agents, the summoners – cared for little except worldly profit. The *Friar's Tale's* Summoner's mocking denouncement of the very mechanisms of salvation, Confession and Absolution (III, ll. 1440–1442), exemplifies his role as the satiric embodiment of his office's pastoral neglect. Contemporary preachers such as the Dominican Friar John Bromyard (d.1352) followed the same lines of argument as Chaucer, accusing the whole judicial apparatus of promoting vice.[27] The perceived disregard of the local priesthood for the spiritual health of their flocks led some moralists to argue that the appendages of the rural church were no better than demons themselves. Ironically, it is the Summoner's literal reading of the world that prohibits his ability to actually 'see' the supernatural entity in his midst.

Aside from the obvious moral equivalencies between the Summoner and the devil, the most overt form of irony in the *Friar's Tale* involves the hunter of souls becoming prey to an even more insidious hunter of souls.[28] Despite learning about the myriad ways demons are able to ensnare their victims, the Summoner is so devoted to the letter of his occupation that he cannot see past the devil's guise as a 'brother' bailiff.[29] Even in their initial exchanges, when, 'speaking sweetly', the green-coated yeoman mentions that he dwells in a 'far northern land' (the north being the location of hell in Germanic folklore and Biblical exegesis), the Summoner does not realise, or simply does not care, about the danger he is in.[30] A similar lack of awareness – or perhaps just a surfeit of arrogance – can be discerned in his reaction to the yeoman's invitation to visit his homeland:

"Brother," quod he, "fer in the north contree,

Whereas I hope som tyme I shal thee see.

Er we departe, I shal thee so wel wisse

That of myn hous ne shaltow nevere mysse" (I, ll.1413–1416)

Although portentous with meaning, these words generate little in the way of fear for the Summoner. Instead, he merely asks his 'brother' to teach him some new tricks of the trade (III, l. 1420) and shows only greedy, surface inquisitiveness when his companion's true identity is revealed. The devil (somewhat wearily) plays along, knowing the ultimate outcome of the game once they reach Mabely's house. He understands the Summoners *entente* all too well and is willing to bide his time to catch his prey (III, l. 1455).[31] As the demonological digression demonstrates, the interrelated themes of deceitful surfaces and hidden truths frame the hypothesis that the devil's body is more a reanimated corpse than airy shell. The usurpation of the corpse was a form of one-sided exchange, analogous to the acquisition of profit and obverse to the sense of reciprocity that underscores the Maussian reading of the 'gift'.[32] But as seen throughout the *Friar's Tale,* the difference between thievery (ll. 1351) and giving freely (III, ll. 1430,1531) is only a matter of perspective, adding a final ironic flourish to the curse, Mabely's 'free gift', that results in the Summoner being taken to hell.

Chaucer's demonology

The demonological digression is not found in any version of 'The Devil and the Advocate' aside from the *Friar's Tale*. It is pure invention on Chaucer's part. Some scholars maintain it is an irrelevant addition to the story, adding nothing of import and serving only to slow down the pace of the narrative.[33] Others have noted it functioned as a way for Huberd to showcase his theological knowledge, a metatextual strategy for diminishing the pilgrim-Summoner still further.[34] Similarly, its overt didacticism has led to suggestions it operated as a platform for Chaucer to convey his own thoughts on the nature of the devil, a proxy demonstration of his learning.[35] Whatever the mode of discourse on display, the digression itself takes the form of a series of questions and answers, evoking the model of the philosophical dialogue between novice and master, tacitly confirming the Summoner's subservience to an even greater evil than himself. Following the revelation of the devil-yeoman's true nature, the Summoner asks – using the formal pronoun, 'ye'[36] – whether demons take on specific forms in hell (III, ll. 1458–1460). Somewhat deflecting the question and not wanting to reveal the secrets of damnation quite just yet, the devil replies that they either *borrow* bodies ('but whan us liketh we kan take us oon') or else make it *seem* as if they have a shape, be it in the likeness of man, ape, or angel. Human senses, he sneers, are incredibly easy to fool. Undeterred and still persisting with the formal register, the Summoner then asks why devils take on different shapes instead of using just the one. "For we [...] wol us swiche forms make / As moost able is oure preyes for to take" (III, l. 1471–1472) comes the forthright reply. In response to the next question concerning why he persist in all this 'labour', the fiend, agitated, remarks that the Summoner does not have the wit to even remotely understand his methods, sufficing only to say that his ability to affect the bodies and souls of others is the function of divine providence. From the devil's perspective, it is an unintended consequence of being one of 'Goddes instrumentz' that his prey sometimes resisted temptation and turned back to the true faith. Indeed, the devil's innate lack of agency in the physical world is confirmed with the admission that 'somtyme be we servant unto man', namechecking St. Dunstan (d.988)[37] and the twelve apostles[38] as those to whom it previously submitted (III, ll. 1501–1502). The ability of fiends to be controlled by men did not only mean holy men: it is an oblique confirmation that sometimes God gives permission for devils to be constrained (and instrumentalised) by necromancers and learned magicians.[39] Indeed, the submission of the fiend to St. Dunstan likely refers not to the infamous episode of his grabbing the devil by the nose with a pair of tongs, but to scurrilous rumours recorded by Eadmer of Canterbury (d.1126) that he dabbled in sorcery, only achieving advancement at Æthelstan's court through the practice of the sinister arts (*sinistris artibus*).[40]

As to be expected, the Summoner is altogether dismissive of the moral purpose behind the devil's incursions. Impatient, but still respectful, he reiterates his interest in the manifest forms that fiends take: "Yet tel me [...] feithfully / Make ye yow newe bodies thus alway / Of elementz?" (III, ll. 1504–1506). It is here that the devil-yeoman builds upon the statement made in line 1462, conforming that they sometimes *aryse* in dead bodies:

[...] The feend ansered, "Nay.

Somtyme we feyne, and somtyme we aryse

With dede bodys in ful sondry wyse,

And speke as renably and faire and wel

As to the Phitonissa [Witch of Endor] dide Samuel" (III, ll. 1506–1510)[41]

This admission destabilises the tacit acceptance made by the Summoner and reading audience that the devil-yeoman has constructed for himself a purely elemental body. As shall be discussed in more detail shortly, nowhere in the text does Chaucer angle towards such a definitive interpretation. The Summoner's misreading of surfaces, despite being all surface himself, forms one of the fundamental conceits of the poem. It is unlikely that his initial appraisal of devil-yeoman as being in a 'mannes shap' (III, l. 1458), all form but no fixed substance, can be taken as accurate. The lack of certainty when it came to discerning the ontology of supernatural entities is encapsulated in lines 1511–1512, the ironic dismissal of the belief that a demon-in-disguise appeared to Saul rather than the actual spirit of Samuel. The digression concludes with the ominous warning that not only will the Summoner soon be able to see the devil-yeoman and his brethren in their native forms, but that through personal experience he will possess a greater knowledge of the underworld than Dante, Vergil, and all the chairs of divinity combined. Of course, such an outcome depended on the devil's (ultimately correct) reading of the Summoner's intention not to forsake his company (III, ll. 1517–1522).

What, then, are we to make of this extract? How does it affect our reading of the body and preternatural abilities of the devil-yeoman? Thomas Aquinas (d.1274) and Vincent of Beauvais (d.1264) have traditionally been taken as the main authorities from whom Chaucer sourced his demonological knowledge. Paula Aitken argues that the replies given by the devil most closely correspond to the statements found in Vincent of Beauvais's *Speculum Maius*, specifically book two of the *Speculum Naturale*.[42] Chaucer, it seems, was well acquainted with Vincent of Beauvais's work, having namechecked both Vincent and the *Speculum Historiale* in line 307 of the 'G-Text' prologue to *The Legend of Good Women*.[43] This said, the demonological information contained in the *Speculum Naturale* forms part of a wider theological tradition, a shared set of conceptual motifs, that can be ultimately traced back to Augustine and the early Biblical commentators. Late medieval disquisitions on the nature of demons were especially influenced by the definitions laid out in the *Summa Theologiae* and *De Malo* of Thomas Aquinas.[44] Whilst Aquinas quietly rejects the Augustinian notion that devils were condemned to reside in the air and were constituted from the same material qualities as their 'prison' (*carcer*),[45] the argument that demons, as immaterial intelligences,[46] were able to *assume* bodies of condensed air certainly informs the Summoner's questions about whether their Hellish forms differed from the elemental bodies they wore on earth. The devil's reply (III, ll.1462–1466) is similarly an accurate summation of the information contained in Ia.114, art. 4 of the *Summa Theologiae*:

> This [the apparent transmutation of matter] may come about it two ways; first, internally as when demons can effect a change in a man's imagination and even in his bodily senses, so that something appears to be other than it is [...]. Second, externally: for since a demon can fabricate a body out of air and, taking it on, appear visible in it, so also he can similarly clothe any material thing in a material form so that it appears in the guise of the latter.[47]

Aquinas confirms that evil spirits are able to manipulate (and infiltrate) the internal workings of the human body, altering its humoural makeup and causing sensory hallucinations. The ability of demons to manipulate the body's senses is another theological commonplace, originating in the writings of the church fathers. Aquinas gives the topic additional consideration in the *De Malo,* arguing that the manipulation of the flow of the bodily spirits was able to fetter a person's reason (*impediri rationis actum*) and create the emotional imbalances needed for the imprinted images to 'stick'.[48] Melancholia, an 'irrational' state of mind arising from the predominance of black bile that could lead to despair unless properly treated, was often assigned a demonic causation. Vincent of Beauvais similarly states that evil spirits could invade the blood – i.e. the humours – in order to impress (*imprimit*) images on the minds of their victims.[49] Many of the same views are considered in the writings of contemporary medical practitioners who, although wary of ascribing a demonic causation to melancholic hallucinations, at least understood that such beliefs were prevalent amongst the patients they treated.[50] The English physician John of Gaddesden (d.1361), for example, notes that he once treated a melancholic woman convinced she was being stalked by a devil dressed in black.[51]

The second remark made in the Aquinas extract, above, concerning the 'taking on' (*assumens*) of airy forms, certainly lends an orthodox interpretation to Chaucer's 'but whan us liketh we kan take us oon' (III. 1. 1462). 'Liketh', meaning 'desire', suggests an immediacy of action that accords with the reading of such bodies as being fabricated at will. However, it should be emphasised that the Middle English verb 'taken' has strong connotations of physicality,[52] a much more aggressive (and possessive) mode of action than the Latin *assumere* (meaning 'to receive'; 'to accept'), used by both Thomas Aquinas and Vincent of Beauvais.[53] The idea that the devil-yeoman can assume (or seems to assume) various forms is predicated only on the next line, l. 1463, 'or elles make yow seme we been shape'. The conceptual dissonance between 'taking' and 'assuming' is repeated in lines 1507–1508, with the feigning of bodies (i.e. the assumption of a *simulated* form) placed in contrast to the overtly physical act of 'arising' in a corpse. In keeping with the poetic theme of the misreading of surfaces, line 1462 is ambiguous enough to allow for (and encourage) multiple interpretations.

Theological orthodoxies inform other key aspects of the digression, including the belief that demons were employed as weapons for good (*ST*, Ia. 114 art. 1, res.), and could only work their 'divers art' at God's behest (*ST*, Ia. 114 art. 4, res. 2). The theory that demons possessed subtler, keener intellects than humans accounts, in part, for the devil-yeoman's ability to discern the Summoner's true *entente*, the easy confidence of knowing he will soon claim another soul (*ST*, Ia. 172, art. 5; *De Malo*, q. 16, art. 7). The *De Malo* describes the differences thus:

> But human beings can with certainty know in causes things that belong to the causes as proceeding necessarily from them. And devils or angels, who know the power of natural causes better than human beings do, can much more certainly know such things. And things that happen for the most part can be known in their causes with some probability and not complete certainty, but more certainly by good or bad angels than by human beings. And we should note that knowing a future thing in its cause is simply knowing the present inclination of the cause to produce its effect.[54]

Through the careful observation of material signs, human behaviours, and by drawing upon their ancient knowledge, demons were able to assess whether their victims had the moral fortitude to overcome temptation. Bartholomaeus Anglicus (d.1272), another authority known to Chaucer, synthesises Isidore of Seville[55] and Augustine[56] in noting that the combination of experience, sharp wit, and an understanding of human psychology allowed demons to accurately predict the future.[57] Although they were prevented from actually seeing inside a human soul – only God had that privilege – evil spirits had other ways to manipulate their prey and ascertain 'intent'. The devil-yeoman's insistence that the Summoner, a proxy demon himself, *shall* soon find himself in hell is based on an appraisal of the all too obvious signs. Chaucer, then, enhances the ironic resemblance between the Summoner and devil by having one 'brother' unable to read signs and the other a master of the art.

From the ability to shapeshift to the insidious manipulation of the body and soul, the devil-yeoman does not exist outside of the criteria laid out in learned discourse except, of course, in the explicit referral to the ambulation of the dead. Although the theological traditions of Thomas Aquinas accepted the idea that the devil can invade the body-fortress, there is tantamount silence, even opposition, where the logical extension to this line of thinking – the false resurrection of the corpse – is concerned. William of Auvergne, Bishop of Paris (d.1249) and one of the greatest theologians of his age, is adamant that neither demon nor soul can inhabit a defunct body. Of course, the fact that such distinctions had to be made is proof that there was much belief to the contrary.[58] Sermon stories remained one of the key vehicles through which the habitual fear of demonic 'invasion', a fundamental church teaching, coalesced within wider intertextual concerns about bad death and restless corpses. As noted by Przemyslaw Mroczkowski, the 'language of the pulpit' permeates the *Friar's Tale*.[59] It need not be reiterated that the tale itself is based on the structure of a popular exemplum. Chaucer, it is safe to say, consulted more than just Vincent of Beauvias and Thomas Aquinas in the construction of the digression including, perhaps, sermon stories on the walking dead. Within the social logic of the story it is entirely appropriate that Huberd, an itinerant preacher, should apply some local flavour to his intellectual evisceration of the pilgrim-Summoner. If the ambiguity of the phrase 'take us oon' precludes an interpretation of line 1462 as truly referring to a demonically-activated corpse, there are no such concerns for lines 1507–1508. The symbolic connection between the devil and the Summoner becomes much more pronounced if the devil-yeoman can be read as being *embodied*. Just as the Summoner acts like a revenant in roving around the local parish (Holderness?) spreading misery and discontent, so it is fitting that his devilish mirror ironically manifests itself within its own socially-pestilential body. The 'taking' of dead bodies emphasises the juxtaposition between the outer shell and inner agent. It is a much more sophisticated deployment of the 'appearance/intent' dichotomy than if the devil-yeoman's form was simply 'assumed'. The additional connotation of one-sided exchange – theft – provides further conceptual links to the wider economic behaviours exhibited by the Summoner and devil-yeoman.

The previous chapter confirmed that the belief in restless corpses was fairly prominent in fourteenth-century England, made manifest across a wide variety of genres. Preachers' manuals, of course, provide some of the most detailed and enlightening case studies. The sermon for the dedication of a church (*De dedicacione ecclesia*) in John Mirk's *Festial* (c.1380s) demonstrates that not all revenants were considered diabolical in nature. Although Mirk only obliquely states that the *spyryte* of an unshriven thief from Lilleshall was embodied, he pointedly introduces the exemplum by saying that there are many that 'walketh aftyr þat þey ben ded'. Likewise, the manner of the haunting – it ȝede ('walked') around the village from sundown to sunlight – certainly suggests that is presented a bodily threat. Mirk's burial sermon (*In die sepulture alicuius Mortui*) is much less opaque, confirming that devils were able to 'take' corpses that hadn't been subject to the Last Rites: "Ðan com a fend and toke þis cors þat was not anoylud, and ȝode into itte and so forth into þe toun".[60] Before it entered the body, the demon was said to have appeared 'leke an ape', a common literary topos that also finds voice through Chaucer's devil-yeoman (III, ll. 1464).[61] Even though the aforementioned *Festial* exempla served the same basic moral function – to demonstrate the ineffable power of the sacraments – Mirk was able to alternate between a demonic and non-demonic causation for revenants depending on the specific pastoral message he was trying to convey. More critically where the intertextual influences on the *Friar's Tale* are concerned, it is important to recognise that the initial 'surface' reading of each entity did not reveal their true *entente*. This only became apparent following their conjuration by the church authorities (a parish priest and anchorite, respectively). An inability to discern between benign and malignant intentions was a common concern in medieval supernatural encounters.[62] Other fourteenth-century texts display the same sense of uncertainty as Mirk's. The exemplum from the BL MS Royal 18b.xxxii sermon collection (c.1400) mentioned briefly on the introductory chapter records how a curate confronted a monstrous apparition in a graveyard. Only after commanding it to speak did he realise it was not the devil but the man he had recently buried, condemned to wander because he died in a state of sin.[63] As also noted previously, John Bromyard's *Summa predicantium* recounts a darkly comic exemplum of a man who fakes his own death in collusion with his wife, but is killed by a servant after unintentionally moving on the bier. The tale concludes with the servant's statement that he successfully 'chased the devil from [the] corpse'.[64] In both cases the percipient instinctively ascribes a demonic agency to the unusual body.

If, as speculated, the devil-yeoman can be read as a type of revenant, how can we account for the Summoner's inability to recognise such an obvious surface fact? Surely a rotting cadaver would provoke a sense of alarm in even the most oblivious or greedy church agent? The idea that demonically-activated corpses could clothe themselves in a second, airy skin, one that fostered the illusion of life whilst concealing a rotten centre, is a common conceit in moralistic exempla, founded on the orthodox belief that evil spirits could overlay material things with false material forms.[65] Caesarius of Heisterbach's *Dialogus miraculorum* (c.1220–35) describes how a devil was exorcised from the body of a churchman who possessed a suspiciously beautiful singing voice. Following the devil's departure, the (dead?) body collapsed into a putrid (*foetente*) mess.[66] In a further exemplum from the *Dialogus miraculorum*, a priest praying for the soul of Hermann I, Langrave of Thuringa (d.1217) receives a vision explaining that the Langrave actually died a year before his apparent bodily death; his corpse animated in the intervening months by a demon in place of the soul.[67] Caesarius substantiates the theological truth of this tale with reference to an episode from the *Life* of St. Patrick, concerning a man who killed one of his stable grooms and whose soul was also replaced by an evil spirit. The demon moved about in the body of the murderer for many years.[68] On being exorcised by St. Patrick, the body lost cohesion and crumbled into dust (*pulverem*). The (seeming) inhibition of bodily decay is an ability not just confined to the workings of the devil. The alliterative poem *St. Erkenwald* (c.1386) details the exhumation of a preserved body from the foundations of a pagan temple, the future site of St. Paul's cathedral. Having been conjured to speak by the eponymous Erkenwald, the corpse explains that although he died before the coming of Christ he lived a just and honourable life as an upholder of the law. As such, his body (and clothes) were preserved by holy grace whilst his soul remained in limbo (ll. 266–272).[69] At the very end of the poem the judge's body is baptised in Erkenwald's tears. Giving a final thanks to God, the cadaver darkens, shrivels, and finally crumbles to dust. Although, admittedly, there is a marked ontological difference between the *miraculous* preservation of the corpse and the tricks used by the devil to obscure the senses, the fact remains that the topos of the undecayed restless corpse had a powerful symbolic value in moralistic discourse, whether it connoted a saint, virtuous pagan, or sinner. It is telling that the characters in the Caesarius exempla were completely unaware of the dangers in their midst until revelation during prayer (in the case of Hermann I), the intervention of a living saint (in the case of the murderous Irishman), and a mistake on the demon's part (i.e. its singing voice was too perfect to belong to a human). Much like the *Friar's Tale's* 'gay yeman' (III, ll. 1380), a fine visage could hide all manner of evil. *Discretio spirituum* – the need to correctly categorise spirits – is the structuring principle that informs the Summoner's greedy questioning of his companion. However blithe and self-serving in this instance, the base tenor of the interrogation (*'What exactly are you'?*) was a sentiment that would have been shared by many in the same situation, anticipating the types of question that would soon become standardised in the 'discernment literature' emerging from the Parisian schools, specifically the works of Henry of Langenstein (*De discretione* spirituum, c.1383), Pierre d'Ailly (*De falsis prophetis II* c.1385) and the Chancellor, Jean Gerson (*De distinctione verarum visionum, a falsis*, c.1401, and *De probatione spirituum*, c.1415).[70]

Thus, the reference to the conjuring of Samuel at the very end of the demonological digression can be read as an encapsulation – indeed, distillation – of the base theme of the dialogue as a whole: the difficulty of establishing an exact ontology for demonic entities. In contrast to the belief of some scholars,[71] lines 1510–1512 should not be viewed as an artless insertion on Chaucer's part. The Witch of Endor is the preeminent Biblical precedent for exploring the question of supernatural identity. Since the very earliest exegetical commentaries there had been disagreements as to whether the summoning of Samuel represented a true act of necromancy – prophecy though conversations with the dead – or if was merely a demonic deception.[72] The story as detailed in 1 Samuel 28 records how Saul, fearing the approaching Philistine army, travelled to Endor to consult with a medium. Wary of the consequences, the witch nonetheless obeys Saul's' command to conjure up the ghost of Samuel. Appearing as an 'old man wearing a robe' (*Vir senex ascendit, et ipse amictus est pallio*), 'Samuel' castigates the king for disturbing his slumber and delivers the prophecy that due to his negligence in dealing with the Amalekites, he will not only lose his kingdom to David, but will die, along with his three sons, at the hand of the Philistines.

The Jewish historian Flavius Josephus (d. AD 100) does not question the truth of Samuel's identity, nor the idea that he was compelled to appear at the necromancer's behest.[73] Likewise, Origen (d.253) favours a literal of the reading of the text, arguing that the witch did indeed conjure up the ghost of Samuel. Writing a century later, Eustathius of Antioch criticises Origen's approach, deciding instead that due to plagiarisms of language 'Samuel' did not speak a true prophecy and was therefore a demon-in-disguise.[74] The *Liber antiquitatum biblicarum* of Pseudo-Philo (c.50–150 AD) offers a slightly different commentary, intimating that Samuel was raised up through the will of God rather than the art of the witch herself.[75] John of Salisbury (c.1158) was one of many medieval theorists who agreed with the demonological explanation of events, noting that the real spirit of Samuel would never have allowed Saul to bow down and 'adore' him (*et inclinavit se, et adoravit*), thereby revealing its malignant nature.[76] By contrast, Peter Comestor's widely-circulated *Historia Scholastica* (c.1173) was one of the most influential sources for maintaining the position that Samuel's ghost was indeed who it claimed to be.[77] Comester also devotes attention to the theory that it was Samuel's *body* alone that was raised up, vivified spiritually (i.e. physiologically) while his soul remained elsewhere.[78] According to Robert M. Correale, Chaucer's reference to the Witch of Endor likely derives from Nicholas Trevet's *Les Cronicles* (c.1307), a universal history that also provided the source material for the *Man of Law's Tale*. Trevet's remark that 'et si ne fu ceo pas Samuel' is certainly echoed in the devil-yeoman's 'And yet wol some men seye it was nat he / I do no fors of youre dyvynytee' (III, ll. 1511–1512). As Correale notes, Trevet was a Master of Theology at Oxford, making him a likely target for the sardonic reference to 'some men'.[79] Even without tracing the full exegetical tradition of 1 Samuel 28, it is apparent from the above evidence that there did not exist a definitive treatment of the Witch of Endor in the Middle Ages. Only with the coming of the Reformation and the diabolisation of the female magical practitioner did scholars start to agree on a more malign interpretation of the story.[80]

To return to the *Friar's Tale*, the devil-yeoman's reading of the Witch of Endor is incredibly ironic, especially given his previous statement that fiends disguised themselves as men to better ensnare their prey (III, ll. 1464). It is here that we arrive at something of a paradox: the devil-yeoman is nothing if not truthful in his previous disquisitions and later premonitions, yet contrary to his own teachings he takes the spirit of Samuel at face value. A literal reading of the Witch of Endor necessitates an acceptance of surface appearances over hidden motivations. Such is the worldview that the devil – wearing, incidentally, the assumed or stolen body of a yeoman – is keen to exploit. The contradiction of the devil-yeoman's reading of Samuel may be a sly joke at Nicholas Trevet's expense,[81] but at the same time it forces the reader – if not the disinterested Summoner – to question their own acceptance of the authority of the devil's (surface) words and deeds. Demons, of course, lied with the truth (*De Malo*, qu. 16 art. 12).[82] By not picking up on these and other warning signs, the Summoner has all but confirmed his readiness to be transformed from subject to object, to be taken body and soul to hell. Failure in the act of *discretio spirituum* effortlessly ties together the interrelated themes of profit accumulation, vain surfaces, and bodily usurpation, stressing the narrative importance of the demonological digression. Understood in this way, the very phrase 'whan us liketh we kan take us oon' becomes less a dry academic state-ment, a rote answer to an obvious question, and more a casual threat in keeping with lines 1513–1522: devils do indeed take the right sort of bodies at their leisure.

Conclusion: commerce and the undead corpse

The rivalry between Huberd and the pilgrim-Summoner is the structuring prin-ciple that binds the various narrative units of Fragment III together. Professional enmity, specifically the disdain for the corruption of the rural church, underscores Huberd's attacks, just as the pilgrim-Summoner's hatred of the mendicant orders fuelled his. Chaucer's anti-fraternalism is well-established,[83] a factor that accounts for the irony (and hypocrisy) of the Friar's diatribes.[84] The *General Prologue* emphasises Huberd's complicity in the destabilisation of the economic model of salvation. Indeed, it is said that he often gave lenient penances in exchange for lavish gifts (I, ll.223–224), usually at the expense of any outward (and thus spiritually truthful) expressions of remorse. The performance of contrition was a central feature of the late medieval rite of penance. Weeping was a public sign of humility, true sorrow for one's sins. Only through suffering in the manner of Christ could spiritual debt be absolved.[85] Huberd's desire for profit over 'wepynge and preyeres' (I, l. 231), 'silver' over spiritual substance (I, l. 232), constitutes the same abuse of office as that of the pilgrim-Summoner: penance turned to parody and reduced to a barren 'surface' transaction. If on one level the devil-yeomen acts as a tantamount mouthpiece for Huberd,[86] then a sense of brotherhood – moral equivalency between friars and summoners – is established both without and within the frame story.[87]

Whatever the extent of Huberd's hypocrisy, his distaste for the moral lassitude of summoners find further expression in base economic language used through-out the *Friar's Tale*. The Summoner is a 'theef' like Judas (III, ll. 1350–1351) and well-acquainted with 'briberyes' (III, ll. 1367, 1378). His brother, the devil, extorts, intimidates and connives to offset his meagre 'wages', 'tak[ing] al that men wol me give' (III, ll. 1426, 1430). Profit is sought above all else ('wynne', III. 1421, 1453; 'purchas', III, l.1451;). As intimated previously, the devil uses the verb 'take' to describe both the accumulation of wealth – human souls – and the (forceful?) manner in which he sometimes acquires physical form. It is no coincidence that the first and only time the Summoner expresses a desire to 'take' occurs during the formulisation of the pact of brotherhood, a linguistic clue that portends his eventual damnation:

> "And bothe we goon abouten oure purchas.
>
> Taak thou thy part, what that men wol thee yive,
>
> And I shal myn; thus may we bothe lyve.
>
> And if that any of us have moore than oother,
>
> Lat hym be trewe and parte it with his brother." (III, ll.1530–1534)

A cursory reading of line 1531 presents something of an anomaly. 'Giving' and 'taking' reside on opposite ends of the power spectrum in traditional theories of gift exchange. To 'give' puts an onus on the receiver to reciprocate in kind,[88] while the social violence inherent in 'taking' obliges the injured (or indebted) party to take back what is theirs.[89] Social control is retained by the active agent. In this conceptual framework there is no such thing as a free gift. According to Jacques Derrida the only true way to break the cycle of debt and obligation is to be unaware that a gift is being given in the first place.[90] Such a scenario is impossible in the *Friar's Tale*. Not only does the act of giving to the devil involve conscious *entente* – i.e. to be emotionally complicit in the exchange – but the devil-yeoman makes it clear that hell does not operate on the basis of reciprocity, only the single-minded generation of profit (the accumulation of damned souls). The Summoner, too, elides the reciprocal processes of the Christian spiritual economy by accumulating profit rather than offsetting the debt of sin.[91] Rising up in dead bodies is a type of violent exchange, theft, that only occurs if the taken object was physically or metaphysically 'open' in some way.[92] John Mirk's burial sermon unambiguously states that dying in a state of sin allowed the devil to infiltrate the dead. Casearius of Heisterbach's story about the diabolical puppetry of Herman I's corpse also illustrates the ease with which devils could overcome a sinner's bodily defences. In a similar vein, the oath that sends the Summoner to ell ultimately depends on his own spiritual intransigence (or 'openness'). So devoted is he to extracting as much profit as possible from the poor widow that he damns himself through the declaration that the 'foule feend me fecche' should he give up his prize. The conditions of his own curse are such that the contingency clause offered by Mabely – 'but he wol hym reprente' (III, l. 1629) – still assures him of his downfall. At this point the Summoner is quite literally damned if he does and damned if he doesn't. Revealing his *entente* serves only to recontextualise the ties of brotherhood and place him at the centre of an economic game between Mabely and the devil-yeoman (III, ll. 1610–1611).[93] Spiritually unfortified, the Summoner is transformed from active agent, subject, into inactive commodity, object. On confirmation of Mabely's desire to go through with the exchange (adding in her pan for good measure), the devil-yeoman is only too eager to take what has been given freely. The Summoner's *body* is now resolutely his (III, l. 1635). Emphasis is given only to his surface gains ('thy body and this panne be myne by right'), leaving the narrator – whether in character as Huberd or metatextually as Chaucer – to interpolate that the Summoner went to hell 'body and soule' (III, l.1640). From the perspective of gift theory there are no imbalances of power between the giver (Mabely) and the taker (the devil). The whole affair is mediated through the transcendental arbiter, God.

In sum, the belief that cadavers could be ambulated by evil spirits provides a framework for exploring the intersecting worlds of spiritual and material economics, a subtext for why the devil was able to ensnare the Summoner's physical form as well as his soul. The ability of demons to 'take' the bodies of sinners is a literary commonplace, the metaphysical logic of which extends back to the demonological teachings of Augustine, consolidated through the *summae* of Thomas

Aquinas, and made manifest in homiletic and historiographical exempla, most notably in tales of the restless dead. The sins of the Summoner – that is, the accumulated debt of his own impious agency – were the mechanism that transformed his body into an 'open', passive object to be taken at the devil's will. His inability to discern (or his sheer indifference to) the danger presented by the devil-yeoman is a consequence of the separation of surface action from moral core, an obverse to the heartfelt curses that ultimately proved his undoing. It is one of the most telling ironies of the *Friar's Tale* that a figure entirely devoted to the acquisition of wealth becomes just another commodity in the end.

Notes

1 All references to the works of Geoffrey Chaucer are taken from *The Riverside Chaucer*, ed. by Larry D. Benson and F. N. Robinson, third edition (Boston, MA: Houghton Mifflin, 1987). All line numbers from the cited poems will be included in parenthesise in the main body of the text.

2 See, for example, R. T. Lenaghan, 'The Irony of the Friar's Tale', in *The Chaucer Review* 7 (1973), 281–94; Earle Birney, '"After his Ymage": The Central Ironies of the Friar's Tale', in *Essays on Chaucerian Irony*, ed. by Beryl Rowland (Toronto, ONT: Toronto University Press, 1985), pp. 85–108. For a recent reading of the idea of debt and exchange in the *Friar's Tale*, see Anna Schurmann, 'Demonic Ambiguity': Debt in the Friar-Summoner Sequence', in *Money, Commerce, and Economics in Late Medieval English Literature*, ed. by Craig E. Bertolet and Robert Epstein (Basingstoke: Palgrave Macmillan, 2018), pp. 77–91

3 Paula Aitken is one of the only scholars who has discussed the meaning of this dialogue in much detail. See 'Vincent of Beauvais and the Green Yeoman's Lecture on Demonology', *Studies in Philology* 35 (1938) 1–9.

4 The practice of discerning between 'good' and 'bad' spirits is a Biblical tradition deriving from 1 Cor. 12:10, 'to another [person, the power of] the discernment of spirits' (alii discretio spirituum), and 1 John 4:1, 'Dear friends, do not believe every spirit, but test the spirits to discern if they are from God' (Carissimi, nolite omni spiritui credere, sed probate spiritus si ex Deo sint).

5 For the tacit acceptance that the Summoner encounters an airy shape-shifter, see Penn R. Sittya, 'The Green Yeoman as Loathly Lady: The Friar's Parody of the Wife of Bath's Tale', *PMLA* 90 (1975), 386–394 (at p. 388); Larry Scanlon, *Narrative, Authority and Power: The Medieval Exemplum and the Chaucerian Tradition* (Cambridge: Cambridge University Press, 1994) p. 156.

6 See the discussion by Richard H. Passon, 'Entente in Chaucer's "Friar's Tale"', *The Chaucer Review* 2 (1968), 166–171.

7 For a recent overview of this topic, albeit one that is conspicuous by its silence on the exchange mechanisms in the *Friar's Tale*, see Robert Epstein, *Chaucer's Gifts: Exchange and Value in the Canterbury Tales* (Cardiff: University of Wales Press, 2018).

8 A transcription of the text can be found in Lutz Röhrich, *Erzählungen des späten Mittelalters und ihr Weiterleben in Literatur und Volksdichtung bis zur Gegenwart*, 2 vols (Bern: Francke, 1962–1967), II (1967), pp. 251–56.

9 Peter Nicholson, 'The Friar's Tale', in *Sources and Analogues of the Canterbury Tales*, 2 vols, ed. by Robert E. Correale and Mary Hamel (Woodbridge: Brewer, 2003–2005), I (2003), pp. 87–99 (at pp. 87–90). For a more comprehensive overview of the analogues to the *Friar's Tale*, looking mainly at the Germanic sources, see Archer Taylor, 'The Devil and the Advocate', *PMLA* 36 (1921), 35–59.

10 'Retulit mihi quidam abbas ordinis Cisterciensis ante annos paucos in Diocesi Bremensi'. For the full Latin and English versions of the Caesarius text, see *The Literary Context of Chaucer's Fabliaux: Text and Translations*, ed. by Larry D. Benson and Theodore M. Anderson (Indianapolis & New York: Bobbs-Merrill, 1971), pp. 362–65.

11 For a full explanation of the functions of the office, see the study by Louis A. Haselmayer, 'The Apparitor and Chaucer's Summoner', *Speculum* 12 (1937), 43–57.

12 Discussed in Benson and Anderson, *Literary Context of Chaucer's Fabliaux,* p. 363; Nicholson, *Sources and Analogues*, pp. 87–91.

13 Nicholson, *Sources and Analogues*, p. 87.

14 Middle English Dictionary (hereafter MED), ed. Frances McSparran et al. (Ann Arbor, MI: University of Michigan, 2001), quiten, v. https://quod.lib.umich.edu/cgi/m/mec/med-idx?type=id&id=MED35686 [accessed 8 September, 2018].

15 Given the antagonism between the pilgrim-Summoner and Huberd, some scholars have taken this 'contree' to be Holderness in East Yorkshire, the named setting of Friar John's (the proxy Huberd's) jurisdiction in the *Summoner's Tale* (III. l. 1710). See *The Riverside Chaucer*, p. 875.

16 For the historical context of the abuse of the summoner's office in late medieval England, see Thomas Hahn and Richard W. Kaeuper, 'Text and Context: Chaucer's *Friar's Tale*', *Studies in the Age of Chaucer* 5 (1983), 67–101.

17 Birney, 'Central Ironies', p. 89; D. W. Robertson Jr, 'Why the Devil Wears Green', *Modern Language Notes* 69 (1954), 470–72.

18 As Daniel T. Kline astutely notes the different types of oath making in the *Friar's Tale* reveals much about each character's spirituality and true intent. The carter and widow make heartfelt oaths to the 'correct' patron saint, while the Summoner's invocation of Sts James (III. l 443) and Anne (III. l.1613), the patron saints of orphans, widows, and grandmothers, is an ironic reflection of his degenerate nature, at surface odds with his predatory *entente*. See in the first instance Daniel T. Kline, '"Myne by right": Oath-Making and Intent in *The Friar's Tale*', *Philological Quarterly* 77 (1998), 271–93 (at pp. 281–82).

19 For the irony of this oath, see n. 18.

20 Explanations for the gloss's change in modality are varied. H. Marshall Leicester Jr believes that Huberd uses it as a rhetorical device to advertise the fact that his wrath against the pilgrim-Summoner has been mitigated. Mary Carruthers argues that the Friar ironically misunderstands his own exemplum – the devil, of course, is not acting like a tempter at all (discounting the offer to share his gold and silver in l. 1400). However, in hiding Huberd's intent to attack the pilgrim-Summoner behind the generic moral formula of the exemplum-form, it can be argued that Chaucer is subtletly evoking the 'inner intent/outer appearance' dichotomy on a wider structural level. See H. Marshall Leicester Jr., '"No Vileyns Word": Social Context and Performance in Chaucer's "Friar's Tale"', *The Chaucer Review* 17 (1982), 21–39; Mary Carruthers, 'Letter and Gloss in the Friar's and Summoner's Tales', *The Journal of Narrative Technique* 2 (1972), 208–14.

21 The 'multiple voices' present in the tale have been given close analysis in Katie Homar, 'Chaucer's Novelized, Carnivalized Exemplum: A Bakhtinian Reading of the Friar's Tale', *The Chaucer Review* 45 (2010), 85–105.

22 Hahn and Kaeuper, 'Text and Context', pp. 92, 100.

23 'auxint les ditz Somnours facent lour sommons as diverses gentz par malice, come ils sont en alantz a lour charuetz en les champes, & aillours, & les surmettont diverses crimes torcenouses, & la facent les povres gentz de faire fin, q'ils appellont The Bischope Almois; ou autrement le dit Somnour les face sommons de xx ou xl leukes de la, einz & aucun foitz en deux lieux a un jour, a grant desease, empovreisment, a oppression des ditz povres Comunes'. For the English translation, see Hahn and Kaeuper, 'Text and Context', p. 82. The original French plea (no. 46) is taken from

Rotuli Parliamtenorum; ut et Petitiones, et Placita in Parliamento, 6 vols. (London, 1776–1777), III, p. 43.

24 Hahn and Kaeuper, 'Text and Context', pp. 84–86, 98.

25 For the figure of the pilgrim-Summoner in the General Prologue, see Ian Forrest, 'The Summoner', in *Historians on Chaucer: The 'General Prologue' to the Canterbury Tales,* ed. by. Stephen H. Rigby and Alastair J. Minnis (Oxford: Oxford University Press, 2014), pp. 421–42; Jill Mann, *Chaucer and the Medieval Estates Satire: The Literature of Social Classes and the General Prologue to the Canterbury Tales* (Cambridge: Cambridge University Press, 1973), pp. 137–44.

26 For a further reading of this maxim, see Mann, *Medieval Estates Satire,* p. 142.

27 Haselmayer, 'The Apparitor and Chaucer's Summoner', p.57; John Bromyard, *Summa predicantium* (Venice, 1586), I, ch. xvii, fol. 43v–45v.

28 Birney, 'Central Ironies', p. 89; Hahn and Kaeuper, 'Text and Context', p. 93.

29 This is an especially egregious misreading of the situation. In medieval folklore it was believed that demons had the propensity to take the form of forest hunters to better ensnare their prey. See Robertson, 'Why the Devil Wears Green', p. 472. Indeed, the royal forest was a liminal zone – straddling the boundary between the natural and cultural worlds – in which encounters with demons were deemed liable to take place. In a wonder story dating to 1337 and first recorded in the continuation of Walter of Guisborough's *Chronicon* (c.1346), a woman named Johanna was tricked into having sex with a demon (*incubo*) in Woolmer Forest, South Downs, after it had taken the form of her lover, William. Johanna fell sick and died within three days of the assault, her body having turned heavy, bloated, and black. See Walter of Guisborough (otherwise known as Walter of Hemingburgh), *Chronicon domini Walteri de Hemingburgh,* 2 vols. ed. by Hans Claude Hamilton (London: Sumptibus Societatis 1848–1849), II (1849), pp. 314–15. The story was also recorded by Thomas Walsingham (d.1422). See *Historia Anglicana,* vol. 1. ed. by Thomas Henry Riley, RS 28 (London: Longman,1863), pp. 199–200.

30 For the Biblical reading of the devilish connotations of the north, see Jeremiah 6: 1: quia malum visum est ab aquilone, et contritio magna ('for disaster and destruction are about to come out of the north') and Isaiah 14: 13: Qui dicebas in corde tuo: In caelum conscendam, super astra Dei exaltabo solium meum; sedebo in monte testamenti, in lateribus aquilonis (And you [the devil] said in your heart: I will ascend into heaven, I will raise my throne above the stars of God, I will sit in the mountain of the covenant, in the sides of the north)

31 Lenaghan, 'The Irony of the "Frair's Tale"', p. 288.

32 Marcel Mauss's formulations of the gift as a type of inalienable exchange that cements social bonds has remained a central, if contended, part of sociological and anthropological research. See Marcel Mauss, *The Gift: The Form and Reason for Exchange in Archaic Societies,* trans. by W. D Halls (London Routledge, 1990). For the interrogation of Maussian concept of the gift in the context of the *Canterbury Tales,* especially the idea of 'quiting' (the repayment of insults), see Epstein, *Chaucer's Gifts,* pp. 67–96.

33 Marshall Leicester, 'No Vileyns Word', p. 27.

34 Paul E. Beichner, 'Baiting the Summoner', *Modern Language Quarterly* 22 (1961), 367–76.

35 David Raybin, '"Goddes Instruments": Devils and Free Will in the Friar's and Summoner's Tales', *The Chaucer Review* 46 (2011), 93–110; Anne E. McIlhaney, 'Sentence and Judgment: The Role of the Fiend in Chaucer's "Canterbury Tales"', *The Chaucer Review* 31 (1996), 173–83 (at p. 175).

36 By contrast, the devil uses the informal *thee* and *thou* in all his interactions with the Summoner (see for example, III, ll. 1401, 1415, 1425, 1453, 1468), a pronoun also employed when speaking to social inferiors. For an analysis of how different pronouns could be utilised for dramatic effect in medieval literature, see Allan A. Metcalf, 'Sir Gawain and You', *The Chaucer Review* 5 (1971), 165–78.

37 Saint Dunstan (c.909–988) was an English saint, educated in the royal court, whose cult proved immensely popular in the Middle Ages. He was the subject of numerous *vitae* and, in accordance with the typical hagiographic formula, scored many triumphs over the devil. One of his most famous encounters sees Dunstan grabbing a shape-shifting demon by the nose with a pair of red-hot tongs. For a collation of Dunstan *vitae* by 'Author B', Osbern of Canterbury, Eadmer of Canterbury, William of Malmesbury and John Capgrave, see *Memorials of Saint Dunstan, Archbishop of Canterbury*, ed. by William Stubbs, RS 74 (London: Longman, 1874).

38 See for example Luke 9: 1: 'Convocatis autem duodecim Apostolis, dedit illis virtutem et potestatem super omnia daemonia, et ut languores curarent' (Then he called his twelve apostles together, and gave them power and authority over all devils, and to cure diseases).

39 Research into late medieval ritual magic is vast. In the first instance, the work of Richard Kieckhefer, *Magic in the Middle Ages*; and *Forbidden Rites: A Necromancer's Manual of the Fifteenth Century* (University Park, PA: Penn State University Press, 1998). See Frank Klaassen, *The Transformations of Magic: Illicit Learned Magic in the Later Middle Ages and Renaissance* (University Park, PA: Penn State University Press, 2013).

40 Indeed, the famous 'miracle' of Dunstan's harp playing on its own accord was taken by his enemies at court as evidence it had been subject to a devilish spell (*diabolico carmine*). See Eadmer of Canterbury, *Vita Sancti Dunstani Archiepiscopi Cantuariensis*, in *Memorials of Saint Dunstan*, pp. 170–71.

41 It should be recognised that 'Phitonissa' is a medieval variant of the Vulgate's *pythonem* (loosely, 'medium'), a term ultimately deriving from the famed priestess of Apollo, Pythia (i.e. the Oracle of Delphi).

42 Aitken, 'Vincent of Beauvais', p. 9.

43 What seyth also the epistel of Ovyde / Of trewe wyves and of here labour? / What Vincent in his Estoryal Myrour?' (*LGW* G, ll. 305–307). See also W. K. Wimsatt, Jr, 'Vincent of Beauvais and Chaucer's Cleopatra and Croesus', *Speculum* 12 (1937), 375–81.

44 Aquinas's most explicit summary of demonic bodies can be found in book sixteen of *De Malo*, See *The "De Malo" of Thomas Aquinas*, ed. by Brian Davies; trans. by Richard Regan (Oxford: Oxford University Press, 2001).

45 See Augustine, *De Civitate Dei*, XXI.10, in *Opera omnia, vol. 7*, PL 41 (Paris, 1845), col.724: 'Nisi quia sunt quaedam sua etiam daemonibus corpora, sicut doctis hominibus uisum est, ex isto aere crasso atque umido, cuius inpulsus uento flante sentitur' (Unless devils have a kind of body made of that dense and humid air which we feel strikes us when the wind is blowing). For the lower air as prison, see Augustine, *De Genesi ad litteram*, III.10, in *Opera Omnia*, vol. 3., pt. 1, PL 34 (Paris, 1841), col. 285: 'nec aeris saltem spatia superiora atque puriora, sed ista caliginosa tenere permissi sunt, qui eis pro suo genere quidam quasi carcer est, usque ad tempus iudicii' (Nor were they allowed to occupy the higher and purer regions of the air, but only the lower, darker parts, which serves as a tantamount prison for them until the day of Judgement).

46 For a discussion on the disembodiment of angels and demons in the official theological discourses of the thirteenth century, see especially Dyan Elliott, *Fallen Bodies: Pollution, Sexuality, and Demonology in the Middle Ages* (Philadelphia, PA: University of Pennsylvania Press, 1999), pp. 127–56.

47 'Quod quidem potest dupliciter contingere: Uno modo, ab interiori; secundum quod daemon potest mutare phantasiam hominis et etiam sensus corporeos, ut aliquid videatur aliter quam sit [...] Alio modo, ab exterior. Cum enim ipse possit formare corpus ex aëre cuiuscumque formae et figurae, ut illud assumens in eo visibiliter appareat; potest eadem ratione circumponere cuicumque rei corporeae quamcumque formam corpoream, ut in eius specie videatur', in *Summa Theologiae, Volume 15: The World Order (Ia. 110–119)*, pp. 84–85.

48 *De Malo*, qu.3, art. 4.

49 'Dicitur tamen diabolus se inserere sanguinibus, id est humoribus, quia in virtute imaginativa, que abundat humoribus, imprimit imagines rerum delectabilium, ex quibus surgunt male cogitationes dum anima circa eas occupatur', in Vincent of Beauvais, *Speculum Naturale,* (Venice: Hermannus Liechtenstein,1494) II.118 (at fol. 26r).

50 See the overview by Catherine Rider, 'Demons and Mental Disorder in Late Medieval Medicine', in *Mental (Dis)Order in Late Medieval Europe*, ed. by Sari Katajala-Peltomaa and Susanna Nirranen (Leiden: Brill, 2014), pp. 47–69 (at pp. 57, 67).

51 'sicut de una muliere quam habui in cura mea vidi quod non audebat loqui de diabolo nec respicere per fenestram extra ne videret diabolum timens de omni homine nigris vestito ne esset ille', in John of Gaddesden, *Rosa anglica practica medicina*e (Venice: 1506), fol. 132r.; transcribed also in Rider, 'Demons and Mental Disorder', p. 57.

52 MED, 'taken', v. (1a) https://quod.lib.umich.edu/cgi/m/mec/med-idx?type=id&id=MED44420 [accessed 8 September 2018].

53 'Qui tamen de hoc aere in quo habitant corpora *assumnunt* cum hominibus apparent', in Vincent of Beauvais, *Speculum Naturale*, II. 125 (at fol. 27r). Discussed also in Aitken, 'Vincent of Beauvais', p. 3. Italics my emphasis.

54 'Ea vero quae sunt in causis suis ut ex necessitate ab eis provenientia, possunt per certitudinem cognosci in causis suis ab homine, et multo certius a Daemone vel ab Angelo, quibus magis est nota virtus causarum naturalium quam hominibus. Ea vero quae contingunt ut in pluribus, possunt cognosci in causis suis non per omnimodam certitudinem, sed per coniecturalem quandam cognitionem; certius tamen ab Angelis bonis vel malis, quam ab hominibus. Considerandum tamen, quod cognoscere futurum in causa sua, nihil est aliud quam cognoscere praesentem inclinationem causae ad effectum', in De Malo, q. 16, art. 7, res.

55 Isidore of Seville, *Etymologies*, VIII.xi. 15–16.

56 Augustine, *De Genesi ad litteram,* II. 17.

57 Bartholomaeus Anglicus, *Liber De proprietatibus rerum* (Strasbourg: Husner, 1491) II.19. See also *On the Properties of Things: John Trevisa's translation of Bartholomaeus Anglicus De proprietatibus rerum: A Critical Text*, ed. by Michael C. Seymour; trans. by Gabriel M. Liegey, 3 vols, (Oxford: Clarendon, 1975–1988).

58 William of Auverge, *De universo*, in *Guilielmi Alverni episcopi Parisiensis, Opera Omnia*, Vol. 1 (Paris, 1674), 2.3.24 (at col. 2: 1069 B-C), discussed in Thomas de Mayo, 'William of Auvergne and Popular Demonology', *Quidditas* 28 (2007), 61–88.

59 Przemyslaw Mroczkowski, '"The Friar's Tale" and its Pulpit Background', in *English Studies Today: Second Series,* ed. by G. A. Bonnard (Bern: Francke, 1961), 107–20 (at p. 117).

60 Erbe, *Festial*, pp. 281, 295.

61 The devil appearing in the likeness of an ape is a longstanding tradition in monastic miracle collections. See, for example, Herbert of Clairvaux' *De miraculis libri tres* (c.1178), a work written primarily for the edification of Cistercian novices. In one of the stories, a monk on his deathbed sees the devil, in ape-form, licking a piece of cloth he had sewn onto his scapular without permission. See *S. Bernardi abbatis primi Clarae-Vallensis opera omnia*, PL 185, ed. by J. P. Migne (Paris, 1860), II. 34 (at cols.1344–1345).

62 Kathryn Edwards, 'How to Deal with the Restless Dead? Discernment of Spirits and the Response to Ghosts in Fifteenth-Century Europe', *Collegium* 19 (2015), 82–99 (at p. 89).

63 *Middle English Sermons: Edited from British Museum MS Royal 18 B. xxiii*, p. 205.

64 'Sed diabolum de corpore mariti tui fugavi' in Bromyard, *Summa predicantium*, I, xxvii, fol. 84v. It is feasible that Bromyard was making an ironic reference to similar story recounted by Caesarius of Heisterbach, who describes how the devil raised the corpse a sinful knight, Everard, upright on a bier, terrifying those present. Fearful of the demonic 'mockery' on display (*ludificationem*), the mourners decided to bound the corpse before burial. In *Dialogus miraculorum*, II dist. XII.11, (at p. 324).

65 See n. 47.
66 Caesarius of Heisterbach, *Dialogus miraculorum*, II dist. XII.4, (at pp. 317–18). It should also be noted that Book Five of the *Dialogus miraculorum* contains numerous exempla on the dangers of cursing and offering 'gifts' to the devil. However, the moral of the exemplum in Book Five Chapter 12 where a father tells his son to 'go to the devil' (*vade diabolo*) does not mention the murky issue of intent, only that God may have wanted to highlight the folly of foolish speech. See *Dialogus miraculorum*, I, dist. V.12 (at p.291).
67 'Cessa pro eo orare,quia anno integro antequam sepeliretur mortuus est, cuius coros malignus spiritus loco animae vegetabat', in Caesarius of Heisterbach, *Dialogus miraculorum*, II, dist. XII.3 (at p. 317).
68 'In cuius corpore diabolus multis annis pro anima habitans', in Caesarius of Heisterbach, *Dialogus miraculorum*, II, dist. XII.3, (at p. 317).
69 'St. Erkenwald', in *The Complete Works of the Pearl Poet*, ed. by Malcom Andrew, Ronald Waldron, and Clifford Peterson; trans. by Casey Finch (Berkeley, CA: University of California Press, 1993), pp. 324–29.
70 Nancy Caciola, *Discerning Spirits: Divine and Demonic Possession in the Middle Ages* (Ithaca, NY: Cornell University Press 2006), pp. 284–85; Wendy Love Anderson, *The Discernment of Spirits. Assessing Visions and Visionaries in the Late Middle Ages* (Tübingen: Mohr Siebeck, 2011), pp. 159–89.
71 Marshall Leicester, 'No Vileyns Word', p. 28.
72 For an overview, see Charles Zika, 'The Witch of Endor Before the Witch Trials', in *Contesting Orthodoxy in Medieval and Early Modern Europe: Heresy, Witchcraft and Magic,* ed. by Louise N. Kallestrup and Raisa M. Toivo (Cham, CH: Palgrave Macmillan, 2017), pp. 167–91.
73 *Flavius Josephus: Translation and Commentary*, ed. by Steve Mason; *Volume 4: Judean Antiquities*, trans. and commentary by Christopher Begg (Leiden: Brill, 2005), 6 (14.2).334–35 (at p. 192).
74 Margaret M. Mitchell, 'Patristic Rhetoric on Allegory: Origen and Eustathius put 1 Samuel 28 on Trial', *The Journal of Religion* 85 (2005), 414–45.
75 'Et ideo noli gloriari rex, neque tu mulier. Vos enim non deduxistis me, sed ea traditio in qua dixit mihi Deus cum viverem' (And so do not boast, King, nor you, woman. It is not you who have brought me, but rather that order that God spoke to me while I was still alive), in *A Commentary on Pseudo-Philo's Liber Antiquitatum Biblicarum, with Latin Text and English Translation,* 2 vols, ed. and tran by Howard Jacobson (Leiden: Brill, 1996), I. ch. 64.7 (at p. 86).
76 John of Salisbury, *Joannis Saresberiensis Opera Omnia,* PL 199, ed. by J. P. Migne (Paris, 1855), cols. 468D.
77 Zika, 'The Witch of Endor', pp. 171, 177.
78 'Alii vero, quod corpus tantum suscitatum est cum spiritu vivifico anima in loco suo manente, et quiescente', in Peter Comestor, *Historia Scholastica Theologiae Disciplinae,* in PL 198 (Paris, 1855), Liber I Regum, ch. XXVI (at col. 1321C)
79 Robert M. Correale, 'Chaucer's Manuscript of Nicholas Trevet's "Les Cronicles"', *The Chaucer Review* 25 (1991), 238–65 (at p. 256).
80 Zika, 'The Witch of Endor', p. 186.
81 Correale, 'Chaucer's Manuscript', p. 256.
82 Quod per ipsa vera quae Daemon manifestat, intendit hominem ad mendacium perducere ('Devils strive to lead human beings to lies by means of the very truths devils manifest')
83 The pilgrim-Summoner's 'repayment' to Huberd is Chaucer's most trenchant satire against the mendicant orders. See especially John V. Fleming, 'The Antifraternalism of the 'Summoner's Tale', *The Journal of English and Germanic Philology* 65 (1966), 688–700
84 Arnold Williams, 'Chaucer and the Friars', *Speculum* 28 (1953), 499–513 (at p. 511).

85 Research on late medieval penitential practice and the performance of contrition is vast. In the first instance, see Christopher Swift, 'A Penitent Prepares: Affect, Contrition, and Tears' in *Crying in the Middle Ages: Tears of History*, ed. by Elina Gertsman (Woodbridge; Boydell, 2012), pp. 79–101 (at pp. 83–84).

86 Beichner, 'Baiting the Summoner', p. 373.

87 For a psychoanalytical exploration of their relationship, Jean E. Jost, 'Ambiguous Brotherhood in the Friar's Tale and Summoner's Tale', in *Masculinities in Chaucer: Approaches to Maleness in the Canterbury Tales and Troilus and Criseyde*, ed. by Peter G. Beidler (Cambridge: Brewer, 1998), pp. 77–90.

88 Mauss, *The Gift*, p. 5.

89 For case studies on the act of 'taking' in medieval societies, see Andrew Cowell, *The Medieval Warrior Aristocracy: Gifts, Violence, Performance, and the Sacred* (Woodbridge: Boydell, 2007), especially chapter three, '"Violence and "Taking": Towards a Generalized Symbolic Economy', pp. 52–63; William I. Miller, 'Gift, Sale, Payment, Raid: Case Studies in the Negotiation and Classification of Exchange in Medieval Iceland', *Speculum* 61 (1986), 18–50.

90 Jacques Derrida, *Given Time: I. Counterfeit Money*, trans. by Peggy Kamuf (Chicago: University of Chicago Press, 1992), p. 14.

91 Schurmann, 'Demonic Ambiguity', p. 84.

92 For the ability of demons to inhabit sinful 'open' bodies, see Nancy Caciola, *Discerning Spirits*, pp. 31–78, 157–58.

93 Passon, 'Entente in Chaucer's Friar's Tale', p. 169; Kline, 'Myne by Right', p. 287.

Primary sources

Augustine, *Sancti Aurelii Augustini Hipponensis episcopi Opera omnia*, PL 32–47, ed. by J. P. Migne (Paris, 1841–1849).

Bartholomaeus Anglicus, *Liber De proprietatibus rerum* (Strasbourg: Husner, 1491).

Bartholomaeus Anglicus, *On the Properties of Things: John Trevisa's translation of Bartholomaeus Anglicus De proprietatibus rerum: A Critical Text*, ed. by Michael C. Seymour; trans. by Gabriel M. Liegey, 3 vols (Oxford: Clarendon, 1975–1988).

Caesarius of Heisterbach, *Caesarii Heisterbacensis Monachi Ordinis Cisterciensis Dialogus Miraculorum*, ed. by Joseph Strange, 2 vols (Cologne: Lempertz, 1851).

The Complete Works of the Pearl Poet, ed. by Malcom Andrew, Ronald Waldron, and Clifford Peterson; trans. by Casey Finch (Berkeley, CA: University of California Press, 1993).

Flavius Josephus, *Flavius Josephus: Translation and Commentary*, ed. by Steve Mason; *Volume 4: Judean Antiquities*, trans. and commentary by Christopher Begg (Leiden: Brill, 2005).

Geoffrey Chaucer, *The Riverside Chaucer*, ed. by Larry D. Benson and F. N. Robinson, 3rd ed. (Boston, MA: Houghton Mifflin, 1987).

Herbert of Clairvaux, *S. Bernardi abbatis primi Clarae-Vallensis Opera Omnia*, PL 185, ed. by J. P. Migne (Paris, 1860).

Isidore of Seville, *The Etymologies of Isidore of Seville*, ed. by Stephen A. Barney (Cambridge: Cambridge University Press, 2006).

John Bromyard, *Summa predicantium* (Venice, 1586).

John Mirk, *Mirk's Festial: A Collection of Homilies*, ed. by Theodor Erbe, EETS Extra Ser., 96 (London: Kegan Paul, 1905).

John of Salisbury, *Joannis Saresberiensis Opera Omnia*, PL 199, ed. by J. P. Migne (Paris, 1855).

Memorials of Saint Dunstan, Archbishop of Canterbury, ed. by William Stubbs, RS 74 (London: Longman, 1874).

Middle English Sermons: Edited from British Museum MS Royal 18 B. xxiii, ed. by Woodburn O. Ross, EETS, Original Ser., 209 (London: Kegan Paul, 1940).

Peter Comestor, *Historia Scholastica Theologiae Disciplinae*, PL 198, ed. by J. P. Migne (Paris, 1855).

Pseudo-Philo, A *Commentary on Pseudo-Philo's Liber Antiquitatum Biblicarum, with Latin Text and English Translation*, 2 vols, ed. and trans. by Howard Jacobson (Leiden: Brill, 1996).

Rotuli Parliamtenorum; ut et Petitiones, et Placita in Parliamento, 6 vols (London, 1776–1777).

Thomas Aquinas, *St. Thomas Aquinas, Summa Theologiae, Volume 15: The World Order (Ia. 110–119)*, ed. and trans. by M. J. Charlesworth (London: Blackfriars, 1970).

Thomas Aquinas, *The "De Malo" of Thomas Aquinas*, ed. by Brian Davies; trans. by Richard Regan (Oxford: Oxford University Press, 2001).

Vincent of Beauvais, *Speculum Naturale* (Venice: Hermannus Liechtenstein, 1494).

Walsingham, Thomas, *Historia Anglicana*, 2 vols, ed. by Thomas Henry Riley, RS 28 (London: Longman, 1863–1864).

Walter of Guisborough, *Chronicon domini Walteri de Hemingburgh*, 2 vols, ed. by Hans Claude Hamilton (London: Sumptibus Societatis, 1848–1849).

William of Auverge, *De universo*, in *Guilielmi Alverni episcopi Parisiensis, Opera Omnia*, 1 vol (Paris, 1674).

Secondary sources

Aitken, Paula, 'Vincent of Beauvais and the Green Yeoman's Lecture on Demonology', *Studies in Philology* 35 (1938), 1–9.

Beichner, Paul E., 'Baiting the Summoner', *Modern Language Quarterly* 22 (1961), 367–76.

Birney, Earle, '"After his Ymage": The Central Ironies of the Friar's Tale', in *Essays on Chaucerian Irony*, ed. by Beryl Rowland (Toronto, ON: Toronto University Press, 1985), pp. 85–108.

Caciola, Nancy, *Discerning Spirits: Divine and Demonic Possession in the Middle Ages* (Ithaca, NY: Cornell University Press, 2006).

Carruthers, Mary, 'Letter and Gloss in the Friar's and Summoner's Tales', *The Journal of Narrative Technique* 2 (1972), 208–14.

Correale, Robert M., 'Chaucer's Manuscript of Nicholas Trevet's "Les Cronicles"', *The Chaucer Review* 25 (1991), 238–65.

Cowell, Andrew, *The Medieval Warrior Aristocracy: Gifts, Violence, Performance, and the Sacred* (Woodbridge: Boydell, 2007).

De Mayo, Thomas, 'William of Auvergne and Popular Demonology', *Quidditas* 28 (2007), 61–88.

Derrida, Jacques, *Given Time: I. Counterfeit Money*, trans. by Peggy Kamuf (Chicago: University of Chicago Press, 1992).

Edwards, Kathryn, 'How to Deal with the Restless Dead? Discernment of Spirits and the Response to Ghosts in Fifteenth-Century Europe', *Collegium* 19 (2015), 82–99.

Elliott, Dyan, *Fallen Bodies: Pollution, Sexuality, and Demonology in the Middle Ages* (Philadelphia, PA: University of Pennsylvania Press, 1999).

Epstein, Robert, *Chaucer's Gifts: Exchange and Value in the Canterbury Tales* (Cardiff: University of Wales Press, 2018).

Fleming, John V., 'The Antifraternalism of the "Summoner's Tale"', *The Journal of English and Germanic Philology* 65 (1966), 688–700.

Forrest, Ian, 'The Summoner', in *Historian on Chaucer: The 'General Prologue' to the Canterbury Tales*, ed. by Stephen H. Rigby and Alastair J. Minnis (Oxford: Oxford University Press, 2014), pp. 421–42.

Hahn, Thomas and Richard W. Kaeuper, 'Text and Context: Chaucer's *Friar's Tale*', *Studies in the Age of Chaucer* 5 (1983), 67–101.

Haselmayer, Louis A., 'The Apparitor and Chaucer's Summoner', *Speculum* 12 (1937), 43–57.

Homar, Katie, 'Chaucer's Novelized, Carnivalized Exemplum: A Bakhtinian Reading of the Friar's Tale', *The Chaucer Review* 45 (2010), 85–105.

Jost, Jean E. 'Ambiguous Brotherhood in the Friar's Tale and Summoner's Tale', in *Masculinities in Chaucer: Approaches to Maleness in the Canterbury Tales and Troilus and Criseyde*, ed. by Peter G. Beidler (Cambridge: Brewer, 1998), pp. 77–90.

Kieckhefer, Richard, *Forbidden Rites: A Necromancer's Manual of the Fifteenth Century* (University Park, PA: Penn State University Press, 1998).

Kieckhefer, Richard, *Magic in the Middle Ages* (Cambridge: Cambridge University Press, 1989).

Klaassen, Frank, *The Transformations of Magic: Illicit Learned Magic in the Later Middle Ages and Renaissance* (University Park, PA: Penn State University Press, 2013).

Kline, Daniel T., '"Myne by right": Oath-Making and Intent in *The Friar's Tale*', *Philological Quarterly* 77 (1998), 271–93.

Lenaghan, R. T., 'The Irony of the Friar's Tale', *The Chaucer Review* 7 (1973), 281–94.

The Literary Context of Chaucer's Fabliaux: Text and Translations, ed. by Larry D. Benson and Theodore M. Anderson (Indianapolis & New York: Bobbs-Merrill, 1971), pp. 362–65.

Love Anderson, Wendy, *The Discernment of Spirits. Assessing Visions and Visionaries in the Late Middle Ages* (Tübingen: Mohr Siebeck, 2011).

Mann, Jill, *Chaucer and the Medieval Estates Satire: The Literature of Social Classes and the General Prologue to the Canterbury Tales* (Cambridge: Cambridge University Press, 1973).

Marshall Leicester Jr., H., '"No Vileyns Word": Social Context and Performance in Chaucer's "Friar's Tale"', *The Chaucer Review* 17 (1982), 21–39.

Mauss, Marcel, *The Gift: The Form and Reason for Exchange in Archaic Societies*, trans. by W. D. Halls (London: Routledge, 1990).

McIlhaney, Anne E. 'Sentence and Judgment: The Role of the Fiend in Chaucer's "Canterbury Tales"', *The Chaucer Review* 31 (1996), 173–83.

Metcalf, Allan A., 'Sir Gawain and You', *The Chaucer Review* 5 (1971), 165–78.

Miller, William I., 'Gift, Sale, Payment, Raid: Case Studies in the Negotiation and Classification of Exchange in Medieval Iceland', *Speculum* 61 (1986), 18–50.

Mitchell, Margaret M., 'Patristic Rhetoric on Allegory: Origen and Eustathius put 1 Samuel 28 on Trial', *The Journal of Religion* 85 (2005), 414–45.

Mroczkowski, Przemyslaw, '"The Friar's Tale" and Its Pulpit Background', in *English Studies Today: Second Series*, ed. by G. A. Bonnard (Berne: Francke, 1961), pp. 107–20.

Nicholson, Peter, 'The Friar's Tale', in *Sources and Analogues of the Canterbury Tales*, 2 vols, ed. by Robert E. Correale and Mary Hamel (Woodbridge: Brewer, 2003–2005).

Passon, Richard H., 'Entente in Chaucer's "Friar's Tale"', *The Chaucer Review* 2 (1968), 166–71.

Raybin, David, '"Goddes Instruments": Devils and Free will in the Friar's and Summoner's Tales', *The Chaucer Review* 46 (2011), 93–110.

Rider, Catherine, 'Demons and Mental Disorder in Late Medieval Medicine', in *Mental (Dis)Order in Late Medieval Europe*, ed. by Sari Katajala-Peltomaa and Susanna Nirranen (Leiden: Brill, 2014), pp. 47–69.

Robertson Jr., D. W., 'Why the Devil Wears Green', *Modern Language Notes* 69 (1954), 470–72.

Röhrich, Lutz, *Erzählungen des späten Mittelalters und ihr Weiterleben in Literatur und Volksdichtung bis zur Gegenwart*, 2 vols (Bern: Francke, 1962–1967).

Scanlon, Larry, *Narrative, Authority and Power: The Medieval Exemplum and the Chaucerian Tradition* (Cambridge: Cambridge University Press, 1994).

Schurmann, Anna, '"Demonic Ambiguity": Debt in the Friar-Summoner Sequence', in *Money, Commerce, and Economics in Late Medieval English Literature*, ed. by Craig E. Bertolet and Robert Epstein (Basingstoke: Palgrave Macmillan, 2018), pp. 77–91.

Sittya, Penn R., 'The Green Yeoman as Loathly Lady: The Friar's Parody of the Wife of Bath's Tale', *PMLA* 90 (1975), 386–94.

Swift, Christopher, 'A Penitent Prepares: Affect, Contrition, and Tears', in *Crying in the Middle Ages: Tears of History*, ed. by Elina Gertsman (Woodbridge: Boydell, 2012), pp. 79–101.

Taylor, Archer, 'The Devil and the Advocate', *PMLA* 36 (1921), 35–59.

Williams, Arnold, 'Chaucer and the Friars', *Speculum* 28 (1953), 499–513.

Wimsatt Jr., W. K., 'Vincent of Beauvais and Chaucer's Cleopatra and Croesus', *Speculum* 12 (1937), 375–81.

Zika, Charles, 'The Witch of Endor Before the Witch Trials', in *Contesting Orthodoxy in Medieval and Early Modern Europe: Heresy, Witchcraft and Magic*, ed. by Louise N. Kallestrup and Raisa M. Toivo (Cham, CH: Palgrave Macmillan, 2017), pp. 167–91.

6　Nightmares and the supernatural encounter

Introduction

> In these days a wonderful event befell in the county of Buckingham [...]: A certain man died, and, according to custom [...] was laid in the tomb on the eve of the Lord's Ascension. On the following night, however, having entered the bed where his wife was reposing, he not only terrified her on awaking, but nearly crushed her by the insupportable weight of his body

> [His diebus in pago Bukingamensi prodigiosa res accdit [...]: Quidam in fata concedens, juxta morem [...], in vigilia Dominicae Ascensionis sepulturae est traditus. Sequenti vero nocte cubiculum uxoris quiescentis ingressus, excitatem non solum terruit verum etiam paene obruit importabili sui pondere superjacto][1]

The night-time assault motif has enjoyed a long-lasting presence in the religious, medical, and folk traditions of Western Europe. As the etymologies of the terms *ephialtes* (Greek), *incubus* (Latin), *mara* (OE, Norse), *nyghtesmare* (Middle English), *cauchemar* (French), and *martröd* (Icelandic) suggest, the experience of being assaulted by an evil agent during or on the cusp of sleep occurred across a wide chronological and geographical spectrum.[2] Indeed, the Arabic *kabuus* ('pressing ghost'), Japanese *kanashibari* ('to bind with chains'), and the Chinese *bei guai chaak* ('being pressed by a ghost') are afflictions that bear remarkable aetiological similarities to the occidental nightmare.[3] From the perspective of English-language scholarship, investigations into the nocturnal assault have tended to focus on the sources from the Early Modern period, specifically the relationship between the nightmare and the agency of the witch ('hag').[4] Interestingly, accounts of being throttled or suffocated during sleep have often been ignored in research on the Slavic vampire,[5] with much more emphasis being placed on the socio-political context of the wider 'epidemic'.[6] As the opening extract from William of Newburgh's *Historia rerum Anglicarum* (c.1198) intimates, the base components of the phenomenon – the feeling of being crushed or harassed by a shadowy, ghostly agent – can also be detected in medieval iterations of the walking corpse narrative. These cross-cultural commonalities are no mere quirk of historical contingency. The universal nature of the human body is the structuring principle that binds each manifestation of the nightmare together.[7]

Indeed, recent developments in neuropsychology and social anthropology have made explicit the connection between the nightmare experience and the symptoms of sleep paralysis combined with hypnopompic and hypnagogic dream states.[8] In brief, nightmares are said to occur when the REM stage of sleep – characterised by the suppression of muscle activity (sleep paralysis) and rapid eye movements (dreams) – intrudes onto the transitional periods between sleep (the hypnagogic stage) and wakefulness (the hypnopompic stage). Characteristic of this state is a 'sense of presence' and a feeling of dread.[9] During REM sleep the body assumes a state of hyper-vigilance, a physiological necessity for the unconscious detection of external, physical threats. The sufferer of a nightmare is partially conscious of his or her surroundings and is thus aware of the dream-visions and the underlying feeling of danger. Since there is no true external source for the threat and considering that the sufferer is unable to move, the feeling of apprehension is extended to a prolonged feeling of fear, something which is then fleshed out and given substance according to the cultural and phenomenological schema of the percipient. Ambiguous, terrifying visions are not the only aspect of REM sleep to be experienced by the victim. Auditory hallucinations, often taking the form of insensible groaning, scratching and tapping sounds, are sometimes more prominent than the vague and often confusing imagery conjured up by the dream.[10]

The feeling of being crushed or throttled, the defining characteristic as far as the etymology of the word 'nightmare' is concerned, also relates to the processes of sleep paralysis. Muscle relaxation is one of the most prominent physiological changes the body undertakes during REM sleep. The relaxation of the chest muscles forces the sleeper to breathe at a much shallower rate. The inability of the victim to take deep breaths may be interpreted as something – or someone – pressing down on the chest, adding to the already palpable sense of danger.[11]

How the sufferer responded to these cognitive dysfunctions depended on his or her specific cultural experiences and beliefs regarding the origin/perpetrator of the attack. The folklorist David J. Hufford and sociologist Robert Ness, for example, have focused on the ways in which the medical nightmare correlated with contemporary accounts of poltergeist activity and 'hag ridings' in Newfoundland, Canada.[12] Despite some fascinating and pertinent discoveries – such as the hypothesis that the overworked, tired, and mentally fragile were the most susceptible to an attack, and that group hysteria can make the nightmare 'contagious' – never once do Hufford and Ness's interviewees claim that their assailants were the actual, physical corpses of the dead. Such fears were absent from mental schemas of the Newfoundland residents and, as a result, failed to cohere from the symptoms of the experience.[13]

Even in cultural contexts where there was a greater range of possibilities concerning the identity of the assailant, only rarely has the neuropsychological-experiential model been used to explicate the encounter between the supernatural agent and its initial, sleeping victim.[14] Moreover, for all the research into the folklore of 'riding-ghosts',[15] mara,[16] incubi,[17] and hags,[18] sources that reveal the connection between crushing, sleep paralysis, and revenant activity have been given only marginal consideration, especially in medieval contexts.[19] Given the widespread belief in the reality of walking corpses in medieval Europe, the relationship between the restless dead and the nightmare experience may have been a lot more common than we currently appreciate. With nocturnal, bedroom assaults being a standard feature of Early Modern witch and vampire narratives, it can be contended that similar patterns of belief – habitual 'texts' – can be mapped onto the more ambiguous narratological elements from analogous medieval sources.

Taking a necessarily holistic approach to the topic, the first part of the investigation will explore the ways in which the base experience of the nightmare (an understood in neuropsychological research) was interpreted according to classical dream theories, humoural medicine, and church doctrine. Then, with reference to the remedies used to protect the body against 'strange visitors' in Anglo-Saxon medical textbooks[20] and the tales of demonic/ghostly assault from Anglo-Norman literature, it will be seen how the authoritative interpretations of the nocturnal assault were replicated, rejected, or interpolated in the rhythms of daily life. The upsurge of Western interest in vampiric activity following the so-called 'epidemics' of the early 1700s resulted in the publication of detailed body of work on the undead encounter, with multiple references to bedroom assaults. Treatises such as Johann Flückinger's *Visum et Repertum* (1732) and Augustin Calmet's *Dissertations Upon the Apparitions of Angels* (1759) will thus be used to structure the subtextual reading of the agency of the medieval revenant, specifically the wonder stories from William of Newburgh's *Historia rerum Anglicarum*. Ultimately, it will be argued that the nightmare experience can be read as an independent 'text'; a universal function of the human body that is given substance and coherence depending on the habits, experiences, and fears of the percipient. Given the correct socio-cultural circumstances, the nightmare could be subsumed into pervading local fears about the dangerous, ambulatory dead.

Canonical traditions of the nightmare: dreams, humoural theory, and sin

The interpretation of dreams was a popular and lucrative business in the classical and Late Antique worlds. Aristotle (c.350 BC), Artemidorus Daldianus (c.150), Calcidius (c.321) and Macrobius (c.410) were among many philosophers and polymaths who devised a framework for the explanation and interpretation of dreams. Calcidius's *Commentary on the Timaeus* and Macrobius's *Commentarii in somnium Scipionis* were widely disseminated in the Middle Ages, the popularity of the latter surpassing all other works and becoming especially renowned in the late eleventh and early twelfth centuries.[21] In discussing the five main classes of dreams in book one, chapter three, Macrobius provides a vivid description of the nightmare, one which is remarkably similar to the modern medical definition:

> The *Apparition* comes upon one at the moment between wakefulness and slumber, in the so called 'first-cloud' of sleep. In this drowsy condition he

thinks he is still fully awake and imagines he sees spectres rushing at him or wandering vaguely about, differing from natural creatures in size and shape, and hosts of diverse things, either delightful or disturbing. To this class belongs, the *Ephialtes*, which according to popular belief, rushes upon people in their sleep and presses them with a weight which they can feel.

[Φάντασμα vero, hoc est visum, cum inter vigiliam et adultam quietam in quadam, ut aiunt, prima somni nebula adhuc se vigilare aestimans, qui dormire vix coepit, aspicere videtur irruentes in se vel passim vagantes formas a natura seu magnitudine seu specie discrepantes variasque tempestates rerum vel laetas vel turbulentas. In hoc genere est εφιάλτης quem, publica persuasio quiescentes opinatur invadere et pondere suo pressos ac sentientes gravare][22]

Macrobius classifies the nightmare as the lowest form of dream, an insignificant occurrence with no particular function or meaning.[23] This, he suggests, is in stark contrast to the popular perception of the *ephialtes*, which was caused by a malign external agent. John of Salisbury concurs with Macrobius's physiological explanation in book two of the *Policraticus* (c.1159), explaining how the *ephialtes* is an affliction by which a person 'imagines himself to be awake yet feels himself crushed down by someone', noting that suffers should consult a doctor as it a very real form of mental dysfunction.[24] The physiological explanation for the nightmare, one which precludes the notion of supernatural agency, may only be mentioned briefly in the *Policraticus*, but it was employed to great effect in other contemporary interrogations of Macrobius' schema. William of Conches' *Glosae super Macrobium* (c.1140), for example, suggests that the pressure placed on the brain by the anterior ventricle when lying supine, and on the heart by other internal organs when sleeping on the left side, creates the feeling of being pressed. Further interpolators of Macrobius's work argued that the visual and physical symptoms of the nightmare were caused by noxious, undigested vapours migrating to the brain, causing particularly disturbing sense-impressions to be formed.[25] Similar physiological explanations for the nocturnal assault are espoused by Pascalis Romaus in the *Liber Thesauri Occulti* (c.1165) and Pseudo-Augustine in the *Liber de Spiritu et Anima* (c.1170s),[26] the latter using the term *phantasma* (image, phantasm) instead of *visum*.[27] Likewise, Bernard of Gordon (d.1330), writing at the turn of the fourteenth century, rejects the theological and popular perception of the 'incubus' and 'old women' (*vetula*) as nonsense and supports the idea of corrupted humours or digestion problems being the cause of a night-time attack.[28] John of Gaddesden (d.1360) agrees, arguing that a patient may imagine a heavy weight is pressing on his or her chest, but that such a thing may not have actually occurred.[29] In a similar vein, Arnald of Villanova (c.1311) describes how the 'shapes' preserved in the imaginative faculty during the onset of sleep (in modern parlance, the hypnagogic stage) influenced the sense of agency that credulous nightmare suffers ascribed to the hallucination.[30]

These explanations, then, derived from the common milieu of humoural theory and the Aristotelian teachings on sleep which, by the middle of the twelfth century, had begun to be much more widely disseminated in the schools of Western Europe.[31] Indeed, the only recognition of outside agency comes from the oblique, almost scornful references to 'popular belief'.[32] It is notable that whilst some medical commentators preferred the neutral Greek designation '*ephialtes*', others, like Bernard of Gordon, favoured the more loaded term 'incubus'.[33] Although it is true that Caelius Aurelianus's *On Acute Diseases and On Chronic Diseases* (c.450) employs *incubus* as a straightforward translation of *ephialtes* – i.e. as a description of a chronic head disease – the consolidation of Christian practice in the Late Antique period meant that the word began to take on more overtly sexualised and demonic connotations.[34] Even Caelius refers to sexual aspects of the incubus as part of a discussion on the disease's wider symptoms ('some are seized with such grotesque visions that they imagine they see the attacker urging them to satisfy a shameful lust').[35] Isidore of Seville's *Etymologies* makes the association explicit:

> Hairy ones ('satyrs') are called *Panitae* in Greek and incubi in Latin, from copulating indiscriminately with animals. Hence also *incubi* are so called from 'lying upon', that is, violating, for often they are shameless towards women, and manage to lie with them.

> [Pilosi, qui Graece Panitae, Latine Incubi appellantur, sive Inui ab ineundo passim cum animalibus. Vnde et incubi dicuntur ab incumbendo, hoc est stuprando. Saepe enim improbi existunt etiam mulieribus, et earum peragunt concubitum][36]

Thus, for churchmen at least, the incubus became synonymous with sex or illicit sexual contact, as suggested by its cognates *concumbere* (to sleep with) and *concubinus* (concubine).[37] If, as Isidore notes, nightmares were caused by an external agent assaulting a victim in his or her sleep, and considering that all supernatural entities other than God and the good angels were subsumed under the mantle of 'demon', 'fiend', or 'devil', then the doctrinal understanding of the phenomenon becomes clear: the pressing on the chest and terrible night-time visions were the result of fallen angels intent on dragging the victim into sin.

And yet, the motif of the sexual nightmare did not begin with Isidore. Demonic lovers and bedroom fiends had been a part of the Christian *habitus* since the time of Augustine, and maybe even before.[38] Book fifteen, chapter twenty-three of *De civitate Dei* notes the contemporary belief that *Silvanos* and *Faunos*, 'known by the rustics as incubi' (*quos vulgo incubos vocant*), satiated themselves upon unsuspecting women.[39] The mechanics of demonic copulation formed part of wider arguments concerning the sensible forms of good and bad spirits. In *De Genesi ad litteram* (c.415) Augustine posits that the bodies of the fallen angels were formed from the coarser lower air, having lost the purer, ethereal bodies they possessed before the rebellion.[40] Isidore paraphrases Augustine in stating that:

> Before the fall [demons] had celestial bodies. Now they have fallen they have turned to an aerial quality; and they are not allowed to occupy the purer

expanses of air, but only the murky regions, which are like a prison for them, until the day of Judgement.

[Ante transgressionem quidem caelestia corpora gerebant. Lapsi vero in aeriam qualitatem conversi sunt, nec aeris illius puriora spatia, sed ista caliginosa tenere permissi sunt, qui eis quasi carcer est usque ad tempus iudicii][41]

Later commentaries, exemplified by the work of Thomas Aquinas (especially *Summa* Ia. 51, art. 2–3),[42] would speculate that these 'airy' bodies were only temporary, drawn from the immediate environment, and used only to interact with the natural world and corrupt humanity.[43] Regardless, Augustine conceded that he did not know for certain whether 'evil spirits, embodied in a kind of aerial substance, whose force is sensibly felt by the body, are capable of lust and can awake a similar passion in women'.[44] However, when discussing the ability of demons to infiltrate and manipulate the senses during sleep, he does indeed suggest that if the dreamer 'consented' to the images of a sexual dream, then they also consented to sin.[45] Although the manipulation of the senses through the sleeper's spiritual vision was not technically a nightmare, and the 'sensible force' felt by the victim did not necessarily mean they were experiencing an erotic dream, the patristic writings had begun the steady process of merging these two phenomena together.[46]

The influence of religious dogma in documented cases of sleep paralysis is very much apparent. An anecdote from the *De vita sua* (c.1115) of the Benedictine monk Guibert of Nogent (d.1124) is a perfect example of how the Augustinian theological schema could be used to structure the interpretation of the feeling of pressure and hypnagogic hallucinations. Modelled on Augustine's own *Confessiones* – thus providing some clues as to the extent of Guibert's immersion in the saint's theology – the 'Autobiography' has been subject to much scholarly investigation, much of it concerning attempts to psychoanalyse the author.[47] An examination of the incidental details, or 'cultural facts', of the narrative under question can reveal more about the experiential context of the nightmare, the habitual beliefs of a high-status monastic cleric, than if attention was focused on the specific, formal reasons for the *De vita sua*'s creation.

In the first book of his *vita*, Guibert describes how his mother, a God-fearing and pious woman, succumbed to a 'despairing anxiety' (*desperatissima sollicitudo*) over the ransom of his aristocrat father by Count William of Normandy, later the Conqueror. Lying in bed one night, unable to sleep:

The Enemy himself [suddenly] lay upon her and by the burden of his weight almost crushed the life out of her. As she choked in the agony of her spirit, and lost all use of her limbs, she was unable to make a single sound; completely silenced but with her reason free, she awaited aid from God alone. Then suddenly from the head of her bed, a spirit, without doubt a good one, began to cry out in loud and kindly tones 'Holy Mary, help her' [...] When the Enemy had thus been driven out by divine power, the good spirit who had called upon Mary and routed the devil turned to her whom he had rescued and said, 'Take care to be a good women'

[Subito vigilanti illi ipse inimicus incubuit, et gravissimo pene usque ad extinctionem pondere jacentem oppressit. Cum sub hac ejus spiritus suffocaretur angustia, et omnium membrorum ex tota libertate careret, vocis autem cujuspiam sonitum nullatenus emittere posset, solumque Dei muta penitus, sed ratione libera, praestolaretur auxilium, ecce a lectuli ejus capite quidam spiritus, haud dubium quin bonus, sic inclamare non minus affectuosa, quam aperta voce coepit: "sancta Maria, adjuva" [...]. Illo igitur sic divinis virtutibus exturbato, pius ipse spiritus qui Mariam clamaverat et daemonem pepulerat, conversus ad eam quam eruerat "Vide, inquit, ut sis bona femina"][48]

This, I would suggest, is a perfect example of how the conceptual lens of orthodox demonology was able to give a sense of structure, if not providing an absolute template, to the terrifying nightmare experience. Guibert's mother was said to be anxious (*anxietate*) and grieving (*moerore*), a form of socio-psychological stress which research has shown increases the likelihood of an attack.[49] The 'crushing' aspect of the nightmare and the terror of being unable to breathe or move despite being conscious are conveyed with remarkable clarity in this narrative. The 'good spirit' could well be a hypnagogic hallucination, one of the 'delightful or disturbing' spectres which Macrobius states often accompany a nightmare.[50] By claiming that 'the Enemy himself lay upon her and [...] almost crushed the life out of her', Guibert is in no doubt that the attacking agent is a demon. Whilst Guibert does not comment on the sexual aspects of the assault, the use of the loaded verb 'incubuit', combined with the reference in book three to 'demons who covet the love of women and even have intercourse with them', make the intentions of the 'Enemy' all too clear.[51] In a separate section of his *vita*, Guibert stresses that his mother was obsessed with divine punishment and the fate of her soul, and 'conceived a fear of God's name since the very beginning of her childhood'.[52] The fact that the mercy of God turned out to be the one true remedy when all hope was lost, and that to avoid future molestation she had to remain 'a good [devout] woman', provides further proof of the orthodox way in which the attack was understood. To a high-ranking cleric and his God-fearing mother, there were only certain ways of 'moving through' the various social, cultural and theological structures at their disposal. An admiration for orthodox teaching (including, therefore, Augustinian demonology), the fear of damnation, and the avocation of harsh asceticism were at the very centre of their belief systems.[53] A violent, ethereal incubus-demon was the only feasible interpretation for the assault.

Benedict of Peterborough's account of the miracles of Thomas Becket (c.1172) also includes reference to a 'pressing' demon. In contrast to the singular attack experienced by Guibert's mother, Benedict records how a knight by the name of Stephen of Hoyland suffered bouts of 'oppression and suffocation' (*oppressus vel suffocates*) at night for almost thirty years. Diagnosed by doctors as suffering from an *ephialtes* – for which Benedict helpfully includes the parenthetical Latin translation 'superincumbentem' – Stephen was unable to be cured by medical means. Instead, he found that his symptoms became temporality relieved after praying 'for the love of the Archbishop of Canterbury', then living in exile. Following Becket's martyrdom, Stephen decided to celebrate a Mass in the archbishop's honour. Only then did the attacks cease. The demon was still able to appear in the form of a 'dwarf' (*nani*), but a further invocation to Becket forced it to permanently depart.[54] The ability of the Martyr to alleviate nocturnal assaults is further attested in William of Canterbury's own collection of Becket miracle stories (c.1172). A fifteen-year-old novice from Pontefract Priory, Nicholas, complained of being strangled by evil spirits during sleep (*Ecce tenent me jugulum meum coarctantes*). The application of one of the saint's relics to the afflicted area – the neck –cured Nicholas of his torments, the spectres (*lemures*) no longer permitted to do harm.[55] For monastic writers with a vested interest in promoting Becket's cult, it was narratologically impossible for a nightmare to signify anything other than a demon to be vanquished.

By the middle of the thirteenth century, the influence of Aristotelian teachings on spiritus and matter, combined with the increasing importance of the body for salvation, forced theologians to question traditional ideas about the aerial and corporeal nature of demons.[56] In academic circles this seachange put greater emphasis on the humoural interpretation for the feeling of pressure during sleep. However, this is not to say the attribution of demonic agency to sleep paralysis ceased to remain a possibility – a potential experiential route – in the clerical worldview.[57] William of Auvergne, bishop of Paris, spends a considerable amount of time in his *De universo* (c.1249) discussing the medical origins of the *ephialtes*, but nonetheless stresses that divine providence sometimes allows evil spirits (*malignis spiritibus*) kill men with compressions, oppressions, suffocations, and similar such methods.[58] The existence of a related demon, the *lamia*,[59] an entity deriving from classical mythology which appeared in the guise of an old woman and murdered children in their sleep was for William also never in doubt.[60] The pervasiveness of Augustinian teachings on malign spirits – and their impact on the interpretation of other unusual nighttime events, such as out-of-body experiences and sudden infant death – can further be detected in Gervase of Tilbury's *Otia Imperialia* (c.1214). Written some three decades before *De universo*, Gervase's 'Recreation for an Emperor' is a prime source for local, oral accounts of the nightmare. In trying to rationalise the phenomenon in book three, chapter eighty-six, Gervase comes across as somewhat of a traditionalist:

> Physicians maintain that lamias, which are popularly known as *masks* or, in the French language, *stries*, are simply nocturnal hallucinations which, as a result of the thickening of the humours, disturb people's spirits in their sleep and cause heaviness. Augustine, on the other hand, cites an opinion expressed by earlier authors, that they are demons which were once undeserving souls and now occupy airy bodies.

[Lamias, quas uulgo mascas aut, in Gallica lingua, strias nominant, fisici dicunt nocturnas esse ymaginationes, que ex grossite humorum animas dormientum turbant et pondus faciunt. Verum Augustinus ipsas ex dictis auctorum ponit demones esse, qui ex animibus male meritis corpora aerea implent][61]

Ruminating on the nature of angelic and demonic bodies in a later part of the chapter, Gervase again defers to the authority of Augustine – specifically, book fifteen, chapter twenty-three of *De civitate Dei* – in noting that there was a wide-spread folk belief in Silvani and Pans, 'which are the creatures that people call incubi (*Siluanos et Panes, quos incubos nominant*)'.[62]

Gervase does not attempt to define an exact ontology for the lamia (his designation for the physiological nightmare), nor does he arrive at a singular reading for the incubus (the sexual demon). And yet, it is notable that he provides only the briefest of information on the common medical definition – the idea that a humoural imbalance can cause sensory hallucinations – whilst devoting much more attention to traditional demonological theory and accounts of contemporary wonders, such as stories of men and women who travel around the world to crush people in their sleep (*dormientes opprimunt*).[63] This bias towards a preternatural reading of the nocturnal assault is a function, perhaps, of the context in which the *Otia Imperialia* was written. As noted explicitly in the preface to book three, the main purpose of the text was to provide the Holy Roman Emperor Otto IV (r.1209–1215) with pleasurable respite from the stresses of the imperial court. Thus, it is not surprising that the base, medicalised understanding of the nocturnal assault receives only marginal consideration. Wonder stories, vouchsafed by age, scripture or first-hand testimony, provided a more fruitful source of mental nour-ishment.[64] Whatever the discursive principles on display, Gervase's claim that he himself witnessed a woman from Arles fall into a lake mid-flight suggests that the reality of such events was entrenched in the mental schemas of the learned and unlearned alike.[65]

It is clear from these sources that the interpretation of the nightmare was dependent on the social, cultural, and educational situation of the author. Secular physicians were in broad agreement that the feeling of being crushed during sleep was caused by imbalanced humours, while theological and moral treatises seemed to favour the agency of unclean agents, be they satyrs, silvani, lamiae, or incubi. These terms also present something of a quandary. To what extent did the *vulgares,* the medieval masses, actually use the terms 'incubi' and 'lamiae' when describing (or experiencing) a nocturnal assault? The 'cultural facts' of the experience easily transliterate into classical typologies, but may not accurately represent how a victim untutored in Augustinian demonology or Greek myth con-ceptualised the *specific* identity of the assailant. Bernard of Gordon's dismissal of the reality of the *vetula* ('old woman') and Gervase of Tilbury's reference to the *masca* ('mask', 'witch') and *stria* ('witch', 'blood-sucker'[66]) are indicative of the ways in which the phenomenon was conceptualised in different socio-cultural are-nas.[67] Indeed, the terms *masca* and *striga* make an early appearance in Northern

European written culture, finding mention in such desperate texts as Aldhem's *Carmen de Virginitate* (c.705)[68] and the *Edictum Rothari* (c.643).[69] Recycling information previously included in the *Admonitio Synodalis* (c.800s) and Hincmar of Reims's first episcopal capitulary (852),[70] the *Decretum* of Burchard of Worms (c.1008–1012) condemns drunken priests who, as part of the revelries that occur on the anniversary of a person's death, bring out 'masks representing evil spirits that are called *Talamascas* in the vernacular'.[71] For some scholars, the *masca* represents a native – i.e. etymologically Germanic – alternative to 'incubus'.[72] Even Guibert of Nogent, a trained theologian and Benedictine monk, seems to use 'incubuit' only in its verb-form, the attacking agent instead designated as the 'Enemy' (*inimicus*, I.13) or simply 'demon' (*daemonia*, III.19).[73]

Where a medical interpretation of the nightmare was not forthcoming (or even considered inappropriate), the identity of the attacking agent remained wholly ill-defined, seeming to comprise interrelated aspects of the ghost, demon and witch. Such ambiguities are especially apparent in insular contexts. If, as will be discussed shortly, Germanic/folkloric ideas about the effect of outside entities on the health of the body were able to syncretise with, and circulate within, imported classical/Christian ideas about the macro- and microcosm, then even if the nightmare was seen to be caused by demonic or spectral interference, it could be cured – and the demon assuaged – by recourse to natural remedies as well to the active agency of God.[74] As intimated by the inability of the medical authorities to ease Stephen of Hoyland's suffering in the above-mentioned miracle story, neither the classically-trained medical practitioners nor the religious authorities seemed willing to account for the relationship between the preternatural causation of the nightmare and the natural relief of its symptoms, favouring one system of thought over another. Bernard of Gordon et al. could not abide the idea that the *ephialtes* was anything other than a physiological dysfunction of the mind/body, just as Guibert of Nogent and Benedict of Peterborough were adamant that only prayer could combat the threat of pressing demons. Although it is true that the use of 'natural' methods to treat supernatural complaints can be discerned in the subtext to William of Newburgh's 'Buckinghamshire' and 'Melrose Abbey' revenant narratives, specifically the pragmatic need to dismember the corpse following the initial bedroom assault,[75] care must be taken to differentiate between village-wide environmental catastrophes and the single, night-time incursions that are indicative of sleep paralysis. However, this is not to suggest that these experiences could not and did not converge. Regardless of the aetiology of the encounter, it is telling that medieval descriptions of the undead tend not to illustrate the precautionary measures taken *before* the attack, only the contingency measures taken *after* the socio-physiological contagion had begun to spread.

The fluid ontological relationship between the onset of illness, the nightmare experience and the influence of the evil agent (whether conceived as a revenant-analogue, hag, or insubstantial spirit), is much more apparent in the corpus of Anglo-Saxon and early Anglo-Norman medical textbooks.[76] There are numerous remedies in *Bald's Leechbook*, the *Lacnunga* and the *Old English Herbarium* that deal with nocturnal assaults and bad dreams. The causes of these illnesses range from the *maran* and *ælfe* to the more ambiguous 'nocturnal visitor/wanderer'. This latter term may also allude to the close, causal connection that seemed to exist between the nightmare experience and anthropomorphised agents. Whilst the connection between sleep demons and the undead has been previously discussed in the context of Icelandic supernatural beliefs, little attention has been paid to how the insular sources articulated this taxonomic overlap.[77]

Insular traditions and the nightmare

The two components of Bald's *Leechbook* (*I* and *II,* surviving in a single tenth-century manuscript, BL Royal 12, D xvii, but originally compiled in the reign of King Alfred), the separate *Leechbook III* (included in the same manuscript as *Leechbooks I* and *II*), the *Lacnunga* (found in the eleventh-century BL MS Harley 585), and the *Herbarium* (an eleventh-century vernacular interpolation of the Latin *Herbarium of Pseudo-Apuleius*), provide a wealth of information about medical practices in the years pre- and postdating the Conquest.[78] Indeed, it would be unwise to assume that as soon as the Norman regime arrived and, later, when newly translated works began to circulate in the British Isles, that a generation's worth of practical knowledge – based partly on Latin texts – suddenly became redundant, or that prior beliefs were completely subsumed by advances in medical theory. Just because a remedy was dismissed as being theoretically dubious did not mean it ceased to be used in practice.[79] Remedies against nocturnal agents, whether transmitted orally or copied from earlier manuscript sources, may well have retained a presence in the repertoires of Anglo-Norman medicine. An evaluation of recipe lxv.5 from *Leechbook II* and the entry for betony in the *Old English Herbarium* (Cotton Vitellius C III, 'MS V') suggests that there were numerous ways to assuage an 'elf' or 'visitor' in one's midst:

Leechbook II
Against an elf [*ælfe*] and against a strange visitor (enchantments?) [*uncuþum sidsan*] rub myrrh in wine and a mickle of white frankincense, and shave off a part of the stone called agate [jet] into the wine, let him drink this for three mornings after his night's fast, or for nine, or for twelve.[80]

Old English Herbarium
This wort which, which is named betony, is produced in meadows [...]; it is good both for a person's soul or body. It shields him against monstrous nocturnal visitors/walkers [*unhyrum nihtgengum*] and against frightful visions and dreams.[81]

As noted above, the terminologies used to describe the nightmare in insular medical manuals are somewhat fluid. Scribal interpolations, the recognition that an illness could have had a variety of causes, and the possibility that the name given to the attacking agent varied according to the compilers' (oral) source, can account for these discrepancies. *Mare/maran*, the most common appellation, is some-times used on its own,[82] or else associated with a secondary or tertiary descriptor, including '*nihtgengum*' and '*nihtgengan*'.[83] Where references to the *maran* are absent, these latter terms betray a sense of tangibility that the original – trans-literated by contemporary scholars into *incubus* – sometimes lacks.[84] While this may not be the case for '*uncuþum sidsan*', a phrase which is ambiguous at best, a related term, *ælf-sidan*, has nonetheless been taken to mean 'the influence of elves' or 'nightmare'.[85] The use of jet shavings in the *Leechbook* remedy provides a further, if oblique, indication that the *uncuþum sidsan* was indeed a form of nocturnal assault.

Classically-derived lapidary traditions, of which the learned compiler of the *Leechbook* may have had at least some knowledge, have long been aware of jet's apotropaic properties.[86] Book thirty-six of Pliny's *Natural History* ascribes many notable qualities to this black, coal-like mineral: it is noted to 'drive off snakes and relieve suffocation of the uterus [...] moreover, when thoroughly boiled with wine it cures toothache and, if combined with wax, scrofulous tumours'.[87] Medieval compilations made only the slightest revisions to this description, interpolating and building upon the classical material using concepts from their own experien-tial frameworks. Thus, as well as driving off serpents, Isidore of Seville claims that jet 'reveals those who are possessed by demons'.[88] Marbode of Rennes' influential *De Lapidibus* (c.1080) likewise mentions that *gagate* 'chases away the powers of Hell' (1.278).[89] The anonymous Peterborough Lapidary (c.1400) makes a similar claim, adding that 'also who bereþ þis ston abowte his nek, þer schall no serpent do him harme'.[90] Jet, then, did not have to be consumed, but could also be used as an apotropaic binding amulet. Albertus Magnus (d.1280), the thirteenth-century Dominican theologian and renowned practical scientist, writes that jet 'is reported to put serpents to flight; and is a remedy for disorders of the stomach and belly, and for phantasms due to melancholy, which some people call demons'.[91] While Albertus himself was hesitant to ascribe demonic agency to *phantasmata*, favouring instead a humoural interpretation for such images, his reference to 'some people' (*quidam*) suggests that members of the wider com-munity thought otherwise and used jet as a form of bodily protection. A definite relationship between jet, demons, the nightmare, pain relief, and 'binding' can thus be detected in the common medical repertoires of Western Europe.[92] This is not to suggest that the compiler of the *Leechbook* was fully immersed in the work of Damigeron and Pliny, only that knowledge of the efficacy of stones was able to circulate within the various oral and written cultures of English society, and that the inherent properties of jet – especially its ability to emit heat and a distinct smell of sulphur when burned – structured both the local (Germano-Christian) and authoritative (classical-Christian) attitudes to disease/nightmare prevention.

Albertus Magnus's description of jet consolidates the various oral and learned traditions of the nightmare into one concise, detailed passage, something which can be used to highlight the specific function of the jet shavings in the *Leechbook* recipe.[93] A remedy for the belly implies a need to fortify the body against poor digestion and imbalanced humours, the result of which could cause unreliable dream images, demons, or nightmares to appear.[94] The ingestion of jet shaving in the *Leechbook* remedy represents a similar need to calm the stomach, rebuild the body's integrity and, in doing, assuage the 'influence of the elf'.[95] Albertus's diagnosis of 'melancholy' not only substantiates the idea that the hallucinations were caused by humoural imbalance, but also that a deviant moral outlook presented a very real danger to the sufferer's physical and spiritual well-being. Melancholy allowed for the body to be assailed by demons (see Guibert's remark that 'it is the habit of the devil [*diabolo*] to invade souls weakened through grief [*tristitia*]'),[96] subjected the victim to despair and, in certain circumstances, led to self-murder. Suicide, of course, was the single greatest sin in Christendom.

The belief that the nightmare experience was caused by supernatural agency – 'incubi' in Isidore of Seville's parlance, 'daemonia' in Guibert's, and the 'ælfe' in the *Leechbook* – by no means contradicts the purely physiological viewpoints. If the 'Buckingham Ghost' narrative from William of Newburgh's *Historia* can be used as an example of local belief, then the nightmare (or evil agent) was seen to cause the complaint, whereas according to the medical and religious authorities the complaint (the imbalanced humours; sin) precipitated the dream visions and/ or nocturnal demon. The compiler of the *Leechbook* recognised that he needed to negotiate between the various traditions of medical practice and shaped the recipe according to the needs and fears of his local clientele. Jet shavings, then, served the dual function of tempering the physiological distress and 'binding' the nocturnal assailant.

The extract from the *Herbarium* details the affective properties of betony and suggests that the herb was particularly potent against 'frightful visions' and 'monstrous nocturnal visitors/wanderers'.[97] *Unhyrum nihtgengum* is not as ambiguous as *uncuþum sidsan* as far as its (potential) relation to the corporeality of the agent is concerned.[98] Although it would be unwise to ignore Anne van Arsdall's observation that *unhyrum nihtgengum* can be translated as 'evil night spirit', the fact that the compiler used the term *nihtgengum* rather than a variation of *mare*,[99] and seeing as how '*maran*' and '*nihtgengan*' are differentiated in other medicinal contexts,[100] indicates that the 'night visitor' occupied a different ontological category to the mare/incubus.[101] These taxonomic distinctions lend credence to the idea that the nightmare – that is, the actual physical attack – could be caused by a variety of different beings.[102]

What, then, of the *nihtgengum*? The verb *gangan* translates simply as 'to go' or 'to walk',[103] and suggests something about the physical qualities of the agent. A related term, *ganga*, interpolates the base meaning of 'to go/walk' as 'to haunt', signifying an entity whose wanderings were detrimental to the wellbeing of the living.[104] It is interesting, then, that the term *sceaduganga*, or 'shadow-walker' (ll. 702–703) is used as a synonym for Grendel in *Beowulf,* especially since the only extant manuscript of the Old English poem is contemporaneous with the original translation of the *Herbarium*. It is possible that the terms *nihtgengum* and *sceaduganga* bear a conceptual as well as a linguistic similarity. Grendel, indeed, shares a significant number of attributes with the undead corpse, including his propensity to attack at night (l.115), his being fated to wander the hinterlands (l.710), his malice (11.149–154), and his fleshy, corporeal nature (11.739–743). The post-mortem decapitation of his corpse (l.1590) is entirely logical if read against the techniques used to quell the undead in *Grettis Saga* (c.1300s), Walter Map's *De nugis curialium* (c.1182) and Geoffrey of Burton's *Vita sancte Moduenne virginis* (c.1144), to pick but three examples. Finally, the likening of Grendel to a *maera* (11. 103, 762) substantiates his status as a nocturnal 'crushing' demon.[105]

Thus, it would be unwise to dismiss the possibility that the two entities, one a literary construct (Grendel), the other the cause of a medical condition (*niht-gengum*), belonged to the same experiential tradition of the dangerous night-time dead. The use of the term 'nocturnal visitor/wanderer' by the translator of the *Herbarium* suggests that the nightmare was not always conceived of as an *ælfe* or *maran*. It is also possible that these terms were clerical reductions or synonyms for the actual threat: a Grendel-like demon that physically attacked the unwary in their sleep.[106] The bedroom assaults transcribed by William of Newburgh and, indeed, the anonymous Byland Monk (c.1400) suggest that this was not some idle, half-remembered fear passed down through the local belief system. 'Snowball' (Snoweshull), the ghost-afflicted tailor from Byland Story II, offered to give his neighbour some of the writings (*partem de scriptis*) he carried with him at all times all times, lest he too be attacked by 'night-terrors' (*timores nocturnos*). Similarly, Story XI recalls how a group of pilgrims camped in a forest were so fearful of 'night-terrors' (*timorem nocturnum*) that one of the party, Richard Rowntree, volunteered to keep watch whilst the others slept.[107] It is interesting to note that '*timores nocturnos*' is also used in the Latin rubric for betony in the twelfth-century copy of the *Herbarium* (BL MS Harley 6258 B), alongside the Old English '*nihtgengum*'.[108] A conceptual link, based on the habitual belief that an unfortified body suffered the predations of roaming night-time spirits, can thus be traced between the *Herbarium*'s 'visitor' and the Byland Monk's 'ghost' (*spiritus*). And yet, while betony and 'writings' (most likely the opening lines of St. John's gospel) were undoubtedly useful tools for protection,[109] a charm found in MS Bodleian. Rawlinson C 506, fol. 297, a fifteenth-century miscellany, is much more explicit with regards to the later medieval techniques for assuaging a nyghte-mare,

> [One should] take a flynt stone that hath an hole thorow it of hys owen growynge & hange it ouer the stabill dore, or ell ouer ye horse, and writhe this charme: In nomine Patris &c. Seynt Iorge, our ladys knyght, he walked day, he walked nyght, till that he fownde that fowle wyght; & whan he her fownde, he here bete and her bownde, till trewly ther her trowthe sche plyght that sche sholde not come be nyght withinne vij rode of londe space ther as Seynt Ieorge i-namyd was. In nomine Patri &c. And wryte this in a bille and hange it in the hors' mane.[110]

Although it is true that this St. George charm – the earliest extant source for the use of 'mare stones'[111] – is over four hundred years removed from the Anglo-Saxon context of the *Herbarium* remedies, scholars have suggested that the habit of hanging such devices in barns and bedrooms flourished for generations before emerging in the written record.[112] *Fowle wyghts* were no less troublesome in the fifteenth century than the *nihtgengum* had been in eleventh and twelfth. The fear of malign nocturnal agents was a habitual truth that persevered into the High Middle Ages and beyond.

Nightmares and revenants in medieval historiography

The growth of literacy in the political and ecclesiastical communities of Western Europe in the late eleventh century precipitated a desire to commit oral texts to the page.[113] A consequence of the increasing reliance on the written word over ephemeral speech acts saw hitherto undocumented habits of belief become much more visible in the written record. As noted previously, a 'text' can be conceived as an interrelated series of assumptions, beliefs, and fears that were disseminated among a particular social grouping. Once committed to vellum, such 'texts' could be used/amended by the author to influence the dispositions of the communities in which they circulated.[114] Ongoing archaeological investigations into 'deviant' burial practices suggest that rather than viewing later medieval ghost/revenant narratives as *wholly* emerging from socio-religious innovation (for example, as a response to the advent of purgatory and liturgies for the dead), such reforms also provided an outlet, however subtextual, through which age-old 'texts' concerning nocturnal assaults, supernatural agencies, and restless corpses could find new modes of expression.[115]

Indeed, incidental details from the historiographic sources, specifically William of Newburgh's *Historia rerum Anglicarum* (c.1198), can provide a tantalising glimpse into the everyday, often unrecorded relationship between the nightmare experience and encounters with the walking dead. Of the four revenant narratives contained in William's *Historia*, only two detail events that occurred inside the bedroom. As recounted at the beginning of the chapter, the revenant in William's 'Buckingham Ghost' narrative 'entered the bed where his wife was reposing [and] not only terrified her on awaking, but nearly crushed (*obruit*) her by the insupportable weight of his body'. The disturbances only ceased when Hugh of Avalon, the Bishop of Lincoln, ordered that a scroll of absolution be placed in the man's grave.[116] The corpse of the dissolute priest from Melrose was said by William to have hovered nightly around the bedchambers of his former mistress, emitting 'load groans and horrible murmurs' (*ingenti fremitu et horrendo murmure*). Following the exhumation of the troublesome corpse – which was said to be under the control of the devil (*diabolus*) – its restlessness was confirmed by the large quantities of liquid blood in the grave and the wound on the torso, having been attacked by a Melrose Abbey monk during one of its nightly wanderings.[117] The corpse was then taken to public ground and summarily cremated.

Certain motifs are immediately apparent. The possibility that the priest's mistress was suffering from sleep paralysis and REM hallucinations can be presumed from the context of the revenant's initial appearance. The Buckinghamshire revenant and the demon that attacked Guibert's mother also appear at night to a distressed and/or drowsy victim. Indeed, it is significant that the victims in all three narratives were mourning the loss of a husband or illicit lover. With the priest having died in a state of sin, and his mistress fearing for the state of her soul for having instigated an affair with a man of God, it can be hypothesised that the victim was suffering from psychological distress and sleep deprivation which, in the medieval language of humoural/spiritual imbalance, led to an unfortified body and increased the possibility of a night-time attack.[118] The experience, then, was shaped according to prevailing cultural beliefs about 'bad' death, health, and damnation; the identity of the perpetrator structured by the traumatic personal experiences of the victim. In contrast William's testimony on the Buckinghamshire revenant and Guibert's account of his mother's assault, where the crushing of the chest was the most apparent symptom, the aspects of the nightmare given emphasis in the 'Hounds' Priest' narrative were the auditory and visual hallucinations.[119] Indeed, the description of the corpse hovering around the bed is strongly reminiscent of William of Malmesbury's account of the post-mortem activities of the drunken bishop, Brihtwold. The wardens at the church in which Brihtwold was buried were disturbed by strange, ghost-like images (*satisque constat custodes locis umbris fantasticis*), until such time the bishop's body was exhumed and deposited in a swamp far away from Malmesbury Abbey.[120] Pointedly, these description accord to the type of non-significant dream discussed by Macrobius: 'In this drowsy condition he thinks he is still fully awake and imagines he sees spectres rushing at him or wandering vaguely about, differing from natural creatures in size and shape, and hosts of diverse things, either delightful or disturbing'.[121]

The 'contagious' aspect of the nightmare experience is not as apparent in the story of the Melrose revenant as in the other encounters transcribed by William. No-one aside from the priest's mistress is described as being harassed by the corpse. Contrast this to event in Buckinghamshire where, having been repulsed from molesting his wife:

> [The revenant] harassed in a similar manner his own brothers who were dwelling in the same street; but they, following the example of the woman, passed the nights in wakefulness with their companions, ready to meet and repel the expected danger. He appeared, notwithstanding, as if with the hope of surprising them should they be overcome with drowsiness.

> [Sic fratres proprios in eodem vico habitantes similiter fatigavit. Illi vero, juxta muliebris cautelae exemplum, parati ad exeipiendum repellendumque periculum, noctes cum suis ducebant insomnes. Aderat tamen ille tanquam desiderans praeoccupare somnolentos].[122]

This observation about the time and place of the revenant's attacks on his brothers is telling. The last line recalls the Macrobian observation that in a 'drowsy condition [the victim] thinks he is still fully awake', suggestive, perhaps, of the onset of a hypnagogic hallucination. Stress, trauma, and despair – all facets of the social disharmony caused by 'bad' death – were emotions which were undoubtedly shared by the immediate family of the deceased. With the family members becoming physiologically susceptible to a *visum* and unsure about the spiritual status of their kinsman, it is unsurprising that they too succumbed to sleep paralysis/nocturnal attacks and attributed its symptoms to their dead, restless brother. As more villagers felt oppressed and crushed at night, so the revenant's wanderings were perceived to have spread and, eventually, became an epidemic. Hugh of Avalon's intervention prevented the exhumation and dissolution of the offending corpse.

By contrast, the courses of action provoked by the Melrose priest's visitations follow the 'standard' procedure for assuaging the pestilent dead. The suspect body was exhumed, found to display signs of restlessness (the wound), and immediately cremated. The Melrose locals interpreted the nightmare as a threat to their physical health and sense of well-being, and acted on the victim's distress accordingly. Walking corpses were an acute environmental hazard, a physical manifestation of the metaphysical disharmony caused by 'bad' death. The nightmare – that is, the initial nocturnal attack – merely confirmed what was already suspected, and thus the object of this disharmony, the corpse, has to be quickly and efficiently contained. The *possibility* that a social transgressor could walk after death was always present in the local worldview, waiting for the correct social and environmental circumstances to coalesce. A nocturnal attack provoked suspicion that a known sinner, in this case a chaplain who lived and died badly, may not have been following the correct path into death. If the deceased did indeed display signs of restlessness upon their exhumation – an excess of liquid blood and a lack of putrefaction, for example – then the relationship between the nightmare, contagion and the corpse was all but confirmed and the correct apotropaic action taken.

Such habits of belief can readily be discerned in the narratology of early modern vampire encounters.[123] Indeed, the sequence described above is repeated almost verbatim in a 1734 travelogue, 'The Travels of Three English Gentlemen', included in the eleventh volume of *The Harleian Miscellany* (1810). Discussing his experiences of journeying through Eastern Europe, the author John Swinton (1703–1777) paraphrases material from Johann Heinrich Zopf's *Dissertatio de Vampyris Serviensibus* (1733) in noting that:

> The people attacked [by vampires] complain of suffocation, and a great interception of spirits; after which they soon expire. Some of them, being asked, at the point of death, what is the matter with them, say they suffer in the manner just related from people lately dead, or rather the spectres of those people; upon which [the vampire bodies] being dug out of the graves, appear in all parts as the nostrils, cheeks, breast, mouth, & c. turgid and full of blood. Their countenances are fresh and ruddy [...] not the least mark of corruption is visible upon them. Those who are destroyed by them, after their death, become Vampyres; so that to prevent so spreading an evil, it is found requisite to drive a stake through the dead body, from whence, on this occasion, the blood flows as if the person was alive. Sometimes the body is dug out from the grave and burnt to ashes; upon which all disturbances cease.[124]

Similar testimony is recorded in the military surgeon Johann Flückinger's account of a vampire epidemic that engulfed the Serbian village of Medvegia (c.1727–1731). One of the final victims, a young girl named Stanacka, 'awoke at midnight with a terrible cry, fearful and shaking, and complained that she had been chocked (*gewürget*) by the son of a hajduk [soldier] called Milloe, who had died nine weeks earlier, whereupon she had experienced a great pain in the chest and became worse by the hour, until she finally died on the third day'.[125] According to Flückinger, suspected vampires were exhumed and checked for signs of unnatural vitality – i.e. a lack of decay and the presence of fresh blood – before being pierced through the heart with a stake and cremated. First recorded in the Silesian physician Martin Weinrich's preface to the 1612 edition of Gianfrancesco Pico della Mirandola's *Strix* ('witches') and concerning events that Weinrich himself witnessed (c.1591), Henry More's account of the ghost of a shoemaker from Breslau (present-day Wrocław) follows the same narratological formula: 'those that were asleep, [the shoemaker] terrified with horrible visions, those that were waking it would strike, pull or press, lying heavily upon them like an *Ephialtes*, so that there were perpetual complaints every morning of their last nights rest, throughout the whole Town [...]'. Eventually, the shoemaker's corpse was exhumed, dismembered, the uncorrupted heart removed, and 'together with his body they put [it] on a pile of wood and burnt them [both] to ashes'.[126] Augustin Calmet's *Dissertations Upon the Apparitions of Angels*, an exhaustive and widely-read treatise on supernatural phenomena, recounts a story first published in the French magazine *Mecure Galant* in 1693–1694:

> These [Polish and Russian] vampires, or devils in their shape, frequently come out of their graves, and pay a visit to their relations, whom they squeeze and pinch and suck their blood, till they are reduced to the greatest weakness, and fall away gradually to their death. This persecution is not confined to one single person but reaches out to every one of the family, except it [can] be put a stop to by cutting off the head, or taking out the heart of the vampire, who is found in his coffin with his flesh soft, flexible, plump and ruddy, though he has been dead for some considerable time. There generally issues from the body a great quantity if blood [...]'.[127]

As with the previous sources, the disarticulation of the body was the only true means of stopping the pestilence from spreading. Neplach of Opatovice (c.1361),[128] François Richard (1657),[129] Johann Valvasor (1689),[130] Joseph Pitton de Tournefort (1718),[131] and Provisor Frombald (c.1725)[132] provide equally vivid testimony for the identification and containment of crushing/hitting ghosts.

Although the nature of the medieval testimonies precludes anything as detailed and coherent as the Slavic/Early Modern vampire tracts, it can be argued that the identification and containment of restless corpses occurred in a similar fashion. The base structure of the insular revenant encounter corresponded almost exactly to the narratology of the Eastern European vampire outbreak. The initial attack (the nightmare; 'bad' death) preceded a wider contagion (the spread of the nightmare and/or the pestilence) and culminated in the 'binding' of the suspect corpse (the final apotropaic response, often prompted by signs of restlessness on the body).[133] While it is unlikely that this pattern can be replicated across all cross-cultural instances of revenant activity – especially in cases where a nocturnal assault or high death count is absent – when nightmares, disease, and ill-timed death did indeed combine the model is certainly persuasive.

Conclusion

This chapter has acted as an overview of the canonical and non-canonical conceptions of the nightmare text in the Middle Ages. Sleep paralysis was, and is, a universal physiological disorder that had no definitive explanation. Imbalanced humours, mental anguish, and demonic sexual contact were just some of the meanings ascribed to the phenomenon by the medical and theological authorities of the era. Theory, however, very rarely conformed to everyday practice. Different ways of 'moving through' one's immediate social field created different rhetorics, or patterns, of belief. It took only a small mental interpolation for the incubus/nightmare to be reconceived as a demonically-activated *body*, a rhetoric which could circulate within the ingrained local traditions of disease causation, ambulatory corpses, and nocturnal agents. Aspects of this synthesis can be discerned in the bedroom location of the initial encounters, the common interpretation of the revenant as a demon-in-disguise and, it can be theorised, the use of jet objects as apotropaic grave goods. Indeed, if jet 'chase[d] away the powers of Hell' in life,[134] either in amulet-form or as an ingredient in a medical recipe, then this habit of belief could be re-employed to bind the revenant to the grave or prevent it from being infiltrated by demons altogether. One of the more evocative examples of the apotropaic use of *gagate* can be discerned in the cemetery of St. James's Priory, Bristol. A pentagonal jet pendant (c.1300), upon which had been inscribed a Maltese cross and pi-like symbols, was recovered from the coffin of an adult female (SK64). The presence of folded silver coins dating to 1190 on the woman's shoulder blades reinforces the notion that these goods formed part of an overarching strategy to protect the corpse from evil.[135] The protective properties of jet could be just as effective in death.

In consideration of the number of encounters with the undead (both in medieval and Early Modern contexts) that begin with the perpetrator attacking a single victim at night, the link between the nightmare experience and the revenant may have been a lot more pervasive than the historical sources suggest. Future investigations into the archaeology of popular magic may yet reveal the prevalence of anti-demon/nightmare remedies in the wider repertoires of corpse protection, indicated, perhaps, by the presence of jet or betony in the burial matrix.[136] From an insular perspective at least, the Anglo-Saxon medical manuals and William of Newburgh's *Historia* provide a tantalising glimpse into how the nocturnal assault experience – the somatic text – synthesised within pervading local fears about malign agents, illness, and 'bad' death.

Notes

A version of this chapter was published previously as Stephen Gordon, 'Medical Condition, Demon or Undead Corpse? Sleep Paralysis and the Nightmare in Medieval Europe', *Journal of the Social History of Medicine* 28 (2015), 425–44. Reproduced by permission of Oxford University Press.

1 Newburgh V. 22 (p. 474).

2 Cognates of 'mara', which itself derives from the Indo-European word *moros* (to drive out) or *mar* (to crush) are found in many northern European languages.

3 Shelley R. Adler, *Sleep Paralysis: Night-Mares, Nocebos, and the Mind-Body Connection* (New Brunswick, NJ: Rutgers University Press, 2011), pp. 14–16.

4 See especially the work conducted by Owen Davies, 'The Nightmare Experience, Sleep Paralysis and Witchcraft Accusations', *Folklore* 114 (2003), 181–203. The term 'hag' derives from the OE *hægtesse*, meaning 'witch' or 'fury'. See Joseph Bosworth, 'An Anglo-Saxon Dictionary Online.' *hægtesse*. ed. by Thomas Northcote Toller and Others. Comp. by Sean Christ and Ondřej Tichý. Faculty of Arts, Charles University in Prague, 21 March 2010. < http://bosworth.ff.cuni.cz/017878 > [Accessed 22 January 2019].

5 For a notable exception to this rule, see Stephen Gordon, 'Emotional Practice and Bodily Performance in Early Modern Vampire Literature', *Preternature: Critical and Historical Studies on the Preternatural* 6 (2017), 93–124 (especially pp. 111–13).

6 Alongside the work of Michael Pickering (2013; 2014), see also Marie-Hélène Huet, 'Deadly Fears: Dom Augustin Calmet's Vampires and the Rule over Death', *Eighteenth-Century Life* 21 (1997), 222–32; Koen Vermier, 'Vampires as Creatures of the Imagination: Theories of Body, Soul, and Imagination in Early Modern Vampire Tracts (1659–1755)', in *Diseases of the Imagination and Imaginary Disease in the Early Modern Period*, ed. by Yasmin Haskell (Turnhout: Brepols, 2011), pp. 341–73; Peter J. Bräunlein, 'The Frightening Borderlands of Enlightenment: The Vampire Problem', *Studies in History and Philosophy of Biological and Biomedical Sciences* 43 (2012), 710–19.

7 Adler, *Sleep Paralysis*, p. 2.

8 J. Allan Cheyne, Steve D. Rueffer and Ian R. Newby-Clark: 'Hypnagogic and Hypnopompic Hallucinations during Sleep Paralysis: Neurological and Cultural Construction of the Nightmare', *Consciousness and Cognition* 8 (1999), 319–37; and 'Relations among Hypnagogic and Hypnopompic Experiences associated with Sleep Paralysis', *Journal of Sleep Research* 8 (1999), 313–17; J. Allan Cheyne, 'Sleep Paralysis and the Structure of Waking-Nightmare Hallucinations', *Dreaming* 13 (2003), 163–79.

9 Cheyne *et al.*, 'Cultural Construction of the Nightmare', p. 322.

10 Cheyne *et al,* 'Sleep Paralysis', p. 316.

11 Adler, *Sleep Paralysis*, p. 80.

12 David J. Hufford, 'A New Approach to the "Old Hag": The Nightmare Tradition – Re-Examined', in *American Folk Medicine: A Symposium*, ed. by Wayland D. Hand (Berkeley, CA: University of California Press, 1976), pp. 73–85; and *The Terror that Comes in the Night: An Experience-centered Study of Supernatural Assault Traditions* (Philadelphia, PA: University of Pennsylvania Press, 1982), p. 55; Robert C. Ness, 'The Old Hag Phenomenon as Sleep Paralysis: A Biocultural Interpretation', *Culture, Medicine and Psychiatry* 2 (1978), 15–39.

13 Ness, 'The Old Hag Phenomenon', p. 31.

14 See Davies, 'Nightmare Experience', pp. 194–95.

15 Eivind Haga, 'The Nightmare – A Riding Ghost with Sexual Connotations', *Nord Psykiatrisk Tidsskrift* 43 (1989), 515–20.

16 Catharina Raudvere, 'Analogy Narratives and Fictive Rituals: Some Legends of the *Mara* in Scandinavian Folk Belief', *ARV: Nordic Yearbook of Folklore* 51 (1995),

41–62; Alaric Hall, 'The Evidence for Maran, the Anglo-Saxon "Nightmares"', *Neophilologus* 91 (2009), 299–317.

17 Maaike van der Lugt, 'The *Incubus* in Scholastic Debate: Medicine, Theology and Popular Belief', in *Religion and Medicine in the Middle Ages*, ed. by Peter Biller and Joseph Ziegler (Woodbridge: York Medieval Press, 2001), pp. 175–200

18 Owen Davies, 'Hag-riding in Nineteenth-Century West Country England and Modern Newfoundland: An Examination of an Experience-centred Witchcraft Tradition', *Folk Life* 35 (1997), 36–53.

19 Gordon, 'Early Modern Vampire Literature', pp. 111–13; Nicolas K. Kiessling, 'Grendel: A New Aspect', *Modern Philology* 65 (1968), 191–201; and *The Incubus in English Literature: Provenance and Progeny* (Pullman, WA: Washington State University Press, 1997), pp.16–20.

20 Oswald Cockayne, *Leechdoms, Wortcunning and Starcraft of Early England*, 3 Vols, RS 35 (London: Longman, 1864–66).

21 Alison M. Peden, 'Macrobius and Medieval Dream Literature', *Medium Aevum* 54 (1985), 59–73.

22 Macrobius, *Commentary on the Dream of Scipio*, ed. and trans. by W. Harris Stahl (New York: Columbia University Press, 1952), I. 3. 7, (at p. 89). For the Latin, see *Commentarii in Somnium Scipionis*, in *Macrobii Ambrosii Theodosii Opera quae supersunt*, 2 vols, ed. by Ludwig Von Jan (Quedlinburg, 1848), I., pp. 26–27.

23 Macrobius' classified dreams as being either significant or non-significant. There were three types of 'significant' dream. The *oraculum*, or oracular dream, occurred when a character in the dream-vision revealed what may or may not come to pass. The *visio*, or prophetic dream, occurred when the content of a dream was proven to be true. The *somnium*, or enigmatic dream, occurred when the true meaning of the vision was obscured by ambiguity and symbolism. Non-significant dreams, meanwhile, included the *insomnium*, an irrational dream caused by emotional excess and which Macrobius takes to be of no particular import, and the *Visum*, or Nightmare, described above.

24 'In quo genere et ephialtem, quo quis uariis pressuris quodam quasi interuigilio, sed somno potius inquieto, opinans se uigilare cum dormiat, putatur ab aliquo interim praegrauari, connumerandum arbitrantur. Quae quidem omnia medicorum potius indigent cura, quam uentilatione nostra, praesertim cum nichil in eis uerum appareat, nisi quod uerissimae sunt et molestissimae passions', Ioannes Saresberiensis, *Policraticus, I-IV*, CCCM 118, ed. K.S.B. Keats-Rohan (Turnhout: Brepols, 1993), II.15 (at p. 94).

25 Van der Lugt, 'Incubus', pp. 187–88.

26 Steven F. Kruger, *Dreaming in the Middle Ages* (Cambridge: Cambridge University Press, 1992), p. 71.

27 Pseudo-Augustine, *Liber de Spiritu et Anima*, in *Sancti Aurelii Augustini Hipponensis episcopi, Opera omnia*, vol. 6, PL 40 (Paris, 1841), col. 798.

28 Bernard of Gordon, *Lilium medicinae*, (Lyon, 1550), II.24: 'Incubus est phantasma in somnis [...]. Vulgares autem dicunt quod est aliqua vetula calcans et comprimens corpora, et hoc nihil est.' (The Incubus is an apparition [that occurs] during sleep [...]. But the common people believe that the Incubus is an old woman who tramples and pressed down on the body. This is nonsense). Cited from Van der Lugt, 'Incubus', p. 176.

29 H. P. Cholmeley, *John of Gaddesden and the Rosa Medicinae* (Oxford: Clarendon, 1912), p. 46.

30 Cited in William F. MacLehose, 'Fear, Fantasy and Sleep in Medieval Medicine', in *Emotions and Health, 1200–1700*, ed. by Elena Carrera (Turnhout: Brill, 2013), pp. 67–94 (at p. 84).

31 Kruger, *Dreaming*, pp. 70–122. Indeed, the Aristotelian texts known in the Middle Ages as the *Parva Naturalia – On Sleep, On Dreams* and *On Divination Through Sleep* – are explicit on the mechanisms for the creation of dream imagery. According

to Aristotle, the 'turbulence' from the heat created by the digestion of food disturbed the sense-impressions present in the sensory organs, creating incoherent and terrifying dream-images (*phantasmata*). See Aristotle, *On Sleep and Dreams*, ed. and trans. by David Gallop (Warminster: Aris & Phillips, 1996), 3. 37 (at pp. 97–98).

32   Van der Lugt, 'Incubus', p. 176.
33   Van der Lugt, 'Incubus', pp. 188–89.
34   Charles Stewart, 'Erotic Dreams and Nightmares from Antiquity to the Present', *The Journal of the Royal Anthropological Institute*, New Ser., 8 (2002), 279–309 (at p. 288).
35   Quidam denique ita inanibus adficiuntur visis, ut et se videre credant irruentum sibi et usam turpissimae libidinis persuadentem, in Caelius Aurelianus, *On Acute Diseases and On Chronic Diseases*, ed. and trans. by I. E. Drabkin (Chicago, IL: Chicago University Press, 1950), III. 56 (at pp. 474–75),
36   Isidore of Seville, *Etymologies*, VIII. xi.103.
37   Stewart, 'Erotic Dreams', p. 286.
38   The pagan diviner Artemidorus Daldianus was one of the first people to conflate the nightmare, specifically the act of pressing, with sexual content: 'Ephialtes is identified with Pan but he has a different meaning. If he oppresses or weighs a man down without speaking, it signifies tribulations and distress [...] if he has sexual intercourse with someone it foretells great profit, especially if he does not weigh that person down', in Artemidorus Daldianus, *The Interpretation of Dreams: Oneirocritica*, ed. and trans. by Robert J.White (Park Ridge, NJ: Noyes, 1975), 2. 37 (at pp. 118–119).
39   Augustine, *De civitate Dei*, XV.23, in *Opera omnia*, vol. 7. PL 41 (Paris, 1845), col. 468.
40   Augustine, *De Genesi ad litteram libri XII*, III.10 in *Opera omnia*, vol. 3, pt. 1, PL 34 (Paris, 1845), col. 285.
41   Isidore of Seville, *Etymologies*, VIII. xi. 17.
42   For Aquinas (Ia. 51, art. 3), babies seemingly borne from sexual contact with incubi can be explained by the demon first assuming a female form, taking the seed of men, before changing into male form to seduce and impregnate the female victim. See *Summa Theologiae, Volume 9: Angels (1a; 50–64)*, ed. and trans.by Kenelm Foster (London: Eyre & Spottiswoode, 1968), p. 42.
43   For an overview of this development, see Elliott, *Fallen Bodies*, pp. 137–41.
44   Non hinc aliquid audeo definire, utrum aliqui spiritus elemento aerio corporati (nam hoc elementum etaim cum agitatur flabello, sensu corporis tactuque sentitur), possint etiam hanc pati libidinem ut quomodo possunt, sentientibus feminis misceantur, Augustine, *De Civitate Dei*, XV.23, PL 41, col. 468.
45   Dyan Elliott, 'Pollution, Illusion, and Masculine Disarray: Nocturnal Emissions and the Sexuality of the Clergy', in *Constructing Medieval Sexuality*, ed. by Karma Lochrie, Peggy McCracken, and James A. Schultz (Minneapolis, MN: University of Minnesota Press, 1997), pp. 1–23 (at p. 5).
46   In book twelve of *De Genesi ad litteram*, Augustine locates the visions one experienced during sleep within the bounds of Spiritual vision, the mid-point between Intellectual (divine) and Corporeal (gross) vision. The visions in a dream (and spiritual visions in general) are neither abstract nor corporeal, but the incorporeal *likeness* of things. External forces, such as angels or demons, could manipulate the content of dreams for good or ill. See Augustine, *De Genesi ad litteram*, XII.16–19, PL 34, cols. 466–70.
47   See M. D. Coupe, 'The Personality of Guibert de Nogent Reconsidered', *Journal of Medieval History* 9 (1983), 317–29.
48   For the English translation, see Guibert of Nogent, *Self and Society in Medieval France: The Memoirs of Abbot Guibert of Nogent (1064-c.1125*, ed. and trans by John Benton (New York: Harper & Row, 1970), 1. 13 (at pp. 70–71); for the Latun, see *Histoire de sa vie (1053–1124)*, ed. by Georges Bourgin (Paris: Picard, 1907),

pp. 43–44 [hereafter *Autobiography*]. Compare this incubus attack to an account of a nightmare suffered by a female victim in twentieth-century New York: 'She would feel someone climbing onto her bed and on top of her. The pressure of this weight on her would be great, yet no one could be seen. As her eyes remained open she would hallucinate other figures in the room. She would attempt to shout, but at most she would be capable of moaning', in Jerome M. Schneck, 'Sleep Paralysis without Narcolepsy or Cataplexy: Report of a Case', *Journal of the American Medical Association* 173 (1960), 1129–30.

49 Ness, 'The Old Hag Phenomenon', p. 21; Adler, *Sleep Paralysis*, pp. 87–88, 107.

50 Macrobius, I. 3. 7 (at p. 89).

51 'Daemonia autem mulierum amores, et ipsos etiam concubitus affectantia ubique affatim celebrantur', in *Autobiography,* III. 19 (Benton, p 223; Bourgin, p. 225)

52 'Tamen divini nominis timorem in ipsis pueritiae parturivit initiis', in *Autobiography,* I. 12 (Benton, p. 64; Bourgin, p. 36).

53 Coupe, 'Guibert de Nogent', p. 325.

54 Benedict of Peterborough, *Miracula Sancti Thomae Cantuariensis,* in *Materials for the History of Thomas Becket, Archbishop of Canterbury,* 7 vols. ed. by James Craige Robertson, RS 67 (London: Longman, 1875–1885), II (1876), pp. 44–45.

55 William of Canterbury, *Miracula S. Thomae Cantuariensis,* in *Materials for the History of Thomas Becket,* 7 vols, ed. by James Craige Robertson, RS 67 (London: Longman, 1875–1885), I (1875), pp. 380–81.

56 The corporeality of angels and demons was, for example, rejected by Thomas Aquinas (Ia, 50, art. 2). Aquinas suggests that people believe that angels are formed from matter because of the limitations of human perception, stating that we 'cannot apprehend them as they are in themselves'. In reality, angels, and demons, are intelligible forms and thus non-material.

57 Kruger, *Dreaming*, p. 87.

58 Verumtamen dubitare non debet, quin malignis spiritibus interdum providentia creatoris permittat compressiones, & oppressiones facere, necnon & suffocationes, & alterius modi extinctiones hominum, William de Auvergne, *De universo, 2.3.24,* also cited in de Mayo, 'William of Auvergne and Popular Demonology', p. 87.

59 In Greek mythology, Lamia was the daughter of a Libyan king seduced by Zeus, whose offspring from the union were murdered by Zeus's wife, Hera, in a jealous rage. In an alternate version of story, it is Lamia herself who is compelled to kill her children. Either way, having been consumed by grief and anger she transforms into a terrifying monster and compelled thereafter to kill the children of others. See Sarah Iles Johnston, *Restless Dead: Encounters Between the Living and the Dead in Ancient Greece* (Berkeley, CA: University of California Press, 1999), pp. 173–74.

60 Mayo, 'William of Auvergne and Popular Demonology', pp. 79–80.

61 *Otia Imperialia,* III. 86 (at p. 723).

62 *Otia Imperialia* III. 86 (at pp. 728–29).

63 *Otia Imperialia,* III. 86 (at p. 723). The feeling of weightlessness, often conceived as an out-of-body experience, is another symptom of the nightmare. Cheyne's studies on sleep paralysis illustrate how the feeling of 'rising' and bliss sometimes counterbalances the feeling of terror and heaviness. Perhaps the most famous account of the night-time flight – and one of the first extant accounts of witchcraft – can be found in the *Canon Episcopi* (*c.*900s): 'during the night, with Diana, the pagan goddess, in the company of a crowd of other women, [wicked women claim] they ride the backs of animals, traversing great distances during the silence of the deep night, obeying Diana's orders as their mistress and putting themselves at her service during certain specified nights', in Lea, *Materials Toward a History of Witchcraft I,* pp. 178–80.

64 'Our primary purpose is to present the marvels (*mirabilia*) of every province to our discerning listener, in order that His Imperial Highness may have a source of refreshment (*recreet*) for his thoughts' (in *Otia Imperialia,* III. Preface (at, pp. 558–59).

65 *Otia Imperialia*, III. 93 (at p. 743).

66 'Striga' is an ambiguous term deriving from the bird-like Strix of Classical antiquity. In certain literary context it seems to have denoted 'vampiric corpse' as well as 'witch'. See n.129 and the chronicler Johan Weikhard Valvasor's account of the seventeenth-century Carnolian *štrigon*, Jure Grando.

67 Van der Lugt, 'Incubus', p. 176.

68   The masca is mentioned by Aldhelm in 'De octo vitiis principalibus', the final section of the *Carmen de Virginitate:* '...when the bold solider does not fear the larva or the masca' (cum larvam, et mascam miles non horreat audax). See Aldhelm, *Sancti Aldhelmi Ex Abbate Malmesburiensi Episcopi Schireburnensis Opera Quae Extant Omnia*, ed. by J. A. Giles (Oxford, 1844), p. 214.

69 The 'Edicts of King Rothair' are famous for being the first written compilation of Lombard law codes. For the *masca*, see no. 376: 'No one may presume to kill another man's female slave as if she were a [vampire?], which the people call 'witch'' (Nullus presumat haldiam alienam aut ancillam, quasi strigam, quaem dicunt mascam, occidere), in *The Lombard Laws*, ed. and trans. by Katherine Fischer Drew (Philadelphia, PA, University of Pennsylvania Press, 1973), pp. 126–27. For the Latin, see 'Edictus Rothari', in. *MGH*, LL 4, ed. by Friedrich Bluhme (Hannover, 1868), pp. 3–90 (at p. 87).

70 Robert Amiet, 'Une "Admonitio Synodalis" de l'époque carolingienne: Étude critique et Édition', *Mediaeval Studies* 26 (1964), 12–82 (at p. 51); Hincmar of Reims, 'Erstes Kapitular, in *MGH*, Cap. Episc 2 (Hannover: Hahnsche, 1995), pp. 34–45 (at p. 41).

71 'larvas daemonum, quas vulgo Talamascas dicunt', in Burchard of Worms, *Opera*, PL 140 (Paris, 1853), col. 652B.

72 For an overview of the etymology and connotations of *masca*, see Enid Welsford, *The Court Masque: A Study in the Relationship Between Poetry & the Revels* (Cambridge: Cambridge University Press, 1927), pp. 94–97.

73 Van der Lugt, 'Incubus', p. 181.

74 See Audrey L. Meaney, 'The Practice of Medicine in England about the year 1000', *Journal of the Social History of Medicine* 13 (2000), 221–37.

75 Newburgh V. 23–24 (pp. 475, 479).

76 Karen L. Jolly, *Popular Religion in Late Anglo-Saxon England: Elf Charms in Context* (Chapel Hill, NC: University of North Carolina Press, 1996), p. 147.

77 Kiessling, *The Incubus in Medieval Literature*, p. 17; Ármann Jakobsson, 'The Taxonomy of the Non-existent: Some Medieval Icelandic Concepts of the Paranormal, *Fabula* 54 (2013), 199–213.

78 The *Old English Herbarium* survives in four manuscripts: BL Cotton Vitellius C III; Hatton 76 Bodley; Harley 585 (all *c*.1020s), and Harley 6258B (*c*.1200). For more details, see Anne van Arsdall, *Medieval Herbal Remedies: The Old English Herbarium and Anglo-Saxon Medicine* (London: Routledge, 2002), pp. 104–5.

79 John Riddle, 'Theory and Practice in Medieval Medicine', *Viator* 5 (1974), 157–84.

80 Wið ælfe 7 wið uncuþum sidsan gnid myrran on win 7 hwites recelses em micel 7 sceaf gagates dæl þæs stanes on þæt win drince .III. morgenas neaht nestig oþþe .VIII. Oþþe .XII.', in *Leechdoms* vol. 2, 'Leech Book II', Ch. LXV. 5 (at pp. 296–97).

81 Ðeos wyrt þe man betonican nemneð, heo biþ cenned on mædeum [...] seo deah gehwæþer ge þæs mannes sawle ge his lichoman, hio hyne scyldeþ wið unhyrum nihtgengum 7 wið egeslicum gesihðum 7 swefnum, in *Leechdoms* vol 1, 'Herbarium', pp. 70–71. It should be recognised that the entry for betony originally circulated as a separate text, *De Herba Vettonica* (c.400), before being appended to the beginning of the *Pseudo-Apuleius Herbarium* at an early point in its textual history.

82 *Leechdoms* vol. 2, 'Leech Book I', Ch. LXIV (at pp. 140–41).

83 *Leechdoms* vol. 2, 'Leech Book III', Ch. I (at pp. 306–7). Critically, '*nihtgengan*' appears without reference to *mare/maran* in 'Leech Book III', Ch. LIV and LXI (at pp. 342–45).

84 For the contemporary transliteration of *maera* into *incubi*, see *A Late Eighth-Century Latin-Anglo-Saxon Glossary*, ed. By J. H. Hessels (Cambridge: Cambridge University Press, 1906), p. 49.

85 Joseph Bosworth, 'An Anglo-Saxon Dictionary Online.' *Ælf-siden* < http://bosworth .ff.cuni.cz/finder/3/%C3%86lf-siden> [Accessed 19 January 2019].

86 Among the first major extant works to note the magical properties of stones were Damigeron's *De Virtutibus Lapidum* and Dioscorides of Anazarba's *Materia Medica* (*c*.50–70 BC). Books XXXVI and XXXVII of Pliny's *Natural History* built upon the previous work and became the paradigm for future compilations. For the Classical influence on medieval lapidaries, see Peter Kitson, 'Lapidary Traditions in Anglo-Saxon England: part I, the background; the Old English Lapidary', *Anglo Saxon England 7* (1978), 9–60.

87 'fugat serpentes ita recreatque volvae strangulationes [...] idem ex vino decoctus dentibus medetur strumisque cerae permixtus', in Pliny, *Natural History, Volume X: Books 36–37*, ed. and trans. by D. E. Eichholz (Cambridge, MA Harvard University Press, 1962), XXXVI.141 (at pp.114–15). The *Natural History* was known to have circulated in Anglo-Saxon England; indeed, Pliny is one of the only classical authorities mentioned in the *Leechbook*. The practice of boiling jet with wine to cure toothache certainly bears some relation to the above-mentioned Old English recipe, and suggests that the *Leechbook*'s compiler consciously improvised the base formula of the Classical recipe to suit the needs (and fears) of his local clientele. See Debby Banham, 'Dun, Oxa and Pliny the Great Physician: Attribution and Authority in Old English Medical Texts', *Journal of the Social History of Medicine* 24 (2011), 57–73 (at pp. 62–63).

88 *Etymologies*, XVI. iv. 3.

89 'Idem demonibus contrarius esse putatur' (XVIII. De gagate), in Marbode of Rennes, *De Lapidibus: Considered as a Medical Treatise with Text, Commentary and C. W. King's Translation; together with Text and Translation of Marbode's Minor Works on Stones*, ed. by J. M. Riddle, *Sudhoffs Archiv* 20 (Wiesbaden: Steiner, 1977), pp. 1–144 (at p. 56).

90 Jan Evans and Mary S. Serjeantson, *English Medieval Lapidaries*, EETS o.s, 190 (London: Oxford University Press, 1933), 90–91.

91 'Fertur etiam quod fugat serpentes, et valet etiam contra stomachi et ventris subversionem, et contra phantasmata melancholica quae quidam daemones vocant', in *Mineralium*, in *B. Alberti Magni, Opera Omnia* Vol. 5. ed. by Augustine Borgnet (Paris, 1890), II. ii.7 (at p. 37). For the English translation, see Albertus Magnus, *Book of Minerals*, ed. and trans. by Dorothy Wyckoff (Oxford: Clarendon, 1967), p. 93.

92 Audrey L. Meaney, *Anglo-Saxon Amulets and Curing Stones*, BAR British Ser., 96 (Oxford: Archaeopress 1981), p. 72.

93 Albertus's claim that he derived some of his knowledge of stones from his own observations suggests that the 'some people' to which he alludes could in fact be *vulgares* whom he met with on his travels.

94 For the link between poor regimen and 'unreliable' dreams, see Kruger, *Dreaming*, pp. 72–87.

95 Louise Vinge, *The Five Senses: Studies in a Literary Tradition* (Lund: CWK Gleerp, 1975), p. 60.

96 *Autobiography*, I. 13 (Benton, pp. 70–71; Bourgin, p. 43).

97 For a *Leechbook* nightmare remedy that uses betony, see *Leechdoms* vol. 2, 'Leech Book I', Ch, LXIV (at pp. 140–1): 'If a mare ride a man, take lupins and garlic and betony and frankincense, bind them on a faun's skin, let a man have the worts on him, and let him go to his home.'

98 For the manuscript tradition of the *Old English Herbarium* and its Latin antecedents, see Hubert J. D. Vriend, *The Old English Herbarium and Medicina de Quadrupedibus*, EETS, o.s 286 (Oxford: Oxford University Press, 1984).

99 Indeed, *nihtgengum* seems to be a conscious interpolation of the original Latin *nocturnas ambulationes* ('night walkers'), as read in the oldest extant manuscript of the Pseudo-Apuleius tradition, Leiden MS Vossanius Latinus Q 9 (c.600). See Vriend, *The Old English Herbarium*, pp. xlviii, 31.

100 *Leechdoms* vol. 2, 'Leech Book III', Ch. I (at pp. 306–7).

101 Anne van Arsdall makes a conscious decision to use the term 'nightmare' for *nihtgengum* in her translation of the *Herbarium* betony entry. See *Medieval Herbal Remedies*, p. 139, n. 71.

102 Jakobsson, 'Taxonomy of the Non-Existent', p. 205.

103 Joseph Bosworth, 'An Anglo-Saxon Dictionary Online.' *GANGAN*. <http://bosworth. ff.cuni.cz/013271> [Accessed 27 September 2018]

104 Lecouteux, *The Return of the Dead*, pp. 132, 197.

105 Kiessling, 'Grendel', pp. 193–94.

106 H. Stuart also notes that the terms for supernatural entities in Anglo-Saxon textbooks betray a sense of clerical reductionism. See 'The Anglo-Saxon Elf', *Studia Neophilologica* 48 (1976), 313–20.

107 James, 'Twelve Medieval Ghost Stories', pp. 416, 421.

108 Vriend, *The Old English Herbarium*, pp. 1, 31.

109 The ghost states that it was able to appear to Snowball because 'today you have not heard mass or the gospel of St. John' (*ewangelium Iohannis scilicet 'In principio'*). See James, 'Twelve Medieval Ghost Stories', p. 416.

110 Jacqueline Simpson and Stephen Roud, *Dictionary of English Folklore* (Oxford: Oxford University Press, 2000), p. 259.

111 For later iterations of the St George nightmare charm, see Jacqueline Simpson, 'The Nightmare Charm in King Lear', in *Charms, Charmers and Charming: International Research on Verbal Magic*, ed. by Jonathan Roper (Basingstoke: Palgrave Macmillan, 2009), pp. 100–107. See also Earl of Ducie, 'Exhibition of Three 'Mare-Stones', or 'Hag-Stones'', *The Journal of the Anthropological Institute of Great Britain and Ireland* 17 (1888), 134–37.

112 Meaney, *Curing Stones*, p. 99.

113 Stock, *Listening for the Text*, p. 34.

114 Schmitt, *Ghosts in the Middle Ages*, pp. 59–78.

115 See the discussions in Stephen Gordon, 'Dealing with the Undead, pp. 127–28. See also Andrew Reynolds, *Anglo-Saxon Deviant Burial Customs* (Oxford: Oxford University Press, 2009), 68–92.

116 Newburgh V. 22 (p. 475).

117 'Quod cum egesta humo nudassent, ingens in eo vulnus quod acceperat, et cruoris plurimum qui ex vulnere fluxerat, in sepulchro invenerunt', Newburgh, V. 24 (p. 479).

118 Cheyne *et al.*, 'Cultural Construction of the Nightmare', pp. 322, 333; Adler, *Sleep Paralysis*, p. 87.

119 Cheyne, 'The Structure of Waking-Nightmare Hallucinations', p. 164.

120 GpA V. 258.

121 Macrobius, I. 3. 7.

122 Newburgh, V. 22 (p. 474).

123 Gordon, 'Early Modern Vampire Literature', pp. 93–124.

124 'The Travels of Three English Gentlemen', in the *Harleian Miscellany*, Vol. 11, ed. by William Oldys (London, 1810), pp. 218–354 (at p. 231). For the attribution of the tract to Swinton, see Trevor Shaw, 'John Swinton, F. R. S., Identified as the Author of a 1734 Travel Journal', *Notes and Records of the Royal Society of London* 53 (1999), 295–304.

125 'Um Mitternacht aber ist sie mot einem entsetzlichen Geschrey, Furcht und Zittern, aus dem Schlaff aufgefahren, und geklaget, daß sie von einem 9. Wochen verstorbenen Heyducken Sohn, nahmens Milloe, sey um den Hals gewürget worden, worauf sie einen grossen Schmertzen auf der Brust empfunden und von Stund zu Stund sich

schlechter befunden, bis sie endlich den dritten Tag gestorben', in Flückinger, *Visum et Repertum,* pp. 5–6.

126 Henry More's *An Antidote against Atheism,* 2nd ed. (London, 1655), III. 8 (at pp. 209–13). For the original Latin text, see Matin Weinrich, 'proaemium', in Gianfrancesco Pico della Mirandola, *Strix* (Strasbourg, 1612 [1523]), pp. 1–60.

127 Calmet, *Dissertations Upon the Apparitions of Angels,* pp. 212–3. The removal of the revenant's heart can also be discerned in William of Newburgh's 'Ghost of Anantis' narrative and the account of the walking dead discussed in Geoffrey of Burton's *Vita sancte Moduenne virginis*

128 Neplach notes that every night the dead shepherd Myslata rose from the grave, wandered through the streets of Blow and 'throttled' (*iugulando*) the local village folk, in *Chronicon,* p. 480.

129 'Mais en peu des temps le mort fit paroistre qu il estoit: car ill commenca à donner tant d'espouuante, qu'entrant de nuict dans les maisons, criant, hurlant and frappant...', François Richard, 'De Feux Resuscitez', in *Relation de ce qui s'est passe de plus remarquable a Saint-Erini isle de l'Archipel* (Paris, 1657), pp. 208–26 (at p. 215).

130 Valvasor's history of Carnolia (present-day Slovenia) includes an account of a *štrigon* ('vampire') named Jure Grando (d.1656) who, returning from the grave, subjecting his wife to horrifying sexual assaults (*Nothzüchtig*). See Johan Weikhard Valvasor, *Die Ehre Hertzogthums Krain,* 4 Vols (Rudolfswerth, 1877–1879 [1689]), III. XI (at pp. 317–19).

131 Describing a *vrykolakas* outbreak he observed on his travels through the Greek Islands, de Tournefort writes: 'the [burning of the dead man's heart] did not make him more tractable; he went on with his racket more furiously that ever: he was accused of beating folks in the night...' See Joseph Pitton de Tournefort, *A Voyage into the Levant* (London, 1741 [1718]), Vol. 1, letter three (at pp. 103–7).

132 Frombald notes how the suspected vampire, Peter Plogojoviz 'laid down upon and throttled' (*gelegt und gewürget*) his victims in their sleep, until they too fell into sickness and died, in 'Copia eines Schreibens aus dem Gradisker District in Ungarn', p. 11, col. 2.

133 Gordon, 'Early Modern Vampire Literature', p. 113.

134 Marbode of Rennes, *De Lapidibus,* p. 56.

135 Reg Jackson, *Excavations at St. James's Priory, Bristol* (Oxford: Oxbow, 2006), p. 142.

136 For the use of protective magic in medieval mortuary practices, see Roberta Gilchrist, 'Magic for the Dead? The Archaeology of Magic in Later Medieval Burials' *Medieval Archaeology* 52 (2008), 119–59; Gordon, 'Disease, Sin and the Walking Dead', pp. 63–66.

Primary sources

Albertus Magnus, *Book of Minerals,* ed. and trans. by Dorothy Wyckoff (Oxford: Clarendon, 1967).

Albertus Magnus, *Mineralium,* in B. Alberti Magni, *Opera Omnia,* 38 vols, ed. by Auguste Borgnet (Paris: Vivès, 1890–1899).

Aldhelm, *Sancti Aldhelmi Ex Abbate Malmesburiensi Episcopi Schireburnensis Opera Quae Extant Omnia,* ed. by J. A. Giles (Oxford: Veneunt apud J. H. Parker, 1844).

Aristotle, *On Sleep and Dreams,* ed. and trans. by David Gallop (Warminster: Aris & Phillips, 1996).

Artemidorus Daldianus, *The Interpretation of Dreams: Oneirocritica,* ed. and trans. by Robert J. White (Park Ridge, NJ: Noyes, 1975).

Augustine, *Sancti Aurelii Augustini Hipponensis episcopi Opera omnia,* PL 32–47, ed. by J. P. Migne (Paris, 1841–1849).

Benedict of Peterborough, *Miracula Sancti Thomae Cantuariensis*, in *Materials for the History of Thomas Becket, Archbishop of Canterbury*, 7 vols, ed. by James Craige Robertson, RS 67 (London: Longman, 1875–1885).

Beowulf, ed. and trans. by Michael Swanton (Manchester: Manchester University Press, 1997).

Bernard of Gordon, *Lilium medicinae* (Lyon, 1550).

Burchard of Worms, *Burchardi Vormatiensis Episcopi, Opera*, PL 140, ed. by J. P. Migne (Paris, 1853).

Caelius Aurelianus, *On Acute Diseases and On Chronic Diseases*, ed. and trans. by I. E. Drabkin (Chicago, IL: Chicago University Press, 1950).

Calmet, Augustin, *Dissertations Upon the Apparitions of Angels, Dæmons, and Ghosts, and Concerning the Vampires of* Hungary, *Bohemia, Moravia, and Silesia – Translated from the French* (London: Cooper, 1759).

Cockayne, Oswald, *Leechdoms, Wortcunning and Starcraft of Early England*, 3 vols, RS 35 (London: Longman, 1864–1866).

'Edictus Rothari', in *MGH, LL 4*, ed. by Friedrich Bluhme (Hannover, Impensis Bibliopolii Hahniani, 1868), pp. 3–90.

Evans, Jan and Mary S. Serjeantson, *English Medieval Lapidaries*, EETS o.s 190 (London: Oxford University Press, 1933).

Flückinger, Johann, *Visum et Repertum* (Nuremburg, 1732).

Frombald, 'Copia eines Schreibens aus dem Gradisker District in Ungarn,' in *Wienerisches Diarium*, 21 July 1725, pp. 11–12.

Gervase of Tilbury, *Otia Imperialia: Recreation for an Emperor*, ed. and trans. by S. E. Banks and J. W. Binns (Oxford: Clarendon, 2002).

Guibert of Nogent, *Histoire de sa vie (1053–1124)*, ed. by Georges Bourgin (Paris: Picard, 1907).

Guibert of Nogent, *Self and Society in Medieval France: The Memoirs of Abbot Guibert of Nogent (1064–c.1125)*, ed. and trans. by John Benton (New York: Harper & Row, 1970).

Hincmar of Reims, 'Erstes Kapitular', in *MGH, Cap. episc 2* (Hannover: Hahnsche, 1995), pp. 34–45.

Isidore of Seville, *Etymologies*, ed. and trans. by S. A. Barney et al. (Cambridge: Cambridge University Press, 2006).

Isidore of Seville, *Isidori Hispalensis Episcopi, Etymologiarum Sive Originum Libri XX*, 2 vols, ed. by W. M. Lindsay (Oxford: Clarendon, 1911).

John of Salisbury, Ioannes Saresberiensis, *Policraticus, I–IV*, CCCM 118, ed. by K. S. B. Keats-Rohan (Turnhout: Brepols, 1993).

Joseph Bosworth, 'An Anglo-Saxon Dictionary Online', ed. by Thomas Northcote Toller et al. Comp. by Sean Christ and Ondřej Tichý. Faculty of Arts, Charles University in Prague, 21 March 2010, http://bosworth.ff.cuni.cz/.

A Late Eighth-Century Latin-Anglo-Saxon Glossary, ed. by J. H. Hessels (Cambridge: Cambridge University Press, 1906).

The Lombard Laws, ed. and trans. by Katherine Fischer Drew (Philadelphia, PA: University of Pennsylvania Press, 1973).

Macrobius, *Commentarii in Somnium Scipionis*, in *Macrobii Ambrosii Theodosii Opera quae supersunt*, 2 vols, ed. by Ludwig Von Jan (Quedlinburg, Basse, 1848).

Macrobius, *Commentary on the Dream of Scipio*, ed. and trans. by W. Harris Stahl (New York: Columbia University Press, 1952).

Marbode of Rennes, *De Lapidibus: Considered as a Medical Treatise with Text, Commentary and C. W. King's Translation; together with Text and Translation of Marbode's Minor Works on Stones*, ed. by J. M. Riddle, *Sudhoffs Archiv* 20 (Wiesbaden: Steiner, 1977).

Materials for the History of Thomas Becket, Archbishop of Canterbury, 7 vols, RS 67, ed. by James Craige Robertson (London: Longman, 1875–1885).

More, Henry, *An Antidote against Atheism*, 2nd ed. (London, 1655).

Pitton de Tournefort, Joseph, *A Voyage into the Levant* (London, 1741 [1718]).

Pliny, *Natural History: History, Volume X: Books 36–37*, ed. and trans. by D. E. Eichholz, Loeb Classical Library 419 (Cambridge, MA: Harvard University Press, 1962).

Pseudo-Augustine, Liber, 'de Spiritu et Anima' in *Sancti Aurelii Augustini Hipponensis episcopi, Opera omnia*, 6 vols, ed. by J. P. Migne, PL 40 (Paris, 1841).

Richard, François, *Relation de ce qui s'est passe de plus remarquable a Saint-Erini isle de l'Archipel* (Paris, 1657).

Swinton, John, 'The Travels of Three English Gentlemen', in *The Harleian Miscellany*, 11 vols, ed. by William Oldys (London: Dutton, 1810), pp. 218–354.

Thomas Aquinas, *Summa Theologiae, Volume 9: Angels (1a; 50–64)*, ed. and trans. by Kenelm Foster (London: Eyre & Spottiswoode, 1968).

Valvasor, Johan Weikhard, *Die Ehre Hertzogthums Krain*, 4 vols (Rudolfswerth: Krajec, 1877–1879).

Van Arsdall, Anne, *Medieval Herbal Remedies: The Old English Herbarium and Anglo-Saxon Medicine* (London: Routledge, 2002).

Vriend, Hubert J. D., *The Old English Herbarium and Medicina de Quadrupedibus*, EETS, o.s 286 (Oxford: Oxford University Press, 1984).

Weinrich, Matin, 'Proaemium', in *Gianfrancesco Pico della Mirandola, Strix* (Strasbourg, 1612), pp. 1–60.

William of Auverge, 'De universo', in *Guilielmi Alverni episcopi Parisiensis, Opera Omnia*, 1 vol (Paris, 1674).

William of Canterbury, 'Miracula S. Thomae Cantuariensis', in *Materials for the History of Thomas Becket*, 7 vols, ed. by James Craige Robertson, RS 67 (London: Longman, 1875–1885).

William of Malmesbury, *De Gestis Pontificum Anglorum Libri Auinque*, ed. by N. E. S. A. Hamilton (London: Longman, 1870).

William of Malmesbury, *The Deeds of the Bishops of England*, ed. and trans. by David Preest (Woodbridge: Boydell, 2002).

William of Newburgh, 'Historia rerum Anglicarum', in *Chronicles of the Reigns of Stephen, Henry II., and Richard I*, 2 vols, ed. by Richard Howlett, RS 82 (London: Longman, 1884–1885).

William of Newburgh, 'The History of William of Newburgh', in *The Church Historians of England*, vol. IV, pt. 2, ed. by Joseph Stevenson (London: Seeleys, 1856).

Secondary sources

Adler, Shelley R., *Sleep Paralysis: Night-Mares, Nocebos, and the Mind-Body Connection* (New Brunswick, NJ: Rutgers University Press, 2011).

Amiet, Robert, 'Une "Admonitio Synodalis" de l'époque carolingienne: Étude critique et Édition', *Mediaeval Studies* 26 (1964), 12–82.

Banham, Debby, 'Dun, Oxa and Pliny the Great Physician: Attribution and Authority in Old English Medical Texts', *Journal of the Social History of Medicine* 24 (2011), 57–73.

Bräunlein, Peter J., 'The Frightening Borderlands of Enlightenment: The Vampire Problem', *Studies in History and Philosophy of Biological and Biomedical Sciences* 43 (2012), 710–19.

Cheyne, J. Allan, 'Sleep Paralysis and the Structure of Waking-Nightmare Hallucinations', *Dreaming* 13 (2003), 163–79.

Cheyne, J. Allan, Ian R. Newby-Clark, and Steve D. Rueffer, 'Relations Among Hypnagogic and Hypnopompic Experiences Associated with Sleep Paralysis', *Journal of Sleep Research* 8 (1999), 313–17.

Cheyne, J. Allan, Steve D. Rueffer, and Ian R. Newby-Clark, 'Hypnagogic and Hypnopompic Hallucinations During Sleep Paralysis: Neurological and Cultural Construction of the Nightmare', *Consciousness and Cognition* 8 (1999), 319–37.

Cholmeley, H. P., *John of Gaddesden and the Rosa Medicinae* (Oxford: Clarendon, 1912).

Coupe, M. D., 'The Personality of Guibert de Nogent Reconsidered', *Journal of Medieval History* 9 (1983), 317–29.

Davies, Owen, 'Hag-Riding in Nineteenth-Century West Country England and Modern Newfoundland: An Examination of an Experience-Centred Witchcraft Tradition', *Folk Life* 35 (1997), 36–53.

Davies, Owen, 'The Nightmare Experience, Sleep Paralysis and Witchcraft Accusations', *Folklore* 114 (2003), 181–203.

De Mayo, Thomas, 'William of Auvergne and Popular Demonology', *Quidditas*, 28 (2007), 61–88.

Earl of Ducie, 'Exhibition of Three "Mare-Stones", or "Hag-Stones"', *The Journal of the Anthropological Institute of Great Britain and Ireland* 17 (1888), 134–37.

Elliott, Dyan, *Fallen Bodies: Pollution, Sexuality and Demonology in the Middle Ages* (Philadelphia, PA: University of Pennsylvania Press, 1999).

Elliott, Dyan, 'Pollution, Illusion, and Masculine Disarray: Nocturnal Emissions and the Sexuality of the Clergy', in *Constructing Medieval Sexuality*, ed. by Karma Lochrie, Peggy McCracken, and James A. Schultz (Minneapolis, MN: University of Minnesota Press, 1997), pp. 1–23.

Gilchrist, Roberta, 'Magic for the Dead? The Archaeology of Magic in Later Medieval Burials', *Medieval Archaeology* 52 (2008), 119–59.

Gordon, Stephen, 'Dealing with the Undead in the Later Middle Ages', in *Dealing with the Dead: Mortality and Community in the Middle Ages*, ed. by Thea Tomaini (Leiden: Brill, 2018), pp. 97–128.

Gordon, Stephen, 'Disease, Sin and the Walking Dead in Medieval England, *c.*1100–1350: A Note on the Documentary and Archaeological Evidence', in *Medicine, Healing and Performance*, ed. by Stephen Gordon et al. (Oxford: Oxbow, 2014), pp. 55–70.

Gordon, Stephen, 'Emotional Practice and Bodily Performance in Early Modern Vampire Literature', *Preternature: Critical and Historical Studies on the Preternatural* 6 (2017), 93–124.

Haga, Eivind, 'The Nightmare – A Riding Ghost with Sexual Connotations', *Nord Psykiatrisk Tidsskrift* 43 (1989), 515–20.

Hall, Alaric, 'The Evidence for Maran, the Anglo-Saxon "Nightmares"', *Neophilologus* 91 (2009), 299–317.

Huet, Marie-Hélène, 'Deadly Fears: Dom Augustin Calmet's Vampires and the Rule over Death', *Eighteenth-Century Life* 21 (1997), 222–32.

Hufford, David J., 'A New Approach to the "Old Hag": The Nightmare Tradition – Re-Examined', in *American Folk Medicine: A Symposium*, ed. by Wayland D. Hand (Berkeley, CA: University of California Press, 1976), pp. 73–85.

Hufford, David J., *The Terror that Comes in the Night: An Experience-Centered Study of Supernatural Assault Traditions* (Philadelphia, PA: University of Pennsylvania Press, 1982).

Jackson, Reg, *Excavations at St. James's Priory, Bristol* (Oxford: Oxbow, 2006).

Jakobsson, Ármann, 'The Taxonomy of the Non-Existent: Some Medieval Icelandic Concepts of the Paranormal, *Fabula* 54 (2013), 199–213.

James, M. R., 'Twelve Medieval Ghost Stories', *English Historical Review* 37 (1922), 413–22.

Johnston, Sarah Iles, *Restless Dead: Encounters Between the Living and the Dead in Ancient Greece* (Berkeley, CA: University of California Press, 1999).

Jolly, Karen L., *Popular Religion in Late Anglo-Saxon England: Elf Charms in Context* (Chapel Hill, NC: University of North Carolina Press, 1996).

Kiessling, Nicolas K., 'Grendel: A New Aspect', *Modern Philology* 65 (1968), 191–201.

Kiessling, Nicolas K., *The Incubus in English Literature: Provenance and Progeny* (Pullman, WA: Washington State University Press, 1997).

Kitson, Peter, 'Lapidary Traditions in Anglo-Saxon England: Part I, The Background; The Old English Lapidary', *Anglo Saxon England* 7 (1978), 9–60.

Kruger, Steven F., *Dreaming in the Middle Ages* (Cambridge: Cambridge University Press, 1992).

Lea, Henry C., *Materials Toward a History of Witchcraft*, 3 vols (New York: Yoseloff, 1957).

Lecouteux, Claude, *The Return of the Dead: Ghosts, Ancestors, and the Transparent Veil of the Pagan Mind*, trans. by Jon E. Graham (Rochester, NY: Inner Traditions, 2009).

MacLehose, William F., 'Fear, Fantasy and Sleep in Medieval Medicine', in *Emotions and Health, 1200–1700*, ed. by Elena Carrera (Turnhout: Brill, 2013), pp. 67–94.

Meaney, Audrey L., *Anglo-Saxon Amulets and Curing Stones*, BAR British Ser., 96 (Oxford: Archaeopress, 1981).

Meaney, Audrey L., 'The Practice of Medicine in England About the year 1000', *Journal of the Social History of Medicine* 13 (2000), 221–37.

Ness, Robert C., 'The Old Hag Phenomenon as Sleep Paralysis: A Biocultural Interpretation', *Culture, Medicine and Psychiatry* 2 (1978), 15–39.

Peden, Alison M., 'Macrobius and Medieval Dream Literature', *Medium Aevum* 54 (1985), 59–73.

Pickering, Michael, 'Constructing the Vampire: Spirit Agency in the Anonymous *Actenmabige und Umstansliche Relation von denen Vampiren oder Menschen-Saugern (1732)*', in *Unnatural Reproductions and Monstrosity: The Birth of the Monster in Literature, Film, and Media*, ed. by Andrea Wood and Brandy Schillace (Amherst, NY: Cambria Press, 2014), pp. 69–88.

Pickering, Michael, '"Sie Mußten ins Feuer": Changing Polices Within the Habsburg Monarchy on the Destruction of Vampire Bodies', in *Evil and the State: Interdisciplinary Perspectives*, ed. by Kiran Sarma and Ben Livings (Oxford: Inter-Disciplinary Press, 2013), pp. 11–29.

Raudvere, Catharina, 'Analogy Narratives and Fictive Rituals: Some Legends of the *Mara* in Scandinavian Folk Belief', *ARV: Nordic Yearbook of Folklore* 51 (1995), 41–62.

Reynolds, Andrew, *Anglo-Saxon Deviant Burial Customs* (Oxford: Oxford University Press, 2009).

Riddle, John, 'Theory and Practice in Medieval Medicine', *Viator*, 5 (1974), 157–84.

Schmitt, Jean-Claude, *Ghosts in the Middle Ages: The Living and the Dead in Medieval Society*, trans. by Teresa L. Fagan (Chicago: Chicago University Press, 1998).

Schneck, Jerome M., 'Sleep Paralysis Without Narcolepsy or Cataplexy: Report of a Case', *Journal of the American Medical Association* 173 (1960), 1129–30.

Shaw, Trevor, 'John Swinton, F. R. S., Identified as the Author of a 1734 Travel Journal', *Notes and Records of the Royal Society of London* 53 (1999), 295–304.

Simpson, Jacqueline, 'The Nightmare Charm in King Lear', in *Charms, Charmers and Charming: International Research on Verbal Magic*, ed. by Jonathan Roper (Basingstoke: Palgrave Macmillan, 2009), pp. 100–107.

Simpson, Jacqueline and Stephen Roud, *Dictionary of English Folklore* (Oxford: Oxford University Press, 2000).

Stewart, Charles, 'Erotic Dreams and Nightmares from Antiquity to the Present', *The Journal of the Royal Anthropological Institute*, New Ser., 8 (2002), 279–309.

Stock, Brian, *Listening for the Text: On the Uses of the Past* (Baltimore, MD: John Hopkins University Press, 1990).

Stuart, H., 'The Anglo-Saxon Elf', *Studia Neophilologica* 48 (1976), 313–20.

Van der Lugt, Maaike, 'The Incubus in Scholastic Debate: Medicine, Theology and Popular Belief', in *Religion and Medicine in the Middle Ages*, ed. by Peter Biller and Joseph Ziegler (Woodbridge: York Medieval Press, 2001), pp. 175–200.

Vermier, Koen, 'Vampires as Creatures of the Imagination: Theories of Body, Soul, and Imagination in Early Modern Vampire Tracts (1659–1755)', in *Diseases of the Imagination and Imaginary Disease in the Early Modern Period*, ed. by Yasmin Haskell (Turnhout: Brepols, 2011), pp. 341–73.

Vinge, Louise, *The Five Senses: Studies in a Literary Tradition* (Lund: CWK Gleerp, 1975).

Welsford, Enid, *The Court Masque: A Study in the Relationship Between Poetry & the Revels* (Cambridge: Cambridge University Press, 1927).

Epilogue

From the medieval to the early modern: the persistence of habit

By the turn of the fifteenth century the religious apparatus for dealing with super-natural encounters was well established. Thanks in part to the impact of the edu-cational reformer Jean Gerson and his circle at the University of Paris, mentioned briefly in chapter five, the officially-sanctioned techniques for the discernment of spirits found ready acceptance in the habitual repertoires of everyday life. The procedure was simple: should a lay person make contact with a non-human entity, the priest overseeing the affair was to first test the moral status of the percipient to gauge if her or she were trustworthy and free of sin, which not only affected the validity of the tale but also determined whether they had encountered a good or bad spirit. After being subject to the appropriate questioning and an identity ten-tatively established, the restless dead were to receive the benefits of post-mortem prayer and absolution, whereas demonic entities were to be conjured and exor-cised to depart.[1] This, indeed, is the near exact sequence of events recorded in a story from an anonymous English chronicle detailing the haunting of a pilgrim in Weymouth, c.1456. Confronted on two consecutive nights by a spirit dressed head to toe in white, the pilgrim, understandably fraught, decided to visit the local priest for counsel. Determining from the outset that the pilgrim had a 'goode herte' and was clear of conscience, the priest advised that he should conjure the spirit 'to tell the what he ys' if it reappeared the following night. Sure enough, at nightfall, the spirit came to the pilgrim's bedchamber. On being conjured to speak it confessed that 'I am [...] thy faderes brother'. After ascertaining the truth of this statement through a series of questions – 'how long ys it ago sen thow deyde?'; 'Where ys my fader?'; 'And where ys my moder?'– the pilgrim acquiesced to his dead uncle's wishes that masses be said in his name at the sanctuary of St. James in Spain.[2]

The narratological elements of this encounter are so common as to be to verg-ing on stereotype. It is a clear advertisement of the reality of Purgatory and the efficacy of the cult of St. James.[3] And yet, such (seemingly) inviolate frameworks found themselves under increased scrutiny as the century progressed, a conse-quence of wider socio-political discord. Whilst popular dissatisfaction with the supernatural hierarchy cannot be traced to a singular cause or event, the seeds of change certainly found fertile ground in aftermath of the Council of Constance (1414–1418), one of the most influential (and infamous) ecumenical councils of the later Middle Ages. It was here that the Schism caused by the botched papal election of 1378 and the formation of the antipapal regime in Avignon finally found a resolution with the election of a unified pope, Martin V, in 1417.[4] The impetus to heal the church in all its forms extended to the clarification of some of the more obscure aspects of pastoral care, exemplified by commissioning of the *Ars moriendi* ('Art of Dying') handbook, a text specifically designed to help the laity achieve a 'good' death.[5] With the internecine squabbles of the Schism allowing error to flourish, it was also an occasion where the ratification of doctrine and punishment of unorthodox thinking was firmly on the agenda. On 6 July 1415, one of the delegates, the Czech theologian Jan Hus, was burnt as a heretic. Two months earlier, on 4 May, the council had similarly denounced the teachings of one of Hus's most prominent influences, John Wycliffe (d.1384). It was decreed that Wycliffe's body be removed from consecrated ground, a sentence carried out thirteen years later when the excommunicate's bones were exhumed from Lutterworth churchyard and cremated. Hus and Wycliffe's criticisms of the clergy and the iniquities of Catholic doctrine resonated strongly across the continent. The desire for institutional reform was brewing, helped in part by the popular revulsion at the manner of Hus's death. Dissatisfaction with the creaking church edifice reached its crescendo with the publication of the *Ninety-Five Theses* of Martin Luther (1517). Luther's condemnations were enthusiastically received and led to the ratification of a new religious/political 'text' – a template that had wide-reaching consequences on the practices of everyday life. With nascent printing technologies allowing for a more concerted dissemination of the written word, Luther's polemics gained immediate traction in the secular and ecclesiastical centres of Northern Europe. If Lutheranism found a ready audience in the Germanic and the Scandinavian realms, the English Reformation (c.1534) was much more contingent. Henry VIII's assertion of Royal Supremacy over Rome, his desire to quell opposition to his religious kingship, and his general distrust of the 'foreign' (i.e. monastic and papal) influences in his land were just as important to the processes of reform as the dissatisfaction with superstition.[6] Indeed, Henry was a firm believer in the power of the Mass and, initially, did not agree with the more severe ideologies of the *Ninety-Five Theses*, such as the rejection of the reality of transubstantiation.[7] Whatever the impetus for the establishment of the church of England, the state's appropriation of key (though not all) aspects of the Protestant ideology resulted in the transformation of the official status of the ghost. The rejection of the doctrine of Purgatory as expressed in the church of England's *Thirty-Nine Articles* (1563) denied the possibility that the living could interact with the dead,[8] while the dissolution of the monasteries cut off a prime source for written accounts of supernatural events. In funerary contexts, less emphasis was placed on the eschatological significance of the corpse. The perpetuation of the memory of the deceased and the advertisement of the social status of the living became the defining factors in the body's treatment after death.[9] In the strictest Protestant sense, exemplified by the *De Spectris* of Ludwig Lavater (1570), ghosts were either intangible devilish illusions, hallucinations, or popish tricks designed to propagate the errors of Catholicism. The spirits of the dead went directly to heaven or hell.[10] As a consequence of the almost complete diabolisation of the 'true' supernatural encounter, the Devil (and his main earthly agent, the witch) appeared to have had a greater foothold in the world than ever before. Such pronouncements were, of course, open to debate. Acceptance of the reformist ideals did not lead to a complete revision of practice. Entrenched habits of belief persisted, often coming into conflict with these new doctrinal truths.[11] In situations where the extremes of Protestant theology were unable to suit the needs of the textual community or fully cohere within its prevailing social logic, the likelihood of syncretism with (or subjugation to) pre-existing or concomitant modes of thought tended to rise. The extant corpus of penny pamphlet literature testifies to the amalgamation of Protestant, Catholic, and folkloric genre codes in English writings on the supernatural: despite taking on decidedly devilish qualities, apparitions were by the seventeenth century seen mostly as non-diabolic in nature, working according to the dictates of Providence.[12] In a similar way, the tacit acceptance of revenants also persisted. Just as demonically-activated corpses remained an underlying cause for concern, so the belief that the souls of the dead were attached to their own defunct bodies was also hard to extinguish.

Some examples will suffice to illustrate this point. During the late seventeenth century, near the village of Wesham, Lancashire, there lived a witch known locally as Mag Shelton (birth name Margery Hilton). Shelton was despised by the local community and lived alone in a dilapidated old house called Cuckoo Hall. Amongst her many crimes she was said to have soured milk, lamed cattle, and even magically transformed a full pitcher of milk into a goose – the method by which she regularly stole produce from her neighbours. Suspected of bewitching a cow, she was finally brought to task by the daughter of the cow's owner, who bound Shelton with a powerful counter spell. Feigning friendliness, the girl invited Shelton into her home and offered her a seat by the inglenook fireplace, under which was placed an amulet made from two healds (loom equipment) and a bodkin (needle). The amulet prevented the witch from rising. Unable to move and slowly roasted by the fire, Shelton was freed only after she removed the enchantment from the cow. Fearing for her own safety whilst she still lived in Cuckoo Hall, Shelton made a deal with the hunt-loving Lord of Cottam, William Haydock (d.1707): if she could make a hare appear during one of his circuits, the lord was to provide her a new place of residence within the village of Woolplumpton, which formed part of the Cottam estate (the only proviso being that he not release a certain hound during the chase). On the day of the hunt a hare duly appeared. Forgetting Shelton's warning, Haydock released the hound, causing the hare to flee back in the direction of the witch's house in Wesham. The dog nipped at the hare's hind legs as it jumped through the window. It was noticeable thereafter that the witch always walked with a limp. In the end, Shelton died a lonely and miserable death, her body found crushed between a barrel and the wall of her house. Local gossip insinuated that the devil had finally claimed his due. Despite everything, she was laid to rest in the churchyard of St. Anne's in Woolplumpton.

Her corpse, however, did not stay quietly in the grave. Every time it was buried it reappeared on the cemetery topsoil the following morning. Only after her spirit was assuaged by a priest from Cottam Hall and a large boulder placed over the grave did her wanderings finally cease.[13]

Over six hundred years separate Mag Shelton from the Witch of Berkeley. Whilst much of the narrative re-treads the most common stereotypes of early modern witchcraft encounters – the souring of milk; the laming of cattle; the illusory transformation of a physical object[14] – the description of the corpse being unable to stay at rest is relatively uncommon in accounts of this type. Remove the culturally-specific accoutrements of the tale and the base narrative structure could easily have been written by William of Malmesbury or his contemporaries. A wonder story detailing the fate of an inveterate sinner who died a terrible death, and whose body moved after death until certain apotropaic actions were taken, would not look out of place in either the *Gesta regum Anglorum* or the *Historia rerum Anglicarum*. The Welsh practice of 'sin eating' described by the famed Antiquarian John Aubrey (c.1686), in which bread and beer was eaten over the corpse so as to take on 'all the Sinnes of the Defunct and [free] him or her from *walking* after they were dead',[15] is another indication that the revenant did not disappear from the habitual beliefs of the common folk, despite the increasingly popular viewpoint, espoused most prominently by the philosopher Thomas Hobbes (d.1679), that supernatural powers did not intervene in the world. It was as part of the competing anti-atheist movements of the late seventeenth century that ghost, demon, and witch narratives were enlisted as proof that the architecture of the spiritual world – and thus God – existed.[16] This, indeed, seems to have been the purpose of the 31 October 1691 edition of the London magazine *The Athenian Mercury*, which printed a collection of letters on ghost encounters to 'reduc[e] the many proselytes of Saduccism [atheism] and Hobbitism amongst us'. The account of the ghost of Joseph Chambers, who was said to have 'lean[t] against a Tree, in the very Cap and Dress he was laid out in', is suggestive of a physicality (and a physical danger) not apparent in the other readers' stories. The description of Chambers's ghost being on an 'errand' and forcefully rapping on the front door of his former house also bears this out.[17] For some members of *The Athenian Mercury*'s readership at least, the fear of embodied ghosts still held sway. The folklore surrounding the death of George Hodgson from the village of Dent in Cumbria (1715) similarly speaks to the intransigence of local belief. With rumours circulating the Hodgson, a known curmudgeon, was causing a nuisance even after death, his grave was exhumed and, sure enough, his body was found to be fresh and life-like, his hair and nails 'growing' in a similar manner to that described in contemporaneous accounts of the Slavic vampire.[18] Horrified by what they saw, the villagers reburied Hodgeon at the entrance to the local church with a brass stake driven into his torso. Hodgson's grave marker, in which the top of the stake clearly visible, can still be seen in Dent village today.[19]

These are not the only examples from seventeenth- and eighteenth-century England that suggest a continued, even workaday concern about the tangible undead. Aubrey further writes in his *Miscellanies* (1696) that following the death of Sir Walter Long (d.1610) 'his body did not go Quiet to the Grave, it being Arrested at the church-porch by the Trustees of the first Lady' (i.e. his first wife, Mary).[20] Included in the chapter on apparitions alongside jottings on insubstantial phantoms, strange bedroom visitors, and prophetical beings, the manner of Long's capture is unremarked. That Aubrey does not add any qualification to the story is a testament not only to his uncritical empiricism,[21] but also the fact that accosting walking corpses at the edge of churchyards – near the 'kirkestile', in the parlance of the Byland Monk – remained an unusual but not unexpected occurrence. This seeming nonchalance is in stark contrast to the reaction of Aubrey's contemporary, the philosopher Henry More, who remarks that the post-mortem activity of the shoemaker of Breslau, mentioned in the previous chapter, was 'so notorious, that it is hardly to be parallel'd by any we meet with in Writers'.[22] Much like William of Newburgh, who makes a similar comment about the lack authoritative (i.e. classical) precedents in the *Historia rerum Anglicarum*, the everyday reality of such encounters was dependent on the particular textual community and/or experiential network in which the percipient dwelt. Henry More resided on one side of the spectrum and the family of Walter Long (if not John Aubrey) on the other. To whatever degree and moved by whatever agency, the restless dead remained an indelible part of the folk habitus. As a site of meditation on the traumas of death, they still served an important social function.

In light of the above, it does not pay for medievalists and early modernists to treat the seismic events of the Reformation as the upper or lower limit to one's historical interests. Diachronic investigations which take into account the continuation or re-inscription of habit and belief across time have admittedly become much more frequent in recent years, but the initial instinct to separate human experience into 'medieval' and 'post medieval' certainly remains, especially in the popular mindset. The same is true for the use of the Conquest of 1066 as a site of cultural division between 'early medieval' and 'later medieval' England. As noted by interdisciplinary theorists such as Peter Weingart, it is the constraints of knowledge formation and the need to apply strict delineations to one's research and pedagogical outputs that perpetuate and reinforce these boundaries.[23] Just as they were not constrained by the grave, reanimated corpses remained unbeholden to modernist attempts to control and manage time. For the purpose of exploring how individual authors interrogated the phenomenon – something that has not hitherto been attempted in detail – I made a practical decision to focus on specific case studies from the later Middle Ages. Aside from the necessary scene-setting of the introductory chapter, close textual analysis was preferred over broad survey. Even so, knowledge of how the microcosmic text (the chronicle, the poem, the somatic experience) emerged from the macrocosmic text (belief, habit, convention) provides a methodological baseline for evaluating the restless corpse in its wider diachronic context. The deaths of Mag Shelton, Walter Long, Joseph Chambers, and George Hodgson offer a tentative entry point into the untold story of the early modern English revenant. The material is there, just waiting to be rediscovered. This, of course, is a task for another occasion.

Conclusion

Ultimately, this collection of essays has shown that the embodied ghost could serve a wide range of critical functions. Chroniclers, satirists, homily writers, poets, and medical practitioners overlaid their own biases and discursive intentions onto an entity – in reality, a vague melange of entities – whose form and function were forever contingent and 'open'. Chapter one argued that the danger of letting malignant elements fester within the body-politic can be read in the Witch of Berkeley's forced removal (exorcism?) from the body of the church. The causal relationship between the 'inner' (microcosmic) and 'outer' (macrocosmic) worlds can further be read in chapter two, where the rebellion of William FitzOsbert, the warmongering of kings Richard I and Philip II, and the calamitous stewardship of William Longchamp similarly highlight how the spiritual corruptions of a single person could lead many more people into ruin. To paraphrase Peter the Chanter, the sins of the individual were liable to infect and destabilise the wider Christian community.[24] It is no coincidence that William of Newburgh's revenant stories, allegorical as they are, focus on the environmental and social catastrophes wrought by a *single* walking corpse. Whilst the dissonance between outer appearance (surface) and inner meaning (intent) is a theme that permeates all chapters, it is with the *De nugis curialium* of Walter Map that we can see how the trope was deconstructed to stress that life as a courtier (and, ironically, the life of a Cistercian) was much like being confronted by an undead corpse: appearance did not necessarily correspond to true motivation. Map takes the function of wonders to their logical extreme. Embodied ghosts become signs without referents, able to signify everything and thus signify nothing, a lack of meaning and stability that mirrored Map's own social situation.

Building upon the idea that the sensory appraisal of the undead did not lead to a true understanding of either their motivations *or* surface nature, chapters four and five emphasised the difficulty of discerning between spiritual and devilish agency (chapter 4) and between substantial and insubstantial bodies (chapter five). John Mirk did not think it inappropriate to imply that walking corpses could be motivated by devils *and* the spirits of the deceased. Much like his forbearer William of Malmesbury, Mirk understood that different rhetorical contexts demanded different applications of the truth. In this case, the empty vessel of the ambulatory corpse – the surface 'text' – could be filled with whatever agency was needed to stress the spiritual importance of sanctifying the church (the dedication of a church sermon) and adhering to the correct deathbed rituals (the Burial sermon). Likewise, the demonological digression in Chaucer's *Friar's Tale* should be read less as a clumsy insertion and more an articulation of contemporary concerns about the accurate discernment of spirits. The Summoner's questioning of the devil-yeoman should not be read as a complete disregard of the danger he is in, but an orthodox – if arrogant – interrogation as to what type of body his 'brother' was wearing at a particular moment in space-time: aerial or made of flesh? The final chapter ties together the insights gained over the course of the book and demonstrates how a universal sensory 'text', sleep paralysis combined with hypnagogic and hypnopompic hallucinations, was able to cohere and express itself within the belief systems of individual social actors. The ascription of the feeling of pressure on the chest to the agency of the undead was an interpretation shared by many.

In sum, recourse to different types of written data can provide a more nuanced understanding of the ways in which the belief in the restless dead was conceptualised in the medieval world. The embodied ghost was a potent vehicle for commenting upon such disparate topics as the frailties of the political climate, the need to die a good death, and the fractured nature of the self. In the case of learned medical practitioners and 'progressive' theologians, they could also be employed to denounce the exasperating levels of superstition shown by the more credulous members of society. As a manifestation of social, spiritual and medical disorder, the restless corpse – or, rather, the topos of the restless corpse – found utility by writers of all degree and circumstance. From a modern academic standpoint, an interdisciplinary method, the weaving together of the various strands of the cultural text, is a necessary approach to take when the object of study is under-represented in, yet finds expression across, different disciplinary arenas. Further inroads into the relationship between written and non-written texts and the archaeology of ghost belief can only add to our knowledge base.

As demonstrated throughout this volume, the semiotic instability of the revenant rules out any attempt to codify the mode and manner of a corpse's (seeming) reappearance, or even if its apparent form – tangible; fleshy – corresponded to an actual physical presence. Typological slippages between corporeal and incorporeal bodies, between verified encounters and sensory illusions, permeate wonder stories, religious exempla, poetic artefacts and medical reports alike. The general scholarly consensus that the religious innovations of twelfth and thirteenth centuries led to the disembodiment of the undead may bear out on a macrocosmic level but, as the previous chapters have shown, human souls still had the option of re-entering their own cadavers. Despite themselves becoming disembodied and reduced to pure intelligence, demons never lost the ability to infiltrate and 'shame' the corpses of the sinful dead.[25] Belief, of course, is mutable and palimpsestic, subject to change over time. However, rather than viewing change as a stereotypical, positivist ascent from one mode of thought to another, change can also be recursive, doubling back on itself, knotting, operating at different velocities from one person to the next. From William of Malmesbury to John Mirk, the question as to whether 'open' corpses could be mobilised by demons or the spirits of the dead – if even at all – never found a definitive answer: the knot pulled tight. Appropriately enough, the mood evoked by the narratives discussed in this volume is one of a lingering sense of uncertainty. One thing, however, is for certain: encounters with the restless dead were not to be taken lightly. The words of St. Hugh of Lincoln's advisors ring true at this point. Confronted with the news of a dead man terrorising a small town in Buckinghamshire, Hugh was suitably horrified to learn that cremation was seen as an appropriate form of crisis management. As William of Newburgh describes it, the bishop's retinue merely turned to each other and shrugged: *talia saepius in Anglia contigisse*. This is just what the locals do. Such things often happened in England.

Notes

1 Edwards, 'How to Deal with the Restless Dead?', pp. 82–83.
2 *An English Chronicle of the Reigns of Richard II, Henry IV, Henry V, and Henry VI, written before the year 1471*, ed. by John Silvester Davies (London: Camden Society, 1856), pp. 72–74.
3 Indeed, at the very end of the exemplum the chronicler directly implores his readers to 'worship Seynt James'.
4 In brief, the cardinals who elected Urban VI in 1378 became convinced they had made an error and, declaring their original decision void, elected Clement VII six months later. Urban's refusal to give up the Papal See resulted in a division of loyalties between Rome and Avignon (where Clement VII was based). The Council of Pisa in 1409 succeeded only in electing a third pope, Alexander V, making the situation even worse. Thus a new council was urgently needed to bring the matter to a close. See Phillip H. Stump, *The Reforms of the Council of Constance (1414–1418)* (Leiden: Brill, 1993).
5 For the attribution of the *Ars moriendi* to Jean Gerson's influence at the Council of Constance, see Donald F. Duclow, 'Dying Well: The *Ars moriendi* and the Dormition of the Virgin', in *Death and Dying in the Middle Ages*, ed. by Edelgard E. DuBruck and Barbara I. Gusick (New York: Lang, 1999), pp. 379–429 (at p. 380); for the context of Gerson's pastoral theology, see Dorothy C. Brown, *Pastor and the Laity in the Theology of Jean Gerson* (Cambridge: Cambridge University Press, 1987).
6 Peter Marshall, *Reformation England, 1480–1642* (London: Arnold, 2003), p. 56.
7 George Bernard, 'The Piety of Henry VIII', in *The Education of a Christian Society: Humanism and the Reformation in Britain and the Netherlands*, ed. by N. Scott Amos, Andrew Pettegree and Henk F. K. Van Nierop (Aldershot: Ashgate, 1999), pp. 62–88 (at p. 80).
8 Article XXII: 'The Romysh Doctrine concernyng Purgatory, Pardons, Worshipping, and Adoration as wel of ymages, as of reliques, and also invocation of saintes, is a fond thyng vainly fayned, and grounded upon no warrauntie of Scripture, but rather repugnaunt to the Word of God', in Church of England, *Articles, whereupon it was agreed by the archbysshops and bisshops of both the prouinces, and the whole clergye, in the conuocation holden at London in the yere of our Lord God M.D.lxii accordyng to the computation of the Churche of England* (London, 1563), p. 18
9 Sarah Tarlow, *Ritual, Belief and the Dead in Early Modern Britain and Ireland* (Cambridge: Cambridge University Press, 2011), pp. 21–33.
10 Ludwig Lavater, *De Spectris: Lemuribus et Magnis atque Insolitis Fragoribus* (Geneva, 1570).
11 Jo Bath, '"In the Devill's Likenesse": Interpretation and Confusion in Popular Ghost Belief', in *Early Modern Ghosts: Proceedings of the 'Early Modern Ghosts' conference held at St. John's College, Durham University on 24 March 2001*, ed. by John Newton (Durham: Durham University Centre for Seventeenth- Century Studies, 2002), pp. 70–78; Ronald Hutton, 'The English Reformation and the Evidence of Folklore', *Past & Present* 148 (1995), 89–116.
12 Bath, 'In the Devill's Likenesse', p. 72. To pick one example, the author of pamphlet *Strange and Wonderful News from Lincolnshire...* (London, 1679) makes it clear that 'Ghosts and infernal shapes [are] often Instrumental made, to the discoveries of Vilianous Exploits' when introducing the story of the apparition of Thomas Carter, secretly murdered by his elder brother, William. Following Thomas's death, an 'airey form assumed the shape of [Thomas], with fresh bleeding Wounds' and began to torment the surviving Carter household with dreadful groans and shrieks. The ghost was also said to have transformed into more 'fearful forms', such as a Bear and Lion. Finally, a man who 'pretended to Astrology' (i.e. a magician) conjured Thomas to speak. The ghost answered that it was not in the man's power to lay him until justice had been

served against those responsible for his death. This story, paradigmatic of many, deftly illustrates the often-confused synthesis of diabolical and non-diabolical motifs.

13 Paraphrased from Joseph Gillow, *The Haydock Papers* (London, 1888), pp. 40–44.

14 The foundational reading on this topic remains Keith Thomas's magisterial *Religion and the Decline of Magic: Studies in Popular Beliefs in Sixteenth and Seventeenth Century England* (Harmondsworth: Penguin, 1971).

15 John Aubrey, *Remaines of Gentilisme and Judaisme,* ed. by James Britten (London, 1881[1686–87]), p. 35. Italics my emphasis.

16 An argument synopsised in Gillian Bennett, 'Ghost and Witch in the Sixteenth and Seventeenth Centuries', *Folklore* 97 (1986), 3–14; Jo Bath and John Newton, '"Sensible Proof of Spirits": Ghost Belief during the Later Seventeenth Century, *Folklore* 117 (2006), 1–14.

17 *The Athenian Mercury*, vol. 4 no. 10, 31 October 1691, col. 4.

18 Such growth is due to the tightening of the skin during the natural processes of decay, making it seem as though new hair and nails are being formed, as discussed in Barber, *Vampires, Burial and Death*, p. 119.

19 Mike Appleton, *50 Gems of the Yorkshire Dales: The History & Heritage of the Most Iconic Places* (Stroud: Amberley, 2015).

20 John Aubrey, *Miscellanies* (London, 1696), p. 63.

21 Bath and Newton, 'Sensible Proof of Spirits', p. 9.

22 More, *An Antidote against Atheism,* p. 209.

23 As explained in Peter Weingart, 'A Short History of Knowledge Formation', *The Oxford Handbook of Interdisciplinarity*, ed. by Robert Frodeman, Julie Klein and Carl Mitcham (Oxford: Oxford University Press, 2010), pp. 3–14.

24 Peter the Chanter, *Verbum abbreviatum*, PL 205, col. 535D.

25 Elliott, *Fallen Bodies*, pp. 133–34.

Primary sources

The Athenian Mercury, vol. 4, no. 10, 31 October 1691.

Aubrey, John, *Miscellanies* (London, 1696).

Aubrey, John, *Remaines of Gentilisme and Judaisme*, ed. by James Britten (London: W. Satchell, Peyton, 1881).

Church of England, *Articles, whereupon it was agreed by the archbysshops and bisshops of both the prouinces, and the whole clergye, in the conuocation holden at London in the yere of our Lord God M.D.lxii accordyng to the computation of the Churche of England* (London, 1563).

An English Chronicle of the Reigns of Richard II, Henry IV, Henry V, and Henry VI, Written Before the Year 1471, ed. by John Silvester Davies (London: Camden Society, 1856).

Lavater, Ludwig, *De Spectris: Lemuribus et Magnis atque Insolitis Fragoribus* (Geneva, 1570).

More, Henry, *An Antidote Against Atheism*, 2nd ed. (London, 1655).

Peter the Chanter, *Petri Cantoris Verbum Abbreviatum*, PL 205, ed. by J.-P. Migne (Paris, 1855).

Strange and Wonderful News from Lincolnshire, or a Dreadful Account of a Most Inhuman a Bloody Murther (London, 1679).

Secondary sources

Appleton, Mike, *50 Gems of the Yorkshire Dales: The History & Heritage of the Most Iconic Places* (Stroud: Amberley, 2015).

Barber, Paul, *Vampires, Burial and Death: Folklore and Reality* (New Haven, CT: Yale University Press, 1988).

Bath, Jo, '"In the Devill's Likenesse": Interpretation and Confusion in Popular Ghost Belief', in *Early Modern Ghosts: Proceedings of the 'Early Modern Ghosts' Conference Held at St. John's College, Durham University on 24 March 2001*, ed. by John Newton (Durham: Durham University Centre for Seventeenth-Century Studies, 2002), pp. 70–78.

Bennett, Gillian, 'Ghost and Witch in the Sixteenth and Seventeenth Centuries', *Folklore* 97 (1986), 3–14.

Bernard, George, 'The Piety of Henry VIII', in *The Education of a Christian Society: Humanism and the Reformation in Britain and the Netherlands*, ed. by N. Scott Amos, Andrew Pettegree, and Henk F. K. Van Nierop (Aldershot: Ashgate, 1999), pp. 62–88.

Brown, Dorothy C., *Pastor and the Laity in the Theology of Jean Gerson* (Cambridge: Cambridge University Press, 1987).

Duclow, Donald F., 'Dying Well: The *Ars moriendi* and the Dormition of the Virgin', in *Death and Dying in the Middle Ages*, ed. by Edelgard E. DuBruck and Barbara I. Gusick (New York: Lang, 1999), pp. 379–429.

Edwards, Kathryn, 'How to Deal with the Restless Dead? Discernment of Spirits and the Response to Ghosts in Fifteenth-Century Europe', *Collegium* 19 (2015), 82–99.

Elliott, Dyan, *Fallen Bodies: Pollution, Sexuality and Demonology in the Middle Ages* (Philadelphia, PA: University of Pennsylvania Press, 1999).

Gillow, Joseph, *The Haydock Papers* (London, Burns & Oates, 1888).

Hutton, Ronald, 'The English Reformation and the Evidence of Folklore', *Past & Present* 148 (1995), 89–116.

Marshall, Peter, *Reformation England, 1480–1642* (London: Arnold, 2003).

Newton, John and Jo Bath, '"Sensible Proof of Spirits": Ghost Belief During the Later Seventeenth Century', *Folklore* 117 (2006), 1–14.

Stump, Phillip H., *The Reforms of the Council of Constance (1414–1418)* (Leiden: Brill, 1993).

Tarlow, Sarah, *Ritual, Belief and the Dead in Early Modern Britain and Ireland* (Cambridge: Cambridge University Press, 2011).

Thomas, Keith, *Religion and the Decline of Magic: Studies in Popular Beliefs in Sixteenth and Seventeenth Century England* (Harmondsworth: Penguin, 1971).

Weingart, Peter, 'A Short History of Knowledge Formation', in *The Oxford Handbook of Interdisciplinarity*, ed. by Robert Frodeman, Julie Klein, and Carl Mitcham (Oxford: Oxford University Press, 2010), pp. 3–14.

Index

For Product Safety Concerns and Information please contact our EU
representative GPSR@taylorandfrancis.com
Taylor & Francis Verlag GmbH, Kaufingerstraße 24, 80331 München, Germany